THE COLLECTED
SHORT STORIES
OF LOUIS L'AMOUR

Bantam Books by Louis L'Amour

NOVELS

Bendigo Shafter
Borden Chantry
Brionne
The Broken Gun
The Burning Hills
The Californios
Callaghen
Catlow
Chancy
The Cherokee Trail
Comstock Lode
Conagher
Crossfire Trail
Dark Canyon
Down the Long Hills
The Empty Land
Fair Blows the Wind
Fallon
The Ferguson Rifle
The First Fast Draw
Flint
Guns of the Timberlands
Hanging Woman Creek
The Haunted Mesa
Heller with a Gun
The High Graders
High Lonesome
Hondo
How the West Was Won
The Iron Marshal
The Key-Lock Man
Kid Rodelo
Kilkenny
Killoe
Kilrone
Kiowa Trail
Last of the Breed
Last Stand at Papago
   Wells
The Lonesome Gods
The Man Called Noon
The Man from
   Skibbereen
The Man from
   the Broken Hills
Matagorda
Milo Talon
The Mountain Valley War
North to the Rails
Over on the Dry Side

Passin' Through
The Proving Trail
The Quick and the Dead
Radigan
Reilly's Luck
The Rider of Lost Creek
Rivers West
The Shadow Riders
Shalako
Showdown at
   Yellow Butte
Silver Canyon
Sitka
Son of a Wanted Man
Taggart
The Tall Stranger
To Tame a Land
Tucker
Under the Sweetwater
   Rim
Utah Blaine
The Walking Drum
Westward the Tide
Where the Long Grass
   Blows

SHORT STORY COLLECTIONS

Beyond the Great Snow
   Mountains
Bowdrie
Bowdrie's Law
Buckskin Run
The Collected Short
   Stories of Louis
   L'Amour (vols. 1–7)
Dutchman's Flat
End of the Drive
From the Listening Hills
The Hills of Homicide
Law of the Desert Born
Long Ride Home
Lonigan
May There Be a Road
Monument Rock
Night over the Solomons
Off the Mangrove Coast
The Outlaws of Mesquite
The Rider of
   the Ruby Hills
Riding for the Brand

The Strong Shall Live
The Trail to Crazy Man
Valley of the Sun
War Party
West from Singapore
West of Dodge
With These Hands
Yondering

SACKETT TITLES

Sackett's Land
To the Far Blue
   Mountains
The Warrior's Path
Jubal Sackett
Ride the River
The Daybreakers
Sackett
Lando
Mojave Crossing
Mustang Man
The Lonely Men
Galloway
Treasure Mountain
Lonely on the Mountain
Ride the Dark Trail
The Sackett Brand
The Sky-Liners

THE HOPALONG CASSIDY NOVELS

The Riders of High Rock
The Rustlers of West Fork
The Trail to Seven Pines
Trouble Shooter

NONFICTION

Education of
   a Wandering Man
Frontier
The Sackett Companion:
   A Personal Guide to
   the Sackett Novels
A Trail of Memories:
   The Quotations of Louis
   L'Amour, compiled by
   Angelique L'Amour

POETRY

Smoke from This Altar

THE
COLLECTED
SHORT STORIES
OF
LOUIS L'AMOUR

CRIME STORIES
Volume 6, Part 2

Louis L'Amour

BANTAM BOOKS
NEW YORK

2016 Bantam Books Mass Market Edition

Published in the United States by Bantam Books, an imprint of Random
House, a division of Penguin Random House LLC, New York.

Bantam Books and the HOUSE colophon are registered trademarks
of Penguin Random House LLC.

Originally published as part of *The Collected Short Stories of Louis
L'Amour, Volume 6,* in the United States by Bantam Books, an imprint of
Random House, a division of Penguin Random House LLC, in 2008.

ISBN 978-0-804-17978-2
ebook ISBN 978-0-553-90579-3

Cover design: Scott Biel
Cover art: Gregory Manchess

Printed in the United States of America

randomhousebooks.com

9 8 7 6 5 4 3 2 1

Bantam Books mass market edition: September 2016

CONTENTS

THE COLLECTED
SHORT STORIES
OF LOUIS L'AMOUR

DREAM FIGHTER

H E NEVER EVEN cracked a smile. Just walked in and said, "Mr. Sullivan, I want a fight with Dick Abro."

Now Dick Abro was one of the four or five best heavyweights in the racket and who this kid was I didn't know. What I did know was that if he rated a fight with anybody even half so good as Dick Abro, his name would have been in every news sheet in the country.

At first I thought the guy was a nut. Then I took another look, and whatever else you can say, the kid had all his buttons. He was a tall, broad-shouldered youngster with a shock of wavy brown hair and a nice smile. He looked fit, too, his weight was around one eighty. And Abro tipped the beam at a plenty tough two hundred.

"Listen, kid," I said, shoving my hat back on my head and pointing all four fingers at him. "I never saw you before. But if you were twice as good as you think you are, you still wouldn't want any part of Dick Abro."

"Mr. Sullivan," he said seriously, "I can beat him. I can beat him any day, and if you get me the fight, you can lay your money he will go out in the third round, flatter than ten pancakes."

What would you have said? I looked at this youngster, and then I got up. When I thought of that wide, brown face and flat nose of Abro's, and those two big fists ahead of his powerful shoulders, it made me sick to think what would happen to this kid.

"Don't be a sap!" I said, hard-boiled. "Abro would slap you dizzy in half a round! Whatever gave you the idea you could take that guy?"

"You'd laugh if I told you," he said quite matter-of-factly.

"I'm laughing now," I said. "You come in here asking for a fight with Abro. You're nuts!"

His face turned red, and I felt sorry for the kid. He was a nice-looking boy, and he did look like a fighter, at that.

"Okay," I said. "You tell me. What made you think you could lick Abro?"

"I dreamed it."

You could have knocked me down with an axe. He dreamed it! I backed up and sat down again. Then, I looked up to see if he was still there, and he was.

"It's like this, Mr. Sullivan," he said seriously. "I know it sounds goofy, but I dream about all my fights before I have them. Whenever I get a fight, I just train and never think about it. Then, a couple of nights before the fight, I dream it. Then I get in the ring and fight like I did in the dream, and I always win."

Well, I thought if Dick Abro ever smacked this lad for a row of channel buoys, he'd do a lot of dreaming before he came to. Still, there's a lot of nuts around the fight game. At best, and it's the grandest game in the world, it's a screwy one. Funny things happen. So I tipped back in my chair and looked up at him, rolling a quid of chewing gum in my jaws.

"Yeah? Who'd you ever lick?"

"Con Patrick, in two rounds. Beetle Kelly in four, Tommy Keegan in three. Then I beat a half dozen fellows before I started to dream my fights."

I knew these boys he mentioned. At least, I knew one of them personally and two by their records. None of them were boys you could beat by shadowboxing.

"When'd you have this pipe about Abro?" I asked.

"About a week ago. I went to see the pictures of his fight with the champ. Then, two weeks ago I saw him knock out Soapy Moore. Then I dreamed about fighting him. In the dream, I knocked him out with a right hook in the middle of the third."

I got up. "You got some gym stuff?" I asked.

He nodded. "I thought maybe you'd want to see me box. Doc Harrigan down in Copper City told me to see you soon as I arrived."

"Harrigan, eh?" I rolled that around with my gum a few times. Whatever else Harrigan might be, and he was crooked enough so he couldn't even play a game of solitaire without trying to cheat without catching himself at it, he did know fighters.

We walked down to the gym, and I looked around. There were a couple of Filipinos in the ring, and I watched them. They were sure slinging leather. That man Sambo they tell about in the Bible who killed ten thousand Filipinos with the jawbone of an ass must have framed the deal. Those boys can battle. Then, I saw Pete McCloskey punching the heavy bag. I caught his eye and motioned him over. The kid was in the dressing room changing clothes.

"Listen, Pete," I said. "You want that six-round special with Gomez?"

"I sure do, Finny," he said. "I need it bad."

"Okay, I'll fix it up. But you got to do me a favor. I got a kid coming out on the floor in a couple of minutes, and I want to see is he any good. Watch your step with him, but feel him out, see?"

"I get it. You don't want him killed, just bruised a little, eh?" he said.

The kid came out and shadowboxed a couple of rounds to warm up. Pete was looking him over, and he wasn't seeing anything to feel happy about. The kid was fast, and he used both hands. Of course, many a bum looks pretty hot shadow-boxing.

When they got in the ring, the kid, who told me his name was Kip Morgan, walked over and shook hands with Pete. Then he went back to his corner, and I rang the bell.

McCloskey came out in a shell, tried a left that the kid went away from, and then bored in suddenly and slammed a wicked right to the heart. I looked to see Morgan go down, but he didn't even draw a breath. He just stepped around, and then, all of a sudden, his left flashed out in four of the snappiest, shortest jabs I ever saw. Pete tried to slide under it, but that left followed him like the head of a snake. Then, suddenly, Pete and I saw that opening over the heart again. And when I saw what happened I was glad I was outside the ring.

McCloskey hadn't liked those lefts a bit, so when he saw those open ribs again, he uncorked his right with the works on it. The next thing I knew, Pete was flat on his shoulders with his feet still in the air. They fell with a thump, and I walked over to the edge of the ring. Pete McCloskey was out for the afternoon, his face resting against the canvas in a state of calm repose. I couldn't bear to disturb him.

―――

THAT NIGHT I dropped in on Bid Kerney. Race Malone, the sportswriter, was sitting with him. We talked around awhile, and then I put it up to him.

"What you doing with Abro?" I asked. "Got anybody for him?"

"Abro?" Bid shrugged. "Heck, no. McCall wants the champ, an' Blucher wants McCall. There ain't a kid in sight I could stick in there that could go long enough to make it look good. Even if I knew one, he wouldn't fight him."

"What's in it?" I asked. "You make it ten grand, and I got a guy for you."

Race looked up, grinning. "For ten grand I have, too. Me! I'd go in there with him for ten grand. But how long would I last?"

"This kid'll beat Abro," I said coolly, peeling the paper off a couple of sticks of gum casually as I could make it. "He'll stop him."

"You nuts?" Kerney sneered. "Who is he?"

"Name of Morgan, Kip Morgan. From over at Copper City. Stopped Patrick the other night. Got ten straight kayos. Be fighting the champ in a year."

When I talked it up so offhand, they began wondering. I could see Malone smelling a story, and Bid was interested.

"But nobody knows him!" Bid protested. "Copper City's just a mill town. A good enough place, but too far away."

"Okay," I said, getting up. "Stick him in there with Charlie Gomez. But after he beats Gomez, it'll cost you more."

"If he beats him, it'll be worth it!" Bid snapped. "Okay, make it the last Friday this month. That gives you two weeks."

When I walked out of there, I was feeling good. There

would be three grand in this, anyway, and forty percent of that was a nice cut these days. Secretly, I was wondering how I could work it to make the kid win. He had some stuff. I'd seen that when he was in there with Pete, and while Gomez was tough, there was a chance. Pete was fighting Tommy Gomez, Charlie's brother, so he would be training. That took care of the sparring partner angle.

———

SUDDENLY, I THOUGHT of Doc Van Schendel. He was an old Dutchman, from Amsterdam, and a few years before I'd done him a favor. We'd met here and there around town several times, and had a few bottles of beer together. He called himself a psychiatrist, and in his office one time, I noticed some books on dreams, on psychology, and stuff like that. Me, I don't know a thing about that dope, but it struck me as a good idea to see the Doc.

He was in, with several books on the table, and he was writing something down on a sheet of paper. He leaned back and took off his glasses.

"Hallo, hallo, mein Freund! Sit yourself down and talk mit an oldt man!" he said.

"Listen, Doc, I want to ask you a question. Here's the lay." Then I went ahead and told him the whole story. He didn't say much, just leaned back with his fingertips together, nodding his head from time to time. Finally, when I'd finished, he leaned toward me.

"Interesting, very, very interesting! You see, it iss the subconscious at work! He boxes a lot, this young man. He sees these men fight. All the time, he iss asking, 'How would I fight him?' Then the subconscious takes what it knows of the fighter, and what it knows of boxing, undt solves the problem!"

He shrugged.

"Some man t'ink of gomplicated mathematical problem. They go to sleep, undt wake up mit the answer! It iss the subconscious! The subconscious mindt, always at vork vile ve sleep!"

RACE MALONE WAS short of copy, and he took a liking to Kip Morgan so we drove over together. When we got down to the arena, the night of the fight, it was jammed to the doors. Charlie Gomez was a rugged, hard-hitting heavy with a lot of stuff. If the kid could get over him, we were in the money. Race grabbed a seat behind our corner and the kid and I headed for the changing rooms.

"How is it, Kip?" I asked him. I was bandaging his hands, and he sat there watching me, absently.

"It's okay. I dreamed about the fight last night!"

"Yeah?" I said cautiously. I wasn't very sold on this dream stuff. "How'd you do?"

"Stopped him in the second."

We got our call then, and it wasn't until I was crawling through the ropes after him that it struck me what a sweet setup this was. It was too late to get to a bookie, but looking down I saw Race Malone looking up at us.

"Want a bet?" I asked him, grinning. "I'll name the round."

Race grinned.

"You must think the kid's a phenom," he said. "All right. You name the round, and I'll lay you three to one you're wrong!"

"Make it the second," I said. "I don't want it over too soon."

"Okay," Race grinned. "For two hundred? It's a cinch at any odds."

I gulped. I'd been figuring on a five spot, a fin, like I always bet. That's why they called me Finny Sullivan. But if I backed down, he'd kid me for crawfishing. "Sure," I said, trying to look cheerful, "two yards against your six."

THE BELL SOUNDED, and Gomez came out fast. He snapped a short left hook to the kid's head, and it jerked back a good two inches. Then, before the kid could see, Charlie was inside, slamming away at Morgan's ribs with both hands. The kid pushed the Portugee off and ripped his eye with a left, hooked a short right to the head, and then Gomez caught him with a long overhand right, and the kid sailed halfway across the ring and hit the canvas on his tail!

I grabbed the edge of the ring and ground my teeth. I wasn't thinking of my two yards either, although I could afford to lose two yards as much as I could afford to lose an eye, but I was thinking of that shot at Abro and what a sap I was to get taken in on a dream fighter. Second round, eh? Phooey!

But the kid made it to one knee at seven and glanced at me. He needed rest, but there wasn't time, so I waved him up. He straightened up, and Gomez charged across the ring throwing a wild left that missed by a hairsbreadth, and then the kid was inside, hanging on for dear life!

Gomez shook him loose, ripped both hands into the kid's heaving belly, then jerked a wicked right chop to the chin. The kid toppled over on the canvas. I was sick enough to stop it, but the referee had to do that, so I just sat there, watching that game youngster crawl to his feet. Gomez rushed again, took a glancing left to the face that split his eye some more, and then whipped a nasty right to the body. They were in a clinch with the kid hanging on when the bell rang.

Race Malone looked over at me shaking his head.

"I never thought I'd be smart enough to take you for two hundred, Finny," he said. "At that, I hate to see the kid lose."

So did I.

"Listen, Kip," I said. "You ain't got a chance. I'm going to call the referee over and stop it!"

He jerked up on the stool.

"No you won't!" he snapped. "I'm winning in the next round! I've been ready for this. I knew it was going to happen! Now watch!"

The bell rang, and the kid walked out fast. Charlie Gomez was serious. He was all set to win by a kayo this round, and he knew what it meant. It meant he'd be back in the big money again.

He snapped a vicious left hook, but it missed, and then that flashy left jab of the kid's spotted him in the mouth. I'm telling you, there never was one like it. Bang-bang-bang-bang! Just like a trip-hammer, and then a jolting right to the body that wrenched a gasp from Charlie, and had the fans yelling like crazy men.

Leaping in, Gomez swung a volley of punches with both hands so fast you could hardly see them travel, but the kid slid away, and then stepped back and nearly tore Charlie's head loose with a wicked left hook. Then came a crashing right that knocked Gomez into the ropes, and then a left that laid Charlie's cheek open like it had been cut with a knife!

With Gomez streaming blood, and the fans howling like madmen, the kid stepped in coolly, measured the Portugee with a nice straight left, and fired his right—right down the groove! The referee could have counted to five thousand.

I was trembling so I could hardly control myself, but I calmly turned around to Race.

"I'll take that six yards, son," I told him, in a bored voice. "And I'll treat you to a feed and beer."

Race paid me carefully. Then he looked up.

"Honest to Roosevelt, Finny," he said, "what kind of dope did you slip that kid? It sure snapped him out of it. He acted there for a while like he was in a dream!"

Maybe you don't think I grinned then.

"Maybe he was, Palsy, maybe he was!"

––––––

THE NEXT TWO months slipped by like another kind of dream. Morgan trained hard, and I spent a lot of time with him. If Doc Van Schendel was right, and I was betting he was, there wasn't any hocus-pocus about the kid's fighting. It was just that he had some stuff, a good fighting brain, and he thought fighting so much that his subconscious mind had got to planning his battles.

It isn't so wild as it sounds. You know how a guy scraps, and what to use against him. Dempsey was a rusher who liked to get in close and work there, so Tunney made him fight at long range and then tied him up in the clinches. Every fighter is a sucker for something, and a guy who learns the angles can usually work out a way to beat the other fellow.

The kid had a lot on the ball, and I wanted him to have

more. In those two months while we were building up for Abro, I gave him plenty of schooling. I knew he had the old moxie. He was fast, and he could hit. This dream business was just so much gravy. I'll admit there was an angle that bothered me, but I didn't mention it to the kid. I was afraid he'd get to thinking about it, and it would ruin him. What if he dreamed of losing?

Now wasn't that something? The day I first thought of that wasn't a happy one. But I kept my mouth shut. Race Malone was around a good deal. He liked the kid, and then there was a chance the promoter was slipping him a little geetus on the side for playing Morgan up for the Abro fight. With the sensational win over Gomez and the ten kayos behind him, not much was needed. If it had been, his fight with Cob Bennett would have been enough.

———

COB HAD RATED among the first ten for six or seven years. He was a battle-scarred veteran, whose face was seamed with scar tissue and who knew his way around inside the ropes. A lot of fans liked him, and they all knew he could fight. About a month after the Gomez scrap, I took the kid over to Pittsburgh and stuck him in there with Bennett. It lasted a little over two minutes.

———

IF I LIVE to be a hundred, I'll never forget that Abro fight. The preliminaries had been a series of bitter, hard-fought scraps, and the way things shaped up, anything but a regular brannigan was going to be sort of an anticlimax.

Dick Abro crawled through the ropes, looking tough as always. When he came over to our corner, I confess I got a sinking sensation in the pit of my stomach. Sometimes I think maybe I ain't cut out for this racket. There was going to be four grand in this fight for me, yet when I thought of this kid going out there with that gorilla, I got a qualm or two. I'll admit I didn't let them queer my chances for that four grand, because four grand will buy a lot of onions, but nevertheless, I was feeling plenty sorry for Kip.

Abro grinned.

"Howya, keed?"

He had a face like a stone wall, all heavy bones and skin like leather. "You lika da tough going, huh?"

He gripped Morgan's hand and then spun on his toe and walked back across the ring, easy on his feet as a ballet dancer, and him weighing in at two-oh-eight for this brawl.

When the bell sounded, the kid took his time. Abro wasn't in any hurry either. His big brown shoulders worked easily, his head lowered just enough. Most people figured Abro as a tough slugger, but a guy doesn't get as far as he did without knowing a thing or two. Abro feinted and landed a light left. Then he tried another left but the kid stepped away. Dick walked in, feinted again and jerked a short right hook to the ribs. He dug a hard left into the kid's belly, and then jerked it up to slam against his chin.

Abro was cool. He knew the kid was no bum and was watching his step. The kid's left shot out, twisting as it landed, and I saw Abro's head jerk. He stepped back then, and I could see that it jarred more than he'd expected. Abro shot a steaming left to the head, jerked a right to the chin, then pushed his head against Morgan's shoulder and started ripping punches into his body.

Morgan twisted away, flashed that left to Abro's face twice, making the big fellow blink. I could see his eyes sharpen, saw him move in. Then the kid dropped a short right on his chin, and Dick Abro sat down hard. The crowd came off their seats yelling, and Abro sprang up at the count of one, and slammed a vicious right to the kid's head.

Morgan staggered, and backed away, with Abro piling after him, both hands punching. Then Kip ripped up a short right uppercut, and Abro stopped dead in his tracks. Before he could recover, a sweeping left hook dropped him to the canvas. He was up at five, and working toward the kid cautiously.

But Morgan was ready and stepped in, his left ripping Abro's face like a spur, that short right beating a drumfire of punches into the bigger man's body. Abro staggered and seemed about to go down, but, as the kid stepped in, Dick fired a left at close quarters that set Morgan back on his heels.

Boring in, Abro knocked Morgan back into the ropes with a hard right. The kid was hurt. I could see him trying to cover up, trying to roll away from Abro, who was set for the kill. Always dangerous when hurt, the big fellow had caught Kip just right.

Morgan backed away, desperately trying to hold Abro off with a wavering left. Just as Dick got to the kid with two hard wallops to the body, the bell rang.

"Take it easy, kid," I told him. "Don't slug with this guy. Box him and keep moving this round."

Abro came out fast for the next round, but the kid jabbed and stepped around, jabbed again and stepped around further. He missed with his right and took a stiff left to the ribs. Then Abro leaped in, splitting the kid's lip with a snappy left hook, and as the kid tried to jab, rammed a right into his belly with such force it brought a gasp from his lips. The kid tried to clinch, but Abro shook him off and floored him with a short right.

The kid was hurt bad. He got to his knees at five, and when the referee said nine, swayed to his feet. Dick walked in, hitching up his trunks, looking the kid over. He was a little too sure, and Kip was desperate.

He let go with a wild right swing that fairly sizzled. Abro tried to duck, jumped back desperately, but the kid lunged, and the punch slammed against Abro's ear! The big fellow went down with a crash. Thoroughly angered, he leaped to his feet, groggy with pain and rage, and sprang at the kid, swinging with both hands.

Toe-to-toe they stood and swapped it out. Tough as they come, and a wicked puncher, Dick Abro was fighting the fight of his life. He had to.

Ducking and weaving, swaying his big shoulders with every punch, his face set in grim lines, Kip Morgan was fighting like a champion. They were standing in the center of the ring, fighting like madmen, when the bell sounded. It took the referee, the timekeeper, and all the seconds to pry them apart.

RACE MALONE WAS battering away at his typewriter between rounds, and the kid sat there on his stool, grim as death. When the bell sounded, Abro looked bad. One eye was completely closed, the other cut. His lips were puffed and broken. I think everyone in the crowd that night sensed what was going to happen.

Abro rushed in and swung a left, but the kid slid inside, hooked short and hard with his left, and whipped a jolting, rib-loosening punch into the big man's body. Abro staggered, and his legs went loose. He tried to clinch, but the kid shook him off, took a left without flinching, then chopped a right hook to the chin that didn't travel a bit over six inches. Abro turned half around and dropped on his face, dead to the world.

MAYBE YOU THINK I was happy. Well, I wasn't. The kid was suddenly one of the ranking heavies in the game, but me, I had worries. The more I thought of what might happen if the kid dreamt of losing, the more I worried. We were matched with Hans Blucher, a guy who had beaten Abro, had fought a draw with Deady McCall and been decisioned by the champ. Blucher, in a lot of ways, was one of the toughest boys in the game.

So I went to see Doc Van Schendel.

"Listen, Doc," I said. "Supposing that kid dreams of losing?"

Doc shrugged.

"Vell? Maybe hiss psychology is spoiled by it, yes? Maybe he t'ink these dreams iss alvays true. Probably he vill lose."

"You're a big help!" I said, and walked out. Leaving, I saw Race Malone.

"Hello," he said. "What's the matter? You going to a psychiatrist now? Nuts, are you? I always suspected it."

"Aw, go lay an egg!" I said wittily, and walked away. If I'd looked back I'd have seen Race Malone going into the Doc's office. But I had enough worries.

When I walked into the gym the kid was walloping the

bag. He was listless, and his heels were dragging. So I walked over.

"What's the matter?" I said. "Didn't you get any rest last night?"

"Yeah, sure I did," he growled. It wasn't like the kid to be anything but cheerful.

"Listen," I said. "Tell me the trouble. What's on your mind?"

He hesitated, glancing around. Then he stepped closer.

"Last night I dreamed a fight," he said slowly, "and I lost! I got knocked out . . . I think I'd been winning until then."

I knew it! Nothing lasts. Everything goes haywire. A guy can't get a good meal ticket but what he goes to dreaming bad fights.

"Yeah," I said. "Who were you fighting?"

"That's just the trouble," he said. "I couldn't see who it was! His face was all vague and bleary!"

I grinned, trying to pass it off, hoping he won't worry. "That sounds like Pete McCloskey," I said. "He's got the only face I know of that's vague and bleary."

But the kid doesn't even crack a smile; as if it wasn't bad enough for him to dream of losing a fight, he has to go and dream of losing to somebody he can't see!

If I knew who it was he was going to lose to, we'd never go near the guy. But as it was, there I stood with a losing fighter who didn't know who he was going to lose to!

———

BLUCHER IS THE next guy we fight, and if we beat him, we get Deady McCall and then the champ. There's too much at stake to take any chances. And I can see that dreaming about that knockout has got the kid worried. Every time he fights he'll be in there under the handicap of knowing it's coming and not being able to get out of it.

At best, this dreaming business is logical enough. But there's a certain angle to it that runs into fatalism. The kid might just have found some weakness in his own defense, and thought about it until he got himself knocked out in his dreams.

Me, I don't know a lot about such things, but I got to think-ing. What if he got knocked out when he wasn't fighting?

Pete McCloskey was punching the heavy bag, and when I looked at him, I got a flash of brains. Heck, what's a manager good for if he can't think?

"Listen, Pete . . ." I gave him the lowdown, and he nodded, grinning. After all, Morgan had knocked him so cold he'd have kept for years, and this was the only chance Pete would ever have to get even.

———

WHEN THEY CRAWLED into the ring for their after-noon workout, I chased the usual gang out. I gave Kip some tips on some new angles I wanted him to try. That was the gag for having a secret workout, but I just didn't want them to see what's going to happen.

They were mixing it up in the third round of the workout, and like I told him, Pete was ready. I looked up at Kip and yelled. "Hey, Morgan!"

And when he turned to look at me, Pete let him have it. He took a full swing at the kid and caught him right on the but-ton! Kip Morgan went out like a light.

But it was only for a half minute or so. He came out of it and sat up, shaking his head.

"What—what hit me?" he gasped.

"It was my fault, kid," I told him, and me feeling like a heel. "I yelled, an' Pete here had started a swing. He clouted you."

"Sure, I'm sorry, Kip," Pete broke in, and he looked it, too.

"That's okay." He got up, shaking his head to clear it of the effects of the punch. "No hard feelings."

"That's enough for today, anyway," I told him. "Let it go, and have a good workout tomorrow."

Morgan was crawling from the ring when suddenly he stopped, and his face brightened up.

"Hey, Finny!" He dropped to the floor and grabbed my arm. "I'm okay! You hear? I'm okay! That was the knockout. Now I'm in the clear."

"Yeah, sure. That's great," I told him.

But now, tell me a ghost story, I was still worried. One way or another the kid had convinced me. There might still be that knockout to think about—if there was really anything to it—but he could go in the ring without it hanging over him, anyway. He was in the clear now.

He was in the clear, but I wasn't. You can't be around a big, clean-looking kid like this Kip Morgan without liking him. He was easygoing and good-natured, but in the ring, he packed a wallop and never lacked for killer instinct. And me, Finny Sullivan, I was worried. Sooner or later the kid was going to get it, and I didn't want to be there. Some guys are all the better for a kayo, and maybe he would be. But they are always hard to take.

———

KIP WAS CLIMBING into the ring the night of the Blucher fight when Race Malone reached over and caught me by the coat. He pulled me back and spoke confidentially.

"What's this dope about Morgan dreaming his fights? Before he fights 'em, I mean?"

"Where'd you get that stuff?" I asked. "Whoever heard of such a thing?"

Race grinned.

"Don't give me that. Doc Van Schendel let the kitten out of the bag. Come on, pal, give. This is a story."

"Can't you see I got a fight on?" I jerked a thumb toward the ring. "See you later."

Morgan went out fast in the first round. He was confident, and looked it. Blucher feinted and started to throw a right, but the kid faded away like a shadow. It was just like he was reading Blucher's mind. The German tried again, boring in close, but for everything he tried, the kid had an answer. And Morgan kept that jarring, cutting left, making a mess of Blucher's features.

Honest to Roosevelt, it was just like he'd rehearsed it, and, of course, that's what he'd done. What the kid had, I was hoping, was a photographic memory. He'd see a guy fight a couple of times, and he'd remember how he got away from every punch, how he countered, and what he did under every condition. It was instinctive with him, like Young Griffo slipping punches. Tunney got the job done as thoroughly, only he did it by hard work and carefully studying an opponent.

There's only a certain number of ways of doing anything in the ring, and a fellow fighting all the time falls in habits of doing certain things at certain times. Morgan thought about that, remembered every move a man made, and knew what to do under any circumstance. It was a cinch. Or would be until he met some guy who crossed him up. Some of them you could never figure—like Harry Greb. He made up his own style each time and threw them from anywhere and everywhere.

Blucher stepped in, taking it cautiously, and hooked a light one to the ribs. The kid stabbed a left to the mouth, then another one. Blucher threw a right, and the kid beat him to the punch with a hard right to the heart. Then Morgan put his left twice to the face, and sank a wicked one into the solar plexus. Blucher backed away, covering up. Kip followed him, taking his time. Just before the bell rang, Morgan tried a right to the body and took another left hook.

Glancing down between rounds, I saw Race Malone looking at the kid with a funny gleam in his eye . . . which I didn't like. Put that dream stuff in the papers, and it would ruin the kid. They'd laugh him out of the ring.

The second round started fast. Morgan went out, then dropped into a crouch and knocked Blucher into the ropes with a terrific left hook that nearly tore his head off. Blucher bounded back and tried to get in close, but the kid danced away. Then he came back with that flashy left jab to Blucher's mouth, feinted a right to the heart, and left his head wide open.

Blucher bit, hook, line, and sinker. Desperate, he saw that opening and threw everything he had in the world on a wide left hook aimed for the kid's chin!

It was murder. Morgan had set the German right up by taking those other left hooks, and when that one came he was set. He stepped inside with a short right to the chin, and I'm a sun-kissed scenery-bum if Blucher's feet didn't leave the floor by six inches! Then he hit the canvas like somebody had dropped him off a building, and the kid never even looked down. He just turned and walked to his corner and picked up his towel. He *knew* Blucher was out.

The payoff came in the morning. I crawled out of the hay rubbing my eyes and walked to the door. When I picked up my paper, it opened my eyes quick enough.

DREAM FIGHTER KAYOS BLUCHER
Morgan Fights According to Dream Plan.
Blucher Completely Out-Classed.

I walked back inside and read the rest of it. Race had been getting around. He'd picked up a statement from Van Schendel, whom I'd not asked to keep still, and then had found two or three other guys who knew something about it. Here and there the kid had mentioned it before I took him over. Then Race went down the line of his fights and showed how the kid had won—and how I'd called the round on Charlie Gomez.

It made a swell yarn. There was no question about that. I could see papers all over the country eating it up. Good stuff, if you just wanted to make a couple of bucks, but the wrong kind of publicity for a champ.

Champ? Yes, that's what I figured. I'd been figuring on it ever since the kid took Gomez. This dream stuff didn't mean a thing to me. I was banking on the kid's boxing and his punch. And down in the corner of the sports sheet I saw something else . . .

DEADY MCCALL TO RETIRE
Contender to Marry

That left Kip Morgan the leading contender for the world's heavyweight title. That put Kip in line for a fight for the world's championship, and it had to be within ninety days. I knew the champ, Steve Kendall, had signed with Bid Kerney to defend his title. And Bid had a contract that made the kid his for one more fight in that same period. We had the champ, and we had Bid, and there was no getting away from that.

THAT DREAM STUFF built the fight up beautifully, and everything went fine until about four days before the battle. I dropped around to the dressing room after the kid's workout. He was sharp, ready to go. I'd never seen him look better. His body was hard as iron, and he'd browned to a beautiful golden tint that had all the girls in camp oohing and aahing around. But he looked worried.

"What's the matter, Kip?" I asked him. "Working too hard?"

He shook his head.

"No. I'm worried though. I slept like a log last night—and never dreamed a bit! I was just dead from the time I hit the bed until I woke up this morning."

"So what?" I said, shrugging. "You got four nights yet."

He nodded, gloomily. We talked awhile, and then I went outside. Stig Martin was a hanger-on around the fight game I'd picked up to rub the kid. Maybe he knew his way around too well. But he was an A-1 rubber. He grinned at me.

"How's the kid? Dreaming any?"

"Listen, Duck-Bill," I told him. "You lay off that stuff, see? That dream business is a lot of hooey, get me? Now forget it."

I turned away, but when I got to the door, I glanced back. Stig was standing there with a sarcastic grin on his face that I didn't like. I was about to go back and fire him when Race Malone came up. So I postponed it. Which only goes to show what a sap I was.

———

RACE TOOK ME back to town to get some publicity shots of me signing articles to guarantee that the kid would defend his title against Kendall if he beat him, and it was the next morning before I saw Morgan or Stig again. The minute I saw the kid, I knew something was haywire.

"What's eatin' you?" I asked him, gripping his arm. "You feel all right, don't you?"

"Yeah," he muttered. "Only I haven't dreamed about this fight. I dreamed last night, but it was all a confused mess where nothing got through. Only sometimes I'd think about punches, and I'd hear them saying how I was getting beat. That I was blood all over, that I couldn't take it. Over and over again."

I frowned, pushing my hat back on my head. Stig Martin was standing on the edge of the porch, smoking a cigarette. He was grinning. It made me sore.

"Listen, you," I said. "Take a walk. I'm sick of seeing your face around. Walk around someplace and keep out of the way."

He pouted, and walked off. Something didn't smell right about this deal.

"Listen, kid," I said. "You never mentioned hearing voices before. Before it was all like a motion picture, you said."

He nodded.

"I know. But now I don't see anything. I just hear a lot of confused stuff about me getting whipped."

I could see he was worried. His eyes looked hollow, and his face was a little yellow. I decided to get hold of Doc Van Schendel.

———

WHEN I DROVE back to the camp with Van Schendel the next day, I saw the kid sitting on the steps, twisting his hands and cracking his knuckles nervously. His face was drawn, and he looked bad. Just as we got out of the car, I heard Stig Martin speak to him.

"What of it, kid? Everybody has to lose sometime. You're young. You couldn't expect to take the belt the first time out."

"What's that?" I snapped at him. "Where'd you get that stuff, talking to my fighter like that? Listen, you tramp! Morgan's going to knock the champ loose from his buttons, an' don't forget it!"

Stig got up, sneering.

"Yeah? Maybe. But not if he doesn't have the right dream. He's got to be ready for that . . . got to be ready to lose. If he goes in without his dream, he's going to get beat to a pulp! Right, Kip? For your own good, I suggest you duck this one."

Well, I haven't hit a guy since I used to hustle pool around the waterfront, but I uncorked that one with the works on it. Stig Martin hit the ground all in one bunch. He wasn't out, but he had a lot of teeth that were. He got up and stumbled away, mumbling through mashed lips, and I walked over to the kid, rubbing my knuckles, and hustled him inside. I came out to get Doc and found him looking at Stig's retreating back.

"Who iss dese man?" he asked, curiously. "I see him talking mit Steve Kendall undt Mister Johnson."

"What?" I yelled. "You saw Stig—!" I backed up and sat down cussing myself for a sap. I should have known Martin was a plant. And here I was feeling so good about getting the champ, worrying about dreams and everything, that I let something like that happen. Why, if Doc hadn't seen—

"Hey, wait a minute!" I shouted, scrambling up again. "Where did you see Kendall and his pilot?"

Doc turned, looking at me over his glasses. "Vhy, they was oop to my office. They were asking me questions about zose articles in de newspaper. Vhy, iss it nodt all right?"

Then I just let go everything and sat down. I sat there with the Doc staring at me, kind of puzzled. Finally, I get up courage enough to take it.

"All right," I said. "Tell me. Tell me all about it. What did they ask you, and what did you tell them?"

"They asking me aboot dreams, undt vhat vould happen if he don't dream at all."

The Doc rambled on into a lot of words I didn't understand, and a lot of talk that was all a whistle in the wind to me, and if Race Malone hadn't come up I never would have got it figured out.

"It's simple enough," Race said. "They went to the Doc to find some way of getting your boy's goat. They decided to keep him from dreaming, and they found out dope might do it. If you look into it, I'll bet you find Stig Martin has been slipping the kid something to make him sleep, and sleep heavily."

Then the Doc had told them some people were subject to suggestion when asleep or doped, so (I found this out later) Stig evidently gave the kid a riding all night a couple of times, telling him over and over that he'd lose, that he didn't have a chance. He kept it up even when the kid was awake, and they were together.

After listening to all of this Race shrugged his shoulders.

"It's a lousy stunt, and the nuttiest thing I ever heard of, but it'll make a swell story."

I got up.

"Listen," I said, trying to be calm. "If one word of this ever makes the paper I'll start packing a heater for you, and the first time I see you I'll cut you down to the curb, get me? Those stories of yours spilled the beans in the first place!"

Race promised to say nothing until after the fight, and I walked inside with Doc Van Schendel to look the kid over. We didn't let on about Stig, Kendall, or Johnson. I had a better idea in mind. I asked the Doc to stick around the camp with us, and, feeling guilty for his part in all this, he agreed to help.

———

WHEN WE WENT into town for the fight, I was feeling much happier. The kid was looking pretty good and rarin' to go, with a nervousness that's just right and natural.

I was still pretty nervous myself. This fight wasn't going to be a cinch, by no means. But when the kid crawled into the ring, I was in a much better frame of mind than I had been some days before. Stig Martin contributed his little share to my happiness, too. When I saw him in the hall near the dressing room, I licked my lips.

He didn't see me until I was within arm's length of him, and then it was too late to duck. I slammed him into the wall, then hit him again. He slid down the wall and sat there, blood streaming from his nose.

A big cop looked around the corner, came over, frowning.

"What's going on here?" he demanded.

"I am," I returned cheerfully, and went.

———

IT WILL BE a long time before they have a crowd like that again, and a long time before they see two heavyweights put on such a fight. When we walked down to the ring, the ball-park was ablaze with lights, and there was a huge crowd stretching back into the darkness, a sea of faces that made you feel lost. Then the lights went out, and there was only the intensely white light over the ring, and the low murmur of voices.

Kip Morgan was wearing a blue silk dressing gown, and he crawled into the ring, walking quickly over to the resin box. The champ took his time. I saw him take in the kid's nervousness with a sleepy smile. Then he rubbed his feet slowly in the resin and walked back to his corner.

Then I was talking to the kid, trying to quiet him down, trying to get him settled when I was so jittery that a tap on the shoulder would have set me screaming. I'd been handling scrappers a long time, but this was my first championship battle, and there, across the ring, was the Big Fellow, the world's heavyweight champion himself, the guy we'd been reading about, and seeing in the newsreels. And here was this kid that I'd brought up from the bottom, the kid who was going out there to fight that guy.

I'm telling you, it was something. I saw the champ slip off his robe and noticed that hard brown body, the thick, sloping shoulders, the slabs of muscle around his arms, watched him dancing lightly on his toes, moving his arms high. He was a fighter, every inch of him.

We got our instructions, and both men stared down at the canvas. I whispered a few last-minute instructions to the kid, tossed his robe and towel to a second, then dropped down beside the ring. Morgan was standing up there, all alone now. He had it all ahead of him in the loneliest place in the world. Across the ring the champ was sucking at his mouth-piece, and dancing lightly on his toes. When the bell sounded you could hear it ring out over the whole crowd, and then those guys were moving in on each other.

Did you ever notice how small those gloves look at a time like that? How that dull red leather seems barely to cover their big hands? I did, and I saw the kid moving out, his fists ready. They tried lefts, and both landed lightly. The kid tried another. He was still nervous. I could see that. The champ stepped away from it, looking him over. Then he feinted, but the kid stepped back. He wasn't fooled. The champ moved in, and the crowd watched like they were in a trance. They all knew something was going to happen. They had a hunch, but they weren't hurrying it.

Suddenly, the champ stepped in fast, and his left raked the kid's eye, and a short, wicked right drummed against the kid's ribs. The champ bored in, slamming both hands to the head, then drilled a right to the body. The kid jabbed and walked around him, taking a hard right. The champ landed another right. He was confident, but taking his time.

The kid jabbed twice, fast. One left flickered against the champ's eye, the other went into his mouth—hard. The champ slipped under another left and slammed a wicked right to the ribs and I saw the kid's mouth come open.

Then the champ was really working. He drilled both hands to the body, straightened up and let the kid have a left hook on the chin. The kid's head rolled with the punch and Morgan jarred the champ with a short right. They were sparring in mid-ring at the bell.

The second opened with the champ slipping a left and I could see the gleam of grease on his cheekbones as he came in close. A sharp left jab stabbed Morgan twice in the mouth, and he stepped away with a trickle of blood showing. The champ came in again, jabbed, and the kid crossed a right over the jab that knocked the champ back on his heels.

Like a tiger the kid tore in, hooking both hands to the body. A hard right drove the champ into a neutral corner, and the two of them swapped it out there, punching like demons, their faces set and bloody. When they broke, I saw both were bleeding, the champ from an eye, and the kid from the mouth.

They met in mid-ring for the third and started to swap it out, neither of them taking a back step. Then the champ straightened up, and his right came whistling down the groove. Instinctively, I ducked—but the kid didn't.

Then I was hanging on to the edge of the ring and praying or swearing or something and the kid was lying out there on the canvas, as still as the dead. I was wishing he never saw a ring when the referee said four, and the kid gathered his knees under him. Then the referee said five and the kid got one foot on the floor. At six he was trying to get up and couldn't make it. At eight, he did, and then the champ came out to wind it all up.

Behind me someone said, "There he goes!" and then Kip wavered somehow and managed to slip the left, and before the right cross landed he was in a clinch. The champ pounded the kid's ribs in close, but when they broke the kid came back fast with a hard left hook, then another, and another and another!

The champ was staggering! Kip walked in, slammed a hard right to the head and took a wicked one in return. I saw a bloody streak where the champ's mouth should be, and the kid jerked a short left hook to the chin, and whipped up a steaming right uppercut that snapped the champ's head back.

Morgan kept boring in, his lips drawn in a thin line. All the sleepiness was gone from the champ. Morgan stabbed a left and then crossed a right that caught the champ flush on the nose as he came in. Out behind me the crowd was a thundering roar, and the kid was weaving and hooking, slamming punch after punch to the champion's head and body, but taking a wicked battering in return.

Somewhere a bell rang, and they were still fighting when the seconds rushed in to drag them back to their corners.

The kid was hot. He wouldn't sit down. He stood there, shaking his seconds off, swaying on his feet from side to side, his hands working and his feet shuffling. I was seeing something I never saw before, for if ever fighting instinct had a man, it had Kip Morgan.

When the bell rang I saw the champ come off his stool and trot to the center of the ring, and then the kid cut loose with a sweeping right that sent him crashing into the ropes. Before he could get off them, the kid was in there pounding away with both hands in a blur of punches that no man could evade or hope to stem.

Kendall whipped a right to the kid's body, but he might as well have slugged the side of a boiler, for the kid never slowed up. The champion was whipped, and he knew it. You could see in his face there was only one thing he wanted, and that was out of there. But he clinched and hung on, his eyes glazed, his face a bloody mask, his mouth hanging open as he gasped for breath.

When the bell rang for the fifth, not a man in the house could speak above a whisper. Worn and battered by the fury of watching the fight, they sat numb and staring as the kid walked out there, his face set, his hands ready. There was nothing of the killing fury about him now, and he moved in like a machine, that left stabbing, stabbing, stabbing.

The champ gamely tried to fight back, throwing a hard right that lost itself on air. Then a left set him back on his heels, and as he reversed desperately to regain his balance, the kid stepped back, coolly letting him recover. Then his right shot out and the champion came facedown to the blood-smeared canvas—out cold!

Mister, that was a fight.

Race cornered me first thing.

"Give, Finny," he said, all excited. "What did you do to the kid?"

I smiled.

"Nothing much, Race. I only used the same method Stig Martin used. With Doc's help, we doped him that night, kept repeating over and over that he'd win the fight, that it was surefire for him! The next day he was all pepped up! The Doc and I worked on him after that, putting him into the right kind of physical shape. So how could you stop him in the ring tonight?"

"What a story!" breathed Race. "What a—"

"What a nothing!" I snapped. "No more stories from you, Race Malone. The dream fighter business is going to be all over, anyhow, Race. I'm going to tell Morgan just what happened to him! How long do you think he's going to believe in this dream business after that?

"I'll bet you ten to one it'll knock his dreams out of the ring!"

CORPSE ON THE CARPET

S HE WAS SITTING just around the curve of the bar, a gorgeous package of a girl, all done up in a gray tailored suit. The hand that held the glass gave a blinding flash and when I could see again, I got a gander at an emerald-cut diamond that would have gone three carats in anybody's bargain basement. Yet when she turned toward me, I could see the pin she wore made the ring look cheap.

No babe with that much ice has any business dropping into a bar like the Casino. Not that I'm knocking it, for the Casino is a nice place where everybody knows everybody else and a lot of interesting people drop in. But those rocks were about three blocks too far south, if you get what I mean.

At the Biltmore, okay. At the Ambassador, all right. But once in a while some tough Joes drop in here. Guys that wouldn't be above lifting a girl's knickknacks. Even from a fence there was a winter in Florida in those rocks.

It was then I noticed the big guy further along the bar. He had a neck that spread out from his ears and a wide, flat face. His hands were thick and powerful. And I could see he was keeping an eye on the babe with the ice, but without seeming to.

This was no pug, and no "wrassler." Once you've been in the trade, you can spot them a mile off. This guy was just big and powerful. In a brawl, he would be plenty mean and no average Joe had any business buying any chips when he was dealing.

"Babe," I said, to myself, "you're lined up at the wrong rail. You better get out of here—fast!"

She shows no signs of moving, so I am just about to move in—just to protect the ice, of course—when a slim, nice-looking lad beats me to it.

HE'S TALL AND good-looking, but strictly from the cradle, if you know what I mean. He's been wearing long pants for some twenty-odd years, but he's been living at home or going to school and while he figures he's a smart lad, he doesn't know what cooks. When I take a gander at Blubber Puss, which is how I'm beginning to think about the big guy, I can see where this boy is due to start learning, the hard way.

Me? I'm Kip Morgan, nobody in particular. I came into this bar because it was handy and because there was an Irish bartender with whom I talked fights and football. Like I say, I'm nobody in particular, but I've been around.

This nice lad who's moving in on the girl hasn't cut his teeth on the raw edges of life yet. The babe looks like the McCoy. She's got a shape to whistle at and a pair of eyes that would set Tiffany back on his heels. She's stiff with the boy at first, then she unbends. She won't let him buy her a drink, but she does talk to him. She's nervous, I can see that. She knows the big lug with the whale mouth is watching her.

All of a sudden, they get up and the boy helps her on with her coat, then slides into his own. They go out, and I am taking a swallow of bourbon when Blubber Puss slides off his stool and heads toward the door.

"Bud," I tell myself, "you're well out of this."

Then I figure, what the devil? That rabbit is no protection for a job like that, and Blubber Puss won't play pretty. Also, I have always had confidence in what my left can do to thick lips.

They walk about a block and take a cab. There's another one standing by, and the big Joe slides into it. I am just about to figure I'm out of it when another cab slides up. I crawl in.

"Follow those cabs, chum," I say to the cabbie.

He takes a gander at me. "What do you think this is—a movie?"

"If it was, you wouldn't be here," I tell him. "Stick with them and I'll make it worth your while."

We've gone about ten blocks when something funny happens. The cab the Blubber is in pulls up and passes the other one, going on over the rise ahead of us. While I am still tailing the babe and her guy, and trying to figure that one, I see his cab coming back, and Blubber isn't in it.

Then, we go over the rise ourselves and I see the girl's cab pulling up at the curb near a narrow street. They get out, and we slide past and pull in at the curb. Their side of the street is light, mine is dark, so I know what to do.

The cabbie takes his payoff, and I slip him a two-dollar tip. He looks at it and sneers.

"I thought they always slipped you a five and said keep the change."

I look at him cold. I mean, I chill him. "What do you think this is—the movies?"

The cab slides away and I go around the corner into the same narrow street where the babe and her guy are going, but I'm still on the dark side and there is a row of parked cars along the curb.

It doesn't figure right. If Blubber goes on ahead, that can only mean he knows where the babe and her guy are going. If that is true, that figures Blubber and the girl are working it together. That means mama's boy is headed for the cleaners.

Only the doll doesn't fit. She doesn't look the type. There is more in this, as the guy said eating the grapefruit, than meets the eye.

The babe has pulled up in front of the side entrance of an apartment house and is trying to give her young Lothario the brush. He is polite, but insistent. Then the big lug steps from the shadows and moves up behind the kid.

When he starts moving, I start. The big guy has a black-jack and he lifts it.

I yell, "Look out!"

The kid wheels around, his mouth open, and Blubber Puss turns on me with a snarl. Get that? A snarl. The big ape will have it for days, I figure. When he turned, I plastered it right into his teeth, then fired another into the big guy's digestion.

You know what happened?

Nothing.

It was like slugging the side of a building. That stomach, which I figured would be a soft touch, was hard as nails. I'd thrown my Sunday punch and all I got was rebound.

Now brother, if I nail them with my right and they don't go down, they do some funny things standing up—usually. This big guy took it standing and threw a left that shook me to my socks. Then, he moves in with the blackjack.

The kid starts for him then, but—accidentally, or otherwise— the girl's dainty ankle is there and the kid spills over it onto the sidewalk. I blocked the blackjack with my left forearm and then made a fist and chopped it down to the big lug's eye. I was wearing kid gloves, and they cut to the bone.

Before he can get himself set, I let him have them both in the digestion again. No sale. He tried the blackjack and we circled. I stabbed him with a left, then another. He ducked his head and lunged for me. I caught him by the hair and jerked his face down and my knee up.

When I let go, he staggered back, his nose so flat he had no more profile than a blank check. He was blood all over, and I never saw him look so good. I set myself then and let him have both barrels, right from the hip, and my right smashed his jaw back until his chin almost caught behind his collar-button.

He went down. I'd a good notion to put the boots to him, but I always hate to kick a man in the face when there's a lady around. Doesn't seem gentlemanly, somehow.

I rolled him over on the pavement and he was colder than a pawnbroker's heart. I turned around. The kid is standing there, but the babe has taken a powder.

"Listen," he said, "thanks awfully. But where did she go?"

"Pal," I said, "why don't you let well enough alone? Don't you realize that the doll brought you here for a trimming?"

"Oh, no." He looked offended. "She wouldn't do that. She was a nice girl."

"Buddy, I tailed you and the girl out of the bar because I saw this big mug watching you. Until this guy passed your cab and went ahead, I figured he was after the girl's ice. But he came here, and that could only mean he knew where she was going."

"Oh, no. I don't believe that," he said. "Not for a minute."

"Okay," I answered. "Better scram out of here before the cops come nosing around."

He scrammed. Me, I am a curious guy. The big potato was still bye-bye, so I gave him a frisk. He was packing a gun, which he might have used if I'd given him time. It was a snub-nosed .38. I pocketed the weapon, then found what I wanted. It was a driver's license made out to Buckley Dozen.

Well, Buckley was coming out of his dozen, so I turned away. Then, I saw the diamond pin.

Somehow, the doll had dropped it. Probably when her ankle had tripped the kid. I lifted it off the pavement, went around the corner, and made a half block walking fast. A moment later a cab came streaking by, and Buckley Dozen was in it. But he didn't see me.

———

For a couple of days after that I was busy. Several times I looked at that ice. I figured no dame like that would be wearing anything nearly as good as this looked, so decided it must be glass, or paste. Then I dropped in at the Casino Bar and Emery, the bartender, motioned me over.

"Say, there was a guy in here looking for you. Nice-lookin' kid."

His description fitted the youngster who'd been with the girl.

"Probably figured things out," I said, "and wants to buy me a drink."

"No, it wasn't that. He looked serious, and was awful anxious to see you. He left this address here."

I took the visiting card he handed me, noted the address at a nice apartment away up on Wilshire, and the name Randolph Seagram.

That made me think of the pin again, so on a hunch, I left the bar and started up the street. There was a fancy jewelry store in Beverly Hills, just west past Crescent Heights and Doheny but a million miles away. I went there first, taking a gander at the stuff in the window. Glass or not, this pin in my pocket made the rest of that stuff look like junk. Walking around to the door, I went in.

———

THE FLOOR WAS so polished, I hated to walk on it and everything seemed to be glass and silver.

A clerk walked toward me who looked as if he might consider speaking to either the Rockefellers or the Vanderbilts and asked what he could do for me. I think he figured on taking a pair of tongs and dropping me outside.

"Just give me a quick take on this," I said, handing him the pin, "and tell me what it's worth."

He took a look and his eyes opened like he was looking at this great big beautiful world for the first time. Then, he screws a little business into his eye and looks the pin over.

When he looked up, dropping his glass into his hand, he was mingling extreme politeness and growing suspicion in about equal quantities.

"Roughly, twenty thousand dollars," he said.

———

THE NIGHT BEFORE, I'd been in a poker game and my coat had hung on a hook alongside of a dozen others, with all that ice loose in my pocket! I took it standing.

"I'd like to speak to the manager," I said quickly.

The manager was a tall, cool specimen with gray hair along his temples and looked like he might at least be Count von Roughpants or something.

"Listen," I said, "and while I'm talking, take a gander at this." I dropped the ice on the table.

He looked at it, and when he looked up at me, I knew he was thinking of calling the cops.

"I'm not going to tell you how I got this," I said. "I think maybe the party that owns it is in trouble. I don't have any way of finding out where the party to whom it belongs is— unless you can help me. Isn't it true that pins like this are scarce?"

He lifted an eyebrow. "I would say very rare. In fact, I believe this to be a special design, made to order for someone."

"All right. I want you to make some discreet inquiries. Find out the name of the person it belongs to and where they live. I don't want anybody to know why we're asking. This party may have some relatives or friends who would be worried. When I find out who, what, and why, then I'll know what to do."

"You have some idea to whom it belongs?" he asked.

"I think so. I hope to find out for sure. Meanwhile, do this for me. Take down an accurate description of this pin, then my name and description." I could see the suspicion fading from his eyes. "Then if anything goes haywire, I'll be in the clear."

"And the stone?" he asked.

"I'll see it gets to a safe place."

Leaving the store, I turned into a five-and-dime and after picking up a box several times larger than the pin would need, I wadded the pin in paper, stuffed it in the box, and then had the box wrapped by their wrapping service. Then I addressed it to myself and dropped it in a mailbox.

Emery, the Casino bartender, had said the kid was worried. He might have something.

I caught a cab and gave the address that was on the visiting card the kid had left for me.

None of this was my business. Yet I could not leave it alone. The girl had measured up to be the right sort, yet somehow she was tied up with Blubber Puss, who was a wrong G from any angle.

No girl wears jewelry like that when she's willingly working with a strong-arm guy. There was something that smelled in this deal, and I meant to find out what.

The kid lived in a swank apartment. I stopped at the desk and when the lad turned around I said, "Which apartment is Mr. Seagram in?"

He looked at me coolly. "He lives in C-three, but I don't believe he's in. His office has been calling and hasn't gotten an answer."

"His office?"

"Asiatic Importing and Development Company."

"Oh? Then if they are calling him maybe he didn't go to work this morning."

He frowned. "I'm sure nothing is wrong. Mr. Seagram is often out of town."

"I'll go up," I said.

He was watching me as I started for the elevator. I found C-3 around the corner of the hall, out of sight of the foyer.

There was no answer to my knock, and then I saw that the door wasn't quite closed. I pushed it open and stepped in.

Randolph Seagram lay on the floor near an overturned chair. He was dead, half of a knife sticking from his chest. The lights were on, although it was broad daylight and one whole side of the place was windows.

"Got him last night," I told myself. I took a quick gander around, then stepped to the phone. "Get me the police," I said.

"What's the trouble?" the clerk asked. "We mustn't have the police."

"Listen, brother," I cut in quickly. "You've got to have the police. This guy is stone cold dead on the carpet. Get them on the phone, I'll do the talking."

When he got them, I asked for Homicide.

"Mooney talkin'," a voice said. "What's up?"

"There's a guy down here in apartment C-three of the Cranston Arms," I said, "who came out on the wrong end of an argument. He's lying here on the carpet with a knife in his ribs."

I heard his feet come off the desk with a thud. "Where's that again? Who are you?"

"My name is Morgan," I told him, "Kipling Morgan. Kipling as in Gunga Din."

"Don't let anybody leave," he said. "We'll be over."

Kneeling beside him, I gave the lad a hurried frisk. He didn't have any folding money, and his wallet was lying on the floor. They had nicked him for his dough, too. But it wasn't what I was looking for.

Knowing my own habits, I took a chance on his.

There were three addresses on a worn envelope, three addresses and a telephone number. I stuck the envelope in my pocket.

When the police came in, I was sitting in the chair by the telephone like I hadn't moved.

"Detective Lieutenant Mooney." The guy who said it was short and square-shouldered, but looked rugged enough for two men. He gave the body a quick looking over, picked up the empty wallet, then looked at me. "Where do you fit?" he asked.

"Acquaintance," I said. "Met the guy in a bar on Sixth Street. He left word that he wanted to see me. I came up, he was dead."

"When'd you last see him alive?" Mooney was watching me. He had an eye, this dick did.

"About three days ago." I hesitated then told him how I'd followed him from a bar, and what I'd seen. I didn't mention the diamonds.

"Well," he said, "there wasn't anybody around to help him the second time. Looks like they killed him when he made a fuss."

"I don't think so."

Mooney looked up at me. "Why?"

"Seagram thought the girl was on the level. I think maybe he found her again. If I'm any judge, he was going to try when he left me. Well, he must have found her. Either he learned something he wasn't supposed to know, or they tracked him home and knocked him off."

"Know his family?" Mooney asked.

"Nuh uh."

"Who are you? Your face looks familiar." Mooney was still studying me. I could see he wasn't sure I was in the clear. He was a tight-mouthed guy.

"I used to be a fighter."

"Yeah, I remember." He studied me. "Every once in a while you hear of a fighter turning crooked."

"Yeah? Every once in a while you hear of a banker turning crooked, too, or a cop."

"It doesn't sound right," he said. "You followed them home because you figured it was a heist job. Why didn't you call the police?"

"What world are you living in? You can't walk up to a cop and tell him you think somebody is going to stick up somebody else just because you feel it in here." I tapped myself on the chest. "I knew the signs, and I tailed along."

"You had a fight with the guy?" Mooney asked.

"Yeah." I nodded. "You might check your hospitals. The guy had a broken nose when he left me, and he lost a couple of teeth. He had at least three deep cuts, too."

"You work 'em over, huh?" Mooney turned. "Graham, get started on that."

Mooney took my address and I left. Me, I had an idea or two. The girl didn't fit. Somehow she had got mixed up with the wrong crowd, and she might be afraid to ask for help even if she got the chance because of her folks or husband or someone hearing about it; women are funny that way. Seagram might have seen her again, followed her, and tried to learn something. That was when he tried to get hold of me. Then, he went home and they got him.

Yet Blubber Puss didn't fit into the killing. He was a gun man or muscle man. He wouldn't use a shiv. Also, he must have his face well bandaged by now. He would be too easily remembered.

———

BACK IN MY own place, I dug out a .380 Colt that I had and strapped it into a holster that fit around the inside of my thigh under my pants. This one I carried before, and it was ready to use. There was a zipper in the bottom of my right pants pocket, the gun butt just a little lower. I could take a frisk and it would never be found. On my hip, I stuck the rod I took off Blubber Puss.

By nine o'clock, I had eliminated two of the addresses on the envelope. The third and last one was my best bet. It turned out to be a big stone house in the hills above Hollywood. It was set back in some trees and shrubbery with a high wall all the way around.

The gate was closed and locked tight. I could see the shine of a big black car standing in front of the house, almost concealed by the intervening shrubbery. Turning, I walked along the dark street under the trees. About twenty yards farther along, I found what I sought—a big tree with limbs overhanging the wall.

With a quick glance both ways, I jumped and, catching a

limb, pulled myself up. Then, I crawled along the limb until I was across the wall; I dropped to the lawn.

My idea of the thing was this: Seagram had run into the girl again. Maybe he had talked to her, probably not. But, mindful of what I'd told him, he might have been uncertain of her, and so maybe he had tailed her. Then, he had tried to come in here. Perhaps he had convinced himself she was okay, or he was planning a Galahad. But he had died for messing with something out of his league.

This setup still smelled wrong, though. The house was too big. The layout cost money. No fly-by-night hoodlums who might use a girl as a plant to pick up some change would have a place like this, or a girl with diamonds like she had.

I did an Indian act going through the trees. When I got close, I dropped my raincoat on the grass behind some shrubbery and laid down on it where I could watch the house.

There was a distant mutter of thunder, growing off among the clouds like a sleepy man you're trying to wake but who doesn't want to get up.

The house was big and the yard was beautiful. A drive made a big circle among the trees. Another drive went past the house to a four-car garage. One of the cars was in front of the house. Another one, facing out, stood beside it. The last car had a Chicago license—an Illinois plate with the town name-strip above it.

There were two lighted windows on the ground floor, and I could see another on the second floor, a window opposite a giant tree with a limb that leaned very, very near.

Suddenly, a match flared. It was so sudden I ducked. In the glow of the match, as the guy lighted his cigarette, I could see Blubber Puss. His nose was taped up, and there were two strips of adhesive tape on his cheekbones. His lips were swollen considerably beyond their normal size.

Blubber Puss was standing there in the darkness. He looked like he had been there quite a while.

Footsteps on the gravel made me turn my head. Another man, skinny and stooped, was walking idly along the drive. He stopped close to Blubber, and I could hear the low murmur of their voices without being able to distinguish a word.

After a minute, they parted and began walking off in opposite directions. I waited, watching them go. I took a quick gander at the luminous dial of my wristwatch. After almost ten minutes, I saw Skinny come into sight ahead, his feet crunching along the gravel, and then Blubber Puss came into sight. This time they were closer to me when they met.

"This standin' watch is killin' me," Skinny growled. "What's the boss figure is goin' to happen anyway? We're not hot in this town."

"That's what you say." Blubber's mouth shaped the words poorly. "You suppose they won't have word out all over the country? Then knockin' off that kid was a tough break. Why'd he have to stick his nose into it?"

"That's what comes of not havin' any dough," Skinny said. "We had to make a raise. What easier way to do it?"

"Well," Blubber said, with satisfaction, "we'll get plenty out of this before we're done. Gettin' in here was a break, too. Nobody'd think to look here."

"We better keep movin'," Skinny suggested. "The boss might come out and see us loafin' on the job. Anyway, it's near time for our relief."

The two walked on, in their respective ways. I stared after them trying to make sense from what I'd heard. One thing was sure. A relief for these two meant that at least two more men, aside from the mysterious boss, were inside. At the very least that made me one against five. It was too many, this late in the evening, especially when I hadn't eaten any dinner.

The ground-floor window looked tempting, but I decided against it. I'd not have time for much of a look before Skinny and Blubber would be back around, and the chances of being seen were too great. I didn't care to start playing cops and robbers with real bullets until I knew what the setup was.

Picking up my coat, I slid back into the bushes and weaved my way toward that tall tree. A leafy branch should offer a way into one of the upper rooms. It didn't seem like so desperate a chance as going for the ground-floor window.

A few drops of rain began to fall, but this was no time to be thinking of that. I looped my raincoat through my belt and went up that tree. From a position near the bole, my feet on the big limb, I could see into a window.

There were two people in the room. One of them was the doll who wore the diamonds. The other was a younger girl, not over twelve years old. While I was looking, the door opened and a guy came in with a tray. He put it down, made some crack to the girl, and she just looked at him. I could see her eyes, and the warmth in their expression would have killed an Eskimo.

Maybe I'm dumb. Maybe you'd get the idea sooner than me. But only now was it beginning to make sense; the girls were prisoners in what was probably their own home.

The babe who wore the ice that night had been working as a plant. She may have been forced to do it while they held her sister here. Maybe there were others of the family in there, too.

Who this bunch were and how they got here did not matter now. The thing that mattered was to get those two girls out of there, and now. Once they were safe, then we could get to Mooney and spread the whole thing in his lap.

The trouble was I knew how these boys operated. Randolph Seagram, lying back there on the floor with a knife sticking out of him, was evidence enough. They were playing for keeps, and they weren't pulling any punches. Nobody had rubber teeth in this setup.

Nevertheless, I seemed to be cutting myself in. And that was the big question. After all, I wasn't any private dick. There was no payoff if I was successful and at least one of those guys in that house had reason enough to hate my insides. I could get down out of this tree, go back over the wall, make a call to Mooney, and then go home and get a good night's sleep.

I had a good notion to do it. It was the smart thing to do. Except for one consideration.

This was a tough mob. Maybe they had left the doll alone up to now. It looked as if they had. But there was no reason why they should any longer. They might decide to blow and knock off the babes when they left. They might decide to do worse. And they might make that decision within the next ten minutes.

I am still thinking like that when I hear one of the boys down below running. He's heading toward the gate. Another car comes in and swings up under my tree. Two men get out, one of them carrying a briefcase.

"Something's going down," I tell myself, "something interesting." See? That explains it. I'm just a nosy guy. Curious.

There was a dark window a little to the left of the one to the girls' room. Working out on the limb . . . I was out on a limb in more ways than one. I swung down to the ledge of the dark window. It was a French window, opening on a little, imitation balcony.

With my knife blade, I got it open and stepped down in the room.

For a moment I hesitated, getting my bearings. Then I felt my way through the room to the door.

The hallway was dark, too, and I made my way along it to the stairs, then down. I could see light coming from the crack of a door that was not quite closed and could hear the low murmur of voices.

Four men were inside. That scared me. There were two men outside, and two who had just arrived. Counting the three whom I already knew to be inside and the two who had just arrived, there should now have been five in the room.

That meant that there was another guy loose in the house.

Crouching near the foot of the stairs, I peered into the room and listened. I could see three men. One of them was a hoodlum, or I don't know the type when I see one. The other two were the ones who had come in the car, and I got the shock of my life.

The nearer of the pair, sitting sideways to me, was Ford Hiesel, a famous criminal lawyer, a man who had freed more genuine murderers than any two living men. The man facing me across the table was another famous attorney, Tarrant Houston, elderly, brilliant, and a man who had for a time been a judge and was now director of some of the biggest corporations on the Coast. The fourth man, the one I couldn't see, was speaking.

"You have no choice, Mr. Houston. If you attempt to notify the police, the girls will be killed. Their safety lies in your doing just what you are told.

"As the family's lawyer you are in the perfect position to help us. We know Dwight Harley and his wife are in Bermuda. They've left here one hundred and fifty thousand dollars in negotiable securities. If we took them, we'd get maybe thirty thousand dollars from a fence. But you can get their full value.

"You take these bonds, turn them into cash, and bring it here; I want you to work fast. I may add, that you'll be watched."

"What assurance do I have," Houston demanded, "that you will release the girls after you get the money?"

"Because we have no reason to add murder to this. If we get the money, we leave, and the girls remain here."

"All right." Houston stood up. "Since I have no choice in the matter. I can handle the bonds. But I wish you'd allow me to communicate with Harley."

"Nothing doing." The reply was sharp. "You can handle this. I'm sure you've done transactions for him before."

Crouched there by the steps, I stiffened slightly. That voice. I knew it from somewhere.

What Houston didn't know was that murder was already tied in with this deal, and what I knew was that those thugs would never leave the girls alive when they left.

Nor, the chances were, would Houston make it either.

"What's your part in this, Hiesel?" Houston demanded, as he rose from the table.

The criminal lawyer shrugged. "The same as yours, Houston. These men knew of me. They simply got me to contact you. I don't know the girls. Nor do I know Harley, but I've no desire to see the girls or Harley killed over a few paltry dollars."

"And some of those paltry dollars," Houston replied sharply, "will no doubt find their way into your pockets."

He turned and walked to a door to the outside, and Hiesel followed him.

As they reached the door, I glanced back through the archway into the library where they had talked.

A man was standing there, and he was looking right at me.

The gun in his hand was very large, and I knew his face as well as I knew my own.

It was a round, moonlike face, pink and healthy. There were almost no eyebrows, and the mouth was peculiarly flat. When he smiled, he looked cherubic and pleasant. When his mouth closed and his eyes hardened, he looked merciless and brutal.

He was an underworld character known as Candy Chuck Marvin.

"So," he said, "we've a guest." And he added, as I got up and walked out into the open, "Long time no see, Morgan."

"Yeah," I said. "It has been a long time. I haven't seen you since the Redden mob was wiped out. As I remember, you took a powder at just about that time."

"That's right." He gestured me into the library. The fourth man, the hoodlum in the gray plaid suit, had a gun, too. "And where are the boys who wiped out the Redden mob now?"

IT TOOK ME a minute to get it. "Where are they? Why, let's see." I scowled, trying to recall. "Salter was killed by a hit-and-run driver. Pete Maron hung himself, or something. Lew Fischer and Joey Spats got into an argument over a card game and shot it out, both killed. I guess they are all dead."

"That's right. They are." Candy Chuck smiled at me. "Odd coincidence, isn't it? Fortunately, Pete Maron was light. That hook held his weight. I wasn't sure that it would when I first hung the rope over it. Salter was easy. It's simple enough to run a man down. And it's not too difficult a matter to fake a 'gun battle.' I pay my debts, Morgan."

I smiled at him. Candy Chuck Marvin was cunning, without any mercy, and killing meant nothing to him.

He had been convicted once, when a boy. After that, nobody ever found any witnesses.

"But this time there's going to be a change," I said. "You're turning those girls loose."

He laughed. "Am I?" He sat down on the corner of the desk and looked at me. "Morgan, I've found one of those setups I used to dream about. The boys pulled the Madison Tool payroll job, and they were on the lam. They came to me for a place to hole up. Then I got to talking with the little Harley girl on a train. It was perfect, see? Her parents gone, all the servants on vacations. The two girls were going to Atlanta—on a surprise visit. All we had to do was take them off the train at the next stop, return here and move in, a safe hideout for at least thirty days."

"Looked good, didn't it?" I said. "Until Blubber Puss followed the girl out of that bar."

His eyes hardened. "Was that you who beat up on Buckley? I might have known it." Then he nodded. "Yes," he said ruefully, "that was the bad part. We've got the sixty grand the boys lifted on the payroll, but it's hot money. Using it would be a dead giveaway. There was a little money on the girls, but my boys eat. So I sent the babe out with Buckley in order to pick up some cash."

"Winding up," I said dryly, "by knocking off Seagram."

"You know about that?" He looked at me thoughtfully. "You know too much."

Right then I wouldn't have sold my chances of getting out of this mess for a plugged nickel.

I wasn't kidding myself any about Candy Chuck. Take the wiping out of those killers back East. Nobody had ever tumbled that those killings weren't just like they looked— accident, suicide, and gunfight. Candy Chuck knew all the answers.

"There's no end to it," I told him. "You got in a bind and let Seagram learn too much. So you knocked him off. That got the police stirred up. Now you've got me on your hands. Are you going to knock me off, too? Don't you see? It just leads from one to another. You got sixty grand in hot money, and for all the good it does you now, you might as well have none. You've got a lawyer with a lot of bonds, but you haven't any cash to work with. The trouble with you, Marvin, is that you figure it all your way. Just like when you were so sure I'd throw that Williams fight because you threatened me."

Candy Chuck Marvin's eyes narrowed and his mouth tightened. "You'd have been smart to let me forget that," he said. "I dropped ten grand on that fight."

"You're not the kind of guy who forgets anything," I said. "And you're in the spot, not me."

This hoodlum with the rod is standing by taking it all in. Most of my talk has been as much for his benefit as for Candy Chuck's. I knew Marvin liked to hear himself tell how smart he was. I knew he would keep on talking. The longer he talked, the better chance I had for a break. One was all I wanted, brother, just one!

The hoodlum was beginning to shift his feet in a worried fashion. He was getting ideas. After all, he and his pals were right in the middle of a strange city, the cops were on their trail, they didn't have any money, and they were trusting to Marvin to pull rabbits out of a hat.

Marvin was good. He had hostages. He was living in one of the biggest, finest homes in the city, the last place anybody would look. Tarrant Houston wouldn't peep for fear of getting the girls killed. Nobody was around to interfere, and soon Houston would be cashing in a lot of bonds.

"Think of your men, Marvin," I said. I turned to the hood. "What do you think will happen to you guys if the cops move in? You guys get sold down the river. You take the rap, and the smart boy here has his pretty lawyer to get him out of it. If you ask me, you guys are just losing time from your getaway to let Marvin use you for a fast take—if it works."

"Shut up." Marvin was on his feet.

"Y'know, the guy's got somethin'."

The voice was a new one and we all turned. I jumped inside my skin. Whit Dyer had a rep like Dillinger's. He was no smart Joe, but he had a nickel's worth of brains, a fast gun hand, and courage enough for three.

"I never did like this setup," Dyer went on.

"Don't pay any attention!" Marvin snapped. "Where would you be, Dyer, if I hadn't brought you here?"

"Search me," Dyer admitted. "But not being here might be good. After all, there's just one way in and out of this yard, as you know. One way in, one way out. If they block those, we're stuck."

Then I saw something. Little things jump to your mind in a spot like that. There was a side window and the gate that led to the street looked right on it. A car was coming along that street. If it turned the corner this way, the lights would—

"Look out!" I shouted.

The car turned and the lights flashed in the window. Nerves were tense and my yell and the sudden flash did it. I hit the floor and snaked out that snub-nosed .38.

Whit Dyer took a quick step back and tripped on the rug. Somebody yelled and I saw a leg and let go a shot at it. Then I rolled over and hit my feet, running.

I made the stairs two at a time and was halfway up before Marvin made the door. They still hadn't figured out where that sudden flash of light had come from and for all they knew the place was alive with coppers.

Dyer rolled over and tried a quick shot at me, but I snapped one back and put a hole in the floor an inch from his head. Candy Chuck steadied himself and I knew if he ever got me in his sights, I was a dead pigeon. I jumped upward and somehow got hold of the railing at the top of the stairs. I threw myself out of the way just as his bullet whipped by. Then I was running.

I had to get the girls out of there. Skating to a stop, I grabbed the knob on their door, but it was locked. One look at the door told me there wasn't time to bust it, so I fired at an angle against the lock and then with a heave the door came open.

"Quick!" I said. "This way!"

The Harley girls caught on fast. They didn't waste any time. I shoved them into the room through which I'd entered.

"Get out onto that tree," I whispered. "You've got to! If you can get down without being seen, hide in the shrubbery."

Dyer and Greer were coming up the steps. They were careful. I had that gun and they didn't know how much ammo I had. Actually, it was half empty, but I also had the .380, which was a better gun, and two extra clips for it.

Backing around the corner of the hall, I caught a glimpse

of movement on the stairs and fired. Greer fell and started rolling downstairs. In the suddenly silent house, you could hear his body thump, thump, thump from step to step.

Could the shots be heard on the street? I didn't know. But I did know the house probably had walls a foot thick.

The back stairs. The idea hit me like an axe. There would be another way up, it was that kind of house. But by this time, Blubber Dozen and his skinny friend had been relieved of their guard duty and were coming inside. So that way was cut off.

I was on a long interior balcony from which rooms opened on two sides. The main stairway came up one side, but the railings partially cut off my view of it. I knew I had to get away somehow, but fast, before Dozen and his friend found me.

The hallway was hung with paintings and there were a lot of queer ornaments and art objects standing around. Down beyond me was an old chest of heavy wood and against the wall an Egyptian mummy case.

You didn't need to slug me with a ball bat. I grabbed the lid of that upright mummy case and pulled it open. It was empty, and I stepped in and pulled the lid as near shut as I could and still breathe. Inside the case smelled like a dead Egyptian or something; maybe this one had been embalmed in garlic.

Someone called, "Look out, Ed! He's in the hall!" Then Blubber Puss answered, "Must've ducked into a room. He ain't in sight."

Heavy footsteps came along, and I saw a dark shadow pass the crack I was keeping open. That was Dozen. But it was Whit Dyer's voice I heard now.

"I don't like this," Dyer muttered. "He got Greer."

"He did?" Dozen's voice spoke back. "Whit, I don't like this either. This place will be hotter than a firecracker. Let's take the geetus and blow!"

"Maybe that's the smart thing. I was thinkin', though, if Marvin gets his dough from that mouthpiece of Harley's, he figures on keeping it. I'm for knocking Marvin off and taking the jack."

Honor among thieves? Not so's you'd notice it! They

moved off and I opened the lid just a little wider. And I stepped right into Skinny.

His jaw dropped open so far you could have put a bottle of Pepsi-Cola in edgewise, and he backed up, gulping. I guess he figured the dead was coming to life. He was so startled that I slapped his gun arm away with my left and lowered the boom on his chin with my right.

He went down like he'd been dropped off the Chrysler Tower, but his finger tightened on the trigger and a shot went off.

Somebody yelled down the line and I heard feet beating up the stairs. Those feet were coming toward me.

Grabbing up Skinny's gun, I opened up. I wasn't shooting at anything, just making the boys nervous. I let them have four rounds and then started off down the hall running full tilt. I was almost at its end when the roof seemed to fall in. I took about three steps and then passed out cold.

———

WHEN I CAME out of it, I was lying on the floor in the library and Candy Chuck was sitting over me with a rod. I tried to move, but he had tied my hands behind me and wrapped me up with a couple of yards of clothesline. By craning my neck, I could see that Dyer, Skinny, and Dozen were also in the room.

"Don't squirm," Candy Chuck said politely. "Just rest easy." Then his face tightened and he leaned over and began slapping me. When he stopped, his face was a snarl.

"Where's the babes?" he said.

"What babes?" I asked innocently. "I thought you had 'em."

"Don't give me that," he said. "You hid them someplace. Now give, or I'm going to see how long it'll take to burn your foot off."

He would, too.

"Don't do it," I say. "I can't stand the smell of burning flesh. Reminds me of a guy I saw get it in the hot seat, once. You should be interested in that. It won't—"

He booted me in the ribs, and it hurt.

I stopped. I had no yen to get kicked around, and there was a chance he hadn't found my .380. No normal frisk would turn it up. Yet he might kick it, and then he *would* find it. Those ropes weren't bothering me. I had an idea that given a few minutes alone, I could shed them like last year's blonde.

"Listen, sport," I said, and I was addressing Dyer, Skinny, and Dozen, as well as Candy Chuck. Skinny I noticed had a knot on his head where he had hit the deck, and his jaw was swollen. "Why don't you boys play it smart and drag it out of here with the dough you got?"

"Shut up," Marvin said.

His rosy plan didn't look so good now. He was sore, and he was also uneasy. The girls were gone. With the guards and all he probably figured they hadn't left the grounds but without the girls he wouldn't get the money from Houston.

"I'd take it on the lam," I repeated. Then I added, as an afterthought, "This place is filthy with telephones."

He jumped. Then he jerked erect. "Dozen, you and Palo get busy and hunt those babes! Don't stop until you find 'em. You, too, Dyer."

Dyer didn't move. "Look who's giving orders," he said. "I'm stayin'. This guy on the floor makes sense. I like to listen."

Candy Chuck looked up, and if I had been Dyer, I wouldn't have felt good.

"All right," Candy Chuck said, "stay."

Candy Chuck Marvin was big time. You couldn't dodge that. He had been the brain behind many big jobs, and he had stayed in the clear a long time. Also, he had friends. Whit Dyer was merely a guy with a gat, a guy who would and could kill. And he was only about half smart. When Candy Chuck softened up, I knew that Dyer didn't have long to live.

Candy Chuck Marvin had been a big operator around Chicago, St. Paul, and New York. He had connections. Back in the days when I was slinging leather, I'd seen a lot of him. From all I knew, I figured I was the only guy who ever failed to play ball with him and got away alive. He'd ordered me to throw a fight, and I hadn't done it. Then again, I hadn't been easy to find in those days.

Marvin got up and walked over to the fireplace. There was a little kindling there, and he arranged it on the andirons. Then he calmly broke up a chair and added it to the fuel. He lit a crumpled newspaper and stuck it under the wood. Then he picked up the poker and laid it in the fire. When he put the poker there, he looked at me and grinned.

Me, I was sweating. Not because it was hot, but because I was wondering how I'd take it. You may read about people being tortured, but you never know how you'll react to getting your feet burned until it happens.

———

THE FIRE WAS really heating things up when suddenly, I heard the door close, the sound of footsteps, and there was Hiesel, the runt lawyer. He looked at me, then at Marvin.

"Who's this, Chuck?" he said.

"A nosy guy named Morgan. He got the girls out an' hid 'em someplace." He grinned. "I'm going to warm his feet until he talks."

Hiesel's smooth, polished face tightened. He looked down at me.

"This is the man they have the call out for, Chuck. A police call out for him. You'd better get rid of him."

My eyes went to Hiesel. Get rid of me? Just like that? Brother, I said to myself, if I get out of this I'm going to come around and ask you about that!

"And Chuck—Tarrant Houston's gone to work getting those bonds sold. He's working fast, too. He's afraid for the girls."

"He should be," Marvin answered and smiled. "We'll take care of the girls as soon as he shows with the money. And him, too."

He licked his lips. "That older girl, Eleanor. I'd like to talk with her, in private, before anything is done."

Candy Chuck Marvin looked up. He laughed coarsely. "Talk? I see what you mean. I'd like a private talk with her myself."

That poker was hot by now. Candy Chuck pulled it out of the fire and Ford Hiesel's face turned slightly pale. He left the room and Candy Chuck laughed, and began untying my shoe.

"I wouldn't do that," I said. "I haven't changed my socks since I started chasing you guys."

"Smart guy, huh?"

Candy Chuck's eyes were gleaming. He started to pull off my shoes when a calm, low voice interrupted.

"I wouldn't do that."

We both looked around. Eleanor Harley, her face a bit drawn, but as beautiful as that first day I'd seen her in the bar, was standing in the doorway. Candy Chuck lunged to his feet.

"Come here!" he demanded. But she turned suddenly and ducked out of sight. He ran after her.

It was my chance, and I took it. Kicking my tied feet around, I got the ropes that bound my ankles across the red-hot poker, then struggled to a sitting position and began working at my hands. The knots weren't a good job, and lying there on the floor, I had managed to get them a bit looser.

That clothesline burned nicely, and I could hear Candy Chuck Marvin banging around in a room nearby when the first rope came apart.

I kicked and squirmed, getting the other ropes loose, then managed to struggle to my feet.

Forcing my wrists as low as I could get them, I backed my hips through the circle of my arms. Then falling on my back, I got my hands in front of me by pulling my knees against my chest and shoving my feet down through my arms. Then I went to work on the knots with my teeth.

Then I heard somebody coming and looked around to see Blubber Puss. He opened his mouth to yell and I dove at him, driving my head for his stomach. He no more than had his mouth open before I hit him head down and with everything I had behind it.

He went back through the door with an *oof,* hitting the floor hard. Still fighting those ropes, I kept moving. They came loose as I was rounding into the passage to the back of the house, but suddenly I got an idea and my gun, out. I raced for the library again.

Grabbing up a couple of carpets, I stuffed them onto the fire. They caught hold and began to burn. Then I took another carpet and, spilling a pitcher of water they'd had for mixing drinks over it, I put it on the fire. All that smoke would make people very, very curious.

Somewhere out in the back regions of the house, I heard a girl scream. I wheeled around, and saw Whit Dyer looking at me. He had a gun in his hands and you could see the killing lust in his eyes.

My gun was ready, and I've had lots of practice with it. Dyer jerked his up and I let go from where mine was, just squeezing the shot off. The sound of that .380 and his .45 made a concussion like a charge of dynamite in that closed-in room.

I heard his bullet hit the wall behind me and saw a queer look in his face. Then, looking at the spot over his belt buckle, I squeezed off the rest of the magazine. He grabbed his middle like he'd been eating green apples and went over on the carpet, and I went out the door and into the hall.

Somewhere outside, there was a crash and then a sound of shots. I didn't know what it meant, but I was heading toward that scream I'd heard.

Candy Chuck Marvin had caught Eleanor in the kitchen. She was fighting, but there wasn't much fight left in her. I grabbed Candy Chuck by the scruff of the neck and jerked him back. His gun was lying on the table and I caught it up and heaved it out the window, right through the glass.

Then I tossed my empty gun on the floor under the range. There was a wicked gleam in Candy Chuck's eyes. He was panting and staring at me. He was bigger than me by twenty pounds and he'd been raised in a rough school.

He lunged, throwing a wallop that would have ripped my jaw off. But I slipped it and smashed one into his wind that jerked his mouth open. I hooked my left into his wind and he backed off. I followed him, stabbing a left into his mouth. He didn't have blubber lips but they bled.

I hooked a short, sharp left to the eye, and smashed him back against the sink. He grabbed a pitcher and lunged for me, but I went under it and knocked it out of his hand.

Eleanor Harley was standing there, her dress torn, her eyes wide, staring at us. Then the door opened and Mooney stepped in, two cops right behind him, and Tarrant Houston following them.

Mooney took in the scene with one swift look. Then he leaned nonchalantly against the drain board.

"Don't mind me," he said. "Go right ahead."

Candy Chuck Marvin caught me with a right that knocked me into the range. I weaved under a left and hooked both hands short and hard to the body, then I shoved him away and jabbed a left to his face. Again, and then again. Three more times I hit him with the left, keeping his head bobbing like a cork in a millstream, and then I pulled the trigger on my Sunday punch. It went right down the groove for home plate and exploded on his chin. His knees turned to rubber, then melted under him and he went down.

Me, I staggered back against the drain board and stood there, panting like a dowager at a Gregory Peck movie.

Mooney looked Candy Chuck Marvin over with professional interest, then glanced at me approvingly.

"Nice job," he said. "I couldn't do as good with a set of knucks and a razor. Is he who I think he is?"

"Yeah," I said, "Candy Chuck Marvin, and this time you've got enough on him to hang him."

Ford Hiesel shoved into the room. "Got them, did you?" he said. "Good work!"

Then he saw me, and his face turned sick. He started to back away and you could see the rat in him hunting a way out.

"This guy," I said, "advised Candy Chuck to get rid of me, and told him it would be a good idea to get rid of the girls and Houston—to make a clean sweep!"

Eleanor lifted her head. "I heard him say it!" she put in. "We hid in the closet behind the mirror in the hall."

Ford Hiesel started to protest, but there had been enough talk. I shoved him against the drain board, and when I was between him and the rest of the room, I whipped my right up into his solar plexus. The wind went out of him like a pricked balloon and he began gasping for breath. I turned back to the others, gestured at him.

"Asthma," I said. "Bad, too."

"What about the diamonds?" Mooney asked suddenly. "Why didn't they fence them?"

Eleanor turned toward the detective.

"They talked about it," she said. "But the only man who would have handled the diamonds here was picked up by the police, and Marvin was hoping he could arrange things, meanwhile, to keep them for himself."

Then I told her about the pin, and she came over to me as Mooney commented, "I know about that. A clerk named Davis, at the jewelry store, got in touch with me when they checked and found out the pin belonged to Eleanor Harley. That and the smoke tipped us off to this place."

She was looking up at me with those eyes, almost too beautiful to believe.

"I can't thank you enough for what you've done," she said.

"Sure you can," I said, grinning. "Let's go down to the Casino and talk to a couple of bartenders while we have some drinks. Then, I can tell you all about it."

Ain't I the cad, though?

WITH DEATH IN HIS CORNER

T HE GHOST OF a mustache haunted his upper lip, and soft blond hair rolled back from a high white brow in a delicately artificial wave. He walked toward me with a quick, pleased smile. "A table, sir? Right this way."

There was a small half-circle bar at one end of the place and a square of dance floor about the size of two army blankets.

On a dais about two feet above the dance floor a lackadaisical orchestra played desultory music. Three women and two men sat at the bar and several of the tables were occupied. From the way the three women turned their heads to look, I knew all were hoping for a pickup. I wasn't.

A popeyed waiter in a too-tight tux bustled over, polishing a small tray suggestively. Ordering a bourbon and soda, I asked, "Do you know Rocky Garzo?"

The question stopped him, and he turned his head as if he were afraid of what he would see.

"I don't know him," he said hastily. "I never heard of the guy."

He was gone toward the bar before I could ask anything further, but he knew something was wrong. One look at his face had been enough. The man was scared.

He must have tipped a sign to the tall headwaiter, because when he returned with my drink, the blond guy was with him.

"You were asking for someone?" There was a slight edge to his voice, and the welcome sign was gone from his eyes. "What was the name again?"

"Garzo," I said, "Rocky Garzo. He used to be a fighter."

"I don't believe I know him," he replied. "I don't meet many fighters."

"Possibly not, but it is odd you haven't met him. He used to work here."

"Here?" His voice shrilled a little, then steadied down. "You're mistaken, I believe. He did not work here."

"Apparently, you and Social Security don't agree," I commented. "They assured me he worked here, at least until a day or so ago."

He did not like that, and he did not like me. "Well"—his tone showed his impatience—"I can't keep up with all the help. I hope you find him."

"Oh, don't worry. I will."

He could not get away fast enough, seeming to wish as much distance between us as possible. All Rocky's letter had said was that he was in trouble and needed help, and Rocky was not one to ask for help unless he needed it desperately.

It began to look as if my hunch was right. I am not one to be irritated by small things, but I was beginning to get annoyed. All I wanted was to know where Rocky was and what was wrong, if anything.

Rocky Garzo was a boy who had been around. A quiet Italian from the wrong side of the tracks, but a simple-hearted, friendly sort who could really fight. He wanted no trouble with anyone and, except as a youngster, never had a fight in his life he didn't get paid for. I've heard men call him everything they could think of, and he would just walk away. But when the chips were down, Rocky could really throw them.

Each of us had acted as second to the other, had been in the others' corner many times.

Then fleshpots got him, and the selective service system got me. He was a kid who never had anything until he got into big money in the fight game, and he liked the good food, flashy women, and clothes. His money just sort of dribbled away, and the easy life softened him up. Then the boys began to tag him with the hard ones. It was Jimmy Hartman who wound him up with the flashiest right hand on the Coast.

He quit then. He went to waiting on tables. He was a fast-moving, deft-handed man with an easy smile. He quit drinking, and the result was he was doing all right until something went wrong here at the Crystal Palace.

There was a pretty girl sitting at the table next to mine. She was with a bald-headed guy who was well along in his cups. She was young and shaped to be annoyed, if you get what I mean. Beyond that, I hadn't noticed too much about her.

All of a sudden, she was talking to me. She was talking without turning her head. "You'd better take it out of here," she said. "These boys play rough, even for you, Kip Morgan!"

"What's the catch?" I didn't turn my head, either. "Can't a guy even ask for his friends?"

"Not that one. He's hotter than a firecracker, and I don't mean with the law. Meet me at the Silver Plate in a half hour or so and I'll ditch this dope and tell you about it."

This place was not getting me anywhere. The waiter was pointedly ignoring my empty glass, and in such places as this they usually take it out of your hand before you can put it down. I took a gander at Algy or whatever his name was and saw him talking with a hefty lad at the door. This character had bouncer written all over him and looked like a moment of fun. I hadn't bounced a bouncer in some time.

As I passed them, I grinned at Algy. "I'll be back," I said.

This was the cue the bouncer needed. He walked over, menace in his every move. "You've been here too long an' too much." He made his voice ugly. "Get out an' stay out!"

"Well, I'll be swiped by a truck!" I said. "Pete Farber!"

"Huh?" He blinked at me. "Who are you, huh?"

"Why, Pete! You mean you don't remember? Of course, our acquaintance was brief, and you couldn't see very well through all that blood. Naturally, you didn't see me later because I was home in bed before they brought you out of it."

"Huh?" Then awareness came, and his eyes hardened but grew wary also. He did have a memory, after all. "Kip Morgan!" he said. "Sure, it's Kip Morgan."

"Right, and if you'll recall, Rocky Garzo and I teamed up in the old days. He was going down, and I was coming up, but we were pals. Well, I'm a man who remembers his friends, and I'm getting curious about this stalling I am getting."

"Play it smart," Farber said, "and get out while you're all in one piece. This is too big for you. Also"—he moved closer—"I got no reason to like you. I'd as soon bust you as not."

That made me smile. "Pete, what makes you think you could do something now you couldn't do six years ago? If you want a repeat on that job at the Olympic, just start something."

Pete Farber's next remark stopped me cold.

"You beat me," he said, "but you dropped a duke to Ben Altman. Well, you just forget Garzo, because Altman's still a winner."

When I got outside that one puzzled me. What was the connection between Ben Altman, formerly a top-ranking light heavyweight, and Garzo?

Then I began to remember a few things I'd forgotten. There had been some shakeups in the mobs, and Altman, a boy from the old Albina section of Portland, had suddenly emerged on top. He was now a big wheel.

So Rocky didn't work here anymore. I climbed into a cab and gave the cabbie the address of Rocky's rooming house. He turned his head for a second look. "Chum," he said. "I'd not go down there dressed like you are. That's a rough neighborhood."

"Let's roll, Ajax. Anybody who shakes me down is entitled to what he gets."

———

THE ROOMING HOUSE was a decrepit frame building of two rickety stories. The number showed above a doorway that opened on a dark, dank-looking stairway. The place smelled of ancient meals, sweaty clothing, and the dampness of age. Hesitating a moment, I struck a match to see the steps, then felt my way up to the second floor of this termite heaven.

At the top of the stairs, a door stood partly open, and I had the feeling of somebody watching.

"I'm looking for Rocky Garzo," I said.

"Don't know him." It was a woman's husky voice.

"Used to be a fighter," I explained. "A flat nose and a tin ear."

"Oh, him. End of the hall. He came in about an hour ago."

My second match had flickered out, so I struck another and went down the hall, my footsteps echoing in the emptiness. The walls were discolored by dampness and ancient stains, no doubt left by the first settler.

A door at the end of the hall stared blankly back at me. My fist lifted, and my knuckles rapped softly. Suddenly, I had that strange and lonely feeling of one who raps on the door of an empty house. My hand dropped to the knob, and the door protested faintly as I pushed it open. A slight grayness from a dusty, long-unwashed window showed a figure on the bed.

"Rocky?" I spoke softly, but when there was no reply, I reached for the light switch. The light flashed on, and I blinked. I needed no second look to know that Rocky Garzo had heard his last bell, and from the look of the room he had gone out fighting.

He was lying on his right cheek and stomach and there was a knife in his back, buried to the hilt. It was low down on the left side and seemed to have an upward inclination.

The bedding was mussed, and a chair was tipped on its side. A broken cup lay on the floor. Stepping over the cup I picked up his hand. It wasn't warm, but it wasn't cold, either.

His knuckles were skinned.

"Anything wrong, mister?" It was the woman from down the hall. She was behind me in the light of the door, a faded blonde who had lost the battle with graying hair. Her face was puffed from too much drinking, and only her eyes held the memory of what her beauty must have been.

She was sober now, and she clutched a faded negligee about her.

"Yeah," I said, and something of my feelings must have been in my voice, for quick sympathy showed in her eyes. "He's dead. He's been killed."

She neither gasped nor cried out. She was beyond that. Murder was not new to her, nor death of any kind. "It's too bad," she spoke softly. "He was a good guy."

My eyes swept the room, and I could feel that old hard anger coming up inside me. There had to have been two men.

No man fighting with Rocky ever got behind him. He must have been slugging one when the other stepped in from the hall with the shiv.

"You'd better leave, mister. No use to get mixed up in this."

"No, I'm not getting out. Maybe he wasn't in the chips. Maybe he wasn't strictly class, but he was my friend."

She was uneasy. "You'd better go. This is too big for you."

"You know something about this?"

"I don't know anything. I never know anything."

"Look"—I kept my voice gentle—"You're regular. I saw it in your eyes; you're the McCoy." I waved a hand at Rock. "He was one of the good ones. It isn't right for him to go out this way."

She shook her head. "I'm not talking."

"All right. You call the cops. I'll look around."

She went away, and I heard her dialing the phone. I looked down at Rocky. He was a good Italian boy, that one. He came from the wrong side of the tracks, but he never let it start him down the wrong street. He could throw a wicked right hand. And he liked his spaghetti.

"All right, pal," I said quietly, "I'm still in your corner."

Without touching anything, I looked around, taking in the scene. One hood must have circled to get Rock's back to the door where the other one was waiting.

When you knew about fights, in and out of the ring, and when you knew about killings, it wasn't hard to picture. Rocky had come in, taken off his shirt, and the door opened. He turned, and the guy circled away from him. Rocky had moved in, slugging. Then the shiv in the back.

But those knuckles.

"You put your mark on him. I'll be looking for a hood with a busted face. The left side for sure, maybe the right, too."

The woman came back to the room and stood in the door. "I've been trying to place you. You used to work out at the Main Street Gym. Rocky talked about you. He figured Kip Morgan was the greatest guy on earth."

She looked down, twisting her fingers. Her hands once had been beautiful.

"Listen," she pleaded. "I've had so much trouble. I just can't take any more. I'm scared now, scared to death. Don't tell anybody, not even the police, but there were two of them. Both were well dressed. One was tall with broad shoulders; the other was heavy, much heavier than you."

The siren sounded, then whined away and died at the foot of the steps. Detective Lieutenant Mooney was the first one into the room. "Hi," he said, then looked again. "You, is it? Who's dead?"

"Rocky Garzo. He was a fighter."

"I know he was a fighter. I get out nights myself. Who did it? You?"

"He was my friend. I came out from New York to see him."

They started to give the room the business, and they knew their job, so I just stepped into the hall and kept out of the way. What little I had I gave to Mooney while they were shaking the place down.

"If you want me," I said, "I'll be at the Plaza."

"Go ahead, but don't leave town."

A glance at my watch told me it was only forty minutes since I'd left the Crystal Palace, and I was ten minutes late for my date. The cab took ten more getting me there, but the babe was patient. She was sitting over coffee and three cigarette stubs.

"They called them coffin nails when I was a kid," I told her.

She had a pretty smile. "I thought you had decided not to come. That man I was with was harder to shake than the seven-year itch."

"If you can help me," I said, "it would mean a lot. Garzo was my pal."

"Sure, I know. I'm Mildred Casey, remember? I lived down the block from Rock's old man. You two used to fix my bike."

That made me look again. Blue eyes, the ghosts of freckles over the bridge of her nose, and shabby clothes. An effort to be lively with nothing much to be lively or happy about, but great courage. She still had that, a fine sort of pride. There was hurt in her eyes where her heart showed.

"I remember," I said. She had been a knobby-kneed kid with stars for eyes. "How could I forget? It was your glamour that got me."

She laughed, and it was a pretty sound. "Don't be silly, Kip. My knees were always skinned, and my bike was always busted."

Her eyes went from my face to the clothes I was wearing. "You've done well, and I'm glad." If I do say so, they were good. I'd always liked good clothes, liked the nice things that money could buy. Often they hadn't been easy to have because I also liked being on the level. Two of the boys I'd grown up with had ended in the chair, and another was doing time for a payroll job.

"Kid"—I leaned toward her—"tell me about Rocky. You've got to think of everything, and after you've told me, forget about it unless you talk to the police."

Her face went dead white, but she took it standing. In the world where we'd grown up, you didn't have to draw the pictures.

"Rock worked at the Crystal Palace only three weeks. He was a good waiter, but after his first week, something was bothering him. He talked to me sometimes, and I could see he had something on his mind. Then, one night, he quit and never even came back for his money."

"What happened that night?"

"Nothing, really. After a rather quiet evening, some people came in and sat at one of Rock's tables. Horace, he's the blond boy, made quite a fuss over them, but nothing happened that I could see. Then, all of a sudden, Rock went by me, stripping off his apron. He must have gone out the back way."

"Do you know who they were?"

Milly hesitated, concentrating. "There were four in the party, two men and two women. All were well dressed, and the men were flashing big rolls of bills. One of the men was larger than you. He wore a dark suit. A blond girl was with him, very beautiful."

"The big guy? Was he blond, too? With a broken nose?"

She nodded, remembering his eyes. "Yes, yes! He looked like he might have been a fighter once."

For a moment, I considered that. "Have you ever heard of Benny Altman?"

Her face changed as if somebody had slapped her. "So that was Ben Altman!" She sat very quiet, her coffee growing cold in front of her. "He knew a friend of mine once, a girl named Cory Ryan." She thought for a minute, then added, "The other man was shorter and darker."

She reverted to the former topic. "If you want to know anything about Ben Altman, ask Cory Ryan. He treated her terribly."

"Where is she now?"

"She went to San Francisco about two—maybe it was three weeks ago. I had a wire from her from there."

"Thanks. I'm leaving now, Milly, and the less you're seen with me the better. I'm in this up to my ears."

"Be careful, Kip. He was always bragging to Cory about what he could do and how much he could get away with."

We parted after exchanging phone numbers, and then I caught a cab and returned to the Plaza. Some of my friends were around, but I wasn't listening to the usual talk. The story would break the next day about Garzo's murder, but in the meantime I had much to do.

The one thing I had to begin with was Rock himself. He had always been strictly on the level. I knew that from years of knowing him, but the police would not have that advantage. At the Crystal Palace, he must have stumbled into something that was very much out of line. The arrival of Ben Altman must have proved something he only suspected. I might be wrong about that, but Altman seemed to have triggered something in Garzo's thinking.

During the war and the years that followed, I had seen little of my old friends on the Coast, so I knew little about the activities of Garzo, Altman or any of the others.

"What are you so quiet about?" Harry asked. Harry was the bartender, and he had been behind bars in that part of town for nearly forty years. There was very little he didn't know, but very little he would talk about unless he knew you well, and that meant no more than four or five people in town.

"Remember Rocky Garzo? He was killed tonight. I used to work out with the guy."

"Isn't he the brother of that kid that was shot about a year ago?" Harry asked. "You know? Danny Garzo? He was shot by the police in some sort of a mix-up. Somebody said he was on the weed."

On weed . . . the reefer racket . . . Ben Altman . . . things were beginning to fall into place. I left my drink on the bar. I wasn't much of a drinker, anyway, and I had some calls to make.

Bill would be at the *News* office. As expected, it was on the tip of his tongue. "Danny Garzo? Eighteen years old, supposedly hopped up on weed and knifed some guy in a bar and then tried to shoot it out with the police. He was Garzo's brother."

"What do you know about Ben Altman? I hear he's a big man in the rackets now?"

"Brother"—I could fairly see the seriousness in his face—"if you want to live to be an old man, forget it. That's hot! Very, very hot!"

"Then keep your eyes and ears open, because I am going to walk right down the middle of it. Incidentally, if your boys haven't got it already, Rocky Garzo was murdered. They just found the body."

Rocky's brother, high on marijuana, got himself killed when, according to the report, he had gone off his head and started cutting people. Marijuana was more likely to make you stupid than crazy, but the effect was too often assumed to be like methamphetamines. It made me wonder what drugs he'd actually been taking . . . if any at all.

Rocky Garzo had loved his brother. I remembered the kid only as somebody who played ball in the streets, a dark-eyed, good-looking youngster. Evidently, Rocky had started out looking for the source of the drugs. His looking took him to the Crystal Palace, and then Altman comes in, recognizes Garzo, and has a hunch why he's there. Maybe more than a hunch. Maybe he had come there to check on something, a tip, maybe, that Garzo was asking questions or showing too much interest. Garzo leaves at once, and a short time later he is dead.

Maybe that was right and maybe wrong. If I could actually tie it to Altman, I'd have something. If I had the right hunch, I had another hunch that Mooney wouldn't be far behind me. It was a job for the law, and I believe in letting the law handle such things. However, if I could come up with some leads because of the people I knew—well, it might help.

For two days I sat tight and nothing happened; then I ran into Mooney. He was drinking coffee in a little spot where I occasionally dropped in.

"What's happened with Garzo?" I asked him.

His expression wasn't kind. "I'm on another case."

"You've dropped it?"

"We never drop them."

"I think he had something on Ben Altman. I believe Rocky was playing detective because of what happened to Danny."

"Who are you? Sherlock Holmes? We thought of that. It was obvious, but Altman has an alibi, and so have his boys. The worst of it is, they are good alibis, and he has good lawyers. Before you arrest a man like that, you've got to have a case, not just suspicion. It looks like Altman; it could have been Altman. We'd like it if it was Altman, but it's a dead end."

"So you dropped it."

Mooney studied me over his coffee cup. "Look, Kip. I know you, see? I know you from that Harley case. You have a way of barging into things that could get you killed. I like you, so don't mess with this one. And don't worry about Ben Altman. We'll keep after him."

They would keep after him, and eventually they would get him. Crooks sometimes win battles, but they never win the war. However, I had to be back in New York, and I did not have the time to waste, and the old Rock had been a friend. I like to finish them quick, like Pete Farber.

How about Pete Farber? Did he have an alibi? Or what about Candy Pants, the blond headwaiter?

Then I remembered Corabelle Ryan, Milly's friend, who had known Altman. How much did she know?

One of the greatest instruments in the world is the telephone. It may cause a lot of gray hairs in the hands of an elderly lady with nothing else to do; still, it can save a lot of legwork.

A few minutes on the telephone netted me this. Cory was still, apparently, in San Francisco. Milly had not heard from her again. No, she had no address except that Milly had said she would be at the Fairmont for a few days.

The Fairmont had no such party registered. Nor had anybody by that name been registered there. The mail desk did have a letter for her, but it had been picked up. The man picking it up had a note of authorization. She remembered him well—a short, dark man.

"Cory," I muttered as I came out of the booth, "I am afraid you did know something. I am afraid you knew too much."

WHEN IT WAS dark, I changed into a navy blue gabardine suit and a blue and gray striped tie; then I took a cab to the Crystal Palace. I knew exactly what I was getting into, and it was trouble, nothing but trouble.

Horace was nowhere in sight when I went in, nor was Pete Farber. I got a seat in a prominent position, ordered a bourbon and soda, and began to study the terrain. If all went as expected before the evening was over, they would try to bounce me out of there.

The door from the office opened, and Horace emerged, talking to Farber. They both saw me at the same moment. As they saw me, the door opened, and two men walked in. Between them was Milly.

That did not strike me at first, but the next thing did. They did not stop at the hatcheck counter.

Now no nightclub, respectable or otherwise, is going to let two men and a woman go back without checking something without at least an attempt. The girl just looked at them and said nothing.

Then I got a look at Milly's face. If ever I saw a girl who

was scared to death, it was Milly Casey. They started past me, headed for the office, and I knew Milly was in trouble.

Behind me, I heard a grunt of realization and knew Pete Farber was coming for me. The moment needed some fast work. Just as the two men came abreast of my table, I got up quickly.

"Why, hello! Don't I know you?" I smiled at her. "You're the girl I met at the Derby. Why don't you all sit down and let me buy drinks?"

"We're busy! No time for a drink, bud, so roll your hoop."

Pete's arm slid around my neck from behind, which I had been expecting. Pete was never very smart that way. With my left hand, I reached up and grabbed his hand, my fingers in his palm, my thumb on the back, and with my right hand I reached back and grabbed Pete's elbow. It was a rapid, much-rehearsed move, and as I got my grip, I dropped quickly to one knee and whipped Pete over my shoulder.

He had been coming in, and I used his impetus. He went flying and hit the table in front of me with a crash; the table collapsed like a sick accordion and with about the same sound. Being on my knees, I grabbed the legs of the nearest man with Milly and jerked hard. His head hit the table when he fell, and I was up fast to see Milly break away and the other man clawing for a gun.

It was a bad move, leaving him as open as a Memphis crap game, and I threw my right down the groove with everything on it but my shoelaces. When a man grabs suddenly at his hip, his face automatically comes forward. His did, and brother, it was beautiful!

His face came forward as if it had a date with my fist, and you could have heard the smack clear into the street. His feet went from under him as if they'd been jerked from behind. He went down to all fours. Naturally, I didn't kick him. In police reports that might not look good, so when bent over him, my knee sort of banged into his temple. It was what might have been termed a fortuitous accident.

I'd been told Garzo had gone out the back door, so there had to be one. Grabbing Milly, I started for it. Blond Horace was somewhere behind me, and he was screaming. My last glimpse of the room was one I'd not soon forget. It was the face of a big Irishman, built like a lumberjack, who was staring down at those three hoodlums with an expression of such admiration at the havoc I'd wrought that it was the finest compliment a fighting man could receive.

The kitchen clattered and banged behind us, then the door.

We raced down the alley. We reached the street, slowing down, but just as we reached it, a car swung in and stopped us cold.

It was a shock to them and to us, but I'll hand it to Ben Altman. He thought fast, and there was no arguing with the gun in his mitt. "Get in," he said. "You're leaving too soon."

"Thanks," I told him. "Do you mind if we skip this one? We've got a date, and we're late."

"I do mind," he said. He was taking it big, like in the movies. "We can't have our guests leaving so early. Especially when I came clear across town to see the lady."

Milly had a grip on my fingers, and that grip tightened spasmodically when he spoke. She had heard about him from Cory, but that gun was steady. Had it been aimed at me, I'd have taken a chance.

Footsteps came up the alley behind me, and then a gun was jammed into my back so hard it peeled hide. "Get moving!" It was Pete Farber.

Milly was beside me as they walked us back to the club. She was tense and scared, but game. Just why they wanted her, I did not know. Maybe they believed she knew something, being a friend of Corabelle's.

Back in the office at the Crystal Palace, the two hoods I'd worked over came in. Rather, one walked in, the other was half carried.

So there we were: Ben Altman, his three stooges, Milly and myself.

Now Benny was a lad who could scrap a little himself, and he and I had an old score to settle. He got a decision over me in the ring once although I'd had him on the floor three times in the first four rounds. He had a wicked left, and I think on any other night I could have beaten him. On the night that counted, I did not do well enough after that fast start, and it always griped me because Ben Altman was a fighter I had never liked.

"Looks like you banged the boys around a little," Ben said. "But they'll have their innings before this night is over."

"What's the matter, Ben? Do you have to hire your fighting done now?"

He did not like that, and he walked over to me, staring at me out of those white blue eyes. "I could take you any day in the week and twice on Sunday, so why bother now?"

"With the right referee you could," I agreed, "but there isn't any referee now."

He ignored me and walked over to Milly. "Where's the diary?" he demanded.

"I don't know anything about it." Milly held her head up and faced him boldly, proudly. I never saw anybody more poised. "If Cory kept a diary, she certainly never showed it to me. Why don't you ask her?"

Altman's face was ugly. "You tell me," he said, "or I'll break every bone in your body!"

"He can't ask Cory," I said, "because he's murdered her."

Altman turned on me. "Shut up, damn you!"

"Had help, I'll bet." I was trying to distract his attention from Milly. "Ben never saw the day he could whip a full-grown woman."

He lashed out with a wicked left. He wasn't thinking or reasoning, he just peeled that punch off the top of the deck and threw it at me, and I rolled my head, slipping the punch and letting it go past my ear.

"Missed," I said. "Your timing is off, Ben."

With a kind of whining yelp, he wheeled and grabbed a gun from a drawer and brought it up, his face white to the lips. In that instant, my life wasn't worth the flip of a coin, but Pete grabbed him.

"Not here, Ben! These walls are almost soundproof, but they could hear a gun. Let's get them out of here."

Ben must have caught the expression on Milly's face from the corners of his eyes, because he turned on her.

"Why, no, Pete." Altman was himself again. "We'll keep him here. I think he'll be the way to make this babe talk. She might get very conversational when we start burning Morgan's toes."

Milly Casey, cute as she could be usually, looked sick and scared. "Now tell us where the diary is and we'll let you both go."

"Don't tell him a thing, Milly. That diary is our ace in the hole."

Farber gave me a disgusted look. "Shut up! Don't you realize when you're well off?"

"Sure, and I'd like it if Ben blew his top again and started shooting. We'd have the law all over the place in minutes, quicker than you could trip a blind man."

Altman was mad, but he was cold mad now, and he was thinking. He had a temper, but he had more than an ounce of brains.

As for me, I was sure I had guessed right. Corabelle had been murdered, but was her murder as well covered as that of Garzo? If it had happened out of town, as seemed likely, it might not have gone off so smoothly. It was an idea. Also, two men had done the job on Garzo—which two?

As if in reply to my question, the short, dark man who had been with Altman came into the room, and I saw the side of his face. He had been one of them. Who used the knife?

Altman? That did not seem logical, as Altman was too smart to do his own work. He was a fist and gun man, not apt to use a knife. Yet the man had been tall with broad shoulders and who else fitted that but Ben?

"All right, let's get them out of here," Altman said changing his mind suddenly. "We'll take them where we can do as we like. If they don't talk, we'll just get rid of them and hunt for the diary. After all, how many hiding places can there be?"

"It must be in the place where this babe lived," Pete suggested.

"Now," Ben Altman said.

"Okay, boss, with pleasure!" The blackjack sapped me behind the ear, and I went down hard. I faded and must have gone limp as a wet necktie, but I wasn't quite out because I remember hearing them complaining about my weight.

Next I knew, I was on the floor of a car. They had their feet resting on me, and we were driving. I'd passed out again, because we were already climbing, and I thought I could smell pines. This time, they were really taking us out into the country. All that was happening was like a foggy dream through which a few rays of intelligence found their way.

When I became conscious again, I could hear a faint sound as of someone not far from me, but I kept my eyes closed. I was lying on a rough wood floor with my cheek against it.

"Leave him with the babe," Farber was saying. "Let's rustle some chow."

"Is he still out cold? I haven't looked at him."

"He's cold," Pete said. "I clipped him good, and I'd been wanting to do just that."

They went out and closed the door, and I opened my eyes to slits. They were scarcely open when hands touched me, and I let them close again, liking the hands. Very gently, I was turned over, and praise be, I'd had the sense to keep my eyes closed, for in the next minute, my head was lifted, and Milly was kissing me and calling me a poor, dear fool.

Now in one sense, the term is unflattering, but when a good-looking girl holds your head and kisses you, who is to complain? I stayed right in there, taking it very gamely, until, inspired by what was happening, I decided it was time to do something about it and responded.

Milly let out a gasp and pulled away. "Oh, you—!"

"Ssh?" I whispered. "They'll hear you."

"Oh, you devil! You were awake all the time!"

"Yes, thank the Lord, but Milly, if I was dead and you started fussing over me like that, I'd climb right out of the coffin!"

She was blushing, so to ease her embarrassment, I asked, "How many of them are there?"

"Two. Pete Farber and the one called Joe. They're waiting for Ben Altman to come back. Kip, what are we going to do?"

"I wish I knew." I sat up, and my head swam. "If we could get away from here and lay hands on that diary, Mooney could do the rest. Do you know where we are?"

A quick look around the room had indicated there was

nothing there to be used as a weapon. Carefully, I got to my feet, leaning against the wall as the room seemed to spin.

We had no time. Once Altman returned, and I had no doubt he was searching Milly's apartment for the diary, we simply would have no chance.

"Open the door and walk out there. I'll wait by the door. You go out and turn on the charm. Tell them you're hungry, too, and then keep out of the way."

She went without a second's hesitation, and as she stepped through the door, I heard her say, "What's the matter? Do I have to starve, too? Why don't you give a girl a break?"

"Eat!" Farber's voice was hearty. "Sure! Come on out, babe! It may be hours before the boss gets back, and maybe we could make a deal, you an' me." I could imagine the smirk on his face. "I don't think the boss is goin' about this in the right way."

"You'd better have a look," Joe warned, "and see if the chump is still bye-bye."

"You have a look," Farber said. "When I hit 'em, they stay hit."

Joe's footsteps sounded, and the door opened. Joe stuck his head in, and that was all I needed. The blow landed just below and slightly behind his ear, and he started to fall. I grabbed him before he could hit the floor and threw a punch to the wind.

"How's about it, babe?" Farber was saying. "Ben's a tough cookie, but why should you get knocked off? You give me all the right answers and maybe we can figure out something. An' let me tell you, kid. I'm the only chance you've got."

With Joe's necktie I bound his hands behind him and then tied his ankles with his belt. Milly was keeping Joe busy with conversation and hesitations. I stuffed a handkerchief into Joe's mouth, and started for the door with his gun.

"Hey, Joe!" Farber yelled. "This dame's okay! Come on out!"

Joe's gun was on my hip, but I wasn't thinking of using it yet. Milly was sitting on Pete's lap and was keeping his head turned away from the door.

Something warned him, probably the extended silence. He

turned his head and opened his mouth to yell. Milly was off his lap like a shot, as he lunged to his feet to meet a left hook to the teeth.

Farber was in no shape to either take it or dish it out, but he tried. He didn't reach for a gun; he just came in throwing punches. I stabbed a left to the mouth and threw a bolo punch into his belly, and he went to his knees, but as he fell, his mouth open and gasping, I hooked again to his jaw. For an instant, I waited for him to get up, but his jaw was broken, and he was moaning. Taking the gun out of his pocket, I threw both guns into the brush as we headed for the road.

There was no car. There was a road toward the highway, but we didn't take it. We ran into the woods at right angles to the highway, and I took the lead, running until Milly's face was white and she was gasping.

We slowed to a walk and headed downhill in the right direction. Almost before we realized it, we reached a highway. We were lucky, the first car stopped, and one look at Milly seemed to satisfy him that we needed help.

———

ONCE IN TOWN, I put Milly in a cab to headquarters. "Tell Mooney all about it."

"Where are you going?"

"To your place, after that diary. Do you have any idea where it might be?"

"No . . . I honestly did not know she kept one, although she did sit up late writing sometimes." She paused a moment. "One thing that might help. Did you ever read Poe's 'The Purloined Letter'? It was one of her favorite stories. At least she spoke about it a good deal."

A second cab got me to the apartment house. Having Milly's key, I went right in. Nobody was there; nobody seemed to have been there. Maybe "The Purloined Letter" was a clue; the chances were that it was not. Yet I had some ideas of my own.

Corabelle Ryan had not gone to San Francisco by accident. She was hoping to get away from Altman. She did not get away, but the diary was not with her. Result: It must be where she had lived with Milly.

Wherever it was, I had very little time. From then on, things were going to move fast. Much would depend on how soon Ben found I was on the loose once again. Altman could not know what was in the diary, but he was afraid of what it might be. She might have threatened him with it for her own protection.

It was a two-bedroom apartment, with a living room, kitchenette, and bath. I recognized Milly's room at once from some clothes I'd seen her wear and the fact that it was obviously in use. The other room did not appear to have been occupied for several days.

The bureau offered nothing a quick search could reveal. The pockets of the clothes hanging in the closet took but a minute, boxes on the shelf, under the carpet, behind pictures, the bed itself. I checked her makeup kit, obviously a spare, and one of those small black cases that for a time every showgirl or model seemed to have. Nothing there.

For thirty minutes, I worked, going over that apartment like a custom's agent over a smuggler, and then I heard the faintest click from the lock. When I looked around, a hand was coming inside the door, and then he stepped into the room, a tall man with broad shoulders.

It was Horace, Candy Pants himself, and he held a knife low down in his right hand, cutting edge up. There was no love light in his eyes as he moved toward me.

It was like a French poodle baring his teeth to reveal fangs four inches long. From some, I might have expected it, but not from him. He did not say a word, just started across the room toward me, intent and deadly. He was unlike anyone I had ever seen before, but suddenly I got it. He was hopped up on amphetamines.

With his eyes fixed on mine, he closed in. It was like me that I did not think of the gun I carried. The drugs made him dangerous. Hopped up as he was, he could still handle a shiv, and I moved around, very cautious, studying how I'd better handle him. It was not in me to kill a man if I didn't have to, and quite often there are other ways. His eyes were on my stomach, and that was his target. If you're afraid of getting cut, you shouldn't try to handle a man with a knife, just as you should lay off a fist fighter if you can't take a punch.

Feinting, I tried to get that right hand out away from his body, but he held it close, offering me nothing. He took a step nearer, and the blade came like a striking snake; I felt the point touch my thigh. Jerking back, I swung a left that caught him alongside the head, and he almost went down.

He was catlike in his movements, and he turned to face me. His eyes had noted the blood on my leg, and he liked the sight of it. He moved closer.

He was coming for me now, and grabbing a pillow, I snapped it at his face. He ducked and lunged, and it was the chance I wanted.

Slapping his knife wrist out of line with my body, I dropped my right hand on his wrist and jerked him forward, throwing my left leg across in front of him. He spilled over it to the floor, and he hit hard. The knife slithered from his hand and slid under the bed. He struggled to get up, one of his arms hanging awkwardly—broken, I was sure.

He came up, staggering, and I threw a left into his belly. He fell near the bed, the knife almost under his hand. As I knocked it away, my shoulder hit Corabelle's makeup kit. It crashed to the floor, scattering powder, lipstick and—

My eyes fastened on the mirror, and on a hunch, drawn by the apparent looseness of it, I ripped the mirror from its place, and there, behind it, were several sheets of paper covered with writing, possibly torn from a diary. I grabbed them and backed off.

"All right, I'll take that!"

"You will like—!" It dawned on me that it was not Candy Pants speaking but Ben Altman, and he had a gun. The makeup kit was in my left hand, and I threw it, underhanded, at Ben; then I went for him.

The gun barked, and it would have had me for sure if I had not tripped over Candy Pants, who was trying to get up. Ben kicked at my head, but I threw myself against his anchoring leg, and he went down. We came up together and he swung the gun toward me as I came up, jamming the papers into my pocket.

By that time, I was mad. I went into him fast, the gun blasted again, and something seared the side of my neck like a red-hot iron. My left hooked for his wind, and my right hacked down at his wrist. The gun fell, and I clobbered him good with a right.

Suddenly, the apartment, the knives, guns, and Horace on the floor were forgotten. It was as if we were back in the ring again. He slipped a jab, and the right he smashed into my ribs showed me he could still hit. I belted him in the wind, hooked for the chin, and landed a right uppercut while taking a left and right. I threw a right as he ducked to come in and filled his mouth full of teeth and blood. I finished what teeth he had with a wild left hook that had everything and a prayer on it.

Crook he might be, but he was game, and he could still punch. He came at me swinging with both hands, and I nailed him with a left, hearing the distant sounds of sirens. I was hoping I could whip him before the cops got there.

As for Benny, I doubt if he even heard the siren. We walked into each other punching like crazy men, and I dropped him with a right and started for a neutral corner before I realized there weren't any corners and this was no ring.

He tried another left, and I hit him with a right cross, and his knees buckled. He went down hard and got up too quickly, and I nailed him with a left hook. When Mooney and the cops came in you could have counted a hundred and fifty over him. He was cold enough to keep for years.

Mooney looked at me, awed. "What buzz saw ran into you?"

I glanced in the mirror, then looked away quickly. Altman always had a wicked left.

Handing Mooney the pages from the diary, I said, "That should help. Unless my wires are crossed, it was Candy Pants here who put the knife into Garzo."

Milly came through the open door as I was touching my face with a wet towel, trying to make myself look human. "Come," she said, "we'll go to my room. There's something to work with there, and I'll make coffee."

Rocky Garzo could rest better now, and so could his brother. I could almost hear him saying, as he had after so many fights, "I knew you could do it, kid. You fought a nice fight."

"Thanks, pal," I said aloud. "Thanks for everything."

"What are you talking about?" Milly asked. "Are you punchy or something?"

"Just remembering. Rocky was a good boy."

"I know." Milly was suddenly serious. "You know what he used to say to me? He'd say 'You just wait until Kip gets back, things will be all right!'"

Well, I was back.

DEAD MAN'S TRAIL

KIP MORGAN SAT unhappily over a bourbon and soda in a bar on Sixth Street. How did you find a man who did not want to be found when all you knew about him was that he was thirty-six years old and played a saxophone?

Especially when some charred remains, tagged with this man's name, had been buried in New Jersey? And all you had to go on was a woman's hunch.

Not quite all. The lady with the hunch was willing to back her belief with fifty dollars a day for expenses and five thousand if the man was found.

Kipling Morgan had set himself up as a private detective and this was his first case. Five thousand dollars would buy a lot of ham and eggs, and at the moment, the expense money was important.

"No use to be sentimental about it," he told himself. "This babe has the dough, and she wants you to look. So, all right, you're looking. What is there to fuss about?"

He was conscientious; that was his trouble. He did not want to spend her money without giving something in return. Moreover, he was ambitious. He wanted very much to succeed, particularly such a case as this. He could use some headlines, he could use the advertising.

Kip Morgan ordered another drink and thought about it. He took his battered black hat off his head and ran fingers through his dark hair. He stared at the glass and swore.

FIVE DAYS BEFORE, sitting in the cubbyhole he called an office, the door opened, and a mink coat came in with a blonde inside. She was in her late twenties, had a model's walk, and a figure made to wear clothes, but one that would look pretty good without them.

"Are you Kip Morgan?"

He pulled his feet off the desk and stood up. He had been debating as to whether he should skip lunch and enjoy a good dinner or just save the money.

"Yes," he said, "what can I do for you?"

"Do you have any cases you are working on now?" Her eyes were gray, direct, sincere. They were also beautiful.

"Well, ah—" He hesitated, and his face flushed, and that made him angry with himself. What could he tell her? That he was broke and she was the first client to walk into his office? It would scarcely inspire confidence.

"As a matter of fact," she said, the shadow of a smile on her lips, "I am quite aware you have no other cases. I made inquiries and was told you were the youngest, newest, and least occupied private detective in town."

He chuckled in spite of himself. "That's not very good advertising, is it?"

"It is to me. I want an investigator with ambition. I want a fresh viewpoint. I want someone who can devote all his time to the job."

"That's my number you're calling." He gestured to a chair. "It looks like we might do business. Will you sit down?"

She sat down and showed a lot of expensive hosiery and beautifully shaped legs. "My name is Mrs. Roger Whitson. I am a widow with one child, a boy.

"Four years ago, in New Jersey, my husband, who was a payroll messenger, left the bank acting as a guard for a teller named Henry Willard and a fifty-thousand-dollar payroll.

"They were headed for the plant of what was then called Adco Products. They never arrived. Several days later, hunters found the badly charred body of a man lying beside an overturned and burned car in a gully off a lonely road. The body was identified as that of Henry Willard.

"The police decided my husband had murdered him and stolen the fifty thousand dollars. They never found him or any clue to his whereabouts."

"What do you need me for?" Kip asked. "It sounds like a

police matter. If they can't find him with all their angles, I doubt if I can."

"They can't find him because they are looking for the wrong man," Helen Whitson declared. "Mr. Morgan, you may not have much faith in women's intuition. I haven't much myself, but there's one thing of which I am sure. That charred body they found was my husband!"

"They can identify a body by fingerprints, by dental records."

"I know all that, but it so happened that the dead man's fingertips were badly burned. Their argument was that he burned them trying to force open the car door. It looked to me like somebody did it deliberately.

"They found a capped tooth in the dead man's mouth. Henry Willard had a capped tooth, but so did my husband. There were no dental records on either man, and the police disregarded my statement.

"They discovered fragments of clothing, a key ring, pocketknife, and such things that were positively identified as belonging to Henry Willard. The police were convinced. They would not listen to me because they thought I was covering for my husband.

"Mr. Morgan, I have a son growing up. He will be asking about his father. I will not have him believing his father a criminal when I know he is not!

"My husband was murdered by Henry Willard. The reason he has not been found is because his body lies in that grave. I know Henry Willard is alive today and is safe because they have never even looked for him."

"But," he objected, "you apparently have money. Why should your husband steal, or why should they believe he stole, when you are well-off?"

"When my husband was alive, we had nothing. We lived on his salary, and I kept house like any young wife. After he was killed, I went to New York and worked. I was doing well, and then my uncle died and left me a wealthy woman. I am prepared to retain you for a year, if it takes that long, or longer. I want to find that man!"

The information she could give him was very little. Henry

Willard would now be thirty-six years old. He played a saxophone with almost professional skill. He neither gambled nor drank. He seemed to have little association with women. He had been two inches over six feet and weighed one seventy.

He had, in her presence, expressed an interest in California, but that had been over a year before the crime.

They sat for hours, and Kip questioned her. He started her talking about her life with her husband, about the parties they had, the picnics. Several times, Henry Willard had been along. She had seen him many times at the bank. For over a year, he had, at the request of the company, carried the payroll of Adco Products.

He had never played golf or tennis. He expressed a dislike for horses, and Helen recalled during that long session that he disliked dogs, also.

"He must be a crook"—Kip Morgan smiled—"if he didn't like dogs!"

"I know he was!" Helen stated. She described his preferences for food, the way he walked, and suddenly she recalled, "Here's something! He read *Variety*! I've seen him with it several times!"

Kip Morgan noted it and went on. The man had black hair. Birthmarks? Yes, seen when swimming at the club. A sort of mole, the size of a quarter, on his right shoulder blade.

The question was—how to find a man thirty-six years old who played the saxophone, even if he did have a birthmark? The only real clue was the link between *Variety* and the saxophone. He played with "almost" professional skill. Who added that "almost," and why not just professional skill?

"How about a picture? There must have been one in the papers at the time?"

"No, there wasn't. They couldn't find any pictures of him at the time. Not even in his belongings. But I do have a snapshot. He's one of a group at the club. As I recall, he did not want to be in the picture, but one of the girls pulled him into it."

Kip studied the picture. The man was well muscled, very well muscled. He looked fit as could be, and that did not fit with a bank job or with a man who played neither tennis nor golf. One who apparently went in for no sports but occasional swimming.

"How about his belongings? Were they called for?"

She shook her head. "No, he had no relatives."

"Leave any money? In the bank, I mean?"

"Only about a thousand dollars. When I think of it, that's funny, too, because he was quite a good businessman and never spent very much. He lived very simply and rarely went out."

Through a friend in the musicians' union, Kip tried to trace him down and he came to a dead end. Kip haunted night-clubs and theaters, listened to gossip, worried at the problem like a dog over a bone.

"You know what I think?" he told Helen Whitson the next time he saw her. "I've a hunch this Willard was a smart cookie. No relatives showed up, and that's unusual. No pictures in his stuff. No clues to his past. Aside from an occasional reference to Los Angeles, he never mentioned any place he had been or where he came from.

"I think he planned this from the start. I think he did a very smart thing. I think he stepped out of his own personality for the five years you knew him, or knew of him. I think he deliberately worked into that job at the bank, waited for the right moment, then killed your husband and returned to his former life with the fifty thousand dollars!"

He turned that over in his mind in the bar on Sixth Street. The more he considered it, the better he liked it, but if such was the case, he was bucking a stacked deck. He would be well covered. He was not a drinking man, but he was almost finished with his second drink when the idea came to him. He went to the telephone and called Helen Whitson.

A half hour later, they sat across the table from each other. "I've had a hunch. You have hunches, and so can I.

"Listen to this." He leaned across the table. "This guy Willard is covered, see? He's had four years and fifty thousand dollars to work with. He's supposed to be dead. He will be harder to locate than a field mouse in five hundred acres of wheat. We've got just one chance. His mind."

"I don't understand."

"It's like this. He's covered, see? The perfect crime. But no man who has committed a crime, a major crime, is ever sure he's safe. There is always a little doubt, a little fear. He may have overlooked something; somebody might recognize him.

"That's where he's vulnerable. In his mind. We can't find him, so we'll make him come to us!"

She shook her head doubtfully. "How can we possibly do that?"

"How?" He grinned and sat back in his chair. "We'll advertise!"

"Advertise? Are you insane?"

Kip was smiling. "We'll run ads in the *Times* and the *Examiner, Variety,* too. If he's in Los Angeles, he'll see them. Take my word for it, it'll scare the blazes out of him. We'll run an ad inviting him to come to a certain hotel to learn something of interest.

"He will be shocked. He's been thinking he is safe. Still, under that confidence is a little haunting fear. This ad will bring all that fear to the surface.

"All right, suppose he sees that ad? He will know somebody knows Willard is alive. Don't you see? That was his biggest protection, the fact that everybody believed Henry Willard to be dead. He'll be frightened; he will also be curious. Who can it be? What do they know? Are the police closing in? Or is this blackmail?"

Helen was excited. "It's crazy! Absolutely crazy! But I believe it might work!"

"He won't dare stay away. He will be shocked to the roots of his being. His own anxiety will be our biggest help. He'll try, discreetly, to find out who ran that advertisement. He'll try to find out who has that particular room in the hotel. Finally, he will send someone, on some pretext, to find out who or what awaits him. In any event, we'll have jarred him loose. He'll be scared, and he'll be forced by his own worry to do something. Once he begins, we can locate him. He won't have the iron will it would take to sit tight and sweat it out."

She nodded slowly. "But what if—what do you think he will do?"

Morgan shrugged. He had thought about that a lot. "Who knows? He will try to find out who it is that knows something. He will want to know how many know. If he discovers it is just we two, he will probably try another murder."

"Are you afraid?"

Kip shrugged. "Not yet, but I will be. Scared as a man can be, but that won't stop me."

"And that goes for me, too!" she said.

The ad appeared first in the morning paper. It was brief and to the point, and it appeared in the middle of the real estate ads. (Everybody reads real estate advertisements in Los Angeles.) The type was heavy. It read:

HENRY WILLARD

Who was in Newark in 1943? Come to Room 1340 Hayworthy Hotel and learn something of interest.

Kip Morgan sat in the room and waited. Beside him were several paperback detective novels and a few magazines. His coat was off and lying on the table at his right. Under the coat was his shoulder holster and the butt of his gun, where he could drop a hand on it.

Down the hall, in a room with its door open a crack, waited three newsboys. They were members of a club where Kip Morgan taught boxing. Outside, the newsboy on the corner was keeping his eyes open, and three other boys loitered together, talking.

Noon slipped past, and it was almost three o'clock when the phone rang. It was the switchboard operator.

"Mr. Morgan? This is the operator. You asked us to report if anyone inquired as to who was stopping in that room? We have just had a call, a man's voice. We replied as suggested that it was John Smith but he was receiving no calls."

"Fine!" Kip hung up and walked to the window.

It was working. The call might have come from some curious person or some crank, but he didn't think so.

He rang for a bottle of beer and was tipped back in a chair with a magazine half in front of his face when the door opened. It was a bellman.

Alert, Kip noticed how the bellman stared at him, then around the room. The instant the door closed after him, Kip was on his feet. He went to the door and gave his signal. The bellman had scarcely reached the elevator before a nice-looking youngster of fourteen in a blue serge suit was at his elbow, also waiting.

A few minutes later, the boy was at Kip's door. His eyes were bright and eager.

"Mr. Morgan! The bellman went to the street, looked up and down, then walked to a Chevrolet sedan and spoke to the man sitting in the car. The man gave him some money.

"I talked to Tom, down on the corner, and he said the car had been there about a half hour. It just drove up and stopped. Nobody got out." He reached in his pocket. "Here's the license number."

"Thanks." Kip picked up the phone and called, then sat down.

A few minutes later, the call was returned. The car was a rental. And, he reflected, certainly rented under an assumed name.

The day passed slowly. At dusk, he paid the boys off and started them home, to return the next day. Then he went down to the coffee shop and ate slowly and thoughtfully. After paying his check, he walked outside.

He must not go anywhere near Helen Whitson. He would take a walk around the block and return to the hotel room. It had been stuffy, and his head ached. He turned left and started walking. He had gone less than half a block when he heard a quick step behind him.

Startled by the quickening steps, he whirled. Dark shadows moved at him, and before he could get his hands up, he was slugged over the head. Even as he fell to the walk, he remembered there had been a flash from a green stone on his attacker's hand, a stone that caught some vagrant light ray.

He hit the walk hard and started to get up. The man struck again, and then again. Kip's knees gave way, and he slipped into a widening pool of darkness, fighting to hold his consciousness. Darkness and pain, a sense of moving. Slowly, he fought his way to awareness.

———

"HEY, BILL." THE tone was casual. "He's comin' out of it. Shall I slug him again?" Walls and a roof of graying lumber swam into view.

"No, I want to talk to the guy."

Bill's footsteps came nearer, and Kip Morgan opened his eyes and sat up.

Bill was a big man with shoulders like a pro football player and a broken nose. His cheeks were lean, his eyes cold and unpleasant. The other man was shorter, softer, with a round, fat face and small eyes.

"Hi!" Kip said. "Who you boys workin' for?"

Bill chuckled. "Wakes right up, doesn't he? Starts askin' questions right away." He studied Morgan thoughtfully, searching his mind for recognition. "What we want to know is who you're workin' for. Talk and you can blow out of here."

"Yes? Don't kid me, chum! The guy who hired you yeggs hasn't any idea of lettin' me get away. I'm not workin' for anybody. I work for myself."

"You goin' to talk or take a beatin'?"

His attitude said plainly that he was highly indifferent to the reply. Sooner or later, this guy was going to crack, and if they had to give him a beating first, why, that was part of the day's work.

"We know there's a babe in this. You was seen with her."

"Her?" Kip laughed. "You boys are way off the track. She's just a babe I was on the make for, but I didn't score. Private dicks are too poor.

"This case was handed to me by an agency in Newark, an agency that does a lot of work for banks."

He glanced up at Bill. "Why let yourself in for trouble? Don't you know what this is? It's a murder rap."

"Not mine!" Bill said. The fat man glanced at him, worried.

"Ever hear of an accessory? That's where you guys come in."

"Who was the babe?" Bill insisted.

Kip was getting irritated. "None of your damn business!" he snapped, and came off the cot with a lunge.

Bill took a quick step back, but Kip was coming too fast, and he clipped the big man with a right that knocked him back into the wall.

The fat man came off his chair, and Kip backhanded him across the nose with the edge of his hand. He felt the bone break and saw the gush of blood that followed. The fat man whimpered like a baby, and Kip ducked a left from Bill and slammed a fist into the big man's midsection. Bill took it with a grunt and threw a left that Kip slipped, countering with a right cross that split Bill's eye.

Bill started to fall. Kip grabbed him, thrust him against the wall with his left, and hit him three times in the stomach with all the power he could muster. Then he stepped back and hit him in the face with both hands.

Bill slumped to a sitting position, bloody and battered. Kip glanced quickly at the fat man. He was lying on the floor, groaning. Morgan grabbed Bill and hoisted him into a chair.

"All right, talk!" Morgan's breath was coming in gasps. "Talk or I start punching!"

Bill's head rolled back, but he lifted a hand. "Don't! I'll talk! The money . . . it was in an envelope. The bartender at the Casino gave it to me. There was a note. Said to get you, make you tell who you worked for, and we'd get another five hundred."

"If you're lyin'," Kip said, "I'll come lookin' for you!"

Kip took up his battered hat and put it on his head, then retrieved his gun as he was going out and thrust it into his shoulder holster.

He stepped outside and looked around. He had been in a shanty in the country. Where town was he did not know.

On the dark highway, he shoved the gun back in its holster and straightened his clothing. Pulling his tie around, he drew the knot back into place and stuffed his shirt back into his pants. Gingerly, he felt his face. One eye was swollen, and there was blood on his face from a cut on his scalp. Wiping it away with his handkerchief, he started up the road. He had gone but a short distance when a car swung alongside him.

"Want a lift?" a cheery voice sang out.

He got in gratefully, and the driver stared at him. He was a big, sandy-haired man with a jovial face.

"What happened to you? Accident?"

"Not really. It was done on purpose."

"Lucky I happened along. You're in no shape to walk. Better get into town and file a report." He drove on a little way. "What happened? Holdup?"

"Not exactly. I'm a private detective."

"Oh? On a case, huh? I don't think I'd care for that kind of work."

The car picked up speed. Kip laid his head back. Suddenly, he was very tired. He nodded a little, felt the car begin to climb.

The man at the wheel continued to talk, his voice droning along, talking of crimes and murders and movies about them. Kip, half asleep, replied in monosyllables. Through the drone of talk, the question slipped into his consciousness even as he answered, and for a startled moment, his head still hanging on his chest, the question and answer came back to him.

"Who are you working for?" the driver had asked.

And mumbling, only half awake, he had said, "Helen Whitson."

As realization hit him, his head came up with a jerk, and he stared into the malevolent blue eyes of the big man at the wheel. He saw the gun coming up. With a yell, he struck it aside with his left hand, and his right almost automatically pushed down on the door handle. The next instant, he was sprawling in the road.

He staggered to his feet, grabbing for his own gun. The holster was empty. His gun must have fallen out when he spilled into the road. A gun bellowed, and he staggered and went over the bank just as the man fired again.

How far he fell, he did not know, but it was all of thirty feet of rolling, bumping, and falling. He brought up with a jolt, hearing a trickle of gravel and falling rock. Then he saw the shadow of the big man on the edge of the road. In a minute, he would be coming down. The shape disappeared, and he heard the man fumbling in his glove compartment.

A flashlight! He was getting a flashlight!

Kip staggered to his feet, slipping between two clumps of brush just as the light stabbed the darkness. Every step was agony, for he seemed to have hurt one ankle in the fall. His skull was throbbing with waves of pain. He forced himself to move, to keep going.

Now he heard the trickle of gravel as the man came down the steep bank. Stepping lightly, favoring the wounded ankle, he eased away through the brush, careful to make no sound. Somewhere he could hear water falling, and there was a loom of cliffs. The big man was not using the flashlight now but was stalking him as a hunter stalks game.

Kip crouched, listening, like a wounded animal. Then he felt a loose tree limb at his feet. Gently, he placed it in the crotch of a low bush so it stuck out across the way the hunter was coming. Feeling around, he found a rock the size of his fist.

Footsteps drew nearer, cautious steps and heavy breathing. Listening, Kip gained confidence. The man was no woodsman. Pain racked his head, and his tongue felt clumsily at his split and swollen lips.

Carefully, soundlessly, Kip moved back. The other man did what he hoped. He walked forward, blundered into the limb, and tripped, losing his balance. Kip swung the rock, and it hit, but not on the man's head. The gun fired, the shot missing, and Kip hobbled away.

He reached the creek and followed it down. Ahead of him, a house loomed. He heard someone speaking from the porch. "That sounded like a shot. Right up the canyon!"

He waited; then, after a long time, a car's motor started up. Kip started for the house in a staggering run. He stumbled up to the porch and banged on the door.

A tall, fine-looking man with gray hair opened it. "Got to

get into town and quick! There's going to be a murder if I don't!"

Giving the man's wife Helen Whitson's number to call, he got into the car.

All the way into town he knotted his hands together, staring at the road. He had been back up one of the canyons. Which one or how far, he did not know. He needed several minutes to show the man identification and to get him to drive him into town. It had taken more effort to get the man to lend him a gun.

However, the older man could drive. Whining and wheeling around curves and down the streets, he finally leveled out on the street where Helen Whitson lived. As they turned the corner, Kip saw the car parked in front of the house. The house was dark.

"Let me out here and go for the police!"

Moving quickly despite the injured ankle, Kip crossed the lawn and moved up to the house. The front door was closed. He slipped around to the side where he found a door standing open. As he eased up the steps, he heard a gasp and saw a glimmer of light.

"Hello, Helen!" a man's voice said.

"*You*, Henry!"

"Yes, Helen, it has been a long time. Too bad you could not let well enough alone. If your husband hadn't been such an honest fool, I couldn't have tricked him as I did. And this detective of yours is a blunderer!"

"Where is Morgan? What have you done to him?"

"I'll kill him, I believe. And with you dead, I'll feel safer. I was afraid this might happen so I have plans to disappear again, if necessary. But first I'm going to have to kill you."

Kip Morgan had reached the door, turning into it slowly, silently. Helen's eyes found him, but she permitted no flicker of expression to warn Willard. Then a board creaked, and Willard turned. Before he could fire, Kip knocked the gun from his hand, then handed his own to Helen.

"I want you," Morgan said, "for the chair!"

The big man lunged for him, but Kip hit him left and right in the face. The man squealed like a stuck pig and stumbled back, his face bloody. Morgan walked in and hit him three times. Desperately, the big man pawed to get him off, and Kip jerked him away from the sofa and hit him again.

A siren cut the night with a slash of sound, and almost in the instant they heard it, the car was slithering to a stop outside.

Helen pulled her robe around her, her face pale. Kip Morgan picked up Willard and shoved him against the wall. Hatred blazed in his eyes, but what strength there had been four years before had been sapped by easy living. The door opened, and two plainclothes detectives entered, followed by some uniformed officers.

The first one stopped abruptly. "What's going on here?" he demanded.

"This man is Henry Willard," Kip said, "and there is a murder rap hanging over him from New Jersey. Also, a fifty-thousand-dollar payroll robbery!"

"Willard? This man is James Howard Kendall. He owns the Mario Dine & Dance spot and about a dozen other things around town. Known him since he was a kid."

"He went back East, took the name Willard, and—"

"Brady," Willard interrupted, "this is a case of mistaken identity. You know me perfectly well. Take this man in. I want to prefer charges of assault and battery. I'll be in first thing in the morning."

"You'll leave over my dead body!" Kip declared. He turned to Brady. "He told Mrs. Whitson that he had already made plans to disappear again if need be."

"Morgan, I've known Mr. Kendall for years, now—"

"Ask him what he is doing in this house. Ask him how he came to drive up here in the night and enter a dark house."

Kendall hesitated only a moment. "Brady, I met this girl only tonight, made a date with her. This is an attempt at a badger game."

"Mighty strange," the gray-haired man who had driven Kip to town interrupted. "Mighty strange way to run a badger game. This man"—he indicated Kip—"staggered onto my porch half beaten to death and asked me to rush him to town to prevent a murder. It was he who sent me for the police. This house was dark when he started for it."

"All you will need are his fingerprints," Kip said. "This man murdered a payroll guard, changed clothes with the murdered man. Then he took the money and came back here and went into business with the proceeds from the robbery."

"Ah? Maybe you've got something, Morgan. We always wondered how he came into that money."

Kendall wheeled and leaped for the window, hurling himself through it, shattering it on impact. He had made but two jumps when Morgan swept up the gun and fired. The man fell, sprawling.

Policemen trained their revolvers on Morgan. "You've killed him!" Brady said.

"No, just a broken leg. Call the medics and he's all yours."

As the police left, Kip turned to Helen Whitson. "You did it!" she exclaimed. "I knew you could! And you've earned that five thousand dollars!"

"It's a nice sum." He looked at her again. "When are you leaving?"

"I've got to go back to New York on Monday."

"Don't go yet." He took her by the shoulders. "In a couple of days, my lips won't be so swollen. They aren't right for kissing a girl now, but—"

"But I'll bet you could," she suggested, "if you tried!"

THE STREET OF LOST CORPSES

I N A SHABBY room in a dingy hotel on a street of pawn-shops, cheap nightclubs, and sour-smelling bars, a man sat on a hard chair and stared at a collection of odds and ends scattered on the bed before him. There was no sound in the room but the low mutter of a small electric fan throwing an impotent stream of air against his chest and shoulders.

He was a big man, powerfully built, yet lean in the hips and waist. His shoes were off, and his shirt hung over the foot of the bed. It was hot in the room despite the open windows, and from time to time, he mopped his face with a towel.

The bed was ancient, the washbasin rust-stained, the bedspread ragged. Here and there, the wallpaper had begun to peel, and the door fit badly. For the forty-ninth time, the man ran his fingers through a shock of dark, unruly hair.

Kip Morgan swore softly. Before him lay the puzzle of the odd pieces. Four news clippings, a torn bit of paper on which was written all or part of a number, and a crumpled pawn ticket. He stared gloomily at the assortment and muttered at the heat. It was hot—hotter than it had a right to be in Los Angeles.

Occupied though he was, he did not fail to hear the click of heels in the hall outside or the soft tap on his door. He slid from his chair and crossed silently to the door.

Again, the tap sounded. "Who is it?"

"It's me." The voice was low, husky, feminine. "May I come in?"

Turning the key in the lock, he stepped back. "Sure, sure. Come on in."

Nothing about the way she was dressed left anything to the imagination. Her blouse was cheap and the skirt cheaper.

She wore too much mascara, too much rouge, and too much lipstick. Her hose were very sheer, her heels too high.

He waved her into a chair. There was irritation in his eyes. "At least you had sense enough to look the part. Didn't I tell you to stay away from me?" His voice was purposely low, for the walls were thin.

"I had to come!" Marilyn Marcy stepped closer, and despite the heat and the cheapness of her makeup he felt the shock of her nearness and drew back. "I've been worried and frightened! You must know how worried I am! Have you learned anything?"

"Now you listen to me!" His tone was ugly. Her coming into that part of town worried him, and dressed like that? She was asking for it. "I took the job of finding your brother, and if he's alive, I'll find him. If he's dead, I'll find out how and why. In the meantime, stay away from me! Remember what happened to that other dick."

"But you've no reason to believe they killed him because of this investigation!" she protested. "Why should they? You told me yourself he had enemies."

"Sure Richards had enemies. He was a fast operator and a shrewd one. Nevertheless, Richards had been around a long time and had stayed alive.

"As to why they should kill him for looking into this case, I have no idea. All I know is that anything can happen down here, and everything has happened at one time or another. I don't know what happened to your brother or why a detective should get a knife stuck into him for trying to find out. Until I do I'm being careful."

"It's been over a week. I just had to know something! Tell me what you've found out, and I'll go."

"You'll stay right here," he said, "until I tell you to go. You came of your own accord, now you'll leave when I tell you. You'll stay for at least an hour, long enough to make anybody believe you're my girl. You look the part. Now act it!"

"Just what do you expect?" she demanded icily.

"Listen, I'm just talking about the looks of the thing. I'm working, not playing. You've put me on the spot by coming here, as I'm not supposed to know anybody in town. Now sit down, and if you hear any movement in the hall, make with the soft talk. Get me?"

She shrugged. "All right." She shook out a cigarette, offering him one. He shook his head impatiently, and she glared at him. "I wonder if you're as tough as you act?"

"You better hope I am," Kip replied, "or you'll have another stiff on your hands."

He stared grimly at the collection on the bed, and Marilyn Marcy stared at him. Some, she reflected, would call him handsome. Men would turn to look because of a certain toughness that made him seem as if he carried a permanent chip on his shoulder. Women would look, then turn to look again. She had seen them do it.

"Let's look at the facts," he said. "Your brother was an alcoholic, and he was on the skids. Even if we find him, he may not be alive."

"I realize that, but I must know. I love my brother despite his faults, and he took care of me when I was on my way up, and I will not forget him now. Aside from George, he was all I had in the world.

"He was always weak, and both of us knew it, yet when he went into the army, he was a fairly normal human being. He simply wasn't up to it, and when he received word his wife had left him, it broke him up.

"However, if my brother is dead, it was not suicide! It would have to be accident or murder. If it was the former, I want to know how and why; if the latter, I want the murderer brought to trial."

Kip's eyes searched her face as he listened. Having seen her without makeup, he knew she was a beautiful girl, and even before she hired him, he had seen her on the stage a dozen times. "You seem ready to accept the idea of murder. Why would anybody want to kill him?"

"I've heard they kill for very little down here."

"That they do. In a flophouse up the street, there was a man killed for thirty-five cents not long ago. Value, you know, is a matter of comparison. A dollar may seem little, but if you don't have one and want it badly, it can mean as much as a million."

"I've seen the time." Drawing her purse nearer, she counted out ten fives and then ten tens. "You will need expense money. If you need more, let me know."

His attention was on the collection on the bed. "Did Tom ever say anything about quitting the bottle? Or show any desire to?"

"Not that I know of. Each month he received a certain sum of money from me. We always met in a cheap restaurant on a street where neither of us was known. Tom wanted to keep everyone from knowing I had a brother who was a drunk. He believed he'd disgrace me. I sent him enough to live as he wished. He could have had more but he refused it."

Morgan nodded, then glanced at her. "What would you say if I told you that for three weeks prior to his disappearance he hadn't touched a drop?"

Marilyn shook her head. "How could you be sure? That doesn't sound like Tom. Whatever would make him change?"

"If I knew the answer to that I'd have the answer to a lot of things, and finding him would be much easier. Tom Marcy changed suddenly, almost overnight. He cleaned up, had his clothes pressed and his shoes shined. He took out his laundry and then began doing a lot of unexpected running around."

Obviously, she was puzzled, but a sudden glance at her watch and she was on her feet. "I must go. I've a date with George and that means I must go home and change. If he ever guessed I had come down here looking like this, he would—"

Kip stood up. "Sure, you can go." Before she could protest he caught her wrist, spun her into his arms, and kissed her soundly and thoroughly. Pulling away, she tried to slap him, but he blocked it with an elbow. "Don't be silly!" he said. "If you're going to leave here, you'll need to look like you should. That means your lipstick should be smeared, but good!"

He let go of her and stepped back. She stared at him, her eyes clouded and her breast heaving. "Did you have to be so—thorough about it?"

"Never do anything by halves," he said, dropping back into the chair. He looked up at her. "On second thought, I—"

"I'm leaving!" she said hastily, and slipped quickly out of the door.

He grinned after her and wiped the lipstick from his mouth, then stared at the red smear on his handkerchief, his face sobering. He swore softly and dropped back into the chair. Despite his efforts, he could not concentrate.

He walked to the washbasin and wiped away the last of the lipstick.

What did he know, after all? Tom Marcy was an alcoholic with few friends, and only one or two who knew him at all well. Slim Russell was a wino he occasionally treated, and another had been "Happy" Day. Marcy minded his own affairs, drank heavily, and was occasionally in jail for it. Occasionally, too, he was found drunk in a doorway on skid row. The cops knew him, knew he had a room, and from time to time, rather than take him to jail, they'd take him to his room and dump him on his bed.

Then something happened to change him suddenly. A woman? It was unlikely, for he did not get around much where he might have met a woman. Yet suddenly he had straightened up and had become very busy. About what?

The pawn ticket might prove something. The ticket was for Tom Marcy's watch. Obviously, he had reached the limit of his funds when some sudden occasion for money arose, and rather than ask his sister for it, he had pawned his watch.

When he failed to appear at the restaurant, something that had not happened before, Marilyn began to worry.

She returned to the restaurant several times, but Tom Marcy did not show up. When the following month came around, she went again, and again he had not appeared. In the meantime, she had watched the newspapers for news of deaths and accidents. Then she hired a detective.

Vin Richards was a shrewd operative with connections throughout the underworld. A week after taking the case, he was found in an alley not far from the hotel in which Kip Morgan sat. Vin Richards had taken a knife in the back and another under the fifth rib. He was very dead when discovered.

Morgan began with a check of the morgue and a talk to the

coroner's assistants. He had checked hospitals and accident reports, then the jails and the police.

The officers who worked the street in that area agreed that Tom Marcy never bothered anybody. Whenever he could, he got back to his room, and even when very drunk, he was always polite. It was the police who said he had straightened up.

"Something about it was wrong," one officer commented. "Usually when they get off the bottle they can't leave the street fast enough, but not him. He stayed around, but he wouldn't take a drink."

Seven weeks and he had vanished completely; seven weeks with no news. "We figured he finally left, went back home or wherever. To tell you the truth, we miss him.

"The last time I saw him, he was cold sober. Talked with me a minute, asking about some old bum friend of his. He hesitated there just before we drove away, and I had an idea he wanted to tell me something, maybe just say good-by. That was the last time I saw him."

He had disappeared, but so had Vin Richards. Only they found Vin.

"Odd," the same officer had commented. "I would never expect Vin to wind up down here. He used to be on the force, you know, and a good man, too, but he wanted to work uptown. Hollywood, Beverly Hills, that crowd."

The pawn ticket answered one question but posed another. Tom Marcy needed money, so he hocked his watch, something he had not done before. Why did he need money? If he did need it, why hadn't he asked Marilyn?

The news clippings now—two of them were his own idea, one he found in Tom's room. And there was a clue, a hint. His clipping and one of Tom's were identical.

It was a tiny item from the paper having to do with the disappearance of one "Happy" Day, a booze hound and former circus clown. Long known along East Fifth Street and even as far as Pershing Square, he had been one of Marcy's friends.

Marcy's second clipping was about a fire in a town sixty

miles upstate in which the owner had lost his life. There was little more except that the building was a total loss.

The last clipping, one Kip Morgan had found for himself, was a duplicate of one Tom Marcy left behind in the hock-shop. The owner, thinking it might be important, had put it away with Tom's watch and mentioned it to Kip Morgan. At Kip's request, the pawnbroker had shown him the clipping. In a newspaper of the same date as the hocking of the watch, Morgan found the same item. It was a simple advertisement for a man to do odd jobs.

That Marcy had it in his hand when he went to hock his watch might indicate a connection. The pawning of the watch *could* have been an alternative to answering the ad. Yet Marcy had straightened up immediately and had begun his unexplained running around.

Could the advertisement tie in with the disappearance of "Happy" Day? A hunch sent Morgan checking back through the papers. Such an ad appeared in the papers just before his disappearance. Once Kip had a connection, he had followed through. Had there been other disappearances? There had.

Slim Russell, Marcy's other friend, had vanished in the interval between the disappearance of Day and that of Tom Marcy himself. Apparently, it had been these disappearances that brought about the change in Tom Marcy.

Why?

Checking the approximate date of Slim Russell's disappearance, for which he had only the doubtful memories of various winos, he found another such ad in the newspaper.

The newspaper's advertising department was a blind alley. On each occasion, the ad came by mail, and cash was enclosed, no check.

Morgan paced the floor, thinking. Not a breeze stirred, and the day was hot. He could be out on the beach instead of there, sweating out his problem in a cheap hotel, yet he could not escape feeling he was close to something. Also, and it could be his imagination, he had the feeling he was being watched.

Richards, cold and cunning as a prairie wolf, an operator with many connections and many angles, had been trapped and murdered. Before that, three men had disappeared and were probably dead.

Clearing away the Marcy collection, Morgan packed it up, then stretched out and fell into an uncomfortable state of half awake, half asleep.

Hours later, his mind fogged by sleep, he felt rather than heard a faint stirring at the door. His consciousness struggled, then asserted itself. He lay very still, every sense alert, listening.

Someone was at the door fumbling with the lock. Slowly, the knob turned.

Morgan lay still. The slightest creak of the springs would be audible. Perspiration dried on his face and he tried to keep his breathing even and natural. Now the darkness seemed thicker where the door had opened. A soft click of the lock as the door closed.

His throat felt tight, his mouth dry. A man with a knife? Gathering himself, every muscle poised, he waited.

A floorboard creaked ever so slightly, a dark figure loomed over his bed, and a hand very gently touched his chest as if to locate the spot. Against the window's vague light, he saw a hand lift, the glint of a knife. Traffic rumbled in the street, and somewhere a light went on, and the figure beside the bed was starkly outlined.

With a lunge, he threw himself against the standing man's legs. Caught without warning, the man's body came crashing down and the knife clattered on the floor. Kip was up on his feet as the man grasped his fallen knife and turned like a cat. Blocking the knife arm, Kip whipped a wicked right into the man's midsection. He heard the *whoosh* of the man's breath, and he swung again. The second blow landed on the man's face, but he jerked away and plunged for the door.

Going after him, Kip tangled himself in a chair, fell, broke free, and rushed for the door in time to see his attacker go into a door across the hall.

Doors opened along the hall and there were angry complaints. He whipped open the door into which the attacker had vanished, a light went on, and a man was sitting up in bed. A window stood open, but his attacker was gone.

"Who was that guy?" the man in bed protested. "What's goin' on?"

"Did you see him?" The man in bed showed no signs of excitement, nor was he breathing hard.

"See him? Sure, I saw him! He came bustin' in here and I flipped the switch, and he dove out that window!"

The alley was dark and the fire escape empty. Whoever he had been, he was safely away now. Kip Morgan walked back to his room. They had killed Richards when he got too close for comfort, and now they were after him.

When the hotel quieted down, he pulled on his shoes and shirt. He went downstairs into the dingy street; a man was slumped against a building nearby, breathing heavily, an empty wine bottle lying beside him. Another man, obviously steeped in alcohol, lurched against a building staring blearily at Morgan, wondering whether his chance of a touch was worth re-crossing the street.

It was early, as it had been still light when he stretched out on the bed. It was too early for the attacker to have expected Morgan to be in bed unless he already *knew* he was there. That implied the attacker either lived in the hotel or had a spy watching him.

Weaving his way through the human driftwood, Morgan considered the problem. The killer of Richards used a knife, and so had his attacker. It was imperative he take every step with caution, for a killer might await him around any corner. Whatever Tom Marcy had stumbled upon, it had led to murder.

Back to the beginning, then. Marcy had straightened up and quit drinking after the disappearance of Slim Russell. He had known enough to arouse his suspicions and obviously connected it to the disappearance of Happy Day.

It was not coincidence that the two men who vanished had been known to him, for the winos along the streets nearly all knew each other, at least by sight. Many times, they had shared bottles or sleeping quarters, and Marcy might have known sixty or seventy of them slightly.

What aroused Marcy's suspicions? Obviously, he had begun an investigation of his own. But why? Because of fear? Of loyalty to the other derelicts? Or for some deeper, unguessed reason?

Another question bothered Morgan. How had the mysterious attacker identified him so quickly? How had he known about Richards? Richards, of course, had been a private operator for several years, but he, Kip Morgan, had never worked in that area and would be unknown to the underworld except by name from his old prizefighting days.

Something had shocked Tom Marcy so profoundly that he stopped drinking. The idea that was seeping into Morgan's consciousness was one he avoided. To face it meant suspicion of Marilyn Marcy, but how else could the attacker have known of him? Yet why should she hire men, pay them good money, and then have them killed?

If not Marilyn then somebody near her, but that made no sense, either. The distance from East Fifth to Brentwood was enormous, and those who bridged it were going down, not up. It was a one-way street lined with empty bottles.

Instead of returning to his room, Morgan went to the quiet room where Tom Marcy had lived when not drinking heavily. It was a curious side of the man that during his drinking spells, he slept in flophouses or in the hideouts of other winos. In the intervals, he returned to the quiet, cheap little room where he read, slept, and seemed to have been happy.

At daybreak Morgan was up and made a close, careful search of the room. It yielded exactly nothing.

Three men missing and one murdered; at least two of the missing men had answered ads. What of Marcy? Had he done the same?

The idea gave Morgan a starting point, and he went down into the street. The crowding, pushing, often irritable crowd had not yet reached the downtown area. The buses that fed those streams of humanity were still gathering their quotas in the outskirts, miles away.

The warehouse at the address in the advertisement was closed and still. He walked along the street on the opposite side, then crossed and came back down. Several places were opening for business, a feedstore, a filling station, and a small lunch counter across the way.

The warehouse itself was a three-story building, large and old. There was a wooden door, badly in need of paint, a blank, curtained window, and alongside the door a large vehicle entrance closed by a metal door that slid down from above.

Kip crossed the street and entered the café. The place was empty but for one bleary-eyed bum farther down the counter. The waitress, surprisingly, was neat and attractive.

Kip smiled, and his smile usually drew a response from women. "How's about a couple of sinkers? And a cup of Java?"

She brought the order, hesitating before him. "It's slow this morning."

"Do you do much business? With all these warehouses, I should imagine you'd do quite well."

"Sometimes, when they are busy, our breakfast and lunch business can be good. As for the late trade, there's just enough to keep us open. We get some truck and cab drivers in here at all hours, and there's always a few playing the pinball machines."

Kip indicated the warehouse across the street. "Don't they hire men once in a while? I saw an ad a few days ago for a handyman."

"That place?" She shrugged. "It wouldn't be your sort of work. Occasionally, they hire a wino or street bum, and not many of those. I imagine it's just for cleaning up, or something, and they want cheap labor.

"There was a fellow who came in here a few times. I think he went to work over there. At least he waited around for a few days waiting for somebody to show up."

"Did he actually get a job?"

"I believe so. He waited, but when they actually did show up he did not go over. Not for the longest time. He was like all of them, I guess, and really didn't want work all that bad. He did finally go, I think."

"He hasn't been in since?"

"I haven't seen him. But they haven't been working over there, either. If they've been around at all, it was at night."

"They work at night?"

"I don't know about that, but one day I saw the shade was almost to the bottom, and the next day it was a little higher. Again, it was drawn to the bottom."

Kip smiled and asked for a refill. A smart, observant girl.

"I'd make a bet the guy you speak of was the one I talked to. We were looking over the ads together." Kip squinted his eyes as if trying to remember. "About forty? Forty-five, maybe? Medium height? Hair turning gray? Thin face?"

"That's the one. He was very pleasant, but I think he'd been sick or something. He was very nice, but jittery, on edge, like. He was wearing a pin-striped suit, neatly pressed, and you don't see that down here."

"What kind of business are they in?" He turned his side to the counter so he could look across the street. "I could use some work myself, although I'm not hurting."

"You've got me. I have no idea what they do, although I see a light delivery truck, one of those panel jobs, once in a while. One of their men, too, comes in once in a while, but he doesn't talk much. He's a blond, stocky, Swedish type."

Morgan glanced down the counter at the somnolent bum whose head was bowed over his coffee cup.

Through another cup of coffee and a piece of apple pie, they talked. Twice, truck drivers came in, had their coffee and departed, but Kip lingered, and the waitress seemed glad for the company.

They talked of movies, dancing, the latest songs, and a couple of news items.

The warehouse across the street was rarely busy, but occasionally they moved bulky boxes or rolls of carpet from the place in the evening or early morning. Some building firm, she guessed.

The bum got slowly to his feet and shuffled to the door. In the doorway, he paused, and his head turned slowly on his thin neck. For a moment, his eyes met Morgan's. They were clear, sharp, and intelligent. Only a fleeting glimpse and then the man was outside. Kip got to his feet. How much had the man heard? Too much, that was sure. And he was no stew-bum, no wino.

Kip walked to the door and stood looking after the bum, if

such he was. The man was shuffling away, but he turned his head once and looked back. Kip was well inside the door and out of view. Obviously the man had paused in the door to get a good look at Morgan. He would remember him again.

The idea disturbed him. Of course, it might be only casual interest. Nevertheless there was a haunting familiarity about the man, a sort of half recognition that would not quite take shape.

There was no time to waste. The next step was obvious. He must find out what went on inside that warehouse, who the two men were who had been seen around and what was in the boxes or rolls of carpet they carried out. The last carried unpleasant connotations to Kip Morgan. More than ever, he was sure that Tom Marcy had been murdered.

Except for the narrow rectangle of light where the lunch counter was, all the buildings were blank and shadowed when Kip Morgan returned. Nor was there movement along the street, only the desolation and emptiness that comes to such streets after closing hours.

Like another of the derelicts adrift along neighboring streets, sleeping in doorways or alleys, Morgan slouched along the street, and at the corner above the warehouse, he turned and went along the back street to the alley. No one was in sight, so he stepped quickly into the alley and stopped still behind a telephone post.

He waited for the space of two minutes, and nobody appeared. Staying in the deeper shadows near the building Morgan went along to the loading dock at the back of the warehouse.

A street lamp threw a vague glow into the far end of the alley, but otherwise it was in darkness. A rat scurried across the alley, its feet rustling on a piece of torn wrapping paper. Kip moved along the back of the building, listening. There was no sound from within. He tried the door and it was locked.

There was a platform and a large loading door, but the door was immovable. There were no windows on the lower floors, but when he reached the inner corner of the building he glanced up into the narrow space between the warehouse and the adjoining building and saw a second-story window that seemed to be open. The light was indistinct, but he decided to chance it.

Both walls were of brick and without ornamentation but he thought he knew a way. Putting his back against the warehouse and his feet against the opposite building he began to work his way up. It needed but two or three minutes before he was seated on the sill of the warehouse window.

It was open but a few inches, propped there by an old putty knife. Hearing no sound he eased the window higher, stepped in, and returned the window to its former position. Crouching in the darkness, he listened.

Gradually, his ears sorted the sounds—the creaks and groans normal to an old building, the scurrying of rats—and his nostrils sorted the smell. There was a smell of tarpaper and of new lumber. Cautiously, he tried his pencil flash, keeping it away from windows.

He was in a barnlike room empty except for some new lumber, a couple of new packing cases, both open, and tools lying about.

Tiptoeing, he found the head of the stairs and went down. In the front office was an old-fashioned safe, a rolltop desk, and a couple of chairs. The room was dusty and showed no signs of recent use.

It was in the back office where he made his discovery, and it was little enough at first, for the lower floor aside from the front office was unfurnished and empty. And then he glimpsed a door standing open to a room partitioned off in a corner.

Inside was an old iron cot, a table, washstand, and chair. There was a stale smell of sweaty clothing and whisky. The bedding was rumpled. On the floor were several bottles.

Here someone had slept off a drunk, awakening to what? Or had he ever awakened? Or forfeited one kind of sleep for another? The heavy sleep of drunkenness, perhaps, for the silence of death?

Morgan shook his head irritably. What reason had he to believe these men dead? Was he not assuming too much?

He moved around. Kicking a rumpled pile of sacks, he disclosed *a blue, pin-striped suit!*

Tom Marcy had worn such a suit when last seen! Dropping to his knees, Kip made a hasty search of the pockets, but they yielded nothing. He was straightening up when he heard movement from the alley entrance and a mutter of voices.

Dropping the clothing, he took one hasty glance around and darted for the stairway. He went up on his toes, swiftly and silently, then flattened against the wall, listening.

"Hey? Did you hear something?" The voice was low but distinct.

"I heard rats. This old place is full of them! Come on, let's get that pile of junk out and burn it. If the boss found we'd left anything around, he'd have our hearts out. Where'd you leave it?"

"In the room. I'll get it."

He could hear the two men stirring about down below. The blond man mumbling to himself, ignoring the protests of the taller, darker man. Twice, in the glow of their flashlights, Kip got a good look at them.

Footsteps across the floor, then a low exclamation. "Somebody's been here! I never left those clothes like that!"

"Ah, nuts! How do you remember? Who would prowl a dump like this?"

"Somebody's been here, I say! I'm going to look around!"

Morgan was fairly trapped, and he knew it.

They would be coming up the steps in a minute, and he had no chance of getting across that wide floor and opening the window, then climbing down between the walls. Even if the boards did not creak, the time needed for opening and closing the window and the risk of their hearing his feet scraping on the brick wall were too much. He glanced up toward the third floor. Swiftly, he mounted the steps to that unknown floor.

Whatever was going on there was shrewdly and efficiently handled and, at the first hint of official interest, would quiet down so fast that no clue would be left. There were few enough as it was.

Meanwhile, he was working fast. There was a window, and he eased it up. Down was impossible . . . but up?

He glanced up. The edge of the roof was there, only a few feet away and somewhat higher. Scrambling to the sill, his back against the window, he hesitated an instant, then jumped out and up.

It was a wild, desperate gamble; if he fell and broke a leg or was in any way disabled, they would find him and kill him.

He jumped, his fingers clawed for the edge of the parapet on the roof opposite, and caught hold. His toes scraped the wall, then he pulled himself up and swung his feet over the parapet just as the blond man reached the window. For a startled instant, their eyes met, and then he was up and running across the roof. He heard the sharp bark of a pistol shot, but the man could only shoot at where Morgan had been.

Crossing the roof, he looked down at the next one. Only a few feet. He dropped to that roof opposite, but this time he did not run. There was a narrow space there, and he could go down as he had come up. Bracing his back against one side, his feet against the other, he worked his way swiftly down.

He was almost down when he heard running feet on the roof above. Somehow, by a trap door, no doubt, they had reached the roof. "Where'd he go?" The voice was low but penetrating in the silence.

"Across the roofs! Where else! Let him go or we'll have the cops on us!"

"Let's get out of here!"

Dropping to the alley, Kip Morgan brushed himself off and walked to his car, almost a block away. He had barely seated himself when he saw a light gray coupé whisk by. The man nearest him was the blond man, and they did not see him.

Starting his car, he let the gray car get a start, then followed. Habitually, he went bareheaded, but in the car he kept an assortment of hats to be used on just such tailing jobs. He pulled on a wide-brimmed fedora, tilting the brim down.

The gray car swung into Wilshire and started along the boulevard. It was very late, and there was little traffic. Holding his position as long as he dared, he came abreast only one lane away, and passing, turned left and off the street. When he picked them up again, he was wearing a cap and had his lights on dim. Moreover, his car now had a double taillight showing. He had rigged the light himself.

Shortly after reaching Beverly Hills, the gray car turned right, and Kip pulled to the curb, switched hats again, and turned his lights on bright. As the other car pulled up to the curb, he went by, going fast. Turning the corner, he pulled up and parked, then walked back to the corner, pausing in the darkness by a hedge and the trunk of a jacaranda tree.

Another car pulled up and stopped as the two men started across the street. A man and a woman got out. The blond man called out, "Mr. Villani? I got to see you!"

The man was tall and heavily built. He wore evening clothes, and as Morgan slipped nearer, staying in the shadows, he could hear the irritation in the man's voice. "All right, Gus, just a minute."

He turned to the girl he was with. "Would you mind going on in, Marilyn? I'll be right there."

The girl's face turned toward the light, and Kip's pulse jumped. *It was Marilyn Marcy!*

Drawing deeper into the shadows, he chewed his lip, scowling. This just did not make sense.

The two men had come up to Villani, who was speaking. "Gus? How many times have I warned you never to come near me? You know how to get in touch."

Gus's voice was low in protest. "But boss! This is bad! That Morgan guy, he's been into the warehouse!"

"Inside?"

"Uh-huh. I don't know for sure if it was him, but I think it was."

"It was him," the dark man added. "He got away and we had only a glimpse."

Morgan waited, hoping to see Villani's face. This was the boss, the man he had wanted to locate, and he knew Marilyn Marcy.

A low-voiced colloquy followed, but Morgan could hear nothing but the murmur of their voices. "All right, Vinson. Stay with him. We want no failure this time."

The two men started back to their car, and he started to follow them, then decided nothing would be gained. Rather, he wanted to know what was going on there.

As the gray car drove away, Morgan walked past the house into which Villani and Marilyn had disappeared, noting several other cars were parked outside. He went on down to the corner, crossed to a telephone booth and checked for Villani. It was there, the right name, the right address.

George Villani!

Marilyn had a date with George. That tied in, but what did it mean? If she was double-crossing Morgan, what could she hope to gain by it? On the other hand, suppose she did not know? That could be the way these crooks found out about Richards and about him as well. She had simply told her boyfriend.

Morgan walked back to his car, then stopped short, his mouth dry and his stomach gone hollow. The thin, dark man, Vinson, was standing by the tree, and he had a gun in his hand. "Hello, Morgan! Looks like we're going to get together, after all!"

He gestured. "Nice rig you got here—the hats and all. You had us fooled."

"Then what made you stop?" Kip asked pleasantly.

"Your car. It looked familiar, and it was like one we saw when we left the warehouse. For luck we had a look. You shouldn't leave your registration on the steering post."

"Well, so here we are." Morgan could not see the blond man, and that worried him. He had an idea that Gus was the tough one. This guy thought he was tough, and might be, but it was Gus who worried him. "You'd better put that rod away before somebody sees it."

"There's nobody around." Vinson liked that. He clearly thought he had the casual tough guy act down pat. "You've been getting in my hair, Morgan. We don't like guys who get in our hair."

Kip shrugged, and the gun tilted a little. This guy was hair-triggered, and that might be both good and bad. "Getting in people's hair is my business. Where's Tom Marcy?"

"Marcy?" The question surprised Vinson. "I never heard of anybody named Marcy. What's the angle?"

"Why, I am looking for him. That's my job." Morgan was alert and very curious. Obviously, the name surprised Vinson and puzzled him.

Vinson frowned. "I don't get it, pal. We figured you for a—" He paused, catching himself on the word. "We had you figured for the fuzz."

"Look," Morgan protested, "there's something screwy about this. I am looking for Marcy. If you don't know him we've no business together. Let's forget it. You go your way, and I'll go mine, and everybody'll be happy."

"Are you nuts? We're takin' you someplace where we can ask some questions, and we'll get answers." His eyes flickered. "Here comes—"

Morgan moved, swinging down and across with his left hand. He slapped the gun aside and came up under the barrel with his right, missed the grab, but followed through with the butt of his palm under Vinson's chin. The gangster's heels flipped up, and he went down hard, the gun flying from his hand.

From behind him Kip heard running feet, and he threw himself over a hedge, sprinting across the lawn. He ducked behind a huge old tree, grabbed a heavy limb, and pulled himself up. Almost at once, both men rushed on by.

Motionless in the tree, scarcely daring to breathe, he waited. "You fool!" Gus was saying. "You should have shot him!"

He heard them searching through the brush, but the branches above seemed never to occur to them. Nearby, a dog began to bark, and a light went on in a house. With a mutter of angry voices, the two men headed for their car. He heard it start.

Leaning back against the tree trunk, he waited. There was the chance it had been some other car starting or that they had driven but a short distance and were waiting, watching. He was in no hurry now. He had plenty to think about.

George Villani was the boss. In whatever was going on, he was the man who gave the orders and did the planning. When a serious problem came up, they had immediately gone to him. And George Villani was dating Marilyn Marcy.

The whys of that he did not know, but it seemed obvious that through him the killers had learned of Vin Richards, and it must have been Marilyn who told him Morgan was holed up in that hotel.

He lowered himself to the grass, waited an instant to see if he was unobserved, then went along the hedge to the alley.

His car could wait until daylight. If they were watching, and he returned now, they would kill him without hesitation. Once in the alley near the street, he paused.

Marilyn was still next door, and he could hear the sounds of music and laughter from the house. A small party was in progress.

He hesitated, half in the notion of crashing the party, but his shirt was rumpled, and his clothes were dusty from crawling through old buildings. Crossing several streets, he caught a cab and returned to his apartment. For this night the room at the hotel would stay empty.

As he considered the situation, he became convinced Tom Marcy must have come upon some hint of danger threatening his sister. Perhaps he had established a connection between Villani and the disappearances of Day and Russell. Only that seemed a logical explanation for his sudden breaking of old habits and his subsequent investigations. The danger of his sister marrying a murderer had started his interest in the warehouse and the street of missing men.

Back in his apartment he took off his shoes and sat on the edge of the bed. The next day would be soon enough, but at that time he would have to bear down. He must discover why those men had vanished and what had become of Tom Marcy.

He slept, dreaming a dream of flames, of a scream in the night, of—

He awakened suddenly. Vinson was standing over him, and Gus was standing with his back to the door, and they both had guns. He started to sit up, and Vinson hit him a full swing with a boot he had picked up. The blow caught him on the temple, and something exploded in his brain. He lunged to get off the bed, and another blow hit him. His feet tangled in the bedclothes, and he fell sprawling, taking another blow as he fell.

———

WHEN HE REGAINED consciousness, he was lying on his face in the back of a van or delivery truck, and the first thing his eyes recognized was a shoe toe inches from his face. Closing his eyes, he lay still, pain throbbing in his skull.

Somehow they had traced him and gained access to his room without awakening him. Knocked out, he had been loaded in the truck and was being taken . . . where?

Listening, he decided by the lack of traffic sounds and the unbroken rate of speed that they were on a highway.

"What did he say to do with him?" Vinson was asking.

"Hold him. The boss needs to talk to him. He wants to know has he talked to anybody."

Tentatively, Kip tested his muscles. His hands were tightly bound. He relaxed, letting the hammers on his skull pound away. Suddenly, the truck made an abrupt turn, and the road became rough. A gravel road and badly corrugated. The truck dipped several times, then began to climb in slow switchbacks, higher and higher.

The air was clear and cool. The truck made another turn, ran on for a short distance, and then came to a stop. Morgan let his muscles relax completely.

"Haul him out," Vinson said. "I'll light up."

Gus opened the doors from within, dropped to the ground, then grabbed Morgan's ankles and jerked him to the ground. He hit the road with a thump, and it had been all he could do to keep from crying out when his head bumped on the tailboard, then the ground. Gus grabbed him by the shirtfront and dragged him to a dugout where he opened the door and threw him down the steps into darkness. The door closed, the hasp dropped into place, and he was alone.

For what seemed a long time, he lay still; the throbbing in his head became a great sea of pain where wave after wave broke over him. His head felt enormous, and every move generated new agony. Through it, fear clawed its way, tearing with angry fingers at his consciousness.

They would come back, Vinson and Gus. The only way to escape torture and even death was to endure the pain now while he had freedom from their watching eyes.

He lunged, bucking with his bound body, then rolling over three times until he found himself against a tier of boxes or crates. Hunching himself to a sitting position, he began sawing his wrists at the sharp edge of the box. In his desperation, he jerked too far, and the edge scraped his wrist. Wildly, he fought to cut loose the ropes that bound him.

He struggled on. The close confines of the dugout made him pant, and sweat soaked his shirt and ran into his eyes. His muscles grew heavy with weariness, but he fought on, to no avail. So intent was he that he failed to hear the approaching footsteps, failed to hear the opening door. Not until the light flashed in his eyes did he look up. . . .

"Finally woke up, did you?" Gus walked over and jerked him away from the boxes. "Tryin' to escape?" Gus booted him in the ribs.

With a knife, he slashed the ropes that bound Kip's ankles, then jerked him up. Morgan's feet felt heavy, as though he wore diving boots. Gus put a hand between his shoulder blades and pushed him toward the door, and Morgan reached it in a stumbling run. The light of the flash shot past him, revealing the edge of a wash not fifty feet away.

A wash . . . or a canyon. Ten feet or two hundred. His stumbling run became a real run as he hurled himself, bending as far forward as he could, toward that edge and whatever awaited him.

There was a startled curse, then a yell, a momentary pause, and he veered sharply. A bullet slammed past him, and a gun barked. Kip left his feet in a long dive, hitting the edge in a roll that took him over the edge and sliding. He fell, brought up with a crunch and a mouthful of sand at the bottom of the wash. Lunging to his feet, wrists still bound behind him, he charged blindly into the darkness, down the wash. His feet were prickling with a thousand tiny needles at each step, but he ran, desperately, raw breath tearing at his lungs with each step.

Then, aware that his running was making too much sound, he slid to a stop, listening. There were running footsteps somewhere, and a shaft of light shot across the small plateau of a mine dump as the cabin door opened. He heard angry shouts; then a car started.

Kip Morgan had no idea where he was. His brain was pounding painfully, and he smarted from a dozen scratches and bruises. Yet he walked on, fighting his bonds with utter futility. The black maw of another wash opened on his right, and he turned into it. His feet found a steep path, and painstakingly he made his way up. Crouching to keep low, he crossed the skyline of the wash. He had no idea how far he walked, but he pushed on, wanting only distance between himself and his pursuers. As the first faint intimations of dawn lightened the sky, he crept around a boulder and, dropping to a sitting position, was almost immediately asleep.

The hot morning sun awakened him, and he staggered to his feet, aware of a dull throbbing in his hands. Twisting to get a look at them, he saw they were badly swollen and slightly blue. Frightened by the look of them, he looked around. Judging by the sun, he was on the eastern slope of a mountain. All about was desert, with no evidence of life anywhere. Not a sound disturbed the stillness of the morning.

Turning, he started to cross a shoulder of the mountain, sure he would find something on the western side. He must have been brought across to the eastern side during the night.

His mouth was dry, and he realized the intense heat, although only nine or ten o'clock, was having its effect. Stumbling over and through the rocks, he saw a stretch of road. It was the merest trail with no tracks upon it, but it had to go somewhere, so he followed it. When he had walked no more than a mile, he rounded a turn in the road and found himself at an abandoned mine. There was a ramshackle hoist house and gallows frame. He stumbled toward it.

The door hung on rusty hinges, and a rusty cable hung from the shiv wheel. As he neared the buildings, a pack rat scurried away from the door.

The tracks of several small animals led toward the wall of the mountain beyond the small ledge on which the mine stood. Following them, he found a trickle of water running from a rusty pipe thrust into the wall. When he had drunk, he walked back to the hoist house, searching for something with which to cut his bonds. There was always, around such places, rusty tools, tin cans, all manner of castoffs.

On the floor was the blade of a round-point shovel.

Dropping to his knees, he backed his feet toward the shovel and got it between them. Holding it with his feet, he began to saw steadily. The pain was excruciating, but stubbornly he refused to ease off even for a moment, and after a few minutes the rope parted, and he stripped the pieces from his wrists. He brought his hands around in front of him and stared at them.

They were grotesquely swollen, puffed like a child's boxing gloves, with a tight band around his wrists showing where the ropes had pressed into his flesh. Returning to the spring, he dropped on his knees and held his wrists under the cold, dripping water.

For a long time, he knelt, uncertain how much good it was doing but enjoying the feel of the cold water. Slowly, very gently, he began to massage his hands. Finally, he gave up.

Taking a long drink, he turned away from the mine, glancing about for a weapon. He found a short length of rusted drill steel. He thrust it into his belt and headed down the road, carrying his arms bent at the elbows and his hands shoulder high because they hurt less that way. After he had walked a few miles, they began to feel better. A few steps farther, he glimpsed a paved highway, and the first truck along picked him up. "Not supposed to carry anybody," the trucker said, "but you look like you could use help. Filling station at the edge of town. Have to drop you there."

———

BACK IN MARCY'S room, he ran the basin full of warm water to soak his hands. After a while, they began to feel better, and some of the swelling was gone. As they soaked, he considered the situation.

So far, he had learned little, but he seemed to have upset Villani and his men. No doubt they believed he knew more than he did. He was positive they had murdered Tom Marcy, but he had no evidence of any description beyond the presence of a pin-striped suit, which might or might not be Tom's.

He might go and swear out a warrant for kidnaping and assault, but proving it would be something else with the kind of lawyers Villani would have.

What did he know? Digging out the clippings again, he studied them and once more he studied the clipping about the fire. That alone failed to fit. What could be the connection?

Suddenly, it hit him. What if the body in the fire had not been the owner, as was believed? *What if the owner was involved in a plot to rook the insurance companies? With Villani supplying the bodies?*

What about identification procedures? Fingerprints, teeth, measurements? Had the authorities checked out the bodies, or had they simply taken them for what they seemed to be? What did he mean, *bodies*? He had but one fire. Yet suppose there had been more?

Hastily, he dried his hands and took up the phone, dialing the number of the newspaper that published the item. In a matter of minutes, he had the name of the insurance company concerned. The city editor asked, "What's the problem? Is there anything wrong up there?"

Morgan hesitated. The papers had always given him a fair shake during his fighting days, and some of their reporters were better investigators than he was and had ready access to the files.

"I'm not sure, but something smells to high heaven, and somebody is so upset over my nosing around that they've given me a lot of trouble. Three men have disappeared off skid row in the last few months, and somebody doesn't seem to want it investigated."

"Who is this talking?"

"Kip Morgan. I used to be a fighter; now I'm a private investigator."

"I remember you. How about sending a man over to get your story?"

"Uh-uh. Just have somebody quietly check out George Villani, and two strongarm boys named Gus and Vinson." He mentioned the clippings he had found and the fire. Then he gave them the address of the warehouse. "It isn't much, but enough to make me think this may be insurance fraud."

As he hung up, he reflected with satisfaction that now, if anything happened to him, the newspapers at least would have a lead. He needed fifteen minutes by cab to the offices of the insurance company. He had heard a good deal of Neal Stoska, the insurance company's detective.

Stoska was a thin, angular man of fifty-odd, with shrewd, thoughtful eyes. "What is it you wish to know?" He leaned back in his swivel chair, studying Kip's face, then his still-swollen hands.

"Your company insured a building up in Bakersfield that had a fire a short time ago. Is that right?"

"No," Stoska replied. "We insured Leonard Buff, the man who was burned. Tri-State insured the building. Why do you ask?"

"I'm working on something, and there seems to be a connection. Did it look all right to you? I mean, did you sense anything phony about it?"

Stoska was impatient. "Morgan, we can't discuss anything like that with just anybody who walks into this office. If I did suspect anything wrong, we'd be in no position to talk about it until we had some semblance of a case. Have you information for us?"

"Listen . . ." Kip sat back in his chair and told his story from the beginning. The Marcy case, the disappearance of Russell and Day, and what had happened to him. "It's a wild yarn," he added, "but it's true, and I could use some help."

"Your idea is that Marcy's body was in the fire?"

"No, I believe it was Russell's body. I think Marcy discovered something accidentally. My hunch is that he waited in the café for Russell when Slim applied for the job. Slim never came back, and it is possible Marcy saw Villani near the warehouse or with one of the men from the building.

Something aroused his suspicions, and he was a man who loved his sister. In fact, his love for her was the only real thing in his life."

"It's all guesswork," Stoska agreed, "but good guesswork. You had something you wanted me to check?"

"A recheck, possibly. It is the size of Slim Russell and the body you found. Slim was a war veteran, so you can probably get his information that way or from the police. No doubt they picked him up from time to time, and they may have a description."

Stoska reached for the phone and at the same time pressed a button and ordered the file on Buff. "I want all we have on him," he added. "Also, put through a call to Gordon at Tri-State and ask him to come over. Tell him it's important."

A voice sounded on the telephone, and Morgan smiled, for the sharp, somewhat nasal sound had to be Mooney. In reply to Stoska's question, Mooney read off a brief description of Slim Russell. When Stoska hung up, he looked over at Morgan. "It fits," he said. "At least, it's close, very close."

Kip's cab dropped him at Marilyn Marcy's apartment, and he went up fast. She was alone, but dressed to go out.

"What is it?" She crossed the room to him. "You've found him? He's . . . he's dead, is that it?"

"Take it easy." He dropped into a chair. "Fix me a drink, will you? Anything wet." She was frightened of what he had come to tell her, and the activity might relieve the situation. "No, I haven't found him, but you have talked too much."

"I've talked?" She turned on him. "I've done no such thing! Why, I've—"

"Fix that drink and come over here. You did talk, and your talking got Vin Richards killed, and it almost got me killed. Right after you left my room, a guy attacked me with a knife in my hotel room. That was your doing, honey."

"That's nonsense! I told no one!"

"What about George?"

"What about him? Of course, I told him. I've told him everything. I'm engaged to him."

"You won't be for long," he replied grimly. "Now just sit down and get this straight the first time. I haven't time to waste, and I don't want to go into any involved explanations. When I get through talking," he accepted the drink, "you'll probably call me a liar, but that's neither here nor there. You hired me to do a job."

"I don't like the way you talk," she said coldly, "and I don't like you. You're fired!"

"All right, I'm fired, but I am still on this case because it has become mighty personal since I last talked to you. Nobody puts the arm on me and gets away with it.

"Now just listen. You told George Villani about hiring Richards, and within a few days, Richards is dead. You told him about me, and somebody tried to kill me. Who else could have known where I was? Or that I was even hired? Who else knew about Richards?

"And get this: If your brother is dead, it was Villani who killed him or had him killed."

She sat down abruptly, her face pale, eyes wide. She tasted her drink and put it down. "I don't know what's the matter with me. I never drink scotch." She looked at him. "It just doesn't add up. How could George be involved? George didn't even know about Tom. I never told him. And why should he kill him? Why should he kill anybody?"

"Tom loved you. You were his little sister." Morgan watched her over the glass, and he could see she was thinking now. Her anger and astonishment had faded. What if Tom saw you with somebody he knew was bad? Don't ask me how he knew, but Tom Marcy had been around, and he was always skating along the thin edge of the underworld. People down there hear things and they see things and nobody notices them, they're just a bunch of outcasts and drunks.

"I don't believe," he added, "that Villani knew Tom Marcy was your brother. If he knew him it was only as somebody who was interfering. Or that's how it could have been at first. When you told him about Richards and your brother being missing he may have put two and two together."

Briefly he explained but said nothing about talking to the newspapers or the insurance company. "What does Villani do?" he asked then.

"Do?" She shrugged. "He's a contractor of some sort. I

have never talked business with him, but he seems prosperous, has a beautiful home in Beverly Hills, and owns some business property there."

"Well, don't ask him any questions now, just be your own sweet, beautiful self and leave him to me."

The buzzer sounded and she came quickly to her feet. "That's George now. He is coming to pick me up and I'd forgotten!"

"Don't let it bother you, and be the best actress you can be. If he got suspicious now he might start on you. When a man kills as casually as he has he never knows when to stop."

There was a tap on the door and Marilyn crossed to it, admitting George Villani.

He was a big man, broad-shouldered and deep in the chest. His eyes went to Morgan and changed perceptibly. "George? I want you to meet Kip Morgan. He's the detective who is looking for my brother."

"How do you do?" Villani was all charm. "Having any luck?"

"Sure." Unable to resist the needle, Morgan added, "We hope to break the case in a matter of hours."

Villani smiled, but there was no humor in it. "Isn't that what detectives always say?"

Kip Morgan was irritated. He did not like this big, polished, easy-looking man, and some devil within him made him push it further. He had been hit, dragged, and banged around. A good suit of clothes had been ruined and he had a knot on the back of his head. All his resentment began to well to the surface. He knew it was both foolish and dangerous but he could not resist baiting him. Maybe it was this big man who was dating Marilyn, and maybe it was something else.

"Maybe," he replied carelessly. "I don't know what detectives say. I know this one is a cinch. This guy," he was enjoying Marilyn's tenseness, "has been a dope all along. We think he's been supplying bodies to folks who want to collect insurance. He's been getting his bodies off skid row where there are men nobody is supposed to be interested in."

"Seems rather farfetched," Villani said, no suggestion of a

smile now. "Wouldn't the insurance companies become suspicious?"

Kip felt good. He had never been much of a hand at beating around the bush. He was a direct action man and he liked to bull right into the middle of things and keep crowding until his opponent acted without thinking.

"Of course, the insurance companies are suspicious. I helped to make them suspicious. So are the newspapers. Now all we have to do is pick up the boys this man has been working with and make them talk. Once they let their hair down, we will have the man behind it, and fast."

Villani did not like that. He did not like it a bit. Suddenly, he did not want to be going on a date, and it showed. Villani had no reason to believe he was suspected, but he would want to cover up fast, and his next move would be to rid himself of the two who might talk. That done he would be in the clear.

Villani had come to the same conclusion. He turned to Marilyn. "I had no idea you were so busy. Why don't we just skip dinner tonight? I've a few things that need attention and you could finish your conference with Mr. Morgan."

"Why . . . !" Marilyn started to speak but Morgan interrupted.

"That would be a help, although I don't like to intrude. There are several things we have to discuss."

"Fine!" Villani was relieved. "I'll call you, dear." He turned to Morgan. "I wish you success. I hope you find your men."

As the door closed behind Villani, Marilyn turned to Morgan. "He couldn't get away too fast, could he? What is the trouble?"

"No trouble for us. As for Gus and Vinson, I wouldn't want to be in their shoes. He's going to kill them, you know. He'll be headed right for them, right now!"

He finished his drink and got up. "There's nothing I'd like better than to spend the evening with you, but I have to follow him."

She caught up her coat. "Then what are we waiting for?"

"Not you," he protested. "You can't go."

"Tom Marcy was my brother," she said. "If George Villani is all you say he is I want to see for myself."

He hesitated no longer. "It's your funeral, I warned you this was no place for you."

———

VILLANI WAS JUST starting his car when they reached the street, and Marilyn tugged Morgan back into the shadows by the door. "Come on! My car's in the driveway!"

As they turned into the street Villani's car was rounding the corner into the boulevard and traveling fast. Following at a distance, they saw Villani turn off the boulevard and head for his own place.

"If he goes out, we'll take both cars," Morgan suggested. "I'll follow him, you follow me. We don't know what's going to happen."

They sat in darkness waiting for Villani to emerge. Both were tense. Before this night was over there could be serious trouble, for Villani was not a man who was willing to lose. He had too much at stake.

Gus was dangerous, and so was Vinson, in his own way, and he had no business allowing Marilyn to come although he doubted if he could have stopped her and had not wasted breath trying.

Villani left his house on the run and jumped into his car. He did a fast U-turn in the middle of the street, and his headlights sprayed across their car. Kip, seeing what was to come, had ducked down in the seat pulling Marilyn down with him so they could not be seen.

When the lights were gone, Kip sprinted for the car he had abandoned the night before. He moved out from the curb and rounded the corner on two wheels. After half a mile Kip fell behind another car, switched his lights to dim and put on another hat. Gus knew all about his hats but it was unlikely he'd had the chance or thought to mention it to Villani. Behind him, Marilyn moved smoothly through traffic.

Villani seemed to glance back once but gave no indication that he knew he was being followed. He headed over the pass toward the San Fernando Valley and Kip tailed him at a safe distance.

At a filling station near a motel where there were booths, Kip swung to the curb. He ran back and handed a business card to Marilyn. "Take this number and call Stoska. Tell him what has happened and that we're headed for an abandoned mine in this vicinity—" he drew a quick circle on the map and handed it to her, "and ask him to get hold of the sheriff and get him out there!"

Marilyn slid from the seat and even as she took her first step away, Kip was gone, traveling fast after Villani. He overtook him as he was swinging off into the hills, and followed, his lights on bright again. After a short distance he turned into a side road that led to some houses, switched to his dimmers again, and backed out, following again. He turned again, then followed without lights.

Gus and Vinson must still be at the mine, or Villani was expecting them soon. When the car ahead turned off on the mine road Kip followed but a little farther, then turned off on some hard-packed sand among the cacti and parked. From a hidden panel under the dash he took a .45 caliber Colt automatic and followed up the hill. His car was now hidden and to get out, Villani would have to come this way.

All was still at the old mine. The car stood in the open space near the gallows frame, but the delivery truck was nowhere in sight. There was a light in the shack.

Kip Morgan moved into the darkness of the hoist house and waited. Without doubt, Gus and Vinson would be there. Villani had made his rendezvous at a place where their bodies were not likely to be discovered. He could shoot first and fast, then drop the bodies down the old shaft and drive away. The scheme had every chance of succeeding.

What little Kip knew would not constitute evidence tying Villani to the crimes. Unless more evidence could be discovered or Gus and Vinson talked, Villani would go free or not even be accused.

He heard an approaching motor for several minutes before it arrived. It was the truck.

Vinson and Gus got out. They whispered together for a

minute or two, then walked to the shack and went in. Kip moved away from the hoist house and to the wall of the shack. Voices sounded and he pressed his ear to a crack.

"I don't know," Vinson was saying, sullenly, "so don't blame me. He's a hard guy to hold."

Kip found a crack and peered in. Vinson was seated at the table and Villani was pacing. On the shelf behind Vinson lay a piece of drill steel. Vinson's eyes were on his hands. "Gus was there, too!" he protested. "Don't blame me!"

But where was Gus now?

Villani stopped pacing, and his hand reached for the drill steel. He lifted it clear off the shelf and—

Gravel crunched at the corner of the house, and Morgan turned sharply. A gun flamed not a dozen feet away, and only his sudden movement saved him. Instantly, he fired in return. Gus caught himself in midstride and fired again. That bullet thudded into the wall, and Kip fired a second and third time and Gus went down on the gravel.

Flattening against the wall, Morgan peered through the crack. There was no sign of Villani inside the shack, but the door stood slightly open. Vinson was surely dead for no man could survive a skull crushed as was his.

Villani had sent Gus out while he got rid of Vinson, planning to finish Gus later or when he returned. The shots would have warned him that Gus had found something or somebody. Now Villani would know he had at least one man to kill, possibly two.

The slightest move might bring a shot. Kip moved despite the risk, going toward the front of the building, reasoning that Villani would come around the other side as Gus had done. At the front of the house, he took three quick steps to the truck and crouched behind it.

A slow minute dribbled away, then another. Every sense alert, he waited, but there was no nearby sound. Faintly, somewhere far off, he could hear a car. The sound seemed miles away in the clear night air.

"Morgan!" It was Villani. "Is that you out there? Let's talk business!"

Kip kept very still, waiting. For a few seconds there was

no sound, then Villani spoke persuasively. "Morgan, you're being foolish. A thousand dollars if you just let me drive away! Stay on the case, I don't care, but you take the money and I get out of here."

Morgan offered no reply. He could dimly see the area from which the voice came. Only Gus's body was visible, if Gus was actually dead. He had no way of knowing.

"A thousand dollars is a lot of money. You say the word and I'll toss it to you."

"And have you shoot me while I'm in the open? No, thank you!"

Deliberately, he was prolonging the discussion to better locate Villani. Also the sheriff should be on his way.

"I'll wrap it around a stone and toss it to you. You're in no danger."

"You're talking peanuts," Kip said. "Marilyn Marcy might not pay that much but the insurance company will."

There was a brief silence. Was he moving closer? In the vague gray light it was hard to see. There was no moon, only the stars.

"Five thousand might sound better." Morgan held his mouth close to the car, hoping to give it a muffled sound.

Suddenly they both heard the crunch of feet on gravel, and Kip looked around. He started to yell a warning but she was already within sight. Marilyn Marcy was walking fast and she was unaware of the situation.

"Marilyn!" Kip yelled. *"Get back! Get back quick!"*

"No, you don't!" Triumph was hoarse in his tone. "Stay right where you are or I'll kill you!"

Villani was in control, unless—

Kip left the ground in a running dive for the shelter of the building. A gun roared, a hasty shot that missed, and he fired at a dark shadow looming near the corner of the building and heard his shot ring on metal, an old wheelbarrow turned on its side! And then Villani came up from the ground several feet away, and they both fired.

Both should have scored hits but neither did. Kip felt a sharp tug at his sleeve, and then Villani's descending gun barrel knocked his Colt from his hand. As the gun fell he knotted his fist, whipping it forward and up and Villani took it with a grunt, then threw a short hook to the neck, purposely keeping the blow low to avoid hurting his tender fist. The blow staggered Villani, and Kip followed through with his elbow, over, then back, slamming Villani against the building. His gun roared into the ground, the bullet kicking gravel over Kip's shoes. Another blow to the midsection and Villani dropped his gun, reached to grab it off the ground and met Kip's knee in the face. Villani staggered forward and Kip rabbit-punched him behind the neck and the bigger man fell.

Kip scooped both guns off the ground, the fallen man gasping for breath.

Marilyn ran to him. "Kip? Are you hurt? Are you all right?"

"Did you get word to them?"

"They're coming now. I can hear the cars." She came closer. "They told me to wait but I thought I might help."

He looked at her, exasperated, then shrugged.

Villani started to get up.

"Stay where you are," Morgan advised.

"That offer stands." Villani's words were muffled by battered lips. "I've got twenty thousand here. I'll give you half to let me go."

"What became of Tom Marcy?"

"Suppose you find out? You've nothing on me!"

Two cars were pulling into the yard. "No? You killed Vinson. Your fingerprints will be on that drill steel."

Stoska, Mooney, and a half dozen other men came from the cars, pulling Villani to his feet. During the hurried explanations Marilyn stood beside Kip.

He was beginning to feel it now, sore in every muscle, his swollen fists hurting from the fighting and all the tension of the past few days.

"We checked that burned body again," Stoska said, "and there were discrepancies, although they were few. Now we're going to check several other doubtful cases."

Mooney came over to Marilyn. "We found your brother. It was Morgan's tip that started us looking. I'm afraid . . . well . . ."

"He's dead?"

"No, he's not dead, but he's in bad shape. He must have had a run-in with Gus. He took a bad beating and he's in a hospital. They found him last night when a couple of wino friends of his came to the police. They found him and were taking care of him, but they thought he'd just gotten drunk and fallen. When he didn't regain consciousness they got worried and came to us."

"He's all right? Is he conscious?"

"He's conscious, but I won't lie to you. He's in bad shape." Mooney glanced at Kip. "He spotted you. He had been staying away from his old hideouts, tailing Villani and his boys. He saw you in some grease joint across from the warehouse. He almost spoke to you."

"I wish he had." Kip took Marilyn's arm. "It would have saved a lot of trouble."

When they walked almost to the car he commented, "That's why his eyes looked familiar. They were like your eyes. He was sitting there all the time and must have heard me asking questions of the waitress. He couldn't have known why I was interested. Let's go see him."

"Tomorrow. He will be asleep now and sleep will do him more good than anything else. In the meantime you need to get cleaned up, rest a little and have a drink."

"Well," he agreed, "if you twisted my arm."

"Consider it twisted," she said.

STAY OUT OF MY NIGHTMARE

W HEN I WALKED in, Bill was washing a glass. "There's a guy looking for you. A fellow about twenty-five or so. He said to tell you it was Bradley."

"What did he want? Did he say?"

My eyes swept the bar to see if any of my friends were around. None of them was, but about four or five stools away sat a fellow with slicked-back hair and a pasty face.

"He wanted to see you. It seemed pretty serious."

Bill brought a bourbon and soda, and I thought it over. Sam Bradley had been a corporal in my platoon overseas, but we had not seen each other since our return. We had talked over the phone but had never gotten together. I knew that if he wanted me badly, there was something definitely wrong.

A nice guy, Sam was. A good, reliable man and one of the most decent fellows I'd ever met. "I'll look him up," I said. "He's a right guy, and maybe he's in trouble."

"You never can tell." The man with the sickly face intervened. "Right guys can turn wrong. I wouldn't trust my best friend."

The interruption irritated me. "You know your friends better than I do," I told him.

He looked around, and there was nothing nice about his expression. Looking directly into his eyes made me change my mind about him. This was no casual bar rat with a couple of drinks under his belt and wanting to work off a grouch. This guy was poison.

That look I'd seen before, and the man who had it was usually a killer. It was the look of a man who understands only brutality and cruelty. "That sounded like an invitation," he said.

"Take it any way you like. I didn't ask you into this conversation."

"You're a big guy." He watched me like a snake watching a bird. "And I don't like big guys. They always think they've got an edge. Maybe I should bring you down to my size."

He was getting under my skin. I had no idea of anything like trouble when I walked into the Plaza. Now Sam Bradley was on my mind, and I'd no idea of messing around with such a specimen as this. "Your size?" I said. "Nothing is that small."

When he came off that stool, I knew he meant business. Some mean bluff. This torpedo wasn't bluffing. He was going to kill me. He was only a step away when I saw the shiv. He was holding it low down in his right hand, and nobody in the bar could see it but me. He might be a man drunk or all coked up, but he was still smart.

"Put the shiv away, chum." I had not moved from my stool. "You come at me with that and they'll be putting you on ice before dark."

He never said a word, but just looked at me from those flat, ugly eyes. Bill heard me speak of the knife and came down the bar, always ready to stop anything that meant trouble and to stop it before it started.

"Don't do it, pal," I said. "They've got a new carpet on the deck. I don't want to smear it with you."

He came so fast he nearly got me. Nearly, but not quite. His right foot was forward, and when that knife licked out, I chopped his wrist to deflect the blade. My hand closed on his wrist, jerking him toward me, off balance. Then I shoved back quick and at the same time caught him behind the knee with my toe.

He went down hard, the knife flying from his hand as his head thudded against the brass rail. Picking up the knife, I tossed it to Bill. "Put that in your collection."

Getting off the barstool I walked into the sunlight. Cops might come around, and there was no use straining Mooney's friendship further. Grabbing a cab, I headed for Bradley's place.

It was a flat off Wilshire and a nice place. When I pressed

the bell, nothing happened. Ellen must be shopping. Bradley was probably at work. I tried the bell again for luck; I was turning away when I saw the edge of a business card sticking out from beneath the door. It was none of my business, but I stooped and pulled it out. It read, Edward Pollard, Attorney-at-Law.

Under it in a crabbed, tight-fisted script were the words:

WAS HERE AT EIGHT AS SUGGESTED. IF YOU RETURN BEFORE 10 P.M. MEET ME AT MERRANO'S. DON'T DO ANYTHING OR TALK TO ANYONE UNTIL I SEE YOU.

Pollard was a shyster who handled bail bonds and a few criminal cases. We had never met, however. I knew Merrano's, a sort of would-be night club on a side street, a small club but well appointed and catering to a clientele on the fringe of the underworld.

What impressed me about the card was that neither Sam nor his wife had been home since the previous night. Where, then, was Sam? And what had become of Ellen?

Reaching the walk, I thrust the card into my coat pocket.

At that moment, a car wheeled to the curb, and a man spilled out in a run. Brushing by me without a glance, he went to Bradley's door. He did not ring the bell or knock, but stooped quickly and began looking for something on the step or under the door. Not finding it, he got to his feet and tried the door. Only then did he ring the bell. Even as he did so, he was turning away as if he were sure it would not be answered.

He gave me a quick glance as he saw me watching him, then went on by. "Hello, Pollard," I said.

He stopped as if struck and turned sharply. His quick eyes went over me. "Who are you? I never saw you before."

His voice was quick and nervous, and I was talking to a very worried man.

"I was just wondering why a man would try a door before ringing the bell."

"It's none of your business!" he said testily. "It strikes me you've little to do, standing around and prying into other people's affairs."

He did not walk away, however. He was waiting to see what my angle was. So far, he had not decided what I meant to him or what to do about it.

For that matter, neither had I. Actually, I'd no business bothering him. Sam and Ellen might be visiting. There was no sense in building elaborate plots from nothing, yet the fact that Sam had come looking for me and that I had found the card of a man like Pollard under his door was disturbing.

Two facts had been evident. Pollard had not expected Sam to be home, and he had wanted to pick up his card. That might imply he knew where Sam was or what kind of trouble he was in. Why go to all this trouble to pick up a business card unless something was wrong?

"Look, pal," I said, "suppose you tell me what's going on. Come on, give!"

"None of your business!" he snapped, and was getting into the car before I spoke.

"Sam Bradley is a friend of mine. I hope nothing has happened to him or will happen. If anything has happened, I am going to the police. Then I shall start asking questions myself, and buddy, I'll get answers!"

He rolled down the window and leaned as if to speak, then started off with a jerk.

Standing in the street, I thought it over. I had nothing to go on but suspicions, and those without much foundation. Telling myself I was a fool and that Sam would not appreciate it, I went back to the door. The lock was no trick for me, and in something over a minute, I was inside.

The apartment was empty. Hoping Sam would forgive me, I made a hurried check. The beds were unslept in, the garbage unemptied, yet there were no dirty dishes.

Looking through the top drawer of the bureau, I found something. It was a stack of neatly pressed handkerchiefs, but some had been laid aside and something taken from between them. There was a small spot of oil and the imprint of something that had been lying there for some time. That something might have been a .45 army Colt.

My thoughts were interrupted by the rattling of a key in

the door. Hurriedly closing the door, I reached the bedroom door just in time to see the door close behind a girl.

Her eyes caught me at the same instant. She started and dropped her handbag. She was uncommonly pretty, and that contributed to my surprise, for I had seen Ellen Bradley's picture, and this was not she.

My eyes followed as she moved to pick up her dropped bag, and then I looked up into the muzzle of a .32 automatic. "Who are you?" she demanded. "And what are you doing here?"

It had been a neat trick, as smooth a piece of deceptive action as I'd ever seen. Her bag had been dropped purposely to distract my attention. There was nothing deceiving about that gun. It was steady, and it was ugly. Whoever she was, she was obviously experienced and had a quick, agile brain. "Who are you?" she repeated.

"Let's say that I am an old army friend of Sam Bradley's."

Her eyes hardened. "Oh? So you admit you're one of them?" Before I could reply, she said, "I'll just call the police."

"It might be the best idea. But Sam left word he wanted to see me, and if you're a friend of his, we should compare notes. When he said he was in trouble, I hurried right over."

"I'll bet you did! Now back against the wall. I am going to use the telephone, and if you have any doubts whether I'll use this gun, just start something."

I had no doubts.

She took the receiver from the cradle and dialed a number. I watched the spots she dialed and filed it away for future reference. From where I stood, I heard a voice speak but could distinguish no words.

"Yes, Harry, I'm at Sam's . . . no sign of him, but there's somebody else here." She listened, and I could hear someone talking rapidly. She looked me over coolly. "Big fellow, over six feet, I'd say, and broad-shouldered. Gray suit, gray shirt, blue tie. Good-looking but stupid. And," she added, "he got in without a key."

She listened a moment. "Hold him? Of course. I'll not

miss, either. I always shoot for the stomach; they don't like it there."

"I don't like it anywhere," I said.

She replaced the telephone. "You might as well sit down. They won't be here for ten minutes." She studied me as if I were some kind of insect. "A friend of Sam's, is it? I know how friendly you guys are. What are you trying to do? Cut in?"

"Cut in on what?" I asked.

She smiled, not a nice smile. "Subtle as a truck. As if you didn't know!"

"And who," I asked, "is Harry?"

"He's a friend of mine, and from what he said over the phone, I think he knows you. And he doesn't like you."

"I'm worried. That really troubles me. Now give. What's this all about? Where's Sam? Where's Ellen? What's happened to them?"

"Don't play games, mister."

Her tone was bitter, and it puzzled me. Not to say that I wasn't puzzled about the whole action. Sam Bradley was in plenty of trouble, without a doubt, but what sort of trouble?

Although something in her attitude made me wonder if she was not friendly to Sam and Ellen, she had come in with a key, and she had not called the police. Moreover, she was handling the situation with vastly more assurance than the average woman, or man, for that matter. It was an assurance that spoke of familiarity with guns and criminals. Another thing I knew: The number she called had not been that of the police department.

"Look," I said, "if you're a friend of Sam's, we'd better compare notes. When he left here, he took a gun. If Sam has a gun, you can bet he's desperate, because it isn't like him."

At the mention of the gun, her face tightened. "A gun? How do you know?"

I explained. "Now tell me," I finished by asking, "what is this all about?"

Before she could reply, hurried footsteps sounded on the walk, and she stepped back to the door. She opened it, but in the moment before she did, her eyes showed uncertainty, even fear.

Three men stepped into the room, and when I saw them, every fiber turned cold. There wasn't a cop in the country who wouldn't love to get his hands on George Homan. He was the first man through the door, and when I saw him, I lost the last bit of hope that this girl might be friendly. No girl who knew Homan could be a friend to any decent man. Homan was a brutal killer, utterly cold-blooded, utterly vicious.

The second man was tall, with a wiry body and broad shoulders, his features sharp, his eyebrows a straight black bar above his eyes. Then I saw the last man through the door, and he was my friend from the bar, the one who tried to knife me. Now I knew why he wanted my scalp. It was because he had heard me say I was going to find out what Sam's trouble was.

"This is the man, Harry," the girl was saying. "He claims he's a friend of Sam's."

Harry walked over to me, his bright, rodentlike eyes on mine, the hatred in them sharpened by triumph.

"Nice company you keep." I looked past him at the girl. "Did he ever show you the frogsticker he carries? Now I know where you stand, honey. No friend of Sam's would know this kind of rat!"

"Shut your face!" Harry snarled, his mouth twisting. As he spoke, he swung.

It was the wrong thing to do, for gun or no gun, I was in no mood to get hit. For a second, Harry had stepped between me and the gun, but as he stepped in, throwing his right, I dropped my left palm to his shoulder, stopping the punch; then I threw an uppercut from the hip into his belly that had the works on it.

His mouth fell open, and his face turned green as he gasped for air.

Before he could fall, I closed with him, shoving him hard at Homan. The third man I did not know, but George was no bargain, and I wanted him out of the play. I went for my gun fast. Hatchet face yanked his, too, but neither of us fired. We stood there, staring at each other. It was a Mexican standoff. If either fired at that range, both would die.

The girl's gun had dropped to her side. She seemed petrified, staring at me as if a light had flashed in her eyes.

Homan had backed away from Harry, who was groaning on the floor. Hate was in Homan's eyes. "Kill him, Pete! Kill him!"

"Sure"—I was cool now—"if he kills me, we ride the same slide to hell. Shoot and I'll take you all with me. I'm a big guy, and if you don't place them right, it's going to take a lot of lead, and until I fold, I'm going to be shooting."

Harry was on the floor, living up to expectations. He was being disgustingly sick. Homan stepped distastefully away from him. "I'm surprised, George." I was keeping an eye on Pete. "Playing games with a hop head. You know they're unreliable, and you're a big boy now."

"Who is this guy, George?" Pete's eyes were on me. "He's not fuzz."

"Harry had a run-in with him this morning. I saw it, but the guy didn't see me. Harry popped off, and this lug didn't like it. He's Kip Morgan."

That brought a sudden intake of breath from the girl, but my eyes were on Pete, as I was realizing Pete was top man here. Pete was my life insurance.

"That's right. If the name means anything to you, you'll know I am just the kind of damned fool who will shoot if you push me. Take that buzzard off the floor and back out of here. Back out fast."

Pete was a careful man, and Pete was not ready to die. Not yet.

"What if I say nothing doing? What if I tell you to beat it?"

"Then don't waste time—just start shooting. I'll get George and Harry, Pete, but I'll get you first."

"All right." I had guessed Pete would be smart. I'd *gambled* on it. "We'll go. But there's one thing I want to know. What's your angle?"

"Sam Bradley was in my outfit overseas. He was a good guy and a good friend. Anything else?"

"All right. You've proved you're a great big lovable guy. Now get smart and bow out. There's no percentage for you."

"I didn't come into this for laughs," I said. "When Sam

Bradley and his wife are back home and in the clear, then I'll bow out. Until then, I'm in."

"What if I told you he was dead?" Pete said. "And his wife, too?"

That brought another little sound from the girl. I was beginning to wonder about her and just where she belonged. "I wouldn't believe you unless I saw the bodies, and then I'd never rest until you three were dead or in the gas chamber."

"George?" Pete said. "Pick up Harry, put his arm over your shoulder, and walk him to the car. I'll follow. This is no place to settle this." He smiled at me. "There's more of us, and Morgan here has to move around. He can run, and he can hide, but we'll find him."

Homan picked up Harry and started for the door. Harry looked back at me, and his look gave me a chill. I would rather he'd said something.

Pete backed toward the door, keeping his gun on me. "You, too," I told the girl.

She started to protest, but I cut her short. "Get going! Do you think I want you around to shoot me in the back?

"And Pete? Play it smart. If Sam and his wife aren't back in their apartment by midnight, I'm coming for you. I will give you until then."

They went out, and the girl didn't look back. I felt sorry for her, but that might have been because she was pretty. She did not look like a crook, but then, who does?

When they had gone I started after them. I was no closer to knowing what it was all about. Whatever it was, Bradley and Ellen, if not already dead, were in danger. If Pete whoever-he-was was playing with men like George Homan and Harry, he was playing for keeps, and for money, big money.

Before I could move, I had to know what was going on, and I had to find out who the girl was and her connection. Actually, I'd little reason to care. She'd dealt herself into this, one way or the other.

Come to think of it, there was a clue. It was her attitude toward Sam's army friends. What had she meant by her remarks?

Turning around, I began to give that apartment another going-over. In the writing desk, I got my first lead.

It was a circular, or rather, a stack of them. Beside them was a bunch of envelopes and a list of names, several of which I recognized as veterans.

Opening the circular, I glanced over it.

BOOM DAYS BOOM AGAIN

Faro . . . CHUCKALUCK . . . Poker
CRAPS

Come one! Come all!

Proceeds to Wounded Veterans

Dropping into a chair, I read it through; an idea began to germinate.

Where there is gambling, there are sure-thing operators. They flock to easy money like bees to sugar, and unless I was mistaken in my man, Pete was a cinch player. Moreover, I had picked up some talk lately of various gamblers moving in on the vets and taking them for considerable loot. No doubt they had spotted their own players in the crowds and might even have been running the games themselves. Sam Bradley was on several veterans' committees.

Now I needed evidence. Leaving the apartment by the service entrance, I went down the back stairs. Once I reached my car, I checked over the list of names I had brought with me. One, Eugene Shidler, lived not far away. Starting my car, I swung around the corner and headed along the street.

————

SHIDLER CAME TO the door in his shirtsleeves with a newspaper in his hand. He was a short, stocky man, partly bald. Showing him the circular, I asked what he knew about it.

"Only what we all know. We need to raise money to give some of the boys a hand, and Earl Ramsey suggested a real, old-time gambling setup. It would last a week, sponsored by us. He said he knew just the man to handle it, a man who had a lot of gambling equipment he had taken in on a loan. He was pretty sure this man could also provide the dealers, equipment, and refreshments for a small cut of the proceeds.

"Naturally, it looked good to us. We had to do nothing at all when the games started but to come and bring our friends. As we were busy men, that was a big item. Time was the one thing none of us could spare."

"Who was it, the gambler?"

"Pete Merrano."

Pete! . . . *Pete Merrano!* Owner of the Merrano Club! A bookie and small-time racketeer wanting to reach for the big time! Already he had a hand in the numbers and was reported to be financing the importation of cocaine, although keeping free of it himself.

Suppose he had been skimming the games and Sam Bradley discovered it? No sooner did the idea come to mind than I was sure it was the answer.

Shidler looked at me thoughtfully. "What's the matter? Is something wrong?"

There seemed to be something underlying his question, so I said, "Yes, I believe so, but first tell me how it all came out? Did the vets make money?"

"We cleared about a thousand dollars, although some of the boys figured it should have been more. In fact, there was a lot of talk about something crooked, but shucks, you know Sam as well as I do! There isn't a crooked bone in his body!"

"You're right," I said, and then I laid it out for him, all I knew and what I suspected. "Sam and his wife have vanished completely. Merrano, if that was the Pete I'd held at gunpoint, hinted that Sam was dead, but I don't believe that. Anyway, something has Merrano worried, and what it is I have no idea."

Shidler got to his feet. Angrily, he jerked the cigar from his mouth, staring at it with distaste. Glancing toward an inner door, he dropped to the sofa beside me. "If my wife hears of this, I'll never hear the last of it, but I got rooked in that game, but plenty! They took me for five hundred bucks. I owe that to Merrano."

"Then it makes sense. Merrano probably took the lot of you for plenty, and he's counting on you being good sports and keeping your mouths shut. I'd bet he took every one of you for at least as much as you lost."

He nodded. "I lost about a hundred, then drifted into a little side game that Pete was running. I dropped about forty more, then gambled on credit. Merrano holds my IOU for the five hundred."

"Get a few of the boys on the phone and do some checking. Tell them what the story is. Maybe we can get that money back. In the meantime, I am going to find out what became of Sam Bradley."

It was after nine when I returned to my car. The best thing was to talk to Mooney in homicide. He knew me and could start the wheels turning even though it lay outside his department. Although, I reflected, by this time it might not.

First, I would do some checking. There was Earl Ramsey, who had suggested Merrano to run the games and could be in it up to his neck. If Ramsey could be persuaded to tell what he knew, we might be on the track. Before anything else, I must think of Sam and Ellen.

It seemed strange to be riding down a brightly lit street, with all about me people driving to or from home, the theater, dinner, and to realize that somewhere among these thousands of buildings a man and his wife might be facing death. Yet without evidence I could do nothing, and all I had was a hunch that they were still alive.

Checking the list, I found Ramsey's name. The address was some distance away, but worth a visit. If Ramsey were not tied in with the crooks, he might talk.

It was a large, old-fashioned frame dwelling on a corner near a laundry. Parking the car, I got out and rang the bell. Nothing. I went down the steps and looked along the side of the house. There was a light in one of the rear rooms; I went back and pressed the bell again. Three times I rang with no response; then I saw the door was not quite closed. It was open by no more than a crack.

Had it been closed when I arrived? My impression was that it had. That meant someone had opened the door while I stood there! An eerie feeling crept over me, and suddenly I was wishing the street were not so dark. I rang again.

For the second time that day, I pushed open a door I had no right to touch. It swung open, and I peered into a dark living room. "Hello? Mr. Ramsey?"

Silence, then a subdued whispering, not voices but a surreptitious movement.

A clock ticked solemnly, and somewhere I could hear water running in a basin. Uncomfortably, I looked around me. The street was dark and empty except for my own car and another that was parked in darkness farther down. Momentarily distracted from the house, I stared at that car. I had not noticed it when I first drove up.

Suddenly, a hand from the darkness grasped my arm. I started to pull away, but the grip tightened. A voice from the shadows, a voice so old you could almost hear the wrinkles in it said, "Come in, won't you? Did you wish to see Earl?"

It was an old woman's voice, but there was something else in it that set my nerves on edge, and I am not easily bothered.

"Yes, I want to see him. Is he in?"

"He's in the kitchen. He came home to eat, and I put out a lunch for him. Maybe you would like something? A cup of coffee?"

The house was too warm, the air close and stuffy. She walked ahead of me toward a dim rectangle of doorway.

"Just follow me. I never use the lights, but Earl likes them."

She led me along a hall and pushed a door open. As the door opened, I saw Earl Ramsey.

He was seated at a kitchen table, his chin propped on his hand, the other hand against the side of his face. There was a cup before him and an untasted sandwich on his plate. He was staring at me as I came through the door.

"Are you Mr. Ramsey?"

He neither spoke nor blinked, and I stepped past the old woman and stopped abruptly. I was staring into the eyes of a dead man.

Turning, overcome with horror, I looked at the old woman who was puttering among some dirty dishes. "Don't mind him," she said. "Earl was never one for talking. Only when he takes the notion."

My skin crawled. She turned her head and stared at me with expressionless eyes. Gray hair straggled about a face that looked old enough to have worn out two bodies, and her clothing was drab, misshapen, and soiled. She fumbled at her pocket, staring at me.

It gave me the creeps. The hot, stuffy room and this aged and obviously imbecilic woman and her dead son.

Stepping past the table, I saw the knife. It had been driven into the left side of his back, driven up from below as he sat at the table, and driven to the hilt. I touched the hand of Earl Ramsey. It was cold.

The old woman was puttering among the dishes, unaware and unconcerned.

"Have you a telephone?"

She neither stopped nor seemed to hear me, so I stepped past her to the hallway and found a switch. The telephone was on a stand in the corner. I needed but a minute to get Mooney.

"Morgan here. Can you come right over? Dead? Sure he's dead! Yes, I'll wait."

Walking back to the kitchen, I looked around, but there was nothing that might be a clue. Nothing I could see, but then I wasn't a cop. Only, I was willing to bet the killer had come in the door behind Ramsey, dropped a hand on his shoulder, then slammed the knife home. The knife was a dead ringer for the one I'd taken from Harry only that morning.

Several steps led down from that open door behind Ramsey to a small landing. It was dark down there, and a door that would probably let a man out into the narrow space between the house and the laundry next door. I went down the steep steps and grasped the knob to see for myself.

There was a whisper of movement in the darkness, and I started to turn. Something smashed against my skull, and my knees folded under me. As I fell, my arm swept out and grabbed a man around the knees. There was an oath and then a second blow that drove the last vestige of consciousness

from me. I seemed to be sliding down a steep slide into un-
believable blackness.

Yet even as consciousness faded, I heard a tearing of cloth
and the sound of a police siren, far away.

When next I became aware of anything, I was lying on a
damp, hard floor in absolute darkness. Fear washed over me
in a cold wave. With a lunge, I came to a sitting position. My
head swam with pain at the sudden movement, and I put both
hands to it, finding a laceration across my scalp from one of
the blows. My hair was matted with blood. Struggling to my
knees, I was still shaky, and my thoughts refused to become
coherent.

The events of the night were a jumble, the hot, close air of
the kitchen, the hallway, the dead man, the weird old woman,
my call to the police, and the blows on the head.

Somehow I had stumbled into something uglier than expected. A man had been murdered. Perhaps Bradley, too, was
dead.

Feeling for my shoulder holster, I discovered my gun was
missing. That was to be expected. The floor on which I knelt
was concrete, and there was no light. The room had a dank,
musty smell, and I believed for a moment I must be in the
basement of the murder house. Then I placed another smell,
one that I knew well. It was the smell of the sea.

So I had been taken from the house and dumped here?
Why? Had they believed me dead?

Getting up, I waited an instant, then took four careful steps
before encountering a wall. Feeling along the wall, I found
three stone steps and at the top a door. My hands quested
for the knob or latch. There was none. Not even a hinge or a
finger hold anywhere. The door was fitted with admirable
precision.

Working cautiously, for I knew not what lay ahead, I
worked my way around the room, keeping my hands on the
wall. The room was about ten feet wide by twenty feet long
and appeared to be empty, although I had not been down the
center of it. At the far end, there was an opening in the wall
not much above floor level. It was perhaps three feet wide
and covered with a grating of iron bars. They were not thick

bars, but definitely beyond the power of my unaided muscles.

Dropping to my knees, I peered out and could make out a faint line of grayness some distance away and below the level of the floor. My fingers found damp sand around the grate.

Fumbling for a match, I found everything gone from my pockets. Feeling for my inside coat pocket, I found it torn. The labels had been torn from my clothes! That could mean but one thing. I was marked for murder.

The pieces began to fall into place, and as each one fit, I felt a mounting horror. The grate near the floor, the smell of the sea, that damp sand *inside* the window, the faint line of gray! At high tide, this place was under water!

Rushing across the room, I hurled myself at the door, grasping and tearing at the edges, but nowhere could I get a handhold. The door was of heavy plank, a door built to stay where it was placed. In all probability, a watertight door.

I shouted and pounded, but there was no sound. Pausing, gasping for breath, sweat trickling down my face and body, I listened. All was a vast and empty silence. No movement, no sound of traffic. I was alone, then. Alone in a deserted place with no chance of outside help. Then, very slightly at first, I heard a sound. It was a faint rustling, ever so soft, ever so distant. It was the sea. The tide was coming in.

They had known I was alive. They had left me to be drowned by the inflowing water, probably believing I would still be unconscious. Once drowned, they would simply drop my body in the sea, and as it would have all the signs of drowning, my death would be passed off as a suicide or an accident.

How many times, I wondered, had this place already been used for just that purpose? How many had died there, with no chance to escape?

The killers had evidently returned to Earl Ramsey's house and found me there, and when I inadvertently walked into their hands, they simply slugged me and dumped me there. That car parked outside in the dark must have been the car they came in and in which I had been carried away.

Yet I had called Mooney, and Mooney would know something had gone wrong when I was not present, as I had promised I would be.

For the first time in my life, I found myself in a spot that seemed to offer no solution. I had no idea how high the tide would rise in that room. Nor did I know how high were the tides along this coast. It had been years since I looked at a tide table. That the tide would be high enough to drown me, they had no doubts.

Seated on the steps, I tried to puzzle a way out, searching for some means to get the door open or to get past that grate. Yet even as I sat, the room seemed to grow lighter, but for several minutes, the reason did not occur to me. Then I realized the tide was rising and the added light was reflected from the water.

It was only a faint, gray light, but on my knees by the grate I could peer out. The opening was under a wharf or dock, and beyond a short stretch of sandy beach was the lapping water of the incoming tide.

Crossing the room through the middle, I glimpsed something I had not seen before. Putting up a tentative hand, I discovered it was a chain dangling from a beam overhead. It was a double chain. Pulling on it, I heard it rattle in a block above me.

A chain hoist?

No doubt the room had once been used for overhauling boat engines or something of the kind. Running my hand down the chain, I found it ended in a hook. Suddenly there was hope. The chance was a wild one, an absurd one, really. Yet a chance was a chance.

Hauling the chain over to the grate, I hooked in the crossbars and hauled the chain tight. The chance of pulling that grate loose was pitifully small, but I was in no position to pass up any chance at all. My weight was a muscular two hundred pounds, and I gave it all I had. The grate held. Again and again, I tried, hoping the action of the sea water might have weakened the grate or the concrete in which it was set.

No luck. Panting, my shirt soaked with perspiration, I stopped and mopped my face. The water was almost to the edge of the window. It meant little that the water might not rise high enough to drown me. If they returned and found me, I would be killed in any event. I tried again, then gave up the attempt as useless.

Kneeling, I studied the concrete in which the grate was set. There seemed little enough to hold it in place, but it was too much for my strength. With a sledge hammer now—But I had no sledge hammer or anything like it. Moreover, as the grate was set closer to the inside edge, the power must be applied from outside to be most effective. It was useless to consider it.

Or was it? Suddenly, I saw something long and black moving upon the water outside the window. It was some distance away, but each movement of the sea brought it closer. At first, I thought it a man's body. Then I recognized it as timber, much the size of a railroad tie, all of six feet long and perhaps six by six.

The water lapped at the sill below the grate, then retreated. Each time the ripples curled in, the timber came closer.

In an instant, I was on my feet, and recovering the chain from its block, I carried it back to the opening and thrust it through the bars. I made a loop of it; then I waited.

The beam came closer. I tried to snag it with the loop but failed. Again and again, I tried. Sweat poured down my face and body. I wiped it from my brow with the back of my hand. I tried to grasp the timber with my hands by reaching through the crossbars, but failed. Then it actually bumped against the sill, and I grabbed it with both hands. That time, when the water retreated, I held the timber. After a few minutes of struggle, I managed to get a half hitch around the timber. If this did not work, I'd be finished.

Roughly estimating the time, I guessed I might have as much as thirty minutes, perhaps less.

If by that time I had not been successful, the water would have risen so high the timber would be above the opening, and I would be knee-deep in water with my last chance gone.

The waves returned, and that time water spilled over to the floor. Grasping the chain in my hands, I waited for the next wave. When it came, with the beam floating on it, I heaved with all my strength, and the butt of the timber crashed against the iron bars. Relaxing when the wave rolled in next, I gave a second heave. The waves retreated less, and I got in three smashing blows with my crude battering ram before the water rolled back. By now, there was always some water trickling over the sill, and my feet were covered with it.

Water was coming in, and the timber was floating. Again and again, I smashed it against the bars. My muscles ached, and my breath came in gasps. Once, something seemed to give, but there was too little light to see. Feeling with my fingers, my pulse gave a leap. One of the bars had broken free!

Letting go of the chain but anchoring it with a foot, I seized the bars in my hands and gave a tremendous heave. Nothing happened. A second heave and a second bar broke through the crumbling concrete. Now I could bend the bars upward, and using the timber again, I worked on the remaining two bars. When they were bent inward, I grasped them with my hands and pulled them higher. Water was pouring through, but there was room enough for my body. Grasping the sill, I pulled myself through the hole, then lifted my hands to the opening's top and got my feet out. Then I stood up, waist-deep in the dark water. Some distance off was the dim outline of a ladder. I splashed toward it and crawled up to the surface of the dock. Then I sprawled out, exhausted.

It was there she found me.

How long I had been lying there, I do not know, but probably not more than a few minutes. The sound of a car's motor snapped me to awareness. A car meant trouble. Then heels were clicking on the dock, and I came to my feet, staggering. Drunk with fatigue, I stood swaying, ready for battle.

It was the girl, the girl I had met at Sam's. When she saw me, she stopped running. "Oh, you're free! You're safe!"

"You bet I'm free, but it isn't your fault or that of your friends."

"They are not my friends! It wasn't until a few minutes ago somebody made a comment that let me know where you were. I knew they had left you somewhere, but I had no idea where."

"What about Bradley? And his wife?"

"We haven't found them. Nobody seems to know where they are."

"I'll bet your friend Merrano knows!"

She was puzzled. "He might," she admitted. "He acts funny about her. He's looking for Sam, I know."

I had no reason to trust her and did not; however, she did have a car, and I needed transportation. "Let's get back to town. I've got to get some clothes."

She handed me a gun. "It's yours. I stole it back from them."

That didn't make sense, not any way I could look at it. One minute she was with them, sticking me up at gunpoint, and the next she was giving me a gun. I checked the clip. It was loaded, all right.

"How did I rate this trip of yours?" I asked. "Did you come to see if I was drowned?"

"Oh, be still! We're on the same side!" She glanced at me as we got into the car. "My name is Pat Mulrennan."

"That's just ducky," I said. "Now that we're properly introduced we might even start holding hands. No thanks, honey. I'm not turning my back on you."

She sounded honest, and she might be, but nothing about the setup looked good to me except her. But I couldn't forget how chummy she had been with Pete Merrano and Harry, to say nothing of that big-time torpedo, George Homan.

"To be honest, I was not sure you were there, but from a comment, I thought you might be, and I know that Pete has been using that place for something. How I could get you free, I had no idea, but I came, anyway. Then I saw something or somebody lying on the dock."

AT MY APARTMENT, I tried to call Sam, never taking my eyes off Pat. I'll say this for her. I did not trust her, but she was easy to watch. "If you're so friendly, why not tell me where Sam is?"

"I don't know." She sounded sincere. "Please! Forget about yesterday morning! I had no idea you were a friend of

Sam's. For all I knew, you were somebody trying to cut in on Pete's deal."

"And you were acting for Pete?"

"No, I was with him, but I had a job of my own to do. Pete means nothing to me."

She finished saying it as Pete appeared in the door of my bedroom. He had his gun in his hand, and this time, mine was still in its holster. Where he came from, I couldn't guess, unless from the fire escape outside my window. A moment before, I had been in there picking up a clean shirt and had not seen him.

"Is that so?" Pete was watching me but talking to her. "So I mean nothing to you? All right, chick, have it your way. You mean nothing to me, then. When this lad goes out, you go with him."

Not for a second did his eyes leave mine, and believe me, I was doing some fast thinking. "This is no place for a bump-off, Pete." I spoke casually. "There's too many people around. You'd have them all over the place before the sound of the shot died out."

"What if I use a shiv? What if I borrow a note from Harry?" he said, chuckling. "They might even think Harry did it. I hear they're fingering him for the Ramsey killing."

"So that's it? You let your boys take the rap for your killings?"

"Why not? Why have killers unless they are some use to me? Everybody knows what George Homan and Harry are like. Naturally, they take the rap."

"You're probably right," I agreed, "and I must say you've played it the smart way except for one thing. How did Sam get away with the money?"

That was a guess, simply a guess, but it figured to be something like that.

"How do you know he's got the money?" Merrano asked. His gaze was intent. "Maybe you know where the money is? Do you?"

My guess had been right. Somehow Sam had laid hands on the money and disappeared. Knowing Sam, I knew he was saving it for the vets. But it was no wonder Pete Merrano wanted him. "If I turn you and the babe loose, will you tell me where he is?"

"No, but I think you want the money, and I want to see Sam and Ellen safe."

"Suppose, then"—he was watching me—"we trade. I turn Ellen loose if you get me the money. I've been hanging onto her but haven't been able to let Bradley know I have her."

Another point cleared up, but doubt seemed to come into his mind.

"Enough talk," he said irritably. "How do I know you know anything? Turn around."

I turned.

It was still early, and in a matter of minutes, the milkman would be coming. "Look," I said, "Mooney is to meet me here in a few minutes. I just called him."

Gambling that he had seen me on the phone, I was hoping the bluff might work. He could have seen me, and I knew from experience that somebody in the bedroom could not hear what was said unless the speaker purposely talked loud.

"You wouldn't tell me if you knew he was coming," Pete said, but there was doubt in his tone.

"Am I a damned fool? Do you think I want you guys swapping lead with me in the middle? You better take it on the lam while you can, but you turn Ellen loose and I'll see you get your money."

"Other way around, buddy, but get this. She's being watched by George Homan. He will kill her if he's approached. If the police find her, he'll kill her and skip. We've got a getaway all set."

"What about your club?"

He shrugged. "I still owe money on it, and there's fifteen to twenty thousand in that bag Sam's got."

He was moving, toward my bedroom door, I believed.

"You get the dough and call me at home. I'll tell you where to bring it. You've got until noon."

We stood facing the wall, and I counted a slow one hundred, then lowered my hands a little. Nothing happened, so I turned around. Pete was gone.

Undoubtedly, he had been searching the apartment and retreated to the fire escape when he heard me at the door. A glance at my desk drawers and closet showed he had given the apartment a shaking down.

Pete Merrano was worried. His plan for a big cleanup had gone sour when somehow Bradley had realized what was happening and had gotten away with the money. He had put the snatch on Ellen, which had done him no good at all, because he couldn't threaten Sam unless he could find him. Then I barged into the picture and messed everything up by nosing around in all the wrong places. Evidently, Ramsey had gotten cold feet, so they killed him when he wanted out. At least that was how I had it figured.

The next question was what to do now? I'd made a promise I could not back up because I had no idea where Sam was, and I believed Pete was telling the truth when he said George was watching Ellen. That left the situation a nasty one, yet there was, I believed, a way.

"Pat, I'm going to trust you. Get hold of Mooney and tell him what's happened. Tell him I am following my inclinations, and he will know what to do." Knowing Mooney, I could bet on that.

"All right," she said reluctantly, "but be careful. Those boys aren't playing for fun."

She was telling *me*?

We parted, but when I glanced back she was watching me go. For a minute, I thought she looked worried, but that made no sense. My own car was still near Ramsey's, if it hadn't been towed away or stolen, so I hailed a cab.

———

PETE MERRANO HAD been doing all right for himself, or, at least, that was the act. He lived in a picturesque house overlooking Sunset Strip. Leaving the cab a few doors away, I walked up the hill. Skirting the place, I glimpsed a Filipino houseboy coming down the steps from the back door. Turning on the sprinklers to water the lawn, he went around the house. As soon as his back was turned, I went into the house.

There was a pot of coffee on the range, so I took up a cup,

filled it, and drank a couple of swallows, then started up the hall with the coffee in my left hand.

Harry was snoring on a divan in the living room, and Pete was sprawled across the bed with only his shoes and tie off.

The houseboy was working around the yard, so I cut a string from the venetian blinds and very cautiously slipped a loop over Harry's extended ankles. Drawing it as tight as I dared, I tied it.

His gun in its shoulder holster lay on the floor, and with a toe I slid it back under the sofa. Picking up his handkerchief, I placed it within easy reach. Very gently, I took his wrist by the sleeve, lifted it, and placed it across his stomach. I'd just lifted the second to bring it into tying position when he opened his eyes.

By his breath, the glass, and bottle nearby, it was obvious he'd had more than a few drinks before passing out on the divan. His awakening could not have been pleasant. Not only was he awakening with a hangover, but with a man bending over him, he had every reason to believe he was dead or dying.

For one startled instant, he stared. Then his thoughts came into focus, and his mouth opened to yell. The instant he opened his mouth, I shoved the handkerchief into it. He choked, gagged, and grabbed at my wrist, but I jerked a hand free and gave him four stiff fingers in the windpipe.

Grabbing him by his pants at the hips, I jerked him up and flopped him over on his face. He struggled, but he was at least fifty pounds lighter than I and in no condition to put up much of a fight. With my knee in his back, I got a slip knot over one wrist, then the other. In less than a minute, he was bound and gagged.

Pete's voice sounded from the bedroom. Goose flesh ran up my spine. "You sick again, Harry? For the luvva Mike, get into the bathroom! That carpet's worth a fortune!"

Taking my knee from Harry's back, I started for the bedroom, keeping out of line with the door. Merrano was muttering angrily, and I heard his feet on the floor, then his slippers. At the moment, I was thinking of Sam and Ellen and how he had planned to murder me by drowning. There was no mercy in me.

Merrano came through the door scratching his stomach and blinking sleep from his eyes, and I never gave him a chance. Grabbing his shirt-sleeve, I jerked him toward me and whipped one into his belly. The blow was wicked and unexpected, and his mouth fell open, gasping for air, his eyes wide with panic. As he doubled up, I slapped one hand on the back of his head, pushing his face down to meet my upcoming knee.

That straightened him up, blood all over his face and his fingers clawing for his gun. Ignoring the reaching hand, I stepped closer and threw two punches to his chin. His knees sagged, and he hit the floor. Reaching over, I slid the gun from his pocket, then jerked him to his feet.

He was not out, but he had neither the wind nor the opportunity to yell. Grabbing him by the shirt collar, I stood him on his toes. "All right, buddy, you like to play rough. You started bouncing me around, and I don't like it! Now where's Ellen?"

He gasped; the blood running from his broken nose splashed on my wrist. He'd had no chance to assemble his thoughts. Pete Merrano was like all of his kind who live by fear and terror. When that failed, they're backed into a corner. He had been sure he would win. He had still been sure when things started going against him because he simply believed he was too smart. He had forgotten the old adage that cops can make many mistakes, a crook need only make one.

Pete Merrano had made several, and he was realizing that all people can't be scared.

"Where is she?" I insisted.

"Try and find out!" he said past swollen lips.

It was no time for games, so I slugged him in the belly again. "Look, boy," I said, "if that woman's been harmed, the gas chamber will be a picnic compared to what I do to you. Where is she?"

His eyes were insane with fury. "You'd like to know, wouldn't you?" he sneered. "You think you can make *me* talk? Why, you—!"

He jerked away from me, and I let go. He took a round-house swing at me, and I stepped inside of it and hit him with both hands. The punches he'd taken before were kitten blows compared to those. The first smashed his lips into his teeth, which broke under the impact; the second lifted him out of his slippers. He hit the floor as though he'd been dropped off a roof. Jerking him to his feet, I backed him against the wall and began slapping him. I slapped him over and back, keeping my head inside his futile swings, and my slaps were heavy. His head must have been buzzing like a sawmill.

When I let up, there was desperation in what I could see of his eyes. "How does it feel to be on the wrong end of a slug-ging? You boys dish it out, but you can't take it.

"Now where is she? I don't like crooks. I don't like double-crossers. I don't like crooks who pick on women. I'm in good shape, Pete, and I can keep this up all day and all night. Three or four hours of it can get mighty tiresome."

He glared at me, hating and scared. Then something else came into his eyes, and I knew he'd had an idea. "She's at the club," he said, "but you'll never get her. You just get that money, and we'll turn her loose."

Shoving him back on the bed, I let go of him. "Get your coat," I said. "We'll go over there together."

He did not like that, not a little bit, but my gun was in my hand, and he started for the door, glancing at Harry, still lying tied on the divan, as we passed.

We stopped the car a few doors from the club. There was nobody in sight. It was too early for the bar to be open, so I kept the gun in my pocket while Merrano fumbled with his keys.

It was all I could do to keep my eyes open. My muscles felt heavy, and I was dead tired. The long fight to escape from the cellar had taken it out of me, and all I'd needed to have weari-ness catch up with me was that ride in the car.

If Ellen was actually there, Homan would be watching over her, and that, I believed, was what Merrano was depend-ing on. He was planning on my walking into Homan, and both of us knew what that would mean. George would ask no questions. He was trigger-happy and kill-crazy. Nor would Merrano's presence stop him. If he figured he was due for arrest, he would willingly kill Merrano to get at me.

We started across the polished floor. It was shadowed and cool, the tables stacked with chairs, the piano ghostly in the vague light. We headed toward a door that led back-stage from the orchestra's dais. Pete went through the door ahead of me, and a girl screamed. I sprang aside, but not quite enough, for I caught a stunning blow on the skull from a blackjack. George Homan had been waiting right behind the door.

My .45 blasted a hole in the ceiling as I went down, but I was only stunned and shaken by the blow, not knocked out. Scrambling to my feet, I was just in time to see Homan grabbing for a sawed-off shotgun.

That was one time I shot before I thought. That shotgun and his eyes were like a trigger to my tired brain, and I got off three fast shots. Another shot rang out just as my first one sounded. I saw Homan jerk from the impact of the first bullet, smashing his right hand and wrist and going through to the body. The next two bullets caught him as he was fall-ing. The other shot had come from a side door or some-where.

Leaping over Homan's body, I started after Merrano. Ellen Bradley was tied to a chair in the office, and Merrano was grabbing for a desk drawer behind her. Pete got his gun but chose not to fight and dove through a door in the corner be-hind some filing cabinets. His feet clattered on a stair, and I jumped past the filing cabinets and after him.

A dozen steps led down to a street door, and at the bottom, Merrano turned and snapped a hurried shot that missed by two feet; then he jerked the door open as my gun was coming into line. Outside, there was a shout, then a hammering of gunfire from the street.

Standing there gripping my gun, I waited, hesitant to leave Ellen tied and wondering what happened outside. Then the door was blocked by a shadow, and Mooney appeared. "Put it away, Kip," he said. "Merrano ran into the boys. He's bought it."

"How did you get here?" I asked.

Two more men came through the door, and with them was Pat Mulrennan. Our eyes met for an instant, and I thought I saw relief there, but could not be sure. "Where does she fit in?" I asked.

"This is Sergeant Patricia Mulrennan," Mooney said. "She's been working undercover for us. She knew Ellen Bradley, so it was a big help to us."

As he spoke, I began to untie Ellen, but scarcely had I begun when Sam Bradley came in and took the job from my hands. In a moment, they were in each other's arms, laughing or crying, I couldn't tell which.

"You were already on this case? You knew about Merrano?"

"We knew what was going on but had no evidence. It was your tip on the Ramsey killing that gave us a break. Ramsey was a small-time crook, not quite right in the head, but nobody in the service groups knew him as anything but a quiet ex-soldier, and that was usually the case. He had done time, however, and he worked with Pete on small jobs, but when Merrano put the snatch on Ellen Bradley, Ramsey got cold feet. He was going to talk to us, so they killed him.

"That gave us a direct lead because we knew who he had been working with. They killed him, but somehow Merrano found out Ramsey had written a letter to the D.A. telling him all he knew, so they came back to search the house for it. Then they ran into you."

"In the meanwhile, Sam Bradley found out his wife wasn't with her sister, so he came to us and filled us in. After you left Sergeant Mulrennan, she gave us the rest of the story."

Suddenly, I remembered Harry and told Mooney. He ducked out to send men after him, and Ellen came over and said, "Thanks, Kip. Sam told me all you have done."

Mooney had returned, and Pat was standing by the door when Edward Pollard walked in. He had taken three running steps before he saw Mooney and the other officers. The police cars had been at the side or in back, and he had missed them.

He stopped abruptly. From where I stood, he could not see me, and his eyes were on Mooney.

"It would seem I am a bit late, lieutenant, or is Mr. Merrano in? He asked me to represent him in a criminal case."

"Merrano?" Mooney shook his head. "No, he's out of trouble."

"Oh, I'm sorry. Well, nothing for me, then. I'll be going. Good morning."

As he turned, I was moving. That briefcase in the lawyer's hands had begun to seem awfully heavy. He was walking rapidly for the front door when I ducked out the side, and I reached his car just as he did.

Mooney and others had followed, stopping on the walk while I confronted Pollard.

"Take your hand off the door!" he demanded. "I've no time to waste!"

"No, you haven't, Ed, but in a few weeks you will have plenty of time. You'll be doing time.

"I've got the card you left at Bradley's, Ed. You were asking him to come down and walk right into a trap. That card should help to convict you, but I've a hunch we'll find more in the briefcase."

His eyes were desperate. "Get out of my way!"

Mooney had come up behind him. "Maybe we should have a look at the briefcase, Mr. Pollard."

All the spirit went out of him. His face looked gray and old as he turned on Mooney. "Let me go, lieutenant. Let me go. I'll pay. I'll pay plenty."

Mooney opened the briefcase and began leafing through the papers. "You should have thought of this before you planned to gyp a lot of vets out of their money." He glanced up at me. "Morgan, unless I'm mistaken, this is the man who engineered the whole affair. From the looks of this, he was coming to settle up with Merrano."

"Lieutenant, you work it out any way you like. I am going to buy Pat a drink as soon as she's off duty, and then I'm going home and sleep for a week."

"She's off duty as of now," Mooney said, but as we started to walk away, he called after us. "Sergeant? You'd better watch that guy! He's a good man in the clinches!"

Pat laughed, and we kept going. In the clinches, I had an idea Pat could take care of herself.

THE HILLS OF HOMICIDE

T HE STATION WAGON jolted over a rough place in the blacktop, and I opened my eyes and sat up. Nothing had changed. When you are in the desert, you are in the desert, and it looks it. We had been driving through the same sort of country when I fell asleep, the big mesa that shouldered against the skyline ahead being the only change.

"Ranagat's right up ahead, about three, four miles." Shanks, who was driving me, was a thin-faced little man who sat sideways in the seat and steered with his left hand on the wheel. "You won't see the town until we get close."

"Near that mesa?"

"Right up against it. Small town, about four hundred people when they're all home. Being off the state highway, no tourists ever go there. Nothin' to see, anyway."

"No boot hill?" Nearly all of the little mining towns in this section have a boot hill, and from the look of them, shooting up your neighbors must have been the outstanding recreation in the old days.

"Oh, sure. Not many in this one, though. About fifteen or twenty with markers, but they buried most of them without any kind of a slab. This boot hill couldn't hold a candle to Pioche. Over there they buried seventy-five before the first one died of natural causes."

"Rough place."

"You said it. Speakin' of guys gettin' killed, they had a murder in Ranagat the other night. Old fellow, got more money than you could shake a stick at."

"Murder, you say?"

"Uh-huh. They don't know who done it, yet, but you needn't worry. Old Jerry will catch him. That's Jerry Loftus, the sheriff. He's a smart old coot, rustled a few cows himself in the old days. He can sling a gun, too. Don't think he can't. Not that he looks like much, but he could fool you."

Shanks put a cigarette between his lips and lit it with a match cupped in his right hand. "Bitner, his name was. That's the dead man, I mean." He jerked his cigarette toward the mesa. "Lived up there."

"On top?" From where I sat, the wall of sheer, burnt-red sandstone looked impossible to climb. "How'd he get up there?"

"From Ranagat. That's the joker in this case, mister. Only one way up there, an' that way is in plain sight of most of Ranagat, an' goes right by old Johnny Holben's door. Nobody could ever get up that trail without being seen by Johnny.

"The trail goes up through a cut in the rock, and believe me, it's the only way to get on top. At a wide place in the cut, Johnny Holben has a cabin, an' he's a suspicious old coot. He built there to annoy Bitner because they had it in for each other. Used to be partners, one time. Prospected all this country together an' then set up a company to work their mines. 'Bitner and Holben,' they called it. Things went fine for a while, an' they made a mint of money. Then they had trouble an' split up."

"Holben kill him?"

"Some folks think so, but others say no. Bitner's got him a niece, a right pretty girl named Karen. She came up here to see him, and two days after she gets here he gets murdered. A lot of folks figure that was a mighty funny thing, her being heiress to all that money, an' everything."

So there were two other suspects, anyway. That made three. Johnny Holben, Karen Bitner, and my client. "Know a guy named Caronna?"

"Blacky Caronna? Sure." Shanks slanted a look at me out of those watchful, curious eyes. I knew he was trying to place me, but so far hadn't an inkling. "You know him?"

"Heard of him." It was no use telling Shanks what I had come for. I was here to get information, not give it.

"He's a suspect, too. An' in case you don't know, mister, he's not a nice playmate. I mean, you don't get rough with him. Nobody out here knows much about him, an' he's lived in Ranagat for more than ten years, but he's a bad man to fool with. If your business is with him, you better forget it unless it's peaceful."

"He's a suspect, you say?"

"Sure. Him an' old Bitner had a fight. An argument, that is. Bitner sure told him off, but nobody knows what it was about but Caronna; an' Blacky just ain't talkin'.

"Caronna is sort of a gambler. Seems to have plenty of money, an' this place he built up here is the finest in town. Rarely has any visitors, an' spends most of his time up there alone except when he's playin' poker.

"The boys found out what he was like when he first came out here. In these western towns they don't take a man on face value, not even when he's got a face like Blacky Caronna's. Big Sam, a big miner, tangled with him. Sam would weigh about two-fifty, I guess, and all man. That's only a shade more than Caronna.

"They went out behind The Sump, that's a pool hall an' saloon, an' they had it out. Boy, was that a scrap! Prettiest I ever seen. They fought tooth an' toenail for near thirty minutes, but that Caronna is the roughest, dirtiest fighter ever come down the pike. Sam was damn near killed."

"Big guy, you say?"

"Uh-huh. Maybe an inch shorter than you, but wide as a barn door. And I mean a big barn! He's a lot heavier than you, an' never seems to get fat." Shanks glanced at me. "What do you weigh? About one-eighty?"

"Two hundred even."

"You don't say? You must have it packed pretty solid. But don't you have trouble with Caronna. You ain't man enough for it."

That made me remember what the boss said before I left. "His money is as good as anybody's money, but don't you get us into trouble. This Caronna is a tough customer, and plenty smart. He's got a record as long as your arm, but he got out of the rackets with plenty of moola, and that took brains. You go over there and investigate that murder and clear him if you can. But watch him all the time. He's just about as trustworthy as a hungry tiger."

The station wagon rolled down the last incline into the street and rolled to a halt in front of a gray stone building with a weather-beaten sign across the front that said Hotel on one end and Restaurant on the other.

The one street of the town laid everything out before you for one glance. Two saloons, a garage, a blacksmith shop, three stores, and a café. There were two empty buildings, boarded up now, and beyond them another stone building that was a sheriff's office and jail in one piece.

Shanks dropped my bag into the street and reached out a hand. "That will be three bucks," he said. He was displeased with me. All the way over I had listened, and he had no more idea who I was than the man in the moon.

Two thistle-chinned prospectors who looked as if they had trailed a burro all over the hills were sitting on the porch, chewing. Both of them glanced up and stared at me with idle curiosity.

The lobby was a long, dank room with a soot-blackened fireplace and four or five enormous black leather chairs and a settee, all looking as if they had come across the plains fifty or sixty years ago. On the wall was a mountain lion's head that had been attacked by moths.

A clerk, who was probably no youngster when they opened the hotel in '67, got up from a squeaky chair and shoved the register at me. I signed my name and, taking the key, went up the stairs. Inside the room I waited just long enough to take my .45 Colt out of the bag and shove it behind my belt under my shirt. Then I started for the sheriff's office. By the time I had gone the two blocks that comprised the full length of the street, everyone in town knew me by sight.

———

JERRY LOFTUS WAS seated behind a rolltop desk with both feet on the desk and his thumbs hooked in the armholes of his vest. His white, narrow-brimmed hat was shoved back on his head, and his hair and mustache were as white as the hat. He wore cowboy boots, and a six-shooter in an open-top holster.

Flipping open my wallet, I laid it in front of him with my badge and credentials showing. He glanced down at them without moving a hand, then looked up at me.

"Private detective? Who sent for you?"

"Caronna."

"He's worried, then. What do you aim to do, son?"

"Look around. My orders are to investigate the crime, find evidence to clear him, and so get you off his back. From the sound of it"—I was fishing for information—"he didn't seem to believe anybody around here would mind if he was sentenced or not. Guilty or not."

"He's right. Nothing against him myself. Plays a good hand of poker, pays when he loses, collects when he wins. Maybe he buys a little highgrade once in a while, but while the mine owners wish we would put a stop to it, we don't figure that what gold ore a man can smuggle out of a mine is enough to worry about.

"All these holes around here strike pockets of rich ore from time to time. Most of the mines pay off pretty well, anyway, but when they strike that wire gold, the boys naturally get away with what they can.

"The mines all have a change room where the miners take off their diggin' clothes, walk naked for their shower, then out on the other side for their street clothes, but men bein' what they are, they find ways to get some out.

"Naturally, that means they have to have a buyer. Caronna seems to be the man. I don't know that, but I never asked no questions, either."

"Would you mind giving me the lowdown on this killing?"

"Not at all." Loftus shifted his thumbs to his vest pockets. "Pull up a chair an' set. No, not there. Move left a mite. Ain't exactly safe to get between me an' that spittoon."

He chewed thoughtfully for a few minutes. "Murdered man is Jack Bitner, a cantankerous old cuss, wealthy as all get-out. Mine owner now, used to be a prospector. Hard-headed as a blind mule and rough as a chapped lip. Almost seventy, but fit to live twenty years more, ornery as he was. Lived up yonder on the mesa."

Loftus chewed, spat, and continued. "Found dead Monday morning by his niece. Karen Bitner. Killed sometime Sunday night, seems like. Stabbed three times in the back with a knife while settin' at the table.

"Only had two visitors Sunday night. Karen Bitner an' Blacky Caronna. She went up to see the old man about five of the evenin', claims she left him feelin' right pert. Caronna headed up that way about eight, still light at that hour, an' then says he changed his mind about seein' the old man without a witness, an' came back without ever gettin' to the cabin.

"Only other possible suspect is Johnny Holben. Those two old roosters been spittin' an' snarlin' for the last four years, an' both of them made threats.

"Johnny lives on the trail to the mesa, an' he's got ears like a skittish rabbit an' eyes like a cat. Johnny saw those two go up an' he seen 'em come back, an' he'll take oath nobody else went up that trail. Any jury of folks from around Ranagat would take his word for it that a gopher couldn't go up that trail without Johnny knowin' it. As for himself, Johnny swears he ain't been on the mesa in six years.

"All three had motives, all three had opportunity. Any one of the three could have done it if they got behind Bitner, an' that's what makes me suspect the girl. I don't believe that suspicious old devil would let any man get behind him."

"Caronna can't clear the girl, then? If he had gone up to the house and found the old man alive, she'd be in the clear."

"That's right. But he says he didn't go to the house, an' we can't prove it one way or another. The way it is, we're stuck. If you can figure some way to catch the guilty man, you'd be a help." Jerry Loftus rolled his quid in his jaws and glanced at me sharply. "You come up here to find evidence to prove Caronna innocent. What if you find something to prove him guilty?"

"My firm," I said carefully, "only represents clients who are innocent. Naturally, we take the stand that they are innocent until proved guilty, but we will not conceal evidence if we believe it would clear anyone else. If we become convinced of a client's guilt, we drop out of the case. However, a good deal of leeway is left to the operative. Naturally, we aren't here to convict our clients."

"I see." Loftus was stirring that one around in his mind.

"Mind if I look around?"

"Not at all." He took his feet down from the desk and got up. "In fact, I'll go along. Johnny might not let you by unless I am with you."

———

W HEN WE STARTED up the trail, it took me only a few minutes to understand that unless Johnny Holben was deaf as a post it would be impossible to get past his cabin without his knowledge. The trail was narrow, just two good steps from his door, and was of loose gravel.

Holben came to the door when we came alongside. He was a tall, lean old man with a lantern jaw and a handlebar mustache that would have been a dead ringer for the sheriff's except for being less tidy and more yellowed.

"Howdy, Loftus. Who's the dude with you?"

"Detective. Caronna hired him to investigate the murder."

"Huh! If Caronna hired him, he's likely a thief himself." Holben stepped back inside and slammed the door.

Loftus chuckled. "Almost as bad as Old Bitner. Wouldn't think that old sidewinder was worth a cool half-million, would you. No? I guessed not. He is, though. Bitner was worth half again that much. That niece of his will get a nice piece of money."

"Was she the only relative?"

"Matter of fact, no. There's a nephew around somewheres. Big game hunter, importer of animals, an' such as that. Hunts them for shows, I hear."

"Heard from him?"

"Not yet. He's out on the road with a circus of some kind. We wired their New York headquarters."

"Wouldn't be a bad idea to check and see where his show is playing."

Loftus glanced at me. "Hadn't thought of that. Reckon I'm gettin' old. I'll do that tonight."

"Does the girl get all the money? Or does he get some?"

"Don't know. The Bitner girl, she thinks she gets it. Says her uncle told her she would inherit everything. Seems like he had no use for that nephew. So far we haven't seen the will, but we'll have it open tomorrow."

The path led along the flat top of the mesa over the sparse grass and through the scattered juniper for almost a half-mile. Then we saw the house.

It was built on the edge of the cliff. One side of the house was almost flush with the edge, and the back looked out over a natural rock basin that probably held water during the winter or fall, when it rained.

It was a three-room stone house, very carefully built and surprisingly neat. There were a few books and magazines lying about, but everything else seemed to have its place and to be kept there. There was a dark stain on the tabletop that identified itself for me, and some more of the same on the floor under the chair legs. Looking at the dishes, I figured that Bitner was alone and about to begin eating when death had struck.

The one door into the house opened from a screened-in porch to the room where he had been sitting. Remembering how the spring on the door had screamed protestingly when we opened it, there was small chance that anyone could have entered unannounced.

Moreover, a man seated at the table could look out that door and down the path almost halfway to Ranagat.

The windows offered little more. There were three in the main room of the house, and two of those opened over that rock basin and were at least fifteen feet above the ground. Nobody could have entered quietly from that direction.

The third window appeared to be an even less probable entrance. It opened on the side of the house that stood on the cliff edge. Outside that window and about four feet below the sill was a cracked ledge about two feet wide, but the ledge dwindled away toward the back of the house so it was impossible to gain access to it from there. At the front, the porch ran right to the lip of the precipice, cutting off any approach to the ledge from that direction.

Craning my neck, I could see that it was fifty or sixty feet down an impossible precipice, and then a good two hundred feet that was almost as steep, but could be scaled by a daring man. The last sixty feet, though, made the way entirely impracticable.

The crack that crossed the ledge was three to four inches wide and about nine or ten inches deep. In the sand on the edge of a split in the rock was a track resembling that of a large gila monster, an idea that gave me no comfort. I was speculating on that when Jerry Loftus called me.

———

AT THE DOOR I was confronted by three people. Nobody needed to tell me which was Blacky Caronna, and I had already seen Johnny Holben, but it was the third one that caught me flat-footed with my hands down and my chin wide open.

Karen Bitner was the sort of girl no man could look at and ever be the same afterward. She was slim and lovely in whipcord riding breeches and a green wool shirt that didn't have that shape when she bought it. Her hair was red-gold and her eyes a gray-green that shook me to my heels.

Caronna started the show. He looked like a bulldozer in a flannel shirt. "You!" His voice sounded like a hobnailed boot scraping on a concrete floor. "Where have you been? Why didn't you come and look me up? Who's payin' you, anyway?"

"Take it easy. I came up here to investigate a murder. I'm doing it."

Caronna grabbed me by the arm. "Come over here a minute!" He had a build like a heavyweight wrestler and a face that reminded me of Al Capone with a broken nose.

When we were out of earshot of the others, he thrust his face at me and said angrily, "Listen, you! I gave that outfit of yours a grand for a retainer. You're to dig into this thing an' pin it on that dame. She's the guilty one, see? I ain't had a hand in a killin' in—in years."

"Let's get this one thing straight right now," I said. "I didn't come up here to frame anybody. You haven't got money enough for that. You hired an investigator, and I'm him. I'll dig up all I can on this case and if you're in the clear you'll have nothing to worry about."

His little eyes glittered. "You think I'd hire you if I were guilty? Hell, I'd get me a mouthpiece. I think the babe did it. She stands to get the old boy's dough, so why not? He'd had it long enough, anyway. Just my luck the old billygoat would jump me before he gets knocked off. It's inconvenient, that's what it is!"

"What was your trouble with him?"

He looked up at me and his black eyes went flat and deadly. "That's my business! I ain't askin' you to investigate me. It's that babe's scalp we want. Now get busy."

"Look," I said patiently, "I've got to have more. I've got to know something to work on. I don't give a damn what your beef was, just so you didn't kill him."

"I didn't," he said. He hauled a roll from his pocket and peeled off several of the outer flaps, all of them showing a portrait of Benjamin Franklin. "Stick these in your kick. A guy can't work without dough. If you need more, come to me. I can't stand a rap, get me? I can't even stand a trial."

"That's plain enough," I told him, "and it answers a couple of questions I had. Now, one thing more. Did you actually stop before you got to the house? If I knew whether the old man was alive or dead at that hour, I'd know something."

A kind of tough humor flickered in his eyes. "You're the dick, you figure that one out. Only remember: I didn't stick no shiv in the old guy. Hell, why should I? I could have squeezed him like a grape. Anyway, that wouldn't have been smart, would it? Me, I don't lose my head. I don't kill guys for fun."

That I could believe. His story sounded right to me. He could arrange a killing much more conveniently than this one had happened, and when he would not have been involved. Mr. Blacky Caronna, unless I was greatly mistaken, was an alumnus of the old Chicago School for Genteel Elimination. In any rubout job he did he would have a safe and sane alibi.

Yet, one thing I knew. Whether he had killed Bitner or not,

and I doubted it, he was a dangerous man. A very dangerous man. Also, he was sweating blood over this. He was a very worried man.

Loftus was talking to Holben, and Karen Bitner stood off to one side, so I walked over to her. The look in her eyes was scarcely more friendly than Caronna's. "How do you do?" I said. "My name is—"

"I'm not in the least interested in your name!" she said. "I know all about you, and that's quite enough. You're a private detective brought up here to prove me guilty of murder. I think that establishes our relationship clearly enough. Now if you have any questions to ask, ask them."

"I like that perfume you're wearing. Gardenia, isn't it? By Chanel?"

The look she gave me would have curdled a jug of Arkansas corn. "What is that supposed to be—the psychological approach? Am I supposed to be flattered, disarmed, or should I swoon?"

"Just comment. How long has it been since you've seen your uncle? I mean, before this trip?"

"I had never seen my uncle before," she said.

"You have a brother or cousin? I heard there was a nephew?"

"A cousin. His name is Richard Henry Castro. He is traveling with the Greater American Shows. He is thirty-nine years old and rugged enough to give you the slapping around you deserve."

That made me grin, but I straightened my face. "Thanks. At least you're concise. I wish everyone would give their information as clearly. Did you murder your uncle?"

She turned icy eyes on me. Just like the sea off Labrador. "No, I did not. I didn't know him well enough to either murder him or love him. He was my only relative aside from Dick Castro, so I came west to see him.

"I almost never," she added, "murder people on short acquaintance—unless they're detectives."

"You knew you were to inherit his estate?"

"Yes. He told me so three years ago, in a letter. He told me so again on Saturday."

"I see. What's your profession?"

"I'm a secretary."

"You ever let anybody in to see your boss?" I asked. "No, don't answer that. How many times did you see your uncle on this visit?"

"Three times, actually. I came to see him on the day I arrived and stayed approximately two hours. I went to see him the following day, and then the night he was killed."

"How did he impress you?"

She glanced at me quickly. "As a very lonely and tired old man. I thought he was sweet."

That stopped me for a minute. Was she trying to impress me? No, I decided, this girl wouldn't try to impress anyone. She was what she was, for better or worse. Also, with a figure like that she would never have felt it necessary to impress anyone, at least any man.

For almost an hour we stood there; I asked the questions and she shot back answers. She had met her cousin, a big, handsome man given to many trips into the jungle after his strange animals, a few years before. He had his own show traveling as a special exhibit with a larger show. They made expositions and state fairs, and followed a route across country, occasionally playing carnival dates or conventions.

Her short relationship with her uncle had been friendly. She had cooked lunch the day before he was killed, and he had been alive when she had left him on her last visit. He had said nothing to her about his trouble with Caronna, but she knew he was very angry about something. Also, he kept a pistol handy.

"He did? Where is it?"

"In the sideboard, on the shelf with some dishes. He kept a folded towel over it, but it was freshly oiled and cleaned. I saw it when I was getting some cups."

Then Bitner had been expecting trouble. From Caronna? Or was it someone else, someone of whom we had not learned?

———

THAT NIGHT, IN the café, I sat at my table and ran over what little I knew. Certainly, the day had given me nothing.

Yet in a sense it had not been entirely wasted. The three suspects were now known to me, and I had visited the scene.

The waitress who came up to my table to get my order was a sultry-looking brunette with a figure that needed no emphasis. She took my order, and my eyes followed her back toward the kitchen. Then I saw something else. She had been reading a copy of *Billboard,* the show business magazine. Dreams, even in a small town . . . it made me wonder.

Caronna came in. He was still wearing the wool shirt that stretched tight over his powerful chest and shoulders, and a pair of tweed trousers. He dropped into the chair across from me and leaned his heavy forearms on the table. "You got anything?" he said. "Have you got anything on that broad?"

I cut a piece of steak, then looked up at him. "A couple of things. I'm working on them."

He was in a pleasanter mood tonight, and I noticed his eyes straying around, looking for somebody, something. I even had an idea who he was looking for. "They got nothing on me," he said, not looking at me. "The old man an' me, we had a fuss, all right. They know that, an' that I went up the trail to see him. That wasn't smart of me. It was a sucker's trick, but despite that they've got less on me than on that Bitner babe.

"Nobody can prove I went in the house or even went near it. Holben can testify that I wasn't gone long. Your job is to dig up something that will definitely put me in the clear."

"Maybe I've already got something."

He leaned back in his chair, looking me over. It was the first time he'd taken a good look. This Caronna was nobody's fool. He had more up his sleeve than a lot of muscle, but I couldn't see him killing Jack Bitner. Not that way.

Murder was not new to Caronna, but he knew enough about it so he would have had an out. He was in this, up to his neck. That much I believed, and I was sure there was more behind the killing than there seemed. That was when I began to get the idea that Caronna had a hunch who had done the job, and somehow figured to cash in.

The waitress came over, and while I couldn't see their expressions, and she only said, "Anything for you, Mr. Caronna?"

I had a hunch they were telling each other a thing or two. She dropped her napkin then, and Caronna picked it up for her. Where did they think I was born? I caught the corner of the paper in my glance as they both stooped, but the paper was palmed very neatly by Caronna as he returned the napkin to the waitress.

Caronna left after drinking a cup of coffee and rambling on a little. When I went over to pay my check, the *Billboard* was still lying there. Deliberately, although I had the change, I sprung one of Caronna's C-notes on her. I was praying she would have to go to the kitchen for change, and she did.

This gave me a chance at the *Billboard* and I glanced down. It was right there in front of me, big as life:

GREATER AMERICAN
PLAYING TO BIG CROWDS
IN NEVADA

When I got my change I walked outside. The night was still and the stars were out. Up at the mine I could hear the pounding of the compressor, an ever-present sound wherever mines are working.

I really had my fingers on something now, I thought. If Greater American was playing Nevada, then Castro might have been within only a few miles of Ranagat when Bitner was killed.

If Loftus knew that, he was fooling me, and somehow I couldn't picture that sheriff, smart as he was in his own line, knowing about *Billboard*. There was a telephone booth in the hotel, so I hurried over, and when I got the boss in Los Angeles, I talked for twenty minutes. It would take the home office only a short time to get the information I wanted, and in the meantime I had an idea.

Oh, yes. I was going to check Karen Bitner, all right. I was also going to check Johnny Holben. But all my mind was pointing the other way now.

There were several things I had to find out.

Where had Richard Henry Castro been on the night of the murder at the hour of the crime?

What was the trouble between Caronna and Old Jack Bitner?

What was the connection between that walking hothouse plant in the café and Caronna? Or between her and Castro? Or—this was a sudden thought—*both* of them?

Had either Holben or Karen seen anything they weren't telling?

It made a lot to do, but the ball was rolling. From the sign, I saw that the restaurant closed at ten o'clock, so I strolled back to the hotel and dropped into one of the black leather chairs in the lobby and began to think.

———

NOT MORE THAN an hour after my call went in, I got the first part of an answer. The telephone rang, and it was Los Angeles calling me. The Great American, said the boss, had played Las Vegas the day before the murder . . . and its next date had been Ogden, Utah!

In a rack near the desk were some timetables, and some maps put out by filling stations. I picked up one of the latter and glanced over the map. Something clicked in me. I was hot. It was rolling my way, for there was one highway they could have followed, and probably *did* follow that would have carried them by not over a mile from the mesa!

Studying it, I knew I didn't have a lot, although this did bring another suspect into the picture, and a good one. One thing I wanted to know now was the trouble between Caronna and Bitner. I walked restlessly up and down the lobby, racking my brain, and only one angle promised anything at all. Loftus had hinted that Caronna was buying high-grade ore from miners who had smuggled it out of the mines.

Then I looked up and saw Karen Bitner coming down the stairs from her room.

Somehow, the idea of her staying here had never occurred to me, but when I thought about it, where else in this town could she stay?

Our eyes met, and she started to turn away, but I crossed over to her. "Look," I said, "this isn't much of a town, and it's pretty quiet. Why don't we go have some coffee or something? Then we can talk. I don't know about you, but I'm lonely."

That drew a half smile. After a momentary hesitation, she nodded. "All right, why not?"

Over coffee our eyes met and she smiled a little. "Have you decided that I'm a murderer yet?"

"Look," I said, "you want your uncle's murderer found, don't you? Then why not forget the hostility and help me? After all, I'm just a poor boy trying to get along, and if you aren't guilty, you've nothing to fret about."

"Aren't you here to prove me guilty?"

"No. Definitely not. I was retained by Caronna to prove him innocent. Surprising as it may seem, I think he is. I believe the man has killed a dozen men, more or less, but this isn't his kind of job. He doesn't get mad and do things. When he kills it's always for a good enough reason, and with himself in the clear.

"Also, from what he has said, I have an idea that he wants anything but publicity right now. Just why, I don't know, but it will bear some looking over."

"Do you think old Mr. Holben did it?"

That brought me up short. After thinking it over, I shook my head. "If you want my angle, I don't think those old reptiles disliked each other anywhere near as much as they made it seem. I've seen old men like that before. They had some little fuss, but it probably wore itself out long ago, only neither one would want the other to know. Actually, that fuss was probably keeping both of them alive."

"Then," Karen said, "with both Caronna and Holben eliminated, that leaves only myself. Do you think I did it?"

"I doubt it," I said. "I really do. If you were going to kill a man, you'd do it with words."

She smiled. "Then who?"

"That, my dear, is the sixty-four-dollar question."

She smiled, and then her eyes flicked over to our sultry waitress, who was keeping an eye on us from behind the counter. She asked softly, "Who is the Siren of Ranagat? An old flame of yours? Or a new one you've just fanned into being? She scarcely takes her eyes off you."

"My idea is that the lady is thinking less of romance and more of finance. Somewhere in this tangled web she is weaving her own strands, and I don't think my masculine beauty has anything to do with it."

Karen studied me thoughtfully. "You do all right, at that. Just remember that this is a small town, and you'd be a break here. Any stranger would be."

"Uh-huh, and she has a lot of fancy and obvious equipment, but somehow I doubt if the thought has entered her mind. I've some ideas about her."

It was cool outside, a welcome coolness after the heat of the day. The road wound past the hotel and up the hill, and we walked along, not thinking much about the direction we were taking until we were standing on the ridge with the town below us. Beyond, on the other mountain, stretched the chain of lights where the mine stood, and the track out to the end of the dump.

The moon was high, and the mining town lay in the cupped hand of the hills like a cluster of black seeds. To the left and near us lay the sprawling, California-style ranch house where Blacky Caronna lived and made his headquarters. Beyond that, across a ravine and a half-mile further along the hill, lay the gallows frame and gathered buildings of the Bitner Gold Mine, and beyond it, the mill.

On our right, also above and a little away from the town, loomed the black bulk of the mesa. There were few lights anywhere, but with the moon they weren't needed. For a few minutes we stood quiet, our thoughts caught up and carried away by the quiet and the beauty, a quiet broken only by the steady pound of the mine's compressor.

Then, from the shadows behind the buildings along the town's one business street, a dark figure moved. Whether I saw it first, or whether Karen did, I don't know. Her hand caught my wrist suddenly, and we stood there, staring down into the darkness.

It struck me as strange that we should have been excited by that movement. There were many people in the town, most of them still awake, and any one of them might be out and around. Or was there something surreptitious about this figure that gave us an instinctive warning?

I glanced at my watch. By the luminous dial I could see that it was ten minutes after ten. At once, as though standing beside her in the darkness, I knew who was walking down there, and I had a hunch where she was going.

The figure vanished into deep shadows, and I turned to Karen. "You'd better go back to the hotel," I told her. "I know this is a lousy way to treat a girl, but I've some business coming up."

She looked at me thoughtfully. "You mean . . . about the murder?"

"Uh-huh. I think our Cleopatra of the café is about to make a call, and the purpose of that call and what is going to be said interest me. You go back to the hotel, and I'll see you in the morning."

"I will not. I'm coming with you."

Whatever was done now would have to be done fast, and did you ever try to argue with a woman and settle any point in a hurry? So she came along.

We had to hurry, for we had further to go than our waitress, and a ravine to enter and climb out of, and much as I disliked the idea of a woman coming with me into such a situation, I had to hand it to Karen Bitner. She kept right up with me and didn't do any worrying about torn hose or what she might look like when it was over.

THIS CARONNA WAS no dope. Stopped flat-footed by the hedge around his place, I found myself respecting him even more. This was one hedge no man would go through, or climb over, either. For the hedge was of giant suguaro cactus, and between the suguaro trunks were clumps of ocotilio, making a barrier that not even a rattlesnake would attempt. Yet even as we reached it, we heard footsteps on the path from town, and then the jangle of a bell as the front gate opened.

That would be the girl from the café. It also meant that no entry could be gained by the front gate. Avoiding it, I walked around to the rear. There was a gate there, too, but I had no desire to try it, being sure it would be wired like the other.

Then we got a break. There was a window open in the garage. Crawling in, I lifted Karen in after me, and then we walked out the open door and moved like a couple of shadows to the wall of the house. I didn't need to be told that both of us were right behind the eight ball, if caught.

Blacky Caronna wouldn't appeal to the law if he caught us. Knowing the man, I was sure he would have his own way of dealing with the situation.

———

CARONNA WAS SEATED in a huge armchair in a large living room hung with choice Navajo rugs. With his legs crossed, his great shoulders covering the back of the chair, he looked unbelievably huge. He was glaring up at the girl.

Taking a chance, I tried lifting the window. Everything here seemed in excellent shape, so I hoped it would make no sound. I was lucky. Caronna's voice came clearly. "Haven't I told you not to come up here unless I send for you? That damn cowtown sheriff is too smart, Toni. You've got to stay away."

"But I had to come, Blacky. I had to! It was that detective, the one you hired. I saw him looking at my copy of *Billboard*."

"You had that where he could see it?" Caronna lunged to his feet, his face a mask of fury. "What kind of brains you got, anyway?" he snarled, thrusting his face at her. "Even that dope will get an idea if you throw it at him. Here we stand a chance to clean up a million bucks, and if he gets wise, we're through!"

"But they've nothing on you, Blacky," she protested. "Nothing at all."

"Not yet, they ain't, but if you think I'm letting anybody stand in my way on account of that sort of dough, you're wrong, see? This stuff I've been pickin' up is penny-ante stuff. A million bucks, an' I'm set for life. What do you think I brought you up here for? To make a mess of the whole works?

"The way it stands, nobody knows a thing but me. Loftus don't know what the score is, an' neither does this dick, an' they ain't got a chance of finding out unless you throw it in their faces. Let this thing quiet down, an' that dough go where it's gonna go, an' we're set."

"You'd better watch your step," Toni protested. "You know what Leader said about him."

"Leader's a pantywaist. All he can do is handle that pen, but he can do that, I'll give him that much. I'll handle this deal, an' if that baby ever wants to play rough, I'll give him a chance."

"You shouldn't have hired that detective," Toni said worriedly. "He bothers me."

"He don't bother me any." Caronna's voice was flat. "Who would think the guy would pull this truth-and-honor stuff? It looked like a good play. It would cover me an' at the same time cinch the job on that dame, which was the right way to have it. It don't make no difference, though. He ain't smart enough to find his way out of a one-way street."

There was a subdued snicker behind me, and I turned my head and put a hand over her mouth. It struck me afterward that it was a silly thing to do. If a man wants a girl to stop laughing or talking, it is always better to kiss her. Which, I thought, was not a bad idea under any circumstances.

"Now, listen." Caronna stopped in front of her with his finger pointed. "You go back downtown an' stay there until I send for you. Keep your ears open. That café is the best listening post in town. You tell me what you hear an' all you hear, just like you have been. Keep an eye on Loftus, and on that dick. Also, you listen for any rumble from Johnny Holben."

"That old guy? You really are getting scary, Blacky."

"Scary nothing!" he snapped. "You listen to me, babe, an' you won't stub any toes. That old blister is smart. He's been nosin' around some, an' he worries me more than the sheriff. If he should get an idea we had anything to do with that, he might start shootin'. It's all right to be big and rough, but Holben is no bargain for anybody. He'll shoot first and talk after!"

She turned to the door, and he walked with her, a hand on her elbow. At the door they stopped, and from the nearness of their shadows I deduced the business session was over. This looked purely social. It was time for us to leave.

Surprisingly, we got out without any excitement. It all looked pretty and sweet. We had heard something, enough to prove that my first guess was probably right, and it didn't seem there was any chance of Caronna ever knowing we had visited him.

That was a wrong guess, a very wrong guess, but we didn't know at the time.

We didn't know that Karen's shoe left a distinct print in the grease spilled on the tool bench inside that garage window. We didn't know that she left two tracks on the garden walk, or that some of the grease rubbed off on a stone under Blacky Caronna's window.

———

IN THE MORNING I sat over my coffee for a long time. No matter how I sized up the case, it all came back to the same thing. Caronna hadn't killed Old Man Bitner, but he knew who had. And despite the fact that he wasn't the killer, he was in this up to his ears and definitely to be reckoned with.

That copy of *Billboard* was the tipoff. And it meant that I had to get out of here and locate the Greater American Shows, so I could have a look at Dick Castro. Richard Henry Castro, showman and importer of animals.

Caronna came into the café and he walked right over and sat down at the table. I looked up at him. "I can clear you," I said. "I know who the killer was, and you're definitely in the clear. All I need to know now is how he did it."

He dismissed my information with a wave of the hand. His eyes were flat and black. "Here." He peeled off five century notes. "Go on home. You're through."

"What?"

His eyes were like a rattlesnake's. "Get out of town," he snarled. "You been workin' for that babe more than for me. You've been paid—now beat it."

That got me. "Supposing I decide to stay and work on my own?"

"You've got no right unless you're retained," he said. "Anyway, your company won't let you stay without dough. Who's going to pay off in this town? And," he said coldly, "I wouldn't like it."

"That would be tough," I said. "I'm staying."

The smile left his lips. It had never been in his eyes. "I'm giving you until midnight to get out of town," he snarled. Then he shoved back his chair and got up. There was a big miner sitting at the counter, a guy I'd noticed around. When I stopped to think about it, I'd never seen him working.

Caronna stopped alongside of him. "Look," he said, "if you see that dick around here after midnight, beat his ears off. If you need help, get it!"

The miner turned. He had flat cheekbones and ears back against his skull. He looked at me coldly. "I won't need help," he said.

It was warm in the sunlight, and I stood there a minute. Somehow, the sudden change didn't fit. What had brought about the difference in his feelings between the time he had talked with Toni and now? Shrugging that one off, I turned down the street toward the jail.

Loftus had his heels on the rolltop desk. He smiled at me. "Got anything?" he asked.

"Yeah," I said. "Trouble."

"I don't mind admittin'," Loftus said, "this case has got me stopped. Johnny Holben knows somethin', but he won't talk. That Caronna knows somethin', too. He's been buyin' high-grade, most of it from the Bitner Mine. That was probably what their fuss was about, but that ain't the end of it."

"You're right, it isn't." Briefly, I explained about being fired, and then added, "I don't want to leave this case, Loftus. I think I can break it within forty-eight hours. I think I have all the answers figured out. Whether I do it or not is up to you."

"To me?"

"Yes. I want you to make me a deputy sheriff for the duration of this job."

"Workin' right for me?"

"That's right."

He took his feet off the desk. "Hold up your right hand," he said.

———

WHEN I WAS leaving, I turned suddenly to Loftus. "Oh, yes. I'm going out of town for a while. Over to Ogden on the trail of the Greater American Shows."

"There's a car here you can use," he said. "When are you leavin'?"

"About ten minutes after midnight," I said.

Then I explained, and he nodded. "That's Nick Ries, and he's a bad number. You watch your step."

At eleven-thirty I walked to the jail and picked up the keys to the car. Then I drove it out of the garage and parked it in front of the café. It was Saturday night, and the café was open until twelve.

Karen's eyes brightened up when I walked into the café. Toni came over to wait on us. Giving her plenty of time to get close enough to hear, I said to Karen, "Got my walking papers today. Caronna fired me."

"He did?" She looked surprised and puzzled. "Why?"

"He thinks I've been spending too much time with you. He also gave me until midnight to get out of town or that"—I pointed at Nick Ries at the counter—"gives me a going-over."

She glanced at her watch, then at Ries. "Are—are you going?"

"No," I said loud enough for Ries to hear. "Right now I'm waiting for one minute after twelve. I want to see what the bear-that-walks-like-a-man can do besides look tough."

Ries glanced over at me and turned another page of his newspaper.

We talked softly then, and somehow the things we found to talk about had nothing to do with murder or crime or Caronna; they were the things we might have talked about had we met in Los Angeles or Peoria or Louisville.

She was getting under my skin, and somehow I did not mind in the least.

Suddenly, a shadow loomed over our table. Instinctively, my eyes dropped to my wristwatch. It was one minute past twelve.

Nick Ries was there beside the table, and all I had to do was make a move to get up and he would swing.

It was a four-chair table, and Karen sat across from me. Nick was standing by the chair on my right. I turned a little in my chair and looked up at Nick.

"Here's where you get it," he said.

My left foot had swung over when I turned a little toward him and I put it against the rung of the chair in front of Nick and shoved, hard.

It was just enough to throw him off balance. He staggered back a step, and then I was on my feet. He got set and lunged at me, but that was something I liked. My left forearm went up to catch his right, and then I lifted a right uppercut from my belt that clipped him on the chin. His head jerked back and both feet flew up and he hit the floor in a lump.

Shaking his head, he gave a grunt, then came up and toward me in a diving run. I slapped his head with an open left palm to set him off balance and to measure him, and then broke his nose with another right uppercut.

The punch straightened him up, and I walked in, throwing them with both hands. Left and right to the body, then left and right to the head. He hit the counter with a crash, and I followed him in with another right uppercut that lifted him over the counter. He dropped behind it and hit the floor hard.

Reaching over, I got a lemon pie with my right hand and plastered it in his face, rubbing it well in. Then I straightened up and wiped my hands on a napkin.

Toni stood there staring at me as if I had suddenly pulled a tiger out of my shirt, and when I turned, Jerry Loftus was standing in the door, chuckling.

FINDING CASTRO'S SHOW was no trouble. It was the biggest thing on the midway at the fair, and when I got inside I had to admit the guy had something.

There were animals you didn't see in any zoo, and rarely

even in a circus. Of course, he had some of the usual creatures, but he specialized in the strange and unusual. Even before I started looking around for Castro himself, I looked over his show.

A somewhat ungainly-looking animal, blackish in color with a few spots of white on his chest and sides, took my interest first. It was a Tasmanian Devil, a carnivorous animal with powerful jaws noted for the destruction of small animals and young sheep. There was also a Malay Civet, an Arctic Fox, a short-tailed mongoose, a Clouded Leopard, a Pangolin or scaly anteater, a Linsang, a Tamarau, a couple of pygmy buffalo, a babirusa, a duckbilled platypus, a half-dozen bandicoots, a dragon lizard from Komodo, all of ten feet long and weighing three hundred pounds, and last, several monitor lizards, less than half the size of the giants from Komodo, Indonesia.

I glanced up when a man in a white silk shirt, white riding breeches, and black, highly polished boots came striding along the runway beside the pits in which the animals were kept. On a hunch I put out a hand. "Are you Dick Castro?"

He looked me up and down. "I am, yes. What can I do for you?"

"Have you been informed about your uncle, Jack Bitner?"

His handsome face seemed to tighten a little, and his eyes sharpened as he studied me. Something inside me warned: This man is dangerous. Even as I thought it, I realized that he was a big, perfectly trained man, who could handle himself in any situation. He was also utterly ruthless.

"Yes, I received a forwarded message yesterday. However, I had already had my attention called to it in the papers. What have you to do with it?"

"Deputy sheriff. I'd like to ask you a few questions."

He turned abruptly. "Bill! Take over here, will you? I'll be back later." He motioned to me. "Come along."

With a snappy, military stride, he led me to the end of the runway and through a flap in a tent to a smaller tent adjoining. He waved me to a canvas chair, then looked over his shoulder. "Drink?"

"Sure. Bourbon if you've got it."

He mixed a drink for each of us, then seated himself opposite me. "All right, you've got the ball. Start pitching."

"Where were you last Sunday night?"

"On the road with the show."

"Traveling where?"

"Coming here. We drove all night."

"How often do you have rest stops on such a drive as that?"

"Once every hour for a ten-minute rest stop and to check tires, cages, and equipment." He didn't like the direction my questions were taking, but he was smart enough not to make it obvious. "I read in the papers that you had three likely suspects."

"Yes, we have. Your cousin, Johnny Holben, and—" deliberately I hesitated a little—"Blacky Caronna."

He looked at me over his glass, direct and hard. "I hope you catch the killer. Do you think you will?"

"There isn't a doubt of it." I threw that one right to him. "We'll have him within a few hours."

"You say *him*?"

"It's a manner of speaking." I smiled. "You didn't think we suspected you, did you?"

He shrugged. "Everybody in a case like that can be a suspect. Although I'm in no position to gain by it. The old man hated me and wouldn't leave me the dirtiest shirt he had. He hated my father before me. Although," he added, "even if I could have gained by it, there wouldn't have been any opportunity. I don't dare leave the show and my animals. Some of them require special care."

"That Komodo lizard interested me. They eat meat, don't they?"

He looked up under his eyebrows. "Yes. On Flores and Komodo they are said to occasionally catch and kill horses for food. They are surprisingly quick, run like a streak for a short distance, and there are native stories of them killing men. Most such stories are considered fantastic and their ferocity exaggerated. But me, I think them one of the most dangerous of all living creatures." He looked at me again. "I'd hate to fall into that pit with one of them when nobody was around to get me out."

The way he looked at me when he said that sent gooseflesh up my spine.

"Any more questions?"

"Yes. When did you last hear from Blacky Caronna?"

He shifted his seat a little, and I could almost see his mind working behind that suave, handsome face. "Whatever gave you the idea I might hear from him? I don't know the man. Wouldn't know him if I saw him."

"Nor Toni, either?"

If his eyes had been cold before, they were ice now. Ice with a flicker of something else in them. "I don't think I know anyone named Toni."

"You should," I said grimly. "She knows you. So does Caronna. And just for your future information, I'd be very, very careful of Caronna. He's a big boy, and he plays mighty rough. Also, unless I'm much mistaken, he served his apprenticeship in a school worse than any of your jungles—the Chicago underworld of the late Capone era."

That was news to him. I had a hunch he had heard from Caronna but that he imagined him to be some small-time, small-town crook.

"You see," I added, "I know a few things. I know that you're set to inherit that dough, and I know that Blacky Caronna knows something that gives him a finger in the pie."

"You know plenty, don't you?" His eyes were ugly. "This is too tough a game for any small-town copper, so stay out, get me?"

I laughed. "You wrong me, friend. I'm not a small-time cop. I'm a private dick from L.A. whom Caronna brought over to investigate this murder. We didn't get along and he fired me, but then the sheriff swore me in as a deputy."

He absorbed that and he didn't like it. Actually, I was bluffing. I didn't have one particle of evidence that there was a tie-up between Castro and Caronna, nor did I know that Castro was to inherit. It was all theory, even if fairly substantial theory. However, the hint of my previous connection with Caronna worried him, for it could mean that I knew much more about Caronna's business than I should know.

This was the time to go, and I took it. My drive over had

taken some time, and there had been delays. It was already growing late. I got up. "I'll be running along now. I just wanted to see you and learn a few things."

He got up, too. "Well," he said, "I enjoyed the visit. You must come again sometime—when you have some evidence."

"Why sure!" I smiled at him. "You can expect me in a few days." I turned away from him, then glanced back. "You see, when you were in this alone, it looked good, but that Caronna angle is going to do you up. Caronna and Toni. They'd like to cut themselves in on this million or so you'll inherit."

He shrugged, and I turned away. It was not until I had taken two full steps into the deserted and darkened tent that I realized we were alone. While we were talking the last of the crowd had dwindled away, and the show was over.

My footsteps sounded loud on the runway under my feet, but there was a cold chill running up my spine. Castro was behind me, and I could hear the sound of his boots on the boards. Only a few steps further was the pit in which the huge dragon lizard lay.

The dank, fetid odor that arose from the pit was strong in the close air of the darkened tent with all the flaps down. With every sense in me keyed to the highest pitch, I walked on by the pit and turned down the runway to the exit. He drew alongside me then, and there was a queer look in his eyes. He must have been tempted, all right.

"You think I killed Bitner," he said. He had his feet wide apart and he was staring at me.

Why I said it, I'll never know, but I did. "Yes," I said, "I think you killed him."

"You damned fool! If I had, you couldn't prove it. You'd only make an ass of yourself."

That, of course, was the crux of the problem. I had to have evidence, and I had so little. I knew now how the crime had been done. This day had provided that information, but I needed proof, and my best bet was to push him into some foolish action, into taking some step that would give me further evidence. He was, as all criminals are, overly egotistical and overly optimistic, so with the right words I might light a fuse that would start something.

We had turned away from each other, but I could not resist the chance, for what it was worth. *"Ati, ati,"* I said, *"sobat bikin salah!"*

His spine went rigid, and he stopped so suddenly that one foot was almost in the air. He started to turn, but I was walking on, and walking fast. I had told him, "Be careful, you have made a mistake!" in Malayan . . . for the solution to this crime lay in the Far East.

At the edge of the grounds I stopped to light a cigarette. He was nowhere in sight, but I noticed a canvasman I had seen earlier and the man walked up. "How's for a light, mister?"

"Sure," I said. "Wasn't this show in Las Vegas a few days ago?"

"Yeah," he said. "You from there?"

"Been around there a good bit. Have a hard drive over?"

"Not so bad. We stop ever' so often for a rest."

"Who starts you again—Castro? I mean, after a rest stop?"

"Yeah, an' he usually gives us a break once in a while. I mean, sometimes when we're movin' at night he lets us rest a while. Got to, or we'd run off the road."

"Stop many times out of Las Vegas? That desert country must have been quiet enough to sleep."

"We stopped three, maybe four times. Got a good rest out in the desert. Twice he stopped quite a while. Maybe an hour once, maybe thirty minutes again. Boy, we needed it!"

Leaving him at a corner, I walked over to my car and got in. There were several cars parked along the street and in one of them I saw a cigarette glow. Lovers, I thought. And that took my mind back to Karen Bitner. A lot of my thinking had been centered around her these last few hours, and little of it had to do with crime.

THE CAR STARTED easily and I swung out on the highway and headed west. It was a long road I had to drive, across a lonely stretch of desert and mountains with few towns. When I had been driving for about an hour, a car passed me that looked familiar, but there was a girl and man in it. I grinned. Probably the two I'd seen back in town, I thought.

Wheeling the car around a climbing turn, I made the crest and leveled off on a long drive across some rough, broken country. Rounding a curve among some boulders, I saw a car ahead of me and a man bending over a rear wheel. A jack and some tire tools lay on the pavement, and a girl, her coat collar turned up against the cool wind, waved at me to flag me down.

Swinging to the opposite side of the road, I thrust my head out. "Anything I can do?" I asked.

The girl lifted her hand and she held a gun. "Yes," she said, "you can get out."

It was Toni. If the motor had been running, I'd have taken a chance, but I'd killed it when I stopped, believing they needed help. The man was coming toward us now, and with him was still another man who had unloaded from the car. The first was Nick Ries, Caronna's man, but the other I had never seen before. "Yeah," Nick said, "you can get out."

I got out.

My gun was in my hand, and I could have taken a chance on a gun battle, but it was three to one, and they had a flashlight on my face. I'd have been cold turkey in a matter of seconds. With a flit of my right hand I shoved my gun off my lap and behind the cushion, covering the movement by opening the door with my left. I got out and stood there with my hands up while they frisked me. "No rod," the new man told Nick. "He's clean."

"Okay, get him off the road. We've got work to do."

They pushed me around behind some rocks off the road. I could have been no more than fifty yards from the road where we stopped, but I might as well have been as many miles. Nick stared at me, his eyes hard with enjoyment.

"Looks like it's my turn now. Tough guy, huh? All right, you tell us what we want to know, or we'll give you a chance to show us how tough you are." He waved the gun at me. "Did you see Castro? What did you tell him?"

"Sure I saw him. I told him he was the guy who murdered Bitner. I asked him what Caronna wanted from him, and when Caronna got in touch with him last. It struck me," I added, and this was for Toni's benefit, "that he was a pretty smart joe. I think you guys are backing the wrong horse. Anyway," I continued, "I'm riding with him."

"You?" Toni snapped. "What do you mean?"

"Hell," I said, offhand, "figure it out for yourself. I was ready to do business with Blacky, but he wouldn't offer enough dough. Castro's a gentleman. He'll play ball with you. That's what you guys should be doing, getting on his side!"

"Shut up!" Nick snapped. Then he sneered, "You know what happens to guys that double-cross Blacky Caronna? I do. An' I don't want any part of it."

"That's if he's alive," I said. "You guys do what I tell you. You go to Castro."

The line I was using wasn't doing me any good with Nick, I could tell, but I wasn't aiming it at him. I was pretty sure that Toni had her own little game, and that she was playing both ends against the middle. If I could convince her I was playing ball with Castro there was a chance she would lend a hand. A mighty slim chance, but I was in no mood or position to bargain with any kind of a chance.

Of one thing I was sure. When they stopped that car they had no idea of ever letting me get away from this place alive. I had to talk fast. "I never expected," I said, flashing a look at Toni, "to find you out here. If we're going to get anything done, it will have to be done in Ranagat."

"Shut up!" Nick snarled.

"Hold it up a minute, Nick," Toni said. "Let the guy talk. Maybe we'll learn something."

"What I was going to say was this. I'm in this for the dough, like you are. Caronna fires me, so I tie on with Loftus, figuring if I stay where the big dough is, I'll latch onto some of it. So what do I find out? That Loftus and some others have a beautiful case built against Blacky. He's got a bad rep, and the owners are figuring on getting rid of him over this high-grade deal. So they have all gone in together— the mine owners, Loftus, Holben, an' all the rest. They are going to swear Caronna right into the death penalty. By the time that case goes to trial Caronna will be framed so tight he can't wiggle a toe.

"Why do you suppose he wanted me up here? Because he knows they're out to get him. Because he's hotter than a firecracker right now and he can't afford to go on trial.

"What I'm getting at is, why tie yourself to a sinking ship? Caronna's through. You guys can go down with him, or you can swing over to Castro and make more money than you ever will from Caronna."

"But," Ries objected, "the will Castro has leaves the money to him. Why should he give us a split?"

"He's leery of Caronna. Also," I said, grinning, "I've got my own angle, but I'll need help. I know how Castro killed the old man."

"How?" Ries said shrewdly.

I chuckled. In the last few minutes I'd been lying faster than I ever had in my life, but this I really knew. "Don't ask me how. You guys play ball with me, and I'll play ball with you."

"No," Nick said. "We got orders to bump you, and that's what we do."

"Wait, Nick." Toni waved a hand at him. "I've got an idea. Suppose we take this lug back to town. We can cache him in the basement at the café, and nobody'll know. Then we can study this thing over a little. After all, why should Blacky get all the gravy?"

"How do we know this guy is leveling with us?" Nick said. "He gives us a fast line of chatter, an'—"

Toni turned to me. "If you know Castro, and if you're working that close to him, you know about the will. Tell us."

Cold sweat broke out all over me. Here it was, and if I gave the wrong answer they'd never listen to me again. Hell. I wouldn't have time to talk! I'd be too dead.

Still, I had an idea, if no more. "Hell," I said carelessly, "I don't know what anybody else knows, but I know that Johnny Leader wrote that will, and I know that Castro stashed it away when he killed Bitner."

"That's what Caronna figured," Toni said. "This guy is right!"

They didn't see me gulp and swallow. It was lucky I had seen that sign over the small concession on the midway, a sign that said, JOHNNY LEADER, WORLD'S GREATEST PENMAN. And I remembered the comments Caronna had made to Toni about Leader. When I'd glimpsed that sign, it had all come back to me.

At last they let me put my hands down, and we started back to the cars. I wasn't out of the woods by a long way, but I had a prayer now. "Toni," Nick said, "you come with me in this mug's car. Peppy can drive ours. We'll head for Ranagat."

It couldn't have worked out better unless Ries had let Toni and me drive in alone. Nick had Toni get behind the wheel and he put me in alongside of her, then he got in behind. That guy wouldn't trust his grandmother. Still, it couldn't have been much better. My .45 was tucked into the crack behind the seat cushion right where I sat.

As we drove, I tried to figure my next play. One thing I knew, I wasn't taking any chance on being tied up in that basement, even if it meant a shoot-out in the streets of Ranagat. Then I heard something that cinched it.

"Blacky's figurin' on an out," Nick said to Toni. "He don't know about this frame they're springin' on him. He's all set to bump the babe and make it look like suicide, with a note for her to leave behind, confessin' she killed Bitner."

A match struck behind me as Nick lit a cigarette. "He's got the babe, too. We put the snatch on her tonight after he found them tracks she left."

"Tracks?" I tried to keep my voice casual. My right hand had worked behind me as I half turned away from Toni toward Nick, and I had the gun in my hand, under the skirt of my coat.

"Yeah," Nick chuckled. "She got into his place through the garage window an' stepped in some grease on a tool bench. She left tracks."

Toni glared sidewise at me. "Weren't you kind of sweet on her?"

"Me?" I shrugged, and glanced at her with a lot of promissory notes in my eyes. "I like a smart dame!"

She took it big. I'm no Clark Gable or anything, but alongside of Caronna I'd look like Galahad beside a gorilla.

WE ROLLED INTO the streets of Ranagat at about daybreak, and then I saw the sight that thrilled me more than any I could have seen unless it was Karen herself. It was Jerry Loftus. He was standing in the door of his office, and he saw us roll into town. This was a sheriff's office car, and he would know I wouldn't be letting anyone else drive for fun, not with Nick Ries in the back seat, whom he had seen me bash the night before.

Something made me glance around then, and I saw two things. I saw a gray convertible, the one I had seen standing back of Castro's tent, turning into Caronna's drive, and I saw Nick Ries leaning over on his right elbow, fishing in his left-hand pants pocket for matches.

My own right hand held the gun, and when I saw Ries way over on his elbow, I shoved down with my elbow on the door handle. The door swung open, and at the same instant I grabbed at the wheel with my left.

The car swung and smashed into the curb and then over it. We weren't rolling fast, but I hit the pavement gun in hand and backing up, and saw Loftus coming toward us as Peppy rolled down the hill in the following car. "Get that guy!" I yelled.

Nick was screaming mad. "It's a double cross! It's a—" His gun swung up, and I let him have it right through the chest, squeezing the two shots off as fast as I could pull the trigger of my gun.

Nick screamed again and his mouth dropped open, and then he spilled out of the car and landed on his face in the dust and dirt of the gutter.

Another shot boomed behind the car, and I knew it was Loftus cutting loose with his six-shooter. He only shot once.

For once Toni had been caught flat-footed. My twist of the wheel and leap from the car had caught her unawares, and now she stared, for one fatal instant, as though struck dumb. Then her face twisted into a grimace of hate and female fury, and she grabbed at her purse. Knowing where her gun was, I went into action a split second sooner and knocked it from her hand. She sprang at me, screaming and clawing, but Loftus and a couple of passing miners pulled her off me.

"Hold her," I said. "She's in it, too."

"Karen Bitner's disappeared," Loftus told me. "Have you seen her?"

"Caronna's got her."

Diving around the sheriff's car, I sprang for the seat of Peppy's convertible, which had been stopped alongside the street. I kicked her wide open and went up the winding road to Caronna's house with all the stops out. Skidding to a halt in front of the gate, I hit the ground on both feet, and this time I wasn't caring if there was a warning signal on the gate or not. I jerked it open, heard the bell clang somewhere in the interior, and then I was inside the gate and running for the steps.

As I went through the gate I heard something crash, and then a scream as of an animal in pain—a hoarse, gasping cry that died away in a sobbing gasp. I took the steps in a bound and went through the door.

Caronna, his eyes blazing, his shirt ripped half off, was standing in the middle of the room, his powerful, trunklike legs wide spread, his big hands knotted into fists.

In the corner of the room Castro was lying, and I needed only a glance to see that Richard Henry Castro had tackled a different kind of jungle beast, and had come out on the short end. I could surmise what had happened. Castro must have jumped him, and Caronna had torn the man loose and hurled him into that corner and then jumped right in the middle of him with both feet. If Castro wasn't ready for the hospital I never saw a man who was, and unless I was mistaken, he was a candidate for the morgue.

One chair was knocked over, and the broken body of Castro lay on the floor, blood trickling from a corner of his mouth, blood staining the front of his white shirt and slowly turning it to a wide crimson blotch. Yet his eyes were alive as they had never been, and they blazed up to us like those of a trapped and desperate animal brought to its last moment and backing away from the trapper with bared teeth.

Caronna was the thing that centered on my mind and gripped every sense in my being. Somehow, from the first I had known I would fight that man. Perhaps it began when Shanks had told me I wasn't man enough for him. That had rankled.

I stood there looking at Blacky Caronna, a solid block of bone and muscle mounted on a couple of powerful and thick legs, a massive chest and shoulders, and a bull neck that held his blunt, short-haired head thrust forward. He saw me and lunged.

Did I shoot him? Hell, what man who fights with his hands can think of a gun at such a moment? I dropped mine as Caronna lunged for me, and as I dropped it I hooked short and hard with both hands.

My feet were firmly anchored. I was set just right and he was coming in. My left smashed a bit high, slicing a deep cut in his cheekbone, and then my right smacked on his chin. I might as well have hit a wall. He grabbed at my coat, thinking perhaps to jerk it down over my shoulders, but I whipped a right uppercut that clipped him on the chin, and as all my weight was driving toward him, I jerked my chin down on my chest and butted him in the face, blocking his arms with my elbows.

He grabbed my forearms and hurled me away from him so hard that I hit a chair and it splintered under me. He came in with a rush. I hurled my body at his legs. He fell over me, kicking out blindly for my face, and one boot grazed my head, but then I rolled over and came up.

It was wicked, brutal battling. Through a kind of smoky haze in my mind, caused by crashing punches to my head and chin, I drove into him, swinging with both hands, and he met me halfway. It was fist and thumb, gouging, biting, kneeing. Using elbows and shoulders, butting and kicking. It was barroom, backroom, waterfront style, where anything goes and the man who goes down and doesn't get up fast enough is through . . . and he rarely gets up.

A thumb stabbed at my eye in a clinch, and I butted and

gouged my way out of it and then clipped him with a right to the chin as he came in. I struck at his throat with my elbow in close, and then grabbing him by the belt, heaved him from the floor and hurled him back on a table. He kicked me in the chest as I came in, and knocked me into the wall.

My coat and shirt were gone. Blood streaked my body. I could feel a stiffness in the side of my face, and I knew my eye was swelling shut. There was no time to rest, no rounds, no stopping. I stepped in on the balls of my feet and hooked hard to his chin. He blinked and slammed a right at me that I ducked but I caught a sweeping left that rocked me. Weaving to escape his bludgeoning fists, I forced him back against the desk and jamming my left forearm against his throat, I slammed three right hands into his body before he threw me off and charged. I stabbed a left at his face and he took it coming in as though I'd hit him with a feather duster. My right missed and he hit me in the belly with one that knocked every bit of wind out of me.

He hurled me to the floor and jumped for me with both feet, but I jerked up my knees and kicked out hard with both feet. They caught him midway of his jump and put him off balance, and he fell beside me. I rolled over, grabbing at his throat, but he threw a right from where he lay that clipped me, and then I ground the side of his face into the floor by crushing my elbow against his cheek.

We broke free and lunged to our feet, but he caught me with a looping right that staggered me. I backed up, working away from him, fighting to get my breath. My mouth hung open and I was breathing in great gasps, and he came around the wreck of the table, coming for me.

He pushed forward, bobbing his head to make my left miss, so I shortened it to a hook and stepped in with both hands. They caught him solidly, and he stopped dead in his tracks. He shook his head and started for me, his eyes glazed. My left hook came over with everything I had on it, and his cheek looked as if somebody had hit it with an axe.

He took it coming in and scarcely blinked, hurt as he was. For the first time in my life I was scared. I had hit this guy with everything but the desk and he was still coming.

My knees were shaky and I knew that no matter how badly he was hurt, I was on my last legs. He came on in, and I threw a right into his stomach. He gasped and his face looked sick, but he came on. He struck at me, but the power was gone from his punches. I set myself and started to throw them. I threw them as if I was punching the heavy bag and the timekeeper had given me the ten-second signal. I must have thrown both hands into the air after he started to fall, but as he came down, with great presence of mind, I jerked my knee into his chin.

Jerry Loftus came into the room as I staggered back, staring down at Caronna. "I could have stopped it," he said, "but I—"

"Why the hell didn't you?" I gasped.

"What?" His eyes twinkled at the corners. "Best scrap I ever saw, an' you ask me why I didn't stop it!"

"You'd better get cuffs on that guy," I said, disgusted. "If he gets up again I'm going right out that window!"

We found Karen in another room, tied up in a neat bundle, which, incidentally, she is at any time. When I turned her loose, she kissed me, and while I'd been looking forward to that, for the first time in my life I failed to appreciate a kiss from a pretty woman. Both my lips were split and swollen. She looked at my face with a kind of horror that I could appreciate, having seen Caronna.

———

HOURS LATER, SEATED in the café over coffee, Johnny Holben and Loftus came in to join us. Holben stared at me. Even with my face washed and patched up, I looked like something found dead in the water.

"All right," Loftus said doubtfully, "this is your show. We've got Caronna no matter how this goes, due to an old killing back East. That's what he was so worried about. Somebody started an investigation of an income-tax evasion and everybody started to talk, and before it was over, three old murders had been accounted for, and one of them was Caronna's.

"However, while we don't know now whether Castro will

live or not with that rib through his lung, you say he was the one who killed Bitner."

"That's right," I said. "He did kill him."

"He never came up that trail past my place," Holben said.

"But there isn't any other way up, is there?" Karen asked.

"No, not a one," Loftus said. "In the thirty years since I came west with a herd of cattle to settle in this country, I've been all over that mesa, every inch of it, and there's no trail but the one past Holben's cabin."

"Your word is good enough for me," I said, "but the fact is, Castro did not come by any trail when he murdered Old Jack Bitner. How it was done I had no idea until I visited Castro's show. You must remember that he specializes in odd animals, in the strange and the unusual.

"He got his method from India, a place where he had traveled a good deal. When I saw his animals, something clicked into place in my mind, and then something else. I knew then he had scaled the wall under Bitner's window."

"That's a sheer cliff," Loftus protested.

"Sure, and nothing human could climb it without help, but Richard Henry Castro went up that cliff, and he had help."

"You mean, there was somebody in it with him?"

"Nothing human. When I saw his show, I tied it in with a track I saw on the ledge outside Bitner's window. The trouble was that while I knew how it was done, and that his show had been stopped on the highway opposite the mesa, I had no proof. If Castro sat tight, even though I knew how it was done, it was going to be hard to prove.

"Like any criminal, he could never be sure he hadn't slipped up; didn't know who to fear or how much. My problem was to get Castro worried, and his method was one so foreign to this country that he never dreamed anyone would guess. I had to worry him, so in leaving I made a remark to him in Malayan, telling him that he had made a mistake.

"Once he knew I had been in the Far East, he would be worried. Also, he knew that Caronna had seen him."

"Caronna saw him?" Loftus demanded.

"Yes, that had to be it. That was the wedge he was using to cut himself in on Castro's inheritance."

"How could Castro inherit?"

"There's a man in his show named Johnny Leader, a master penman with a half-dozen convictions for forgery on his record. He was traveling with that show writing visiting cards for people, scrolls, etc. He drew up a will for Castro, and it was substituted at the time of the killing."

"Get to the point," Holben said irritably. "How did he get up that cliff?"

"This will be hard to believe," I said, "but he had the rope taken up by a lizard!"

"By a *what*?" Holben demanded.

I grinned. "Look," I said, "over in India there are certain thieves and second-story workers who enter houses and high buildings in just that way.

"Castro has two types of monitor lizards over there in his show. The dragon lizards from Komodo are too big and tough for anyone to handle, and nobody wants to. However, the smaller monitor lizards from India, running four to five feet in length, are another story. It is those lizards that the thieves use to gain access to locked houses.

"A rope is tied around the lizard's body, and he climbs the wall, steered by jerks on the rope from below. When he gets over a parapet, in a crevice, or over a window sill, the thief jerks hard on the rope and the lizard braces himself to prevent being pulled over, and they are very strong in the legs. Then the thief goes up the wall, hand over hand, walking right up with his feet against the wall."

"Well, I'll be damned!" Loftus said. "Who would ever think of that?"

"The day you took me up there," I told him, "I noticed a track that reminded me of the track of a gila monster, but much bigger. The idea of what it meant did not occur to me until I saw those monitor lizards of Castro's.

"Now that we know what to look for, we'll probably find scratches on the cliff and tracks at the base."

Karen was looking at me, wide-eyed with respect. "Why, I never realized you knew things like that!"

"In my business," I said, "you have to know a little of everything."

"I'll stick to bank robbers an' rustlers," Loftus said. "Or high-graders."

"You old false alarm!" Holben snorted. "You never arrested a high-grader in your life!"

We were walking out of the door, and somehow we just naturally started up the hill. Dusk was drawing a blanket of darkness over the burnt red ridges, and the western horizon was blushing before the oncoming shadows.

When we were on top of the hill again, looking back over the town, Karen looked up at me. "Are your lips still painful?"

"Not that painful," I said.

I HATE TO TELL HIS WIDOW

JOE RAGAN WAS drinking his ten o'clock coffee when
Al Brooks came in with the news. "Ollie's dead." He
spoke quietly. "Ollie Burns. Shot."

Ragan said nothing.

"He was shot twice," Al told him. "Right through the
heart. The gun was close enough to leave powder burns on
his coat."

Ragan just sat there holding his cup in both hands. It was
late and he was tired, and the information left him stunned
and unbelieving. Ollie Burns was his oldest friend on the
force. Ollie had helped break him in when he first joined up
after the war. Ollie had been a good officer, a conscientious
man who had a name for thoughtfulness and consideration.
He never went in for the rough stuff, knowing the taxpayers
paid his salary and understanding he was a public servant.
He treated people with consideration and not as if they were
enemies.

"Where did they find him?" he said at last. "How did it
happen?"

"That's the joker. We just don't know. He was found on a
phoned-in tip, lying on the edge of a vacant area near Duns-
muir. What he was doing out there in the dark is more than
anybody can guess, but the doc figures he'd been dead more
than an hour when we found him." Brooks hesitated. "They
think it was a woman. He smelled of perfume and there was
lipstick on his cheek and collar."

"Nuts!" Ragan rose. "Not Ollie. He was too much in love
with his wife and he never played around. I knew the guy too
well."

"Well," Brooks said, "don't blame me. You could be right.
It wasn't my idea, but what Stigler's thinking."

"Where's Mary? Has she been told?" Ragan's first thought was for her. Mark Stigler was not the type to break such news to anyone.

"Uh-huh. Mark told her. Your girl, Angie Faherty, is with her. They were to meet Ollie at a movie at nine, so when he didn't show up she got worried, so they went home. She called the station when he wasn't at home, and a couple of minutes after she called, somebody told us there was a body lying out there in the dark."

"Who called?"

"Nobody knows. The guy said he didn't want to get mixed up in anything and hung up."

"Odd, somebody seeing the body so soon. Nobody walks around there much at night."

Stigler was at his desk when Ragan came in. He looked up, unexpected sympathy in his eyes. "Do you want this case?"

"You know I do. Ollie was the best friend I had in the world, and you can forget the woman angle. He was so much in love with Mary that it stuck out all over him. He wasn't the type to play around. If anything, he was overly conscientious."

"Every man to his own view." Stigler tapped with a pencil. "This is the first man we've had killed in a year, and I want the killer brought in with evidence for a conviction. Understand?"

"Will I work with the squad?"

Stigler shook his head. "You've got your own viewpoint and you've worked with Ollie. You can have all the help you need, but we'll be working on it, too."

Joe Ragan was pleased. This was the way he wanted it but the last thing he expected from Mark Stigler. Stigler was a good homicide man but a stickler for the rulebook, and turning a man loose to work on his own was unheard of from him.

"Mark, did Ollie say anything to you about a case he was working on? I mean, in his spare time?"

"No, not a word." Stigler tapped with the pencil. "On his own time? I didn't know that ever happened around here. You mean he actually went out on his free time and worked on cases?"

"He was a guy who hated loose ends. Ask Mary sometime. Every tool had a place, every magazine was put back in a neat pile on the shelf, every book to its place. It wasn't an obsession, just that he liked things neat, with all the ends tied up. And I know he's had some bug in his bonnet for months now. What it was I have no idea."

"That's something," Stigler agreed. "Maybe he was getting too close to the right answer for somebody's comfort." He lit a cigar, then put it down. "My wife's trying to get me to smoke a pipe," he explained.

"You're right about him being overly conscientious. I recall that Towne suicide, about a year ago. He was always needling me to see if anything new had turned up.

"Hell, there wasn't anything new. It was open-and-shut. Alice Towne killed herself and there was no other way it could have happened. But it seems Ollie knew her and it bothered him a good deal."

"He was like that." Ragan got up. "What have you got so far?"

"Nothing. We haven't found the gun. Ollie's own gun was still in its holster. He was off duty at the time and, like we said, was meeting his wife to go to a show."

"Why didn't he go? I knew about that because my girl was going with them."

"Somebody called him just before eight o'clock. He answered the phone himself and Mary heard him say, 'Where?' A moment later he said, 'Right away.' Then he hung up and asked them if he could meet them in front of the theater at nine. He had an appointment that wouldn't keep."

"I see." Ragan rubbed his jaw. "I'll look into it. If you need me during the next hour, I'll be at Mary's."

"You aren't going to ask her about it now, are you?"

"Yes, I am, Mark. After all, she's a cop's wife. It will be better to get her digging into her memory for facts than just sitting around moping.

"I know Mary, and she won't be able to sleep. She's the kind of woman who starts doing something whenever she feels bad. If I don't talk to her, she'll be washing all the dishes or something."

———

ANGIE ANSWERED THE door. "Oh, Joe! I'm so glad you've come! I just don't know what to do. Mary won't lie down and she won't rest. She—"

"I know." Joe squeezed her shoulder. "We'll have some coffee and talk a little."

Walking through the apartment, he thought about what Stigler had said. Lipstick and perfume. That didn't sound like Ollie. Stigler had never known Ollie the way Ragan had. Ollie had never been a chaser. If there had been lipstick and perfume on him when he was found, it had been put there to throw off the investigation.

And the call. That was odd in itself. It might be that somebody had *wanted* the body found, and right away. But why? The man on the phone might have been the killer, or somebody working with him. If not, what would a man be doing in that area at that hour? For that matter, what was Ollie doing there? It was a dark, gloomy place, scattered with old lumber and bricks among a rank growth of weeds and grass. And right in the middle of town.

"On that call, Angie? Did Ollie say anything else? Give you any idea of what it was all about?"

"No, he seemed very excited and pleased, that was all. He told us he would not be long, but just to be sure to give him until nine. We went to dinner and then to the theater to meet him, but he never showed. He was driving his own car. Mary and I were driving yours."

At the sound of a step in the hall, Ragan looked up. He had known Mary Burns even longer than Ollie. There had been a time when he liked her very much. That was before he had met Angie or she had met Ollie.

She was a dark-eyed, pretty woman with a round figure and a pleasant face. If anyone in the world had been perfectly suited for Ollie, it was Mary.

"Mary," Ragan said, "this may not seem the best time, but I need to ask you some questions."

"I'd like that, Joe, I really would." Her eyes were red and swollen but her chin was firm. She sat down across the table, and Angie brought the coffeepot.

"Mary, you're the only person who knew Ollie better than I did. He was never one to talk about his work. He just did what was necessary. But he had that funny little habit of popping up with odd comments that were related to whatever he was thinking or working on."

"I know." She smiled, but her lips trembled. "He often did that. It confused people who didn't know him."

"All right. We know Ollie was working on something on his own time. I have a hunch it was some case the rest of us had forgotten about. Remember that Building & Loan robbery? He stewed over that for a month without saying anything to anybody, and then made an arrest and had all the evidence for a conviction. Nobody even knew he was thinking about the case.

"Well, I think he was working something like that. I think he was so close on the trail of somebody that they got scared. I think, somehow, they led him into a trap tonight. We've got to figure out what it was he had on his mind."

Mary shook her head. "I have no idea what it could be, Joe. He was working on something, I do know that. I could always tell when something was on his mind. He would sit staring across the top of his newspaper or would walk out in the yard and pull a weed or two. He never liked to leave anything until it was finished. What it was this time, I do not know."

"Think, Mary. Think back over the past few weeks. Try to remember any of those absentminded little comments he made. One of them might be just the lead we need."

Angie filled their cups again. Mary looked up doubtfully. "There was something just this morning, but it doesn't tell us a thing. He looked up while he was drinking his coffee and said, 'Honey, there's two crimes that are almost as bad as rape or murder.'"

"Nothing more?"

"That was all. He was stewing about something, and you

know how he was at times like that. I understood and left him alone."

"Two crimes worse?" Ragan ran his fingers through his hair. "I know what one was. We'd talked about it often enough. He thought, as I do, that narcotics peddling was the lowest crime on earth. It's a foul racket. I wonder if that was it?"

"What could the other crime be?"

He shook his head, frowning. Slowly, carefully then, he led Mary over the past few days, searching for some clue. A week before, she had asked him to meet her and go shopping, and he had replied that he was in the Upshaw Building and would meet her on the corner by the drugstore.

"The Upshaw Building?" Ragan shook his head. "I don't know anything about it. Well"—he got up—"I'm going to adopt Ollie's methods, Mary, and start doing legwork and asking questions. But believe me, I'll not leave this case until it's solved."

Al Brooks was drinking coffee when Ragan walked into the café the next morning. He dropped on the stool beside the vice-squad man and ordered coffee and a side order of sausage.

Al was a tall, wide-shouldered man with a sallow face. He had an excellent record with the force. He grinned at Ragan, but there was a question in his eyes. "I hear Stigler has you on the Burns case. What gives?"

Ragan did not feel talkative. Morning coffee with Ollie Burns had been a ritual of long standing, and the ease and comfort of the big man was much preferred to the sharp inquisitiveness of Al Brooks.

"Strange, Stigler putting you on the Burns case."

"Not so strange." Ragan sipped his coffee, hoping they'd hurry with the sausage. "He figured that being a friend of Ollie's, I might know something."

After a moment, Brooks looked around at him. "Do you?"

Ragan shrugged. "Not that I can think of. Ollie was working on something, I know that."

"I still think it was a woman." Brooks was cynical. "You say he never played around. Hell, what man would pass up a good-lookin' babe? Ollie was human, wasn't he?"

"He was also in love with his wife. The guy had ethics. He was as sincere and conscientious as anyone I ever knew."

Al was disgusted. "Where did all that lipstick come from? Do you think he cornered some gorilla in that lot and the guy kissed him? Are you kidding?"

"You've judged him wrong, Al. My hunch is that was all for effect. The killer wanted us to think a woman was involved.

"Besides," he added, "something they didn't count on. He had a date with his wife and my girlfriend. He was to meet them at nine. Allowing time for going and coming, he wouldn't have had much more time than to say hello and good-by."

Al stared at him for a moment, then shrugged. "Have it your way, but take a tip from me and be careful. If he was working on something that was serious enough to invite killing, the same people won't hesitate to kill again. Don't find out too much."

Ragan chuckled. "That doesn't sound like you, Al. Nobody on the force stuck his neck out more than you did when you pinched Latko."

"That's another thing. I had him bottled up so tight he didn't have a chance. None of his friends wanted any part of it. I had too much evidence."

Ragan got to his feet. "What the hell? We're cops, Al. Taking risks is expected of us."

Al Brooks lifted a hand and walked out. Ragan looked after him. He had never liked Al Brooks, but he was one of the best men on the force. The way he had broken the Latko gang was an example. Aside from a few petty vice raids, it had been Brooks's first job. Two months later he followed it with the arrest of Clyde Bysten, the society killer.

Stigler met him in the hall and motioned him into the office. "Joe, you knew them. How did Ollie get along with his wife?"

Ragan's head came around sharply. "They were the most affectionate people I ever knew. They lived for each other."

Stigler looked up from the papers on his desk. "Then how do you explain that he was shot with his own gun?"

Shock riveted Ragan to the floor. "Shot with *what*?"

"Not with his issue pistol, but another gun he kept at home. It was a .38 Smith & Wesson. We've found the gun, and the ballistics check. The gun is on our records as belonging to Ollie."

"Oh, no!" Ragan's mind refused to accept what he had heard. "Anyway," he added, "Mary was with Angie all the time, from seven until I left them, long after midnight."

Stigler shook his head. "No, Ragan, she wasn't. Your loyalty does you credit, but Mary left Angie at the table to go to the powder room. She was gone so long Angie was afraid she'd gotten sick and went to the rest room. Mary wasn't there."

Ragan dropped into a chair. "I don't get it, Mark, but I'd swear Mary can't be guilty. I don't care whose gun Ollie was shot with."

"What are you trying to do, Joe? Find a murderer or protect Mary?"

Ragan's face flushed. "Now see here, Mark. Ollie's the best friend I ever had, but I'm not going to stand by and see his wife stuck for a crime she could no more commit than I could. It's absurd. I knew them both too well."

"Maybe that was it, Joe. Maybe you knew them too well. Maybe that led to the killing."

Ragan stared at Stigler, unwilling to believe he was hearing correctly. "Mark, that's the most rotten thing that's ever been said to me, and you're no half-baked rookie. You must have a reason. Give it to me."

Stigler looked at him carefully. "Joe, understand this. We have almost no evidence to prove this theory. We do have a lot of hearsay. I might also add that I never dreamed of such a thing until we found that gun in the weeds, and even then I didn't think of you. That didn't come up until Hazel Upton."

"Who's she?"

"She's secretary to George Denby, the divorce lawyer."

"Divorce lawyer?" Ragan stared. "Who would want a divorce lawyer?"

"Miss Upton called us to say that Mary Burns had called when her boss was out, but Mary told her she wanted a divorce from Ollie."

"Somebody is crazy," Ragan muttered. "This is all wrong!"

"We've got a statement from her. We've also got a statement from a friend of Mary's, a Louella Chasen, who said Mary asked her what her divorce had cost and who her lawyer had been. She also implied there was another man."

Ragan was speechless. Even before this array of statements, he could not believe it. He would have staked his life that Ollie and Mary were the happiest couple he had ever known. He looked up. "Where do I come in?"

"You were a friend of the family. You called often when Ollie was away, didn't you?"

"Well, sure! But that doesn't mean we were anything but friends. Good Lord, man . . ."

For several minutes he sat without speaking. He knew how a word here and there could begin to build a semblance of guilt. Many times he had warned himself against assuming too much, and here it was, in his own life.

There was that old affection for Mary, never serious, but something that might come up. He knew what a hard-hitting district attorney could do with the fact that he had known Mary before she met Ollie. They would insinuate much more than had ever existed. Ragan could feel the net tightening around them. Ollie had been shot with his own pistol, and Mary Burns had no alibi. Worse still was the one thing he could not understand, that Mary had actually spoken of divorce.

"Mark," he said slowly, "believe me, there is something very wrong here. I don't know what it is or where I stand with you, but I know as well as I am sitting here that Mary never wanted a divorce from Ollie. I was with them too much. And as for Mary and me, we were never more than friends. Mary knows I am in love with Angie and would marry her tomorrow if she'd have me. She knows that somehow or other we've gotten into the middle of something very ugly."

"Well, keep on with the case, Joe. If you can find out anything that will help, go ahead. But I am afraid Mary Burns is in a bad spot. You can't get around that gun, and you can't escape those statements."

"They lied. They lied and they know they lied."

"For what reason? What would they gain? Why, they didn't even know why we wanted the information! Mary Burns was seen coming out of Denby's office, so we made inquiries. That was when we got the statement from Denby's secretary. Denby was out of the office, so he knew nothing about it."

"Who saw her come out of that office?"

Stigler compressed his lips. "I can't say. It was one of our men and he had a hunch there was something in back of it. As his hunches paid off in the past, we asked him to look into it."

"Al Brooks?"

"Don't start anything, Ragan. Remember, you're not in the clear yourself. You make trouble for Al and I'll have you locked up as a material witness." His face softened. "Damn it, man, I don't want to believe all this, but what can I do? Who had access to that gun? She and you. Maybe your girl-friend, too. There isn't anybody else."

"Then you've got three suspects. I wish you luck with them, Stigler."

———

WHEN HE GOT outside he felt sick and empty. He knew how much could be done with so little. Still, where had Mary gone? And what about this divorce business?

For a moment he thought about driving out to see just what had happened, then he decided against it. Nobody needed to see him and Mary again now. Besides, there was much more to do.

Mary had said Ollie had called her from the Upshaw Building. There was no reason why that should mean any-thing, but it was a place to begin, so he drove over and parked his car near the drugstore where Ollie had met Mary to go shopping.

No matter what had happened since, his every instinct told him to stick to the original case. If Ollie had begun to close in on somebody, all the troubles might stem from that.

The Upshaw Building had a café on the ground floor across the hall from a barbershop. Upstairs there were offices. In the foyer of the building there was a newsstand. Walking over, he began to study the magazines. There was a red-haired girl behind the counter and he smiled at her, then bought a package of gum. He was a big young man with an easy Irish smile, and the girl smiled back.

"Is there something I can find for you? Some particular magazine?"

"I was sort of watching for a friend of mine, a big guy with a wide face. Weighs about two-twenty. Has a scar on his jaw."

"Him? Sure, I remember him. He comes by a lot, although I don't know what for."

"Maybe to see you?" Joe smiled. "I couldn't blame him for that."

"He's nice. Married, though. I saw the ring on his finger."

So Ollie had been here more than once? And just standing around? "He's a friendly guy, my friend is. Likes to talk."

"Yes, he is. I like him. He's sort of like a big bear, but don't you tell him I said so."

"All warm and woolly, huh?"

She laughed. "He did talk a lot, but he's a good listener too." She glanced at Ragan again. "What business is he in? He told me he was looking for an office in this neighborhood."

"He's a lawyer, but he doesn't handle court cases. He works with other lawyers, prepares briefs, handles small cases. He likes to take it easy." Ragan paused. "Did he find an office?"

"I don't know. They're full up here, though he was interested in that office on the fourth floor. Nobody is ever around there, and he was hoping they'd move out. I told him I couldn't see why anybody would want an office they didn't use."

"Does seem kind of dumb, when you're paying rent. That's like buying a car and leaving it in the garage. It doesn't make a lot of sense."

"It sure doesn't. I think Mr. Bradford has been in no more than twice all year. I think he comes over to do his work in the evening. Mrs. Grimes, she cleans up in there, and she says he's been here several times at night. I asked her about the office, thinking maybe I could find out something for your friend. She said they had a special lock on the door, and their own cleaning man who comes once a week."

Joe Ragan steered the talk to the latest movies and her favorite songs, then strolled to the elevator and went to the fourth floor.

He had no idea what he was looking for, except that Ollie Burns had been interested, and Ollie was not a man who wasted his time. Getting off the elevator, he walked briskly down the hall as if looking for a particular place, his eyes scanning the names on the doors.

A closed door with a frosted-glass upper panel was marked JOHN J. BRADFORD, INVESTMENTS. There was a mail slot in the door.

Opposite was an open door where a young man sat at a desk. He was a short, heavyset young man with shoulders like a wrestler. He looked up sharply and there was something so intent about his gaze that Ragan was puzzled by it. He went on down the hall and into the office of JACOB KEENE, ATTORNEY-AT-LAW.

There was no receptionist in the outer office, but when he entered, she appeared. She was not a day over twenty, with a slim and lovely body in a gray dress that left little to the imagination, but much to think about and more to remember. "Yes?"

Ragan smiled. "Now that's the way I like to hear a girl begin a conversation. It saves a lot of trouble. Usually they only say it at the end of the evening."

"Oh, they do?" She looked him over coolly. "Yes, for you I imagine they would." Her smile vanished. "Now may I ask your business, please?"

"To see Mr. Keene. Is he in?"

"Just a minute." She turned, and her figure lost nothing by the move. "A gentleman to see you, Mr. Keene."

"Send him in." The voice was crabbed and brusque.

Joe Ragan stepped by the girl as she stood in the doorway, her gaze cool and unresponsive. Then she stepped out and drew the door shut.

Jacob Keene was a small man who gave the appearance of

being a hunchback, but was not. His face was long and gray, his head almost bald, and he had the eyes of a weasel. He took Ragan in at a glance, motioning to a chair. "Can't get girls these days that don't spend half their time thinking about men," he said testily. "Women aren't like they were in my day." He looked up at Joe, and suddenly the hatchet face broke into a lively smile and his eyes twinkled. "Damn the women of my day! What can I do for you?"

Ragan hesitated, then decided against any subterfuge. "Mr. Keene, I don't think I'm going to fool you, so I am not going to try. I'm looking for information and I'm willing to pay for it."

"Son"—Keene's eyes twinkled with deviltry—"your last phrase touches upon a subject that is close to my heart. Pay! What a beautiful word! Money, they say, is the root of all evil. All right, let's get to the root of things!"

"As a matter of fact, I don't have much money, but what I want will cost you no effort. Shall we say"—Ragan drew ten dollars from his pocket—"a retainer?"

The long and greedy fingers palmed the ten. "And now? This information?"

"I want to know all you know about John Bradford and his business."

Keene's little eyes brightened. Their light was speculative. "Ah? Bradford? Well, well!"

"Also, I'd like to know something about the business across the hall from Bradford, and about the young man at the desk."

Keene nodded. "Sit down, young man. We've much to talk about. Yes, yes, that young man! Notices everything, doesn't he? Most odd, I'd say, unless he's paid to notice. That could be, you know. Well, young man, you have paid me. A paltry sum, but significant, significant.

"Bradford is a man of fifty, I should say, although his walk seems to belie that age. He dresses well, conservative taste. He calls at his office about once a month. The cleaning man takes away the mail."

"The cleaning man?" Ragan was incredulous.

"Exactly. An interesting fact, young man, that has engaged

my fancy before this. Ah, yes, money. We all like money, and my guess would be that our friend down the hall has found a shortcut. People come to his door but they never knock or try to enter, they just slip envelopes through the mail slot."

Keene glanced at his calendar. "Wednesday. Four should come today, but they will not arrive together. They never arrive together. Three are women, one a man."

He drew a long cigar from a box in a drawer and bit off the end. "Nice place I have here, son. I see everyone and everything in that hallway. Two doors here, you see. The one you came in has my name on the door; the outside of this one is just marked 'Private.' If you noticed, there are mirrors on both sides of that door, and they allow me to see who is coming to my office before they arrive. If I don't want to see them, I just press a buzzer and my girl tells them I am out.

"Not much business these days, young man. I tell people I am retired, but I handle a few accounts, long-standing. Keeps me busy, and seeing what goes on in the hallway helps to while the time away."

Keene leaned forward suddenly. "Look, young man, here comes one of the women now."

She was tall, attractive, and no longer young. Ragan's guess was she was over fifty. She walked directly to the door of Bradford's office and dropped an envelope into the slot. Turning then, she went quickly down the hall as if in a hurry to be away. He was tempted to follow her, but on second thought he decided to wait and see what would happen.

It was twenty minutes before the second woman came. Joe Ragan sat up sharply, for this woman was Mary's acquaintance, Louella Chasen: the woman who, according to Stigler, Mary had asked about a divorce lawyer. She, too, walked to the door of Bradford's office and dropped an envelope through the slot.

Keene nodded, his small eyes bright and ferretlike. "See? What did I tell you? They never knock, just drop their envelopes and go away. An interesting business Mr. Bradford has, a very interesting business!"

Three women and a man, Keene had said, and that meant

another woman and man were still to come. He would wait. Scowling thoughtfully, Ragan shook out a cigarette and lighted it. He rarely smoked anymore, and intended to quit, but once in a while . . .

"Look into the mirror now," Keene suggested.

The big-shouldered young man had come into the hall and was looking around. He threw a sharp, speculative glance at Keene's office, then returned to his own.

A few minutes later a tall young man, fair-haired and attractive, dropped his envelope into the slot and left. It was almost a half hour later, and Joe was growing sleepy, when he glanced up to see the last visitor of the day.

She was young and she carried herself well, and Ragan sat up sharply, unbelieving. There was something familiar . . . She turned her face toward Keene's office. It was Angie Faherty, his own girlfriend. She dropped a letter into the slot and walked briskly away.

"Well," Keene said, "you've had ten dollars worth. Those are the four who come today. Three or four will come tomorrow, and so it is on each day. They bunch up, though, on Saturday and Monday. Can you guess why?"

"Saturday and Monday? Could be because they draw their pay on Saturday. They must be making regular investments."

Keene chuckled. "Investments? Maybe. That last young lady has been coming longest of all. Over six months now."

Ragan heaved himself from the chair. "See you later. If anything turns up, save the information for me. I'll be around."

"With more money," Keene said cheerfully. "With more money, young man. Let us grease the wheels of inflation, support the economy, all that."

Angie was drinking coffee at their favorite place when Ragan walked in, and she looked up, smiling. "Have a hard day, Joe? You look so serious."

"I'm worried about Mary. She's such a grand person, and they are going to make trouble for her."

"For Mary? How could they?"

He explained, and her eyes darkened with anger. "Why, that's silly! You and Mary! Of all things!"

"I know, but a district attorney could make it look bad. Where did Mary go when she left you, Angie? Where could she have been?"

"We'll ask her. Let's go out there now."

"All right." He got up. "Have you eaten?"

"No, I came right here from home. I didn't stop anywhere."

"Been waiting long?"

"Long enough to have eaten if I'd thought of it. As it was, all I got was the coffee."

That made the second lie. She had not been here for some time, and she had not come right here from home. He tried to give her the benefit of the doubt. Maybe the visit to the Upshaw Building was so much a habit that she did not consider it. Still, it was out of her way in coming here.

He wanted to believe her. Maybe that's why cops get cynical—they are lied to so often.

All the way out to Mary's, he mulled it over. Another idea kept coming into mind. He had to get into that office of Bradford's. He had to know what those letters contained.

Yet what did he have to tie them to Ollie's death? No more than the fact that Ollie had loitered in the Upshaw Building and had an interest in the fourth floor. Louella Chasen, who came to that office, had volunteered information. She had stated that Mary Burns was asking about a divorce. It was a flimsy connection, but it was a beginning.

He had no other clue to the case Ollie had been working on, unless he went back to the Towne suicide. Mark Stigler had mentioned that Ollie was interested in the Towne case, and it was at least a lead. The first thing tomorrow, he would investigate that aspect.

He remembered Alice Towne. Ollie had known her through an arrest he'd made in the neighborhood. She had been a slender, sensitive girl with a shy, sweet face and large eyes. Her unexplained suicide had been a blow to Ollie, for he liked people and had considered her a friend.

"You know, Joe," he had said once, "I've always thought that might have been my fault. She started to tell me something once, then got scared and shut up. I should have kept after her. Something was bothering her, and if I'd not been in so much of a hurry, she might have told me what it was."

Mary opened the door for them. Joe sat down with his hat in his hand. "Funeral tomorrow?" he asked gently.

Mary nodded. "Will you and Angie come together?"

"I thought maybe you'd like to have Angie with you," he suggested. "I'll be working right up to the moment, anyhow."

Mary turned to him. "Joe, you're working on this case, aren't you? Is there any way I can help?"

Ragan hated it, but he had to ask. "Mary, where did you go when you left Angie the night Ollie was murdered?"

Her face stiffened and she seemed to have trouble moving her lips. "You don't think I am guilty, Joe? You surely don't think I killed Ollie?"

"Mary, they are asking that question, and they will demand an answer."

"They've already asked," Mary said, "and I've refused to answer. I shall continue to refuse. It was private business, in a way, except that it did concern someone else. I can't tell you, Joe."

Their eyes held for a full minute and then Joe got up. "Okay, Mary, if you won't tell, you've got a reason, but please remember: That reason may be a clue. Now let me ask you— did you ever think of divorce?"

"No." Her eyes looked straight into Ragan's. "If people say that, they are lying. It is simply not true."

After Ragan left them, he thought about that. Knowing Mary, he would take her word for it, but would anybody else? In the face of two witnesses to the contrary and the fact that Ollie was shot with his own gun, Mary was in more trouble than she realized.

Moreover, he was getting an uneasy feeling. Al Brooks was hungry for newspaper notices and for advancement. He liked getting around town and liked spending money. A step up in rank would suit him perfectly. If he could solve the murder of Ollie Burns and pin it on Mary, he would not hesitate. He was a shrewd, smart man with connections.

Ragan now had several lines of investigation. The Towne

case was an outside and remote chance, but the Upshaw Building promised better results.

What had Angie been doing there? What did the mysterious letters contain? Who was Bradford?

Taking his car, Ragan drove across town to the Upshaw Building. He had his own ideas about what he would do now, and the law would not condone them. In Keene's office he had noticed the fire escape at his window extended to that of Bradford's office. The lock on the Bradford office door was a good one, and there was no easy way to open it in the time he would have.

After parking his car a block away, he walked up the street to the Upshaw Building. The night elevator man was drowsing over a newspaper, so Ragan slipped by him and went up the stairs to the fourth floor. He paused at the head of the steps, listening. There was not a sound. He walked down the hall to Keene's office and tried the door. It opened under his hand. Surprised and suddenly wary, he stepped inside.

The body of a man was slumped over Keene's desk.

He sat in a swivel chair, face against the desk, arms dangling at his sides. All this Ragan saw in sporadic flashes from an electric sign across the street. He closed the door behind him, studying the shadows in the room.

All was dark and still; the only light was that from the electric sign across the street. The corners were dark, and shadows lay deep along the walls and near the safe.

Ragan's gun was in its shoulder holster, reassuring in its weight. Careful to touch nothing, he leaned forward and spoke gently.

No reply, no movement. With a pen flash he studied the situation.

Jacob Keene was dead. There was a blotch of blood on his back where the bullet had emerged. There was, Ragan noted as he squatted on his heels, blood on Keene's knees and on the floor under him, but not enough. Keene's body, he believed, had been moved. Flipping on the light switch, he glanced quickly around the office to ascertain that it was empty. Then he began a careful search of the room.

Nothing was disturbed or upset. It was just as he had seen

it that afternoon, with the exception that Keene was dead. Careful to touch nothing, he knelt on the floor to examine, as best he could, the wound. The bullet had evidently entered low in the abdomen and ranged upward at an odd angle. The gun, which he had missed seeing, lay on the floor under Keene's right hand.

Suicide? That seemed to be the idea, but remembering the Keene of that afternoon, Ragan shook his head. Keene was neither in the mood for suicide nor the right man for it. No, this was murder. It was up to Ragan to call homicide, but he hesitated. There were other things to do first.

The first thing was to see the inside of that office of Bradford's. He believed Keene had been murdered elsewhere and brought here. He might have been killed trying to do just what Ragan was about to attempt.

Absolute silence hung over the building. Ragan put his ear to the wall, listening. There was no sound. Carefully he eased up the window. Four stories below, a car buzzed along the street, then there was silence. The windows facing him were all dark and empty. As he stepped out on the fire escape, a drop of rain touched his face. He glanced up at the lowering clouds. That would be good. If it rained, nobody would be inclined to glance up.

Flattened against the wall, he eased along to the next window. It was closed and there was no light from within. He tested the window, hoping it was unlocked. It was locked. He took the chewing gum from his mouth and plastered it against the glass near the lock, then tapped it with the muzzle of his gun. The glass broke but could not fall, as it stood against the lock itself. Easing a finger into the hole, he lifted the glass out very carefully, then unlocked the window and lifted it.

Slipping inside, he moved swiftly to the wall and waited, listening. Using utmost care, he began a minute examination.

For an hour he went through the office and found exactly nothing. Nothing? One thing only: a large, damp place where the floor had been wiped clean. Of blood? But blood can never be washed completely away in such a hurried job. Ragan knew what a lab test could prove.

The office was similar to any other, except that nothing seemed to have been used.

There was a typewriter, paper, carbons, extra ribbons, paperclips. The blotter on the desk was also new and unused. The filing cabinets contained varied references to mines and industries. Except for that damp place on the floor, all was as one might expect it to be.

Then he noticed something he had missed. A tiny, crumpled bit of paper lying on the floor under the desk, as though somebody had tossed it to the wastebasket and missed. Retrieving it, Ragan unfolded it carefully and flashed his light upon it.

Ollie Burns's phone number!

Here was a definite lead, but to where? Ragan stood in the middle of the office, wondering where to turn next. Somewhere nearby was the clue he needed. Suddenly there returned to his mind one of the titles of the mining companies he had glimpsed in leafing through the files. Wheeling about, he took a quick step to the filing cabinets and drew out the drawer labeled *T.*

In a moment he had it. *Towne Mining & Exploration.* Under it was a list of code words, then a list of sums of money indicating that fifty dollars per month had been paid until the first of the year, when the payments had been stepped up to one hundred dollars a month. Four months later there was this entry: *Account closed, 20 April.*

His heart was pounding. The suicide of Alice Towne had been discovered on the nineteenth of April!

Towne Mining & Exploration—was there such a firm?

A quick survey showed that on several of the drawers the names of well-known firms were listed, but no payments on any of them. They must be used as a blind, probably for blackmail.

What had Ollie told Mary? *There were two crimes nearly as bad as rape or murder.* Dope peddling and blackmail.

Who else had come to this office? Louella Chasen. Ragan drew out the drawer with the *C,* thumbing through it to a folder marked *Chasen Shipping*. A quick check showed that payments had progressed from ten dollars a month to one hundred over a period of four years.

Louella Chasen was the one who said she had recommended a divorce lawyer to Mary Burns. Would she lie to protect herself? If blackmail could force continual payments, would she not also perjure herself?

Hazel Upton, secretary to Denby, the divorce lawyer. Her name, thinly disguised, was here also.

It was the merest sound, no more than a whisper, as of clothing brushing paper, that interrupted him. Frozen in place, Ragan listened. He heard it again. It came from the office of Jacob Keene, where the murdered attorney still lay.

Ragan's hand went to his gun, a reassuring touch only. This was neither the time nor the place for a gun. The window stood open, and so did the window in the Keene office. If someone was there, he would see the open window, and if that someone leaned out, a glance would show this window to be open too. And if the man who was in the next room happened to be the murderer . . .

Even as he thought of that, Ragan realized there was something else in the files he must see: the file on Angie Faherty.

There was no time for that now, and the door to the hall was out of the question. The only exit from the office was the way he had come.

Like a wraith, he slipped from the filing cabinet to the deep shadow near the safe, then to the blackness of the corner near the window. Even as he reached it he heard the scrape of a shoe on the iron of the fire escape. The killer was coming in.

It was very still. Outside, a whisper of rain was falling and there was a sound of traffic on wet pavement. The flashing electric sign did not light this room, and Ragan waited, poised for action.

A stillness of death hung over the building. The killer on the fire escape was waiting, too, and listening for some movement from Ragan.

Did he know Ragan was there? And who he was? It was a good question.

With a quick glance at the window, Ragan gauged the distance to the telephone. Moving as softly as possible, he glided to the phone. With his left hand he moved the phone to the chair, then lifted the receiver.

Dialing zero, he waited. Tires whined on the pavement below and he spoke quickly. "Police department! Quick!"

In a moment, a husky voice answered. Ragan spoke softly. "Get this the first time. There's a prowler on the fire escape of the Upshaw Building!"

His voice was a low whisper, but the desk sergeant got it, all right. Ragan repeated it and then eased the receiver back on the cradle. From his new position he could see the dim outline of a figure on the fire escape, as whoever it was edged closer.

The police would be here in a minute or two. If only the man on the fire escape would—

He heard the wail of sirens far off, and almost smiled. It would be nip-and-tuck now. The siren whined closer and Ragan heard a muffled curse. Cars slid into the street below and he heard the clang of feet on the fire escape, running down.

For a breath-catching instant he waited, then ducked out of one window and into the next, even as the police spotlight hit the wall. A moment before the glare reached him, he was safely inside. From below he heard a shout. "There he is!" They had spotlighted the other man.

Ragan ducked out the door and ran down the hall, taking the back stairs three steps at a time. When he reached the main floor he saw the watchman craning his neck at the front door, trying to see what was happening. On cat feet, Ragan slipped up behind him. "Did they get him?" he asked.

The watchman jumped as if he'd been shot. He turned, his face white, and Ragan flashed his badge. "Gosh, Officer, you scared the daylights out of me! What's going on?"

"Prowler reported on the fire escape of this building. I'm looking for him."

Sergeant Casey came hurrying to the door. When he saw Ragan he slowed down. Casey was one of Ragan's buddies, for this was a burglary detail. "Hi, Ragan! I didn't know you were here!"

"Did you get him?"

"We didn't, but Brooks almost did."

"Al Brooks?" Ragan's scalp tightened. What had Brooks been doing here? Tailing him? Ragan hadn't thought they might put a tail on him, but Brooks was just the man to do it.

"He was on the street and saw somebody on the fire escape. He started up after him just as we drove up. Fellow got away, I guess."

"Ain't been nobody here," the watchman said. "Only Mr. Bradford, and he left earlier."

"What time was he here?" Ragan asked.

"Maybe eight o'clock. No later than that."

Eight? It was now almost one A.M., and Keene had not been dead long when Ragan found him. Certainly no more than an hour, at a rough guess. His body hadn't even been cold.

Al Brooks came around the corner with two patrol-car officers. He stopped abruptly when he saw Ragan. He was suddenly very careful. Ragan could see the change. "How are you, Joe? I wasn't expecting to see you."

"I get around." Ragan shook out a cigarette.

Casey interrupted. "We'd better go through the building, Joe, now that we're here. The man might be hiding upstairs."

"Good idea," Ragan said. "Let's go!"

Everything was tight and shipshape all the way to Keene's office. Ragan was letting Casey and a couple of his boys precede him. It was his idea to let them find the body. It was Casey who did.

"Hey!" he called. "Dead man here!"

Ragan and Brooks came on the run. "Looks like suicide," Brooks commented. "I doubt if this had anything to do with the prowler."

"Doesn't look like he even got in here," Casey said.

"But the window's op—" Brooks stared. The window was closed. "You know," he said, "when I started up the fire escape, I'd have sworn this window was open."

He returned to the body at the desk. "Looks like suicide," he repeated. "The gun's right where he dropped it."

"Except that it wasn't suicide," Ragan said quietly. "And, Al, you'd better leave this one for homicide." He smiled. "The autopsy will tell us for sure, but this man seems to have been stabbed before he was shot."

"Where do you get that idea?" Brooks demanded.

"Look." Ragan indicated a narrow slit in the shirt, just above the wound. "My guess is he was killed by the stab wound, then shot to make the bullet follow the stab wound. I'll bet the gun belongs to Keene."

Brooks looked around. "How did you know his name?"

"It's on the door. Jacob Keene, attorney-at-law. We don't actually know this is Keene, of course, but I'm betting it is."

Brooks shut up, but the man was disturbed and he was angry. Al Brooks had a short fuse, and it was burning.

Ragan was doing some wondering. What about that prowler? What had become of him? He was carrying on a swift preliminary examination of the office, without disturbing anything, when Mark Stigler arrived. He glanced from Ragan to Brooks. "Lots of talent around," he said. "What is it, murder or suicide?"

The slit in the material of the shirt was barely visible, but Ragan indicated it. "A clumsy attempt to cover up a murder," Ragan commented.

"Could be," Stigler agreed. "Seems kind of farfetched, though. Who was this guy?"

"From his files, he was a sort of shyster, handling a good many minor cases in the past, but he changed here lately, or seemed to. He's semiretired, handling only a few legal affairs for various people."

Stigler's crew went to work while Stigler chewed on a toothpick, listened to the talk, and studied the situation. Al Brooks shoved his hat back on his head and took over.

He had been down on the street when he looked up and saw a prowler outside a window on the third floor. Just as he started up, he heard sirens and the patrol cars appeared. "And just about that time I ran into Joe Ragan. He was already here."

Stigler glanced at Ragan. "How are you coming on the Burns job?"

"Good enough. I'll have it in the bag by the end of the week."

Stigler eyed him thoughtfully. "We've got a strong case against his wife. Brooks thinks she did it. She or somebody close to her."

That meant Ragan, of course.

"Brooks doesn't know what he's talking about. Mary loved her husband, loved him in a way Brooks couldn't even understand."

Brooks's laugh was unpleasant. "For your sake, I hope you are right, but Mary Burns is in this up to her neck, and there *might* just be somebody else involved!"

Ragan walked over to him. "Listen, Al, you do your job and we'll do ours, but just be sure that if you try to pin anything on any friends of mine, you can prove your case. If you've got the goods, all right, but you start a frame and I'll bust you wide open!"

"Cut it out, Ragan!" Stigler said sharply. "Any more talk like that and you'll draw a suspension. I won't have fighting on any job of mine."

"Anyhow," Brooks said quietly, "I don't think you could do it."

Ragan just looked at him. Someday he would have to take Brooks, and he would take him good. Until then he could wait.

Ragan repeated what little he had to Stigler, saying nothing about his previous entry. However, he lingered after Brooks had gone to add a few words.

"I talked to Keene," he said, "and he was a cagey old bird. He gave me the impression that something was going on here that wasn't strictly kosher. He was suspicious of some of the activities on this floor."

"Suspicious? How? Of what?"

"That I don't know, except that the office next to him seems to have been used rarely, and then at night. Although people did come to the door and drop envelopes through the slot."

"So? There's a law says somebody has to use an office because he pays rent?"

Ragan turned away, but Stigler stopped him. "Stay away from Al Brooks, do you hear?" Then, in a rare bit of confidence, he added, "I don't like him any better than you do, but he's been making points with the Commissioners."

Ragan walked back to his car, approaching with care. From now on he must walk cautiously indeed. He was learning things, and he had a feeling it was realized. What he wanted now was to be away where he could think, if he could only—An idea came to him that was insane, and yet . . .

Where had Al Brooks come from? What was he doing in this area, at this hour? His explanation was clear and logical enough, yet a prowler had been on the fire escape, and when the spotlight came on, it had picked up Al Brooks.

Ragan considered that and a few other things about Al Brooks. He dressed better than any man on the force, drove a good car, and lived well. Ragan shook his head. He must be careful and not be influenced by his dislike for Brooks or by Brooks's obvious dislike for him. And the man did have a good record with the department.

It was Al Brooks, however, who had first suggested that Mary Burns might have killed her husband. It was also Al Brooks who had reported seeing Mary coming out of a divorce lawyer's office.

Now that he was thinking about it, a lot of ideas came to mind. Stopping his car at the curb in front of his apartment, Ragan got out and started for the door. There was a strange car parked at the curb a few doors away, and for some reason it disturbed him. He walked over to it. There was no one inside, and it was not locked. He looked at the registration on the steering column. *Valentine Lewis, 2234 Herald Place.*

The name meant nothing to him. He turned away and walked to his private entrance and fitted the key into the lock. As he opened the door he was wondering what the blackmailer could have that would influence both Hazel Upton and Louella Chasen to start the divorce rumor, and if Brooks—

He stepped through the door, and the roof fell on him.

Wildly, grabbing out with both hands, Ragan fell to his knees. He had been slugged and he could not comprehend what was happening, then there was a smashing blow on his skull and he seemed to be slipping down a long slide into darkness.

When he fought his way out of it, he was lying on the floor and his head felt like a balloon. Gray light was filtering into the room. It must be daylight.

He lay still, trying to focus his thoughts. Then he got to his hands and knees, and then to his feet. He staggered to the sofa and sat down hard.

His skull was pounding as if an insane snare drummer were at work inside. His mouth felt sticky and full of cotton. He lifted his head and almost blacked out. Slowly he stared around the room. Nothing had been taken that he could see. He felt for his handkerchief and realized his pockets had been turned inside out.

Staggering to the door, he peered into the street. The strange car was gone.

"Val Lewis," he muttered grimly, "if you aren't guilty, you'd better have a mighty good story, and if you slugged me, God help you!"

Somehow he got out of his clothes and into a shower, and then tumbled into bed. His head was cut in two places from the blows, but what he wanted most was sleep.

It was well past noon when he was awakened by the telephone.

It was Angie. "Joe!" She sounded frightened and anxious. "What's happened? Where are you?"

"I must be home. When the phone rang, I answered it. Where are you?"

"Where am I?" Her tone was angry. "Where would I be? Don't you remember our luncheon date?"

"Frankly, I didn't. I got slugged on the head last night, and—"

"At least," she interrupted, "that's an original excuse!"

"And true. I was visiting an office in the Upshaw Building, and then—"

Her gasp was audible. "Joe? Did you say the Upshaw Building?"

"That's right." Suddenly he remembered her visit there while he and Keene had watched. "Some people up there play rough, honey. A lawyer was murdered up there last night. He knew too much and was too curious about somebody named Bradford."

She was silent. "The slugging," he added, "happened after I got home. I think somebody wanted to find out if I'd carried anything away from that building."

That idea had come to him while he was talking, but it made sense. What other reason was there? Thinking it over, it struck him as remarkable that he had not been killed out of hand. They had probably killed Ollie Burns for little more, or even for less.

She still did not speak, so he asked, "How's Mary? Is she all right?"

"Joe!" She was astonished. "You didn't know? She was arrested this morning. I believe it was Al Brooks."

Brooks? Ragan's grip tightened on the phone until his fist turned white. "All right, that does it. I'm going to blow everything loose now."

"What are you going to do?" Her voice sounded anxious.

"Do? Their whole case is built on a bunch of lies and perjury. I know that Hazel Upton and Louella Chasen were forced into this by a blackmailer."

"Joe, did you say a . . . blackmailer?"

"Yes, Angie, a blackmailer. The same people who hounded Alice Towne to death murdered Ollie Burns and Jacob Keene."

"You mean you *know* all that? Can you prove it?"

"Maybe not right now, but I will, honey, I will!"

It was not until after he hung up that he realized he was still groggy from the blows on the head, and that he had talked too much. He was still suffering from the concussion, but he was mad, also. He had been a damned fool to say so much. After all, she had been blackmailed, too.

He dressed halfway and then went into the bathroom to shave.

His razor smoothed the beard from his face while he turned the case over in his mind. He decided to start with Val Lewis, then work his way to Hazel Upton and Louella Chasen. Also, he was going to talk with that luscious job Keene had for a secretary. And with the sharp-eyed lad who kept an eye on Bradford's door.

For the next two hours Ragan was busy. He visited and questioned several people and spent time checking the files of the *Times*. Also, he visited the address that Valentine Lewis had.

The door was answered by a dyspeptic-looking blonde with the fading shadow of a black eye. She wore a flowered kimono that concealed little.

"I'm looking for Valentine Lewis." Ragan spoke politely. "Is he in?"

"What do you want to see him for?"

"Veterans Administration," Ragan said vaguely.

"That's a lousy joke," she replied coldly. "Val was in San Quentin during the war. Come again."

"Police department." Ragan flashed his badge and started to push by her.

She yelled, strident and angry. "You get out of here, copper! You got no search warrant!"

Ragan took one from his pocket. She didn't get a chance to see more than the top of it, for it was just a form, partly filled out.

She stepped back and asked no more questions, muttering to herself. Ragan needed only a glance around to see that Lewis had enough guns to start World War III.

It was all he needed. He called headquarters and suggested they come down with a warrant for Val Lewis. Any recent ex-convict with a gun in his possession was on his way back to jail.

Blue Eyes stood there looking mean. "You think you're smart, don't you?"

"Whatever I am," he said, "I am not foolish enough to buck the law."

"No," she said, sneering. "You're just a dope. You cops

aren't smart enough to make any money, you just crab it for others."

"You'll have to be plenty smart if you go after Val," she said venomously. "Tough, too. I'd like to see you try it!"

The police cars were arriving. "Lady," Ragan said, "that is just what I am going to do. He works in the Upshaw Building, doesn't he?"

Her surprise showed him he was right. "I am going to send you to headquarters, and then I'm going after your Val. In case you don't know, he slugged me last night. Now it will be my turn."

"Oh? So you're Joe Ragan?" Her face stiffened, realizing she'd made a miscue. "I hope he burns you down!"

Mark Stigler was with them when they came in. He glanced grimly at the assortment of guns. "What is this?" he asked Ragan. "I thought you were working on the Burns murder."

"This is part of it," Ragan said. "See what the girl has to say. I doubt if she wants to be an accessory."

She was really frightened now, but Stigler ignored her. "You think this Val Lewis did it?"

"If he didn't, he knows who did."

All the way to the Upshaw Building, Mark Stigler chewed on his dead cigar while Ragan laid it out for him. He built up the blackmail background, reminded him how Ollie had been bothered by the Towne suicide, and how Ollie had worried the case like a dog over a bone. He told Stigler of his idea that Ollie had been murdered because he had stumbled into the blackmail ring.

He explained about the Bradford office and the letters dropped there and who dropped them. The one thing he did not mention was Angie. She was still his girl, and if she was being blackmailed, he'd cover for her if she wasn't otherwise involved.

"You think there was money in those envelopes?"

"That's right. I believe all those records in the filing cabinets, with the exception of a few obvious company names, are blackmail cases. From what I can remember—and I had only a few hasty glances—the income must run to thousands of dollars a month.

"They weren't bleeding just big shots, but husbands and wives, clerks, stenographers, beauty operators, everybody. I think Bradford, whoever he is, is a smart operator, but he had somebody else with him, somebody who knew Ollie."

"Somebody who could get close to him?"

"Yes, and somebody who believed Ollie was getting close to a solution. Also, it had to be somebody who could get into his house or his locker for that gun."

Stigler rolled his cigar in his lips. "You're telling a good story, but do you have any facts? It all sounds good, but what we need is evidence!"

At the Upshaw Building, Stigler loitered around the corner and let Ragan go after Val Lewis. Lewis was sitting at the open door, as usual. As Ragan turned toward the door of the Bradford office, Lewis got up and came around his desk. "What do you want?" he demanded.

"What business is it of yours?" Ragan asked. "I want into this office. Also"—he turned, with some expectation of what was coming—"I want you for assault and murder!"

Lewis was too confident and too hotheaded for his own good. He started a punch and it came fast, but Ragan rolled his head and let the punch go around it, and hooked a wicked right to the solar plexus that dropped Lewis's mouth open in a desperate gasp for breath. The left hook that followed collapsed the bridge of Lewis's nose as if it were made of paper.

He was big, bigger than Ragan, built like an all-American lineman, but the fight was knocked out of him. Stigler walked up. "You got a key to this place?"

"No, I ain't. Bradford's got it."

"To hell with that!" Ragan's heel drove hard against the door beside the lock. It held, a second and a third time, then he put his shoulder to it and pushed it open. While an officer took Lewis to a patrol car, Ragan went to the filing cabinet.

It was empty.

A second and third were empty, too. Mark Stigler looked from Ragan to the smashed door. "Boy, oh, boy! What now?"

Ragan felt sick. The files had been removed sometime

after he left the place. By now they were hidden or destroyed, and there would be a lot of explaining to do about this door.

Stigler glared at him. "When you pull a boner, you sure pull a lulu!"

"Mark," Ragan said, "get the lab busy on that floor. This is where Keene was murdered. Right there."

"How do you know?"

Ragan swallowed. "Because I was in here last night after the murder."

Stigler's eyes were like gimlets. "*After* the murder? Were you the prowler?"

"No." Ragan filled him in on the rest of it. His meeting with Keene, his return, the discovery of the body, and the mysterious watcher outside.

"Have you any idea who that was?" Stigler fixed him with a cold eye.

"I might have, but I'd rather not say right now."

Oddly, Stigler did not follow that up. He walked around the office, looking into this and that. He was still puttering about when Ragan looked up to see Keene's receptionist standing in the door. "Hi, honey," she said cheerfully. "This is the first time I ever saw this door open."

"Who are you working for now?"

She smiled. "Nobody. Came up to clear my desk and straighten up some work that's left. I'll be out of a job. Need a secretary?"

"Lady," Ragan said, "I could always find a place for you!"

Stigler turned and looked at her from under his heavy brows. "What do you know about this Bradford?" he asked.

"Bradford?" She smiled. "I wondered if you'd ever ask." She indicated Ragan. "Will it do him any good if I talk?"

"Plenty," Stigler said with emphasis.

"All right." She was suddenly all business. "I know that the man who has been calling himself Bradford for the past three months is not the Bradford who opened this office. He is a taller, broader man.

"Furthermore, I know he was in my office after closing time last night, and must have been there after Mr. Keene was murdered."

Stigler took the cigar from his mouth. "How do you figure that?"

"Look." She crossed to the wastebasket below the water cooler and picked out a paper cup. "The man who calls himself Bradford has strong fingers. When he finishes drinking, he squeezes the cup flat and pushes the bottom up with his thumb. It is a habit he has."

She picked up the wastebasket and showed a half-dozen cups to Stigler. He glanced at them and walked next door to Keene's office. She picked up the basket from the cooler and said, "See? One cup left intact, one crushed. On top of the cup that Mr. Keene threw away is this crushed one."

She paused. "I don't know anything about such things, but you might find fingerprints on those cups."

Stigler chewed on his cigar. "We could use you," he said, "in the department."

Outside in the street, Stigler said little. He was mulling something over in his mind. Ragan knew the man and knew he was bothered by something. Finally, Stigler said, as much to himself as to Ragan, "Do you think those records were destroyed?"

"I doubt it. If what that girl says is true, he hasn't been running this business that long. He would need the files to use for himself. I have a suspicion," Ragan added, "that whoever he is, he muscled in."

Stigler nodded. He took the cigar from his teeth. "Joe, I don't know exactly where you're going, but I won't push this case against Mary Burns until I hear more from you. In the meantime, I think we'll check the dead and missing for the last few months."

Stigler got into his car and rolled away, and Ragan stared after him, then realized somebody was at his elbow. It was the receptionist with the figure. "Can I help? I've some free time now."

"Not unless you can remember something more about Bradford and that setup. Did Keene know any more about them?"

"He was curious about a girl who came there, and he had me follow her once."

"What sort of girl?"

"A slender girl with red hair. She wore a green suit and was quite attractive."

For a moment Ragan just stood there. It made no sense, no sense at all.

His eyes turned to the blonde. "What's your name, honey?"

"I was wondering if you even cared," she said, smiling. There was no humor in her eyes, just something wistful, somehow very charming and very young. "I'm Marcia Mahan, and I meant what I said about helping."

Ragan did not know what to do. There was little evidence against Mary. They had the testimony of Hazel Upton and Louella Chasen, but how would they stand up under severe cross-examination? Angie Faherty agreed she had gone to the rest room but had not been there at the time of the killing.

The gun was Ollie's own, so with work they might build a stiff case against Mary. The worst of it was that if she was tried and acquitted, a few would always have their doubts.

He could not stop now. Ollie would have done it for him. Now he was beginning to see where the arrows pointed, and it made him feel sick and empty. One can control events only up to a point.

Other things were clicking into place now. His memory was a good one and had been trained by police work. He remembered something he had overlooked. In those files there had been one with the title BYSTEN PACKING COMPANY.

One of the big cases Al Brooks had broken was that of Clyde Bysten, a blackmail case.

Ragan threw his cigarette into the gutter. He was smoking too much since this case began. "All right, if you really want to help, you can." He wrote an address on a slip of paper. "This is where Alice Towne worked. I want a list of the employees at that office during the time she worked there. Can you do that?"

Marcia nodded. "No problem."

"And meet me at the Peacock Bar at four."

Grabbing a cab, he headed for the bank. Within minutes he was closeted with a vice-president he knew and a few minutes later was receiving the information needed. When he left the bank, he felt he had been kicked in the stomach.

Yet his job was only beginning, and from then until four, he was going through files of newspapers, and using the telephone to save his legs, to say nothing of gasoline. He called business firms, and people he knew, and checked charge accounts and property lists. By four o'clock he had a formidable list of information, blackening information that left him feeling worse than he had ever felt in his life.

Outside the cocktail lounge he waited, thinking over what lay before him. He could see no end in sight. Once more he was going to enter an apartment without a search warrant, only this time he was hoping to find nothing. He was, in fact, planning to enter two apartments.

Marcia was waiting for him, a cup of coffee before her. She placed the list on the table and Ragan scanned it. His heart almost stopped when he saw the name, the one he was positive he would see, and feared to see.

"You look as if you lost your best friend," Marcia said.

———

WHEN RAGAN CAME into homicide, Stigler was behind his desk. "I think I've got it." He shoved a card at Ragan. "Sam Bayless. He did two terms for con games but was hooked into one blackmailing offense that could not be pinned on him. Smooth operator, fits the description we have of Bradford."

"Dead?"

"Found shot to death in the desert near Palmdale. Shot four times in the chest with a .38. We have one of the slugs."

"Good! Can you check it with that gun?"

"We will—somehow. Have you got anything more?"

"Too much." Ragan hesitated, then nodded. "Before the night's over I believe we can cinch this case."

———

IT WAS HIS duty, his duty as a police officer and as a friend of Ollie Burns, a good friend and a decent officer, but he felt like a traitor. It was late when he went to the place near the park and stopped his car. He had rented a car for the evening, and with Marcia Mahan beside him they would seem to be any couple doing a little private spooning, to use an old-fashioned term that he liked.

"What do you want me to do when you go in?" she asked.

"Sit still. If they come back, push the horn button."

The door of the apartment house opened and a man and a woman came out and got into a car. It was Al Brooks—hard, reckless, confident. He did not want to look at the girl, but he had to. It was Angie Faherty.

For an instant, her face was fully under the street light and Ragan saw her eyes come toward his car. She said something to Brooks. Ragan turned toward Marcia. "Come on, honey, let's make it look good."

She came into his arms as if she belonged there, and she did not have to make it look good. It *was* good. The first time their lips met, his hair seemed to curl all the way to the top of his head.

Brooks came across the street toward them, and turned his flashlight into the car. Ragan's face was out of sight against her shoulder, and she pulled her head up long enough to say, "Beat it, bud! Can't you see we're busy?"

Brooks chuckled and walked away and they heard him make some laughing remark to Angie as they got into their car. Then they were driving away.

Marcia unwound herself. "Well! If this is the kind of work detectives do . . ."

"Come here," Ragan replied cheerfully. "They might come back."

"I think you'd better go inside and see what you don't want to see. I'll wait."

Opening the door was no trick. Once inside he took a quick look around. It was all very familiar, too familiar, even to the picture of himself on the piano. That picture must have given Brooks many a laugh.

His search was fast, thorough, and successful. The files were lying in plain sight on a shelf in the closet. He was bundling them up when the horn honked.

They came fast, because when he turned around, he heard the key in the lock. Ragan grabbed the files. One bunch slipped and he reached to catch it and the door slammed open. Al Brooks, his face livid, was framed in the door.

Slowly, Ragan put the files down. "Well, Al, here it is. We've been waiting for this."

"Sure." There was concentrated hatred in his eyes. "And I'm going to like it!"

Brooks had his gun in his hand and Ragan knew he was going to kill.

Brooks fired as Ragan started for him, and something burned Ragan along the ribs. Ragan knocked Brooks back over a chair and went over it after him. They came up slugging. Brooks backed up and Ragan hooked a left to the mouth that smeared it to bloody shreds against his teeth. Brooks ducked to avoid the payoff punch and took it over the eye instead of on the chin. The blow cut to the bone and showered him with blood.

Shoving him away, Ragan swung again and Brooks jerked up a knee for his groin. Turning to avoid it, Ragan turned too far, and Al got behind him, running a forearm across his throat. Grabbing Al's hand and elbow, Ragan dropped to one knee, throwing Brooks over his shoulder.

"What's the matter, chum? Can't you take it? Come on, tough boy! You wanted it, now you're getting it!"

Brooks came in again, but Ragan stabbed a left into his face, then belted him in the wind. Al stumbled forward and Ragan grabbed a handful of hair and jerked Brooks's head down to meet his upcoming knee. It was a neat touch, but hard on the features.

The door smashed open and Mark Stigler came in. Casey was right behind him. "Got him?" Stigler asked.

Ragan gestured and Stigler looked. "Man, oh, man! I've seen a few, but this!"

"There are the files." Ragan pointed. "You'll find the Towne, Chasen, and Upton files there, and a lot of others." He glanced out the door. "Did you . . . ? I mean, was Angie . . . ? What happened to her?"

"She's out there. The girl from Keene's office is with her."

Angie did not look as lovely as he remembered her. In fact,

her eyes were venomous. Her hair was all out of shape and she had a puffed lip.

"What hit you?" Ragan asked.

Marcia smiled pleasantly. "A girl named Mahan. She gave me trouble, so I socked her."

Angie said nothing. She had double-crossed him and helped to frame Mary Burns, but it was not in him to hate her. "Whatever made you pull a stunt like this?" he asked.

She looked up. "You can't prove a thing. You can't blame this on me."

"Yes, we can, Angie," he replied gently. "It is all sewed up. You killed Ollie Burns, then smeared him with lipstick. It was Al who called, but you who met him after you got Mary called away. Mary thought you were in trouble, and when she came back and you were gone, she tried to cover for you. She never dreamed you had killed Ollie.

"You took the gun from their home. Al Brooks wouldn't have had access to it. You would.

"You had a good setup after Al came in with you. You were in it with Bayless or Bradford. You worked with Alice Towne and you wormed the information out of her that she was being blackmailed.

"On one of his vice raids, Al Brooks picked up some information and got hep to what you were doing, and declared himself in. Then he killed Bayless, and you two took over the business. He killed Keene when he caught him in your office after hours, then shot him to make it appear to be suicide."

"Got it all figured, have you?" Brooks said. "Wait until I get out!"

Stigler just looked at him. "They don't get out of the gas chamber, Al. We've got one of the bullets you put into Bayless. It checks with your gun."

"The information that led to your arrest of Latko, Al, came from your blackmailing racket. You had a good thing going there.

"We checked some charge accounts of yours, Angie. Your bank accounts, too. We have all the information we need. We know your brother did time with Bayless."

"My brother?" Her eyes turned wild. "What do you know about him?"

"We picked him up today, and his girlfriend talked. Anyway, we found him with enough guns to outfit an army. He was using the name Valentine Lewis."

Later, when Al Brooks was being booked, he took a paper cup from the cooler and drank, then compressed the cup and pushed the bottom in with his thumb; an unconscious gesture. Seeing it, Stigler looked over at Ragan.

Marcia was standing beside Ragan. "Joe? Shouldn't we go see that officer's wife?"

"All right."

"She's a friend of yours, isn't she?"

"One of the best."

"Will she like me?"

"Who wouldn't?"

They drove in silence and then he said, "How about dinner tomorrow night?"

"At my place?"

"I'll be there."

There was no moon, but they did not need one. There was a little rain, but they did not mind.

COLLECT FROM A CORPSE

PIKE AMBLER CALLED the department from the Fan Club at ten in the morning, and Lieutenant Wells Ryerson turned it over to Joe Ragan. "Close this one fast," he said, "and give me an airtight case."

With Captain Bob Dixon headed for early retirement, Ryerson was acting in charge of the burglary detail. If he made a record, his chance of taking Dixon's job was good.

Ragan knew the Fan Club. A small club working in the red, it had recently zoomed into popularity because of the dancing of Luretta Pace. Ragan was thinking of that when he arrived at the club with Sam Blythe and young Lew Ryerson. Sam was a veteran, Lew a tall young man with a narrow face and shrewd eyes. He had been only four months in the department.

Sam Blythe glanced at the hole chopped in the ceiling and then at the safe. "An easy one, Joe. Entry through the ceiling, a punch job on the safe, nothing touched but money, and the floor swept clean after the job was finished." He walked over to the wastebasket and took from it a crumpled wad of crackly paper. "And here's the potato-chip sack, all earmarks of a Pete Slonski job."

Ragan rubbed his jaw but did not reply.

"It checks with the *modus operandi* file, and it's as open and shut as the Smiley case. I'll call headquarters and have them put out a pickup on Slonski."

"Take it easy," Ragan said. "Let's look this over first."

"What's the matter?" Lew Ryerson was like his brother, too impatient to get things done. "Like Sam said, Slonski's written all over it."

"Yeah, it does look like it."

"It is his work. I'm going to call in."

"It won't do any good," Ragan said mildly. "This job would even fool Slonski, but he didn't do it."

Sam Blythe was puzzled, Ryerson irritated. "How can you be sure?" Ryerson demanded. "It's obvious enough to me."

"This isn't a Slonski job," Ragan said, "unless ghosts can crack safes. Pete Slonski was killed last night in Kansas City."

"What?" Ryerson was shocked. "How do you know that?"

"It was in the morning paper, and as we have a charge against him, I wired the FBI. They checked the fingerprints. It was Slonski, all right, dead as a herring. And dead for a couple of hours before they found him."

Blythe scowled. "Then something is funny. I'd have sworn Slonski did this job."

"So would I," Ragan said, "and now I am wondering about Smiley. He swears he's innocent, and if ever I saw a surprised man, it was Smiley when I put the cuffs on him."

"They all claim to be innocent," Ryerson said. "That case checked out too well, and you know as well as I do you can identify a crook by his method of operation as by his finger-prints."

"Like this one?" Ragan asked mildly. "This looks like a Slonski job, but Slonski's dead and buried."

"Smiley had a long record," Blythe said uneasily. "I never placed any faith in his going straight."

"Neither did I," Ragan admitted, "but five years and no trouble. He'd bought a home, built up a business, and not even a traffic count against him."

"On the other hand," Ryerson said, "he needs money. Maybe he's just been playing it smart."

"Crooks aren't smart," Ragan objected. "No man who will take a chance on a stretch in the pen is smart. They all make mistakes. They can't beat their own little habits."

"Maybe we've found a smart one," Ryerson suggested. "Maybe he used to work with Slonski and made this one look like him for a cover."

"Slonski worked alone," Blythe said. "Let's get some pic-tures and get on with it."

Joe Ragan prowled restlessly while Ryerson got his pictures.

Turning from the office, he walked out through the empty bar and through the aisles of stacked chairs and tables. Mounting the steps from the street, he entered the studio, from which entry had been gained to the office below.

Either the door had been unlocked with a skeleton key, or the lock had been picked. There was a reception room whose walls were covered by pictures of sirens with shadows in the right places and bare shoulders. In the studio itself, there was a camera, a few reflectors, a backdrop, and assorted props. The hole had been cut through the darkroom floor.

Squatting on his heels, Joe Ragan studied the workmanship. A paper match lay on the floor, and he picked it up. After a glance, he put it in his pocket. The hole would have taken an hour to cut, and as the club closed at two A.M. and the personnel left right after, the burglar must have entered between three and five o'clock in the morning.

Hearing footsteps, Ragan turned his head to see a plump and harassed photographer. Andre Gimp fluttered his hands. "Oh, this is awful! Simply awful! Who could have done it?"

"Don't let it bother you. Look around and see if anything is missing and be careful you don't forget and walk into that hole."

Ragan walked to the door and paused, lighting a cigarette. He was a big man, a shade over six feet, with wide, thick shoulders and big hands. His hair was rumpled, but despite his size, there was something surprisingly boyish about him.

Ryerson had borrowed him a few days before from the homicide squad, as Ragan had been the ace man on the burglary detail before being transferred to homicide.

Ragan ran his fingers through his hair and returned to the club. He was remembering the stricken look on Ruth Smiley's face when he arrested her husband. There had been a feeling then that something was wrong, yet detail for detail, the Smiley job had checked as this one checked with Slonski.

Leaving Lew Ryerson and Sam Blythe to question Ambler, he returned to headquarters. He was scowling thoughtfully when he walked into Wells Ryerson's office. The lieutenant looked up, his eyes sharp with annoyance.

"Ragan, when will you learn to knock? What do you want?"

"Sorry." He dropped into a chair. "Are you satisfied with the Smiley case?" Briefly, he explained their discoveries at the Fan Club.

Wells Ryerson waited him out with obvious irritation. "That has nothing to do with Smiley. The man had no alibi. He was seen in the vicinity of the crime within thirty minutes of its occurrence. We know his record, and we know he needs money. The tools that did the job came from his shop. The D.A. is satisfied, and so am I."

Ragan leaned his thick forearms on the chair arms. "Nevertheless," he said, "I don't like it. This job today checks with Slonski, but he's dead, so where does that leave us with Smiley? Or with Blackie Miller or Ed Chalmers?"

Ryerson's anger and dislike were evident as he replied. "Ragan, I see what you're trying to do. You know Dixon is about to retire, and if you can mess up my promotion, you can step up yourself.

"Well, you go back to homicide. We don't need you or anybody like you. As of this moment, you are off the burglary detail."

Ragan shrugged. "Sorry you take it this way. I don't want your job. I asked for the transfer to homicide, but I don't like to see innocent men go to prison."

"Innocent?" Ryerson's tone was thick with contempt. "You talk like a schoolboy! Jack Smiley was in reform school at sixteen and in the pen when he was twenty-four. He was short of cash, and he simply reverted to type. Go peddle your papers in homicide."

Joe Ragan closed the door behind him, his ears burning. He knew how Ryerson felt, but he could not forget the face of Ruth Smiley or the facts that led to the arrest of her husband. Smiley, Miller, and Chalmers had all been arrested by virtue of information from the M.O. file.

It was noon and lunch time. He hesitated to report to his own chief, Mark Stigler. He was stopping his car before the white house on the side street before he realized it.

Ruth Smiley wore no welcoming smile when she opened

the door. He removed his hat, flushing slightly. "Mrs. Smiley, I'd like to ask a few questions if I may. It might help Jack if you answer them."

There was doubt, but a flicker of hope in her eyes. "Look," he explained, "something has come up that has me wondering. If the department knew I was here, they wouldn't like it, as I am off this case, but I've a hunch." He paused, thinking ahead. "We know Jack was near the scene of the crime that night. What was he doing there?"

"We told you, Mr. Ragan. Jack had a call from the Chase Printing Company. He repaired a press of theirs once, and they asked him to come not later than four o'clock, as they had a rush job that must begin the following morning."

"That was checked, and they said they made no such call."

"Mr. Ragan, please believe me," Ruth Smiley pleaded. "I heard him talking I heard his replies!"

Ragan scowled unhappily. This was no help, but he was determined now. "Don't raise your hopes," he said, "but I am working on an angle that may help."

The Chase Printing Company could offer no assistance. All their presses were working, and they had not called Smiley. Yes, he had repaired a press once, and an excellent job, too. Yes, his card had been found under the door when they opened up.

Of course, the card could have been part of an alibi, but that was one thing that had bothered him all along. "Those guys were crooks," he muttered, "yet not one of them had an alibi. If they had been working, they would have had iron-clad alibis to prove themselves elsewhere."

Yet the alternative was a frame-up by someone familiar with their working methods. A call had taken Smiley from his bed to the vicinity of the crime, a crime that resembled his working ways. With the records each man had, there was no way they could escape conviction.

He drove again to the Fan Club. Pike Ambler greeted him. "Still looking? Any leads?"

"A couple." Ragan studied the man. "How much did you lose?"

"Two grand, three hundred." His brow furrowed. "I can't

take it, Joe. Luretta hasn't been paid, and she'll raise a squawk you'll hear from here to Flatbush."

"You mean Luretta Pace? Charlie Vent's girl?"

Ambler nodded. "She was Vent's girl before he got himself vented." He smiled feebly at the pun. "She's gone from one extreme to the other. Now it's a cop."

"She's dating a cop? Who?"

"Lew Ryerson." Ambler shrugged. "I don't blame him. She's a number, all right."

Ragan returned to the office, reported in, and completed some routine work. It was late when he finally got to bed.

He awakened with a start, the telephone jangling in his ears. He grabbed it sleepily. "Homicide calling, Joe. Stigler said to give it to you."

"To me?" Ragan was only half-awake. "Man, I'm off duty."

"Yeah"—the voice was dry—"but this call's from the Fan Club. Stigler said you'd want it."

He was wide awake now. "Who's dead?"

"Pike Ambler. He was shot just a few minutes ago. Get out there as fast as you can."

———

TWO PATROL CARS were outside, and a cop was barring the door. Joe had never liked the word "cop," but he had grown up with it, and it kept slipping back into his thinking. The officer let him pass, and Joe walked back to the office.

Ambler was lying on his face beside the desk, wearing the cheap tux that was his official costume. His face was drained of color now, his blue eyes vacant.

Ragan glanced at the doctor. "How many times was he shot?"

"Three times, and damned good shooting. Right through the heart. Probably a .45."

"All right." Ragan glanced up as a man walked in. It was Sam Blythe. "What are you doing here?"

"Prowling. I was talking to the cop on the beat when we heard the shots. We busted in here, and he was lying like that, with the back window open. We went out and looked around but saw nobody, and we heard no car start."

"Who else was in the club?"

"Nobody. The place closed at two, and the last to leave was that Pace gal. What a set of gams she's got!"

"All right. Have the boys round 'em all up and get them in here." He dropped into a chair when the body had been taken away and studied the situation. A little bit of thinking sometimes saved an awful lot of shoe leather. Blythe watched him through lowered lids.

He got up finally, making a minute examination of the room, locating two of the three bullet holes and digging them from the wall with care to add no scratches. They were .45s and he studied them thoughtfully.

"You know," Blythe suggested suddenly, "somebody could be playing us for suckers, kicking this *modus operandi* stuff around like they are."

"Could be." What was Blythe doing there at this hour? He got off at midnight. "Whoever it is has established a new method of operation. All those jobs—Smiley, Chalmers, and Miller—including the burglary here, all between three and five A.M. The technique is that of other men, but the working hours are his own."

"You think those jobs were frames? Ryerson won't like it."

Ragan shrugged. "I'd like to see his face when he finds I'm back on this job."

"You think it's the same one?" Blythe asked quickly.

"Don't you?"

"I wouldn't know. Those were burglaries. This is murder."

"Sure," Ragan agreed, "but suppose Ambler suspected somebody otherwise unsuspected? Wouldn't the crook have a reason for murder?"

A car slowed out front, and then a door slammed open. They heard the click of angry heels, and Luretta Pace swept into the room. Her long, almond-shaped eyes scanned the room, from Blythe to Ragan. "You've got a nerve! Getting me out of bed in the middle of the night! Why couldn't you wait until tomorrow?"

"It *is* tomorrow," Ragan said. He took out a crumpled pack of cigarettes. "Have one?"

She started to refuse, but something in his amused gray eyes made her resentment flicker out. She turned abruptly, seating herself on the arm of a chair. "All right, ask your questions!"

She had green eyes and auburn hair. Ragan found himself liking it. "First," he suggested, "tell us about the fight you had with Ambler."

Luretta stiffened, and the warmth left her face. "Listen! Don't try to frame me! I won't stand still for it! I was out of here before he was shot, and you know it!"

"Sure, I know it. And I don't think you slipped around back and shot him through the window, either." He smiled at her. "Although you could have done it."

Her face paled, but Luretta had been fighting her own battles too long. "Do you think I'd kill a guy who owes me six hundred bucks? You don't collect from a corpse! Besides, Pike was a good man. He was the first guy I'd worked for in a long time who treated me right.

"You'll hear about it, anyway," Luretta said. "Pike owed me money and couldn't pay up. The money he figured on paying me was in that safe, so when he was robbed, I figured I was working for nothing. I can't afford that, so we had some words, and I told him what he could do with his night club."

"Did he give you any idea when he could pay? Or tell you when he might have the money?"

"Yes, as a matter of fact, he said he would have it all back, every dime. He told me he would pay me tomorrow. I didn't believe him."

"Where do you think he planned to get it?"

"How should I know?" She shrugged a lovely shoulder.

"Then," Ragan asked gently, "he said nothing about knowing who robbed him?"

Sam Blythe sat up abruptly, his eyes on Ragan's, and Luretta lost her smile. She was suddenly serious. "No, not exactly, but I guess what I told you could be taken that way.

Do you think that was why he was killed? Because he knew and tried to get his money back?"

It was a theory and a good one. Suppose Ambler possessed information not available to the police and believed he could get his money returned by promising not to turn in the thief? If he contacted the criminal that could be a motive for murder. Joe understood there could be other reasons for murder, but he believed the relationship between Ambler and Luretta was strictly business . . . but suppose someone else had not?

The only admirer of Luretta's he knew was Lew Ryerson, and that was ridiculous. Or was it?

Such a girl as Luretta Pace could have many admirers. That Sam Blythe thought she was something was obvious. For that matter, he did himself.

It was almost noon when he left the club and walked into the sunlight, trying to assemble his thoughts and assay the value of what he had learned. He was standing on the curb when Andre Gimp came up to him. "Mr. Ragan? Only one thing is missing, and that seems strange, for it was only a picture."

"A picture?" Joe Ragan knew what was coming. "Of whom?"

"Luretta Pace . . . in costume!"

There it was again. The burglary, Luretta Pace, the murder. He drove back to headquarters and found Stigler pacing the floor with excitement. "Hey!" Stigler exploded. "You've got something! The gun that killed Ambler was the same gun that killed Charlie Vent!"

"I thought so when I had them checked. It was a hunch I had."

"You think this ties in with those burglaries?" Stigler asked. Then he smiled. "Wells Ryerson called up, boiling mad. Said you'd been questioning people. I told him homicide was involved now. He shut up like a clam, but he was sure sore." Stigler rolled the cigar in his jaw and asked, "What next?"

"A little looking around and another talk with Luretta Pace."

IN THE ALLEY in back of the Fan Club, he found where a man had been standing behind a telephone pole watching Ambler through the window. A man who smoked several cigarettes and dropped paper matches. Ragan picked up a couple of them; each match stub had been divided at the bottom by a thumbnail and bent back to form a cross. Such a thing a man might do subconsciously, while waiting. Many people, Ragan had noticed, have busy fingers of which they are scarcely aware. Some doodle, and usually in the same patterns.

Ragan placed the matches in a white envelope with a notation as to where they were found. In another envelope, he had an identical match, and he knew where others were to be found.

Later, he went to a small target range in the basement at headquarters and fired a couple of shots, then collected all the bullets he could find in the bales of cotton that served as backstop for the targets.

Luretta met him at the door when he arrived, and he smiled at her questioning glance.

"Wondering?" he asked.

"Wondering whether this call is business or social." She took his hat, then glanced over her shoulder. "Drink?"

"Bourbon and soda." He hesitated. "Better not; I'm still on duty. Just a cup of coffee."

She was wearing sea-green slacks and a pale yellow blouse. Her hair was down on her shoulders, and it caught the sunlight. He leaned back in the chair and crossed his legs, watching her move about.

"Ever think about Charlie?" he asked suddenly.

The hand that held the cup hesitated for the briefest instant. When she came to him with his cup and one for herself, she looked at him thoughtfully. "That's a curious thing to ask. Charlie's been dead for nearly five months."

"You didn't answer my question."

She looked over her cup at him. "Occasionally. He wasn't a bad sort, you know, and he really cared for me. But why bring him up?"

"Oh, just thinking!" The coffee tasted good. "I was wondering if your recent company made you forget him."

Luretta looked him over carefully. "Joe, you're not subtle. Why don't you come right out and ask me what you want to know. I'm a big girl now, and I've been coming to the point with people for a long time."

"I wasn't being subtle. The trouble is, I've a finger on something that is pure dynamite. I can't do a thing until I know more, or the whole thing is liable to fly up and hit me in the face.

"This much I can say. Two things are tied up with the killing of Pike Ambler. One of them is the burglaries; the other one is you."

"Me?" She laughed. "Oh, no, Joe! Don't tell me that! There was nothing between Pike and me, and you don't for the minute think I double in safecracking?"

"No, I don't. Nor do I think there was anything between you and Pike. It's what somebody else may have thought. Moreover, you may know more than you realize, and I believe if I could get inside your memory, I could put the pieces together." He got to his feet and put his cup down. "If anybody should ask you, this call was purely social. If you always look as lovely as you do now, that would be easy to believe."

The buzzer sounded from the door, and when she opened it, Lew Ryerson was there. His eyes went from Ragan to her. He was about to speak, but Ragan beat him to it. "Hi, Lew! Good to see you!"

Ryerson came on into the room, his eyes holding Ragan's. "Heard you were all wrapped up in a murder case?"

"Yeah, just took time off to drop around for coffee."

"Looks like I've got competition." There was no humor in the way he spoke, and his eyes were cold and measuring.

"With a girl like Luretta, you will always have it."

Ryerson glanced at her, his lips thinned down and angry. "I guess that's so, but it doesn't make me like the idea any better."

She followed Ragan to the door. "Don't mind him, and do come back."

There was ugly anger in Ryerson's eyes. "Luretta," he said, "I want you to tell him not to come back!"

"Why, I'll do nothing of the kind!" She turned on Lew. "I told you after Charlie was killed that I do not intend to tie myself down. If Mr. Ragan wants to come by, he's welcome."

"Thanks, honey." Ragan turned to Lew. "See you later, Lew. It's all in fun, you know?"

Ryerson glared. "Is it? I'm not so sure."

———

SAM BLYTHE WAS waiting for him when he walked into the office at homicide. His face was dark and angry. "What goes on here?" he demanded. "Who gave you the right to have my gun tested by ballistics?"

"Nobody," Joe admitted cheerfully. "I knew you didn't carry this one off duty, so I had it checked. I had mine checked, too, as they will tell you, and Stigler's."

"What?" Stigler glared. "You had my gun checked?"

"Sure!" Ragan sat on a corner of the desk. "I needed some information, and now I've got it."

"Aside from this horsing around, what have you done on the Ambler case? Have you found the murderer?"

"Sure, I have."

Stigler jumped, and Blythe brought his leg down from the arm of the chair. "Did you say—you have? You *know* who did it?"

"That's right. I know who did it, and that means I know who killed Charlie Vent, too."

He scowled suddenly, and taking the phone from its cradle, he dialed a number. Luretta answered. "Joe here. Still busy?"

"Yes."

"Luretta, I meant to tell you but forgot. The same man who killed Pike Ambler killed Charlie Vent."

"What?" He heard her astonished gasp, but before she could ask questions, he interrupted.

"Don't ask questions now or make any comments, but you do some thinking, but keep the thinking to yourself. Call me any time of the day or the night, understand?"

He replaced the phone and turned back to Stigler, who took his cigar from his mouth. "All right, give! Who did it?"

"Stigler, you'd call me a liar if I told you. Nor do I have evidence for a conviction, but I've set a trap for him if he will only walk into it. Also, he pulled those jobs for which Blackie Miller, Ed Chalmers, and Jack Smiley are awaiting trial."

"That's impossible!" Stigler said, but Ragan knew he believed. Sam Blythe sat back in his chair watching Ragan but saying nothing, his eyes cold and curious.

"What happens now?" Stigler asked.

"We sit tight. I've some more prowling to do."

"What if your killer skips? I want this case sewed up, Ragan."

"Just what Wells Ryerson told me. You'll both get it." Ragan studied his shoes. "Anything about Charlie Vent's murder ever puzzle you, chief? You'll recall he was shot three times in the face, and that's not a normal way to kill a man."

"I've thought of that. If I hadn't thought it to be a gang killing, I'd have said it was jealousy."

"My idea, exactly. Somebody wanted to muscle in, all right, but on Charlie's girl, not his other activities."

"That doesn't make sense," Blythe protested. "Lew Ryerson's going with her."

"And how many other guys? She's a doll, that one, but she's got a mind of her own, and for the time, she's playing the field."

"Yeah," Sam agreed. "I could name three of them right now."

The phone rang, and Ragan dropped a hand to it. "Joe? This is Luretta. I think I know what you mean. Can you come over about ten tonight?"

"I will, and not a minute late." He hung up, glancing from one to the other. "Ten o'clock, and I think we'll get all the evidence we need. If you guys can sit and wait in a car for a while, I'll give you a murderer."

———

IT WAS DARK under the row of trees that lined the curb opposite the apartment house where Luretta Pace lived, and the dark, unmarked car was apparently empty. Only a walker along the park fence might have seen the three men who waited in the car.

"You're sure this thing is set up, Joe? We can't slip up now!"

"It's set. Just sit tight and wait."

Rain began to fall, whispering on the leaves and on the car top. It was almost 8:40 when Ragan suddenly touched Stigler on the sleeve. "Look!" he whispered.

A man had come around the corner out of the side street near the apartment house. He wore a raincoat, and his hat brim was pulled down. He stepped quickly to the door.

Mark Stigler sat straight up. "Man, that looked just like—!" His voice faded as Ragan's hand closed on his arm.

"It was!" Ragan replied grimly.

A shade in an apartment-house window went up and down rapidly, three times. "Let's go," Ragan said. "We've got to hurry!"

An officer in uniform admitted them to the apartment next door to that of Luretta Pace. A wire recording was already being made, and through the hidden mike in the next apartment, they could hear the voices clearly.

"I don't care who he is!" A man was speaking, a voice that stiffened Sam Blythe to the same realization that had come to Mark Stigler on the outside. "Keep him away from here!"

"I don't intend to keep anybody away whom I like, but as a matter of fact, I don't care for him."

"Then tell him so!"

"Why don't you tell him?" Luretta's voice was taunting. "Are you afraid? Or won't he listen to you?"

"Afraid? Of course not! Still, it wouldn't be a good idea. I'd rather he didn't know we were acquainted."

"You weren't always so hesitant."

"What do you mean by that?"

"Why, you never approved of Charlie, either. You knew I liked him, but you didn't want me to like him."

"That's right. I didn't."

"One thing I'll say for Charlie: He was a good spender. I don't care whether a man spends money on me or not, but it helps. And Charlie did."

"You mean that I don't? I think I've been pretty nice lately."

"Lately. Sometimes I wonder how you do it on your salary."

"I manage."

"As you managed a lot of other things? Like Charlie, for instance?"

For a moment, there was no sound, and Joe Ragan's tongue touched dry lips. Nerve, that girl had nerve.

The tone was lower, colder. "Just what do you mean by that?"

"Well, didn't you? You didn't really believe I thought Charlie was killed in some gang war, did you? Nobody wanted Charlie dead, nobody but you."

He laughed. "I always did like a smart girl! Well, now you know the sort of man I am, and you know just how we stand and what I can do to you or anyone! The best of it is, they can't touch me."

There was a sound like a glass being put down on a table. "Luretta, let's drop this nonsense and get married. I'm going places, and nothing can stop me."

"I won't marry you. This has gone far enough as it is." Luretta's voice changed. "You'd better go now. I never knew just what sort of person you were, although I suspected. At first, I believed you were making things easy for me by not allowing too many questions. Now I realize you were protecting yourself."

"Naturally. But I was protecting you, too."

Joe Ragan got up and took his gun from its holster and slid it into his waistband. Blythe was already at the door. There was a hard set to his face.

"I neither wanted nor expected protection." Luretta was speaking. "I cared for Charlie. I want you to understand that. No, I was not in love with him, but he was good to me, and I hadn't any idea that you killed him. If I had, I would never have spoken to you. Now, get out!"

The man laughed. "Don't be silly! We're staying together, especially now."

"What do you mean?"

"Why, I wouldn't dare let you go now. We'll either get along or you will get what Charlie got." There was a bump as of a chair knocked over, then a shout. *"Stay away from that door!"*

Ragan was moving fast. He swung into the hall and gripped the knob, but it was locked. There was a crash inside, and in a sudden fury of fear for the girl inside, Ragan threw himself against the door. The lock broke, and he stumbled inside.

Lieutenant Wells Ryerson threw the girl from him and grabbed for his gun. Ragan was moving too fast. He slapped the gun aside and hooked a wicked right to the chin, then a left. Ryerson fell back, his gun going off as he fell. He scrambled to his feet, lifting his gun.

Sam Blythe fired in the same instant, and the bullet slammed Ryerson against the wall. The gun dribbled from Ryerson's fingers, and he slid to the floor.

His eyes opened, and for a moment they were sharp, clear, and intelligent. "I told you," he said hoarsely, "to close this one up fast."

His voice faded, and then he struggled for breath. "It looked so . . . easy! The file, those ex-cons on the loose. I could make a record . . . the money, too."

Mark Stigler shook his head. "Ryerson! Who would have believed it?" He glanced at Ragan. "What tipped you off?"

"It had to be somebody with access to the files, and who could be out between three and five A.M. It couldn't be you, Mark, because you're at home with your family every chance you get and your wife would know. Sam, here, likes his sleep too much.

"What really tipped me off was this." Ragan picked up a paper match split into a cross. "It was a nervous habit he had when thinking. Many of us do similar things.

"Matches like that were found on the Smiley and Miller jobs and in the alley near Ambler's office."

"Did Lew know his brother liked Luretta?"

"I doubt it."

"What about Ambler?"

"I think he knew, and somehow he discovered it was Ryerson who cracked his safe. He must have called him. Ryerson did not dare return the call, for then there might be somebody else who knew his secret."

When the body had been taken away, Stigler looked over at Ragan. "Coming with us, Joe? Or are you staying?"

"Neither. We're going to drive over to see Ruth Smiley. I want that to be the first thing we do—turn Jack Smiley loose so he can go back to his family."

Later, in the car, Luretta said, "She'll be so happy! It must be wonderful to make somebody that happy!"

"That's something," Joe Ragan said, "that we ought to talk about."

THE UNEXPECTED CORPSE

SOMEHOW I HAD always known that if she got in a bad spot, she would call on me, just as I knew that I would never turn her down. Maybe it was because I had encouraged her in the old days when being an actress was only a dream she'd had.

Well, it was a dream that had matured and developed until she was there, rising to greater heights with every picture, with every play. It was never news to me when she scored a success. Somehow, there had never been any doubt in my mind.

When my phone rang, I'd just come in. A few of the boys and I had been getting around to some nightspots, and when I came in and tossed my raincoat over a chair, the telephone was ringing its heart out.

It was Ruth. It had been six months since I'd seen her, and I hadn't even known she knew my number; it wasn't in the book.

"Can you come over, Jim? I'm in trouble! Awful trouble!"

Sometimes she tended to dramatize things, but there was something in her voice that warned me she wasn't kidding.

"Sure," I told her. "Just relax. I'll be there in ten minutes."

Light rain was falling and it was quiet outside. A few late searchlights probed the empty sky, and my tires sang on the pavement. I took backstreets because for all I knew, the cops might be having another shakedown of cars, and I didn't want to be stopped. Not that it would mean anything, I wasn't carrying a gun even though I had a permit, but I wanted to avoid delay.

She opened the door quickly when I knocked. The idea that it might be someone else never seemed to enter her head. She was wearing an evening gown, but she looked so much like a frightened little girl that it seemed like old times again.

"What's the trouble?" I asked her.

"There's a . . . there's a dead man in there!" She indicated the door to what I surmised was the bedroom.

"A *dead* man?" Of all the things it might have been, this was one I'd never imagined. I put her aside and went in, careful to avoid touching anything.

The guy was lying on the bed, one leg and one arm dangling over the side. He was dead all right, deader than a mackerel.

My guess would have put him at fifty years old. He might have been a few years younger. He was slim, dapper, and wore a closely clipped gray mustache. His eyes were wide open and blue. There was an amethyst ring on his left hand. Carefully, I felt his pockets. His billfold was still full of money. I didn't count how much, after I saw it was plenty. The label of his suit said that his name was Lawrence Craine.

The name rang a bell somewhere, but I couldn't place it. Spotting a little blood on his shoulder, I saw he had been stabbed behind the collarbone. In such a stab, most of the blood flows into the lungs. That must have been the case, for there was very little blood. At a rough guess, the guy was five-ten or -eleven. He must have weighed a hundred sixty or thereabouts.

Ruth, I still called her that although she was known professionally as Sue Shannon, was sitting as I'd left her, white as death and her eyes big enough and dark enough to drown in.

"Well, tell me about it," I suggested. "Tell me how well you knew him, what he was to you, and what he was doing here."

She had always listened to me. I suspected she had been in love with me once. I know I had with her. However, it was more than that, for we were friends, we understood each other. She tried to answer my questions now, and though her voice shook a little, I could see she was trying to keep herself from getting hysterical.

"His name is Larry Craine. I don't know what he does except that he seems to have a good deal of money. I've met him several times out on the Strip or at the homes of friends. He seemed to know everyone.

"He had found out something about me, something I didn't want anyone to know. He was going to tell, if I didn't pay him. It would have made a very bad story and it was the sort that people would tell around. It would have ruined me.

"I didn't think he would do it, so I told him no. He laughed at me, and gave me until tonight to pay him. I don't know how he got here or how he got in. I went out at eight o'clock with Roger Gentry, but we quarreled and he disappeared. After a while, Davis and Nita Claren drove me home. Then I found him."

"You haven't called the police?"

"The police?" Her eyes were wide and frightened. "Do I have to? I thought that you could hush it up."

"Listen, honey," I said dryly, "this man is *dead*! And he's been *murdered*. The police always seem to be interested in such cases."

"But not here! The body I mean, couldn't you take it some-place else? In stories they do those things."

"I know. But it wouldn't work." I picked up the phone and when I got Homicide, I asked for Reardon, praying he would be in. He was.

"Reardon? Got one for you, and a very touchy case. In the apartment of a friend of mine." I explained briefly, and she stood at my elbow, waiting.

When I hung up, I turned around. "Kid," I warned her, "you're going to have a bad time, so take it standing. The body is here, and if they find out about this blackmail, they've got a motive."

———

WHEN THE SQUAD car pulled into the drive, I was standing there with my arms around her and she was crying. Over her shoulder, I was looking at the wall and thinking, and not about her. I was thinking about this guy Craine. I couldn't make myself think Ruth had done it.

However, there was a chance, even if a slim one. Ruthie, well, she was an impractical girl, and always seemed somewhat vague. But underneath was a will that would move mountains. It wasn't on the surface, but it was there.

Also, she knew a man could be killed in just that way. She knew it because I remembered telling her once when we were talking about some detective stories we'd both read.

Reardon came in and with him were Doc Spates, the medical examiner, a detective named Nick Tanner, a police photographer, and a couple of tired harness bulls.

Sue, I decided to stick to calling her Sue as everyone else would, gave him the story, looking at him out of those big, wistful eyes. Those eyes worked on nearly everyone. Apparently, they hadn't worked on Larry Craine. I doubted if they would work on Reardon who, when it comes to murder, is a pretty cold-blooded fish.

He rolled his cigar in his cheek and listened; he also looked carefully around the room. Reardon was a good man. He would know plenty about this girl before he got through looking the place over.

When she finished, he looked at me. "Where do you figure in this, Jim? What would she be needing with a private eye?"

"That wasn't it. We knew each other back in Wisconsin long before she ever came out here. Whenever she got in trouble, she always called me."

"Whenever . . ."

He looked at me sadly, letting the implication hang. I didn't tell him any more but I knew he would find out eventually. Reardon was thorough. Slow, painstaking, but thorough.

Doc Spates came in, closing up his bag. "Dead about two hours. That's pretty rough, of course. Whoever did it knew what he was doing. One straight, hard thrust. No stabbing around. No other cuts or bruises."

Reardon nodded, chewing his cigar. "Could a woman do it?"

Spates fussed with his bag. "Why not? It doesn't take much strength."

Sue's face was stiff and white and her fingers tightened on my arm. Suddenly I was scared. What sort of a fool's chance I was building my hopes on I don't know, but all of a sudden they went out of me like air from a pricked balloon, and there

I stood. Right then I knew I was going to have to get busy, and I was going to have to work fast.

Just then Tanner came in. He looked at me and his eyes were questioning. He was holding up an ice pick.

"Doc," he said as Spates reached the door. "Could this have done it?"

"Could be." Spates shrugged. "Something long, thin, and narrow. Have to examine it further before I can tell exactly. Any blood on it?"

"A little," Tanner said. "Close against the handle. But it's been washed!"

Reardon was elaborately casual when he turned around. "You do this?" he asked her.

She shook her head. Twice she tried to speak before she could get it out. "No, I wouldn't . . . couldn't . . . kill anyone!"

To look at her the idea seemed preposterous. Reardon was half convinced, but I, knowing her as I did, knew that deep inside she had something that was hard and ready.

"Listen," I said, "let me call Davis Claren and have him come over and pick up Sue. She'll be at his place when you want her."

He looked at me thoughtfully, then nodded. After I'd phoned and come back into the room, I saw he had slumped down on the divan and was sitting there, chewing that unlighted cigar. Sue was sitting in a chair staring at him, white and still. I could see she was near the breaking point and was barely holding herself together.

Only after she had gone off with her friends did he look up at me. "How about you? You do it?"

"Me?" I demanded. "Why would I kill the guy? I never knew him!"

"You knew her," he stated flatly. "She looks like she has a lot of trust in you. Maybe she called on you for help. Maybe she called on you *before* the guy was dead instead of after."

"Bosh." That was the only answer I had to that one.

When he finally let me go, I beat it down to my car. It was after four in the morning, and there was little I could do. It felt cold and lonely in my apartment. I stripped off my clothes and tumbled into bed.

————

THE TELEPHONE JOLTED me out of it. It was Taggart. I should have known it would be him. He was Sue's boss and, as executives went in Hollywood, he was all right. That meant he was basically honest but he wouldn't ever get caught making a statement that couldn't be interpreted at least three different ways. And if the winds of studio politics changed, he'd cut Sue loose like a sail in a storm.

"Sue tells me she called you," he barked. "Well, what have you got?"

"Nothing yet," I told him. "Give me time."

"There isn't any time. The D.A. thinks she did it. He's all hopped up against the Industry, anyway. I'm sending a man over to your office at eight with a thousand dollars. Consider that a retainer!" *Bang;* he hung up the phone.

It was a quarter to eight. I rolled out of bed, into the shower, into my clothes, and through a session with an electric razor so fast that it seemed like one continuous movement. And then, when I was putting the razor away, the name of Larry Craine clicked in my mind.

A week ago, or probably two, I'd been standing in front of a hotel on Vine Street talking to Joe. Joe was a cab starter who knew everybody around. With us was standing a man, a stranger to me, some mug from back East. He spoke up suddenly, and nodded across toward the Derby.

"I'll be damned, that's Larry Craine!" said the man. "What's *he* doing out here?"

"I think he lives here," Joe said.

"He didn't when I knew him!" The fellow growled.

With the thousand dollars in my pocket, I started hunting for Joe. I'd never known his last name, but I got it pretty quick when I looked at a cabbie over a five-dollar bill. It was Joe McCready and he lived out in Burbank.

There were other things to do first, and I did a lot of them on a pay phone. Meanwhile, I was thinking, and when I finally got to Joe, he hesitated only a minute, then shrugged.

"You're a pal of mine," he said, "or I'd say nothing. This lug who spotted Larry Craine follows the horses. I think he makes book, but I wouldn't know about that. He doesn't do any business around the corner."

"What do you know about Larry Craine?"

"Nothing. Doesn't drink very much, gets around a lot, and seems to know a lot of people. Mostly, he hangs around on the edge of things, spends pretty free when there's a crowd around, but tips like he never carried anything but nickels."

Joe looked up at me. "You watch yourself. This guy we were talkin' to, his name is Pete Ravallo. He plays around with some pretty fast company."

He did have Craine's address. I think Joe McCready knew half the addresses and telephone numbers in that part of town. He never talked much, but he listened a lot, and he never forgot anything. My detective agency couldn't have done the business it did without elevator boys, cab starters, newsboys, porters, and bellhops.

That was how I got into Craine's apartment. I went around there and saw Paddy. Paddy had been a doorman in that apartment house for five years. We used to talk about the fights and football games, sitting on the stoop, just the two of us.

"The police have been there," Paddy advised, "but they didn't stay long. I can get y' in, but remember, if y' get caught, it's on your own y' are!"

This Craine had done all right by himself. I could see that the minute I looked around. I took a quick gander at the desk, but not with any confidence. The cops would have headed for the desk right away, and Reardon was a smart fellow. So was Tanner, for that matter. I headed for the clothes closet.

He must have had twenty-five suits and half that many sport coats, all a bit loud for my taste. I started at one end and began going through them, not missing a pocket. Also, as I went along, I checked the labels. He had three suits from New Orleans. They were all pretty shabby and showed much wear. They were stuck back in a corner of the closet out of the way.

The others were all comparatively new, and all made in

Hollywood or Beverly Hills. At first that didn't make much of an impression, but it hit me suddenly as I was going through the fourteenth suit, or about there. Larry Craine had been short of money in New Orleans but he had been very flush in Hollywood. What happened to put his hands on a lot of money, and fast?

When I hit the last suit in line, I had netted just three ticket stubs and twenty-one cents in money. The last suit was the pay-off. When I opened the coat, I saw right away that I'd jumped to a false conclusion. Here was one suit, bought ready-made, in Dallas.

In the inside coat pocket, I found an airline envelope, and in it, the receipt for one passenger from Dallas to Los Angeles via American Airlines. Also, there was a stub, the sort of thing given to you after a street photographer takes your picture. If you want the snapped picture, you can get it and more of them if you wish, if you want to pay a modest sum of money. Craine hadn't been interested.

Pocketing the two articles, I slipped out the back way and let Paddy know I was gone. He looked relieved when he saw me off.

"Nick Tanner just went up," he said.

"Thanks, Paddy," I told him.

I walked around in front and saw Reardon standing by the squad car. Putting my hands in my pockets, I strolled up to him.

"Hi," I said. "How's it going?"

His eyes were shrewd as he studied me. "Not so good for Miss Shannon," he said carefully. "That ice pick did the job, all right. Doc Spates will swear to it. We found blood close up against the handle where it wasn't washed carefully. It's the same type as his blood.

"Also," he added, "we checked on her. She left that party she was at with Gentry and the Clarens early, about three hours before it was over, which would make it along about ten-thirty. She was gone for all of thirty to forty-five minutes. In other words, she had time to leave the party, go home, kill this guy, and get back to the party."

"You don't believe that!" I exclaimed.

He shrugged and took a cigar from his pocket. "It isn't what I believe, it's what the district attorney can make the jury believe. Something you want to think about." He looked up at me from under his eyebrows as he bit off the end of the cigar. "The D.A. is ambitious. A big Hollywood murder trial would give him lots of publicity. The only thing that would make him happier would be a basement full of communists!"

"Yeah." I could see it all right, I could see him riding right to the governor's chair on a deal like that. Or into the Senate. "One thing, Reardon. If she had done it, wouldn't she have had the Clarens come in with her to help her find the body? That would be the smart stunt. And she's actress enough to carry it off."

"I know." He struck a match and lit the cigar, then grinned sardonically at me. "But she's actress enough to fool you, too!"

Was she? I wasn't so sure. I'd known her a long time. Maybe you never really know anyone. And murder is something that comes much too easily sometimes.

"Reardon," I said, "don't pinch Sue. Hold off on it until I can work on it."

He shrugged. "I can't. The D.A.'s already convinced. He wants an arrest. We haven't another lead of any kind. We shook his apartment down, we made inquiries all over town. We don't have another suspect."

"We've been buddies a long time," I pleaded. "Give her forty-eight hours. Taggart's retained me on this case, and I think I've got something."

"Taggart has, eh?" He looked at me thoughtfully. "Don't give me a runaround, now. The district attorney thinks he has a line on it himself. It seems Craine's done some talking around town. He thinks he's got a motive, though he's not saying what it is yet."

"Two days?"

"All right. But then we're going ahead with what we've got. I'll give you until ... let's see, this is Monday ... you've got until Wednesday morning."

———

Sᴜᴇ ᴡᴀs ᴡᴀɪᴛɪɴɢ for me when I got there. She was a beautiful woman, even as tight and strained as she was.

"Is it true? Are they going to arrest me?"

"I hope not." I sat down abruptly. "I'd let them arrest me if I could."

"No, you won't." I looked up and her eyes were sharp and hard. "You came into this because I asked you, and I won't have that happen."

It was the first time I'd seen her show her anger, although I knew she had it. It surprised me, and I sat back and looked at her and I guess my surprise must have shown because she said, defensively, "Don't you talk that way. That's going too far!"

"Well you've got to help me. Just what did Craine want from you?"

"Money." She shrugged. "He told me he wanted ten percent of all I made from now on. He said he had been broke for the last time, that now that he had money he was always going to have money no matter what it cost."

"Did you talk to him many times?"

"Three times. He had some letters. There was nothing bad in them, but the way he read them made them sound pretty bad. It wasn't only that. He knew some stories that I don't want told, about my uncle."

I knew all about that, and could understand.

"But that wasn't all. He told me I had to give him information about other people out here. About Mr. Taggart, for instance, and some of the others. He was very pleased with himself. He obviously was sure he had a very good plan worked out."

"Does Taggart know about this?"

"No one does. You're the only one I've told. The only one I will tell."

"Did Craine ever hint about how he got this money he had?"

"Well, not exactly. He told me I needn't think I could evade the issue because he was desperate. He told me there wasn't anything he would hesitate to do. He said once, 'I've already gone as far as I can go, so you know what to expect if you try to double-cross me.'"

When she left, I offered the best reassurances I could dig out of a mind that was running pretty low on hope. Reardon was careful, and if he couldn't find anything on Larry Craine, there was small chance I could. My only angle was one that had been stirring in the back of my mind all the time.

Where did Larry Craine get his money?

He had been living in Hollywood for several months. He lived well and spent a good bit. That meant that wherever he had come into money, it had been plenty.

To cover all the bases I sent off a wire to an agency in New Orleans.

My next move was a shot in the dark. There was only one person I knew of who had known Craine before he came to Hollywood. I was going to see Pete Ravallo.

He was in a hotel on Ivar, and it didn't take me but two hours and twenty dollars to find him. I rapped on the door to his room, and he opened it a crack. His eyes studied me, and I could see he vaguely remembered my face.

"What'd you want?" he demanded. He was a big guy, and his voice was harsh.

"Conversation," I said.

He sized me up a minute, then let the door open and I walked in. He waved me to a seat and poured himself a drink. There was a gun in a shoulder holster hanging over a chair back. He didn't offer me a drink, and he didn't look very pleased.

"All right," he said. "Spill it!"

"I'm a private shamus and I'm investigating the murder of Lawrence Craine."

You could have dropped a feather. His eyes were small and dark and as he looked at me they got still smaller and still darker.

"So you come to me?" he demanded.

I shrugged. "One night down on the street, I heard you say something about knowing him in New Orleans. Maybe you could give me a line on the guy."

He studied me. Somehow, I felt sure, there was a tie-up, a

tie-up that went a lot further than a casual meeting. Ravallo had been too pleased at seeing Craine. Pleased, and almost triumphant.

"I don't know anything about the guy," he said. "Only that he used to be around the tracks down there. I knew him by sight like I knew fifty others. He used to put down a bet once in a while."

"Seen him since he's been here?" I asked carefully. Ravallo's face tightened and his eyes got mean. "Listen," he said. "Don't try to pin that job on me, see? You get to nosing in my business and you'll wind up wearing a concrete block on your feet! I don't like cops. I like private coppers a lot less, and I like you still less than that! So get up and get out!"

"Okay." I got up. "You'd better tell me what you can, because otherwise I'm going back to New Orleans . . . and Dallas!"

"Wait a minute," he said. He went over behind me to the phone and spun the dial.

"Come on over here," he said into the phone. "I've got a problem."

The hair on the back of my neck suddenly felt prickly and I turned in time to see the sap descending. I threw up an arm, catching him above the elbow. I grabbed his wrist and jerked him forward into the back of the chair, then I lunged forward, hit the carpet with my knees, and, turning, stood up.

Pete Ravallo threw the chair out of his way and came toward me; his voice was cold. "I told you, and now I'm going to show you!" He cocked his arm and swung again.

It was a bad thing for him to do. I hit his arm with my open palm and at the same time I knocked his arm over, I slugged him in the stomach with my left.

He doubled up, and I smacked him again, but the big lug could take it, and he charged me, head down. I sidestepped quickly, tripped over a suitcase, and hit the floor all in one piece. The next thing I knew I got the wind booted out of me and before I could get my hands up, he slugged me five or six times and I was helpless.

He slammed me back against the wall with one hand and then swung the blackjack. He brought it down over my skull, and as everything faded out, I heard him snarling: "Now get lost, or I'll kill you!"

———

WHEN I CAME out of it, I was lying in a linen closet off the hall. I struggled to my feet and swayed drunkenly, trying to get my head clear and get moving. I got out in the hall and straightened my clothes. My face felt stiff and sore, and when I put my hand up to my head, I found blood was caked in my hair and on the side of my face. Then I cleaned myself up as best I could and got out.

It was after eleven, and there was a plane leaving for Oklahoma City at about twelve-thirty. When it took off, I was on it. And the next morning, Tuesday morning, I was standing, quite a bit worse for wear, in front of the *Dallas Morning News*.

When a crook comes into a lot of money, it usually makes headlines. What I had learned so far was ample assurance that what had happened had happened near here. I went to the files of the paper and got busy.

It took me some time, but when I had covered almost two months, I found what I was looking for. It was not a big item, and was well down on an inside page. If I had not been covering it with care, I would never have found the piece at all.

MURDERED MAN BELIEVED
GANG VICTIM

Police today announced they had identified the body of the murdered man found in a ditch several miles south of the city. He proved to be Giuseppe Ravallo, a notorious racketeer from Newark, N.J. Ravallo, who did two terms in the New Jersey State Prison for larceny and assault with a deadly weapon, was reported to have come here recently from New Orleans where he had been implicated in a race-fixing plot.

Ravallo was said to have come to town as the advance man for eastern racketeers determined to move into the area. He was reported, by several local officials whom he approached, to be carrying a considerable amount of money. No money was found on the body. Ravallo had been shot three times in the back and once in the head by a .38-caliber pistol.

So there it was. Just like that, and no wonder Pete Ravallo had wanted to keep me out of the case!

The photo coupon was still in my pocket. At the photographers shop it took me only a few minutes to get it. When I had the picture, I took one look and headed for the airport.

———

IN LOS ANGELES there was a few minutes' wait to claim my luggage, and then I turned toward a cab. I turned, but that was all. A man had moved up beside me. He was small and pasty-faced, and his eyes were wide and strange. There was nothing small about the feel of the cannon he put in my ribs.

"Come on!" he said. "That car over there!"

There are times for bravery. There are also times when bravery is a kind of insanity. Tonight, within limits, I was perfectly sane. I walked along to the car and saw the thick neck of a mug behind the wheel, and then I was getting in and looking at Pete Ravallo. There were a lot of people I would rather have seen.

"I can't place the face," I said brightly, "but the breath smells familiar!"

"Be smart!" Ravallo said. "Go ahead and be smart while you got the chance!"

The car was rolling, and Pasty Face was still nudging me with the artillery.

"Listen, chum!" I suggested. "Move the gun. I'm not going anyplace!"

Pasty Face chuckled. "Oh, yes, you are! You got some things to learn."

We drove on, and eventually wound around in the hills along a road I finally decided was Mulholland Drive. It was a nice place to dispose of a body. I'd probably wind up as part of a real estate plot and be subdivided. In fact, I had a pretty good idea the subdividing was planned for right quick.

When the car pulled in at the edge of the dark road, I knew this was it.

"Get out!"

Ravallo let Pasty Face unload first, and then he put his foot in my back and shoved.

Maybe Pasty Face was supposed to trip me. Maybe Ravallo didn't realize we were so close to the canyon, but that shove with his foot was all I needed. I took it, ducked the guy with the gun, and plunged off into the darkness.

It wasn't a sheer drop. It was a steep slide off into the dark, brush-filled depths of a canyon whose sides were scattered with boulders. I must have run all of twenty feet in gigantic steps before I lost balance and sprawled, headfirst into the brush.

Behind me a shot rang out, and then I heard Ravallo swear.

"After him, you idiots! Get him!"

Kicking my feet over, I fell on the downhill side of the bush and flame stabbed the night behind me, but I wasn't waiting. This was no time to stand on ceremony and I was not going to take a chance on their missing me in the darkness of that narrow canyon. I rolled over, scrambled to my feet, and lunged downhill.

Then I tripped over something and sprawled headlong. A flashlight stabbed the darkness. That was a different story, and I lay still, feeling for what I'd tripped over. It was a thick branch wedged between the sprawling roots of some brush. Carefully, I worked it loose.

Somebody was coming nearer. I lay quiet, waiting and balancing my club. Then I saw him, and he must have moved quietly for he was within two feet of my head!

He took a step and I stuck my club between his feet. He took a header and started to swear. That was all I needed, for I smacked down with that club. It hit him right over the noggin and I scrambled up his frame and wrenched the gun from his hand.

"Stan?" Ravallo called.

I balanced the gun and wet my lips. There were two of them, but I was through running.

I cocked the gun and squared my feet, breaking a small branch in the process.

He fired, but I had been moving even as I realized I'd given away my position. I hit the dirt a half-dozen feet away. My own pistol stabbed flame and he fired back. I got a mouthful of sand and backed up hurriedly. But Pete Ravallo wasn't happy. I heard him whispering hoarsely, and then heard a slight sound downhill from me.

I turned, and Ravallo's gun stabbed out of the dark and something struck me a blow on the shoulder. My gun went clattering among the stones, and I knew from Ravallo's shout that he knew what had happened.

Crouching like a trapped animal, I stared into the blackness right and left. There was no use hunting for the gun. The noise I would make would give them all they needed to shoot at, and Pete Ravallo was doing too well at shooting in the dark.

Fighting desperately for silence I backed up, then turned and worked my way cautiously back through the brush, parting it with my hands, and putting each foot down carefully so as not to scuff any stones or gravel.

I was in total darkness when I heard the sound of heavy breathing, and close by. It was a cinch this couldn't be Pete Ravallo, so it must be the thick-necked mug. I waited, and heard a slight sound. I could barely see the dim outline of a face. Putting everything I had into it, I threw my left!

Beggar's luck was with me and it smashed on flesh and he went sliding down the gravel bank behind him. Instantly, flame stabbed the night. One bullet whiffed close by, and then I began to run. I was lighter than Pete, and my arm was throbbing with agony that seemed to be eased by the movement even as pressure seems to ease an aching tooth. I lunged at that hill and, fighting with both feet and my one good hand, started to scramble back for the top.

Ravallo must have hesitated a moment or two, trying to locate his driver. I was uphill from him anyway, and by the time he started I had a lead of at least forty yards and was pulling away fast. He tried one more shot, then held his fire. A light came on in a distant house.

Tearing my lungs out gasping for air, I scrambled over the top into the road. The car was sitting there, with the motor running, but I'd no thought of getting away. He still had shells, probably an extra clip, too. I twisted into the driver's seat and threw the car into gear and pointed it down the embankment. There was one sickening moment when the car teetered, and then I half jumped, half fell out of the door.

In that wild, fleeting instant as the car plunged headfirst downhill, I caught a glimpse of Pete Ravallo.

The gangster was full in the glare of the headlights, and even as I looked, he threw up his arms and screamed wildly, insanely into the night! And then all I could hear was the crashing tumble of the car going over and over to the bottom of the canyon.

For what seemed a long time I lay there in the road, then crawled to my feet. I felt weak and sick and the world was spinning around so I had to brace myself to stand. I was like that when I heard the whine of a siren and saw a car roll up and stop. There were other sirens farther off.

Reardon was in the third car to arrive. He ran to me.

"What happened? Where's Ravallo?"

I gestured toward the canyon. "How'd you know about him?"

While several officers scrambled down into the canyon, he helped me to the car and ripped off my coat.

"Joe McCready," Reardon said. "He knew you'd gone to Dallas, and he heard the cabbies say that Ravallo was watching the airport. So, I wired Dallas to see if they knew anything about Craine or Ravallo. The paper told me that you found a story about Giuseppe Ravallo's body. So I had some boys watching Pete at this end while we tried to piece the thing together.

"They had gone for coffee and were just getting back when they saw Ravallo's car pulling away. A few minutes' checking and they found you'd come in on the plane. We thought we'd lost you until we got a report of some shooting up this way."

Between growls at the pain of my shoulder, I explained what had happened. There were still gaps to fill in, but it seemed Ravallo had been trying to find out who killed his brother.

"He either had a hunch Craine had done it for the money Giuseppe was carrying, or just happened to see him and realized he was flush. That would be all he would need to put two and two together. However he arrived at the solution, he was right."

Fishing in my coat pocket, I got out the snapshot. It was a picture of Giuseppe Ravallo, bearing a strong resemblance to Pete, sitting at a table with Larry Craine.

"Maybe Craine left New Orleans with Ravallo, and maybe he followed him. Anyway, when Craine left New Orleans he was broke, then he hit Dallas and soon had plenty of money. He bought a suit of clothes there, then came on here and started living high and fast. Ravallo was back behind him, dead."

My arm was throbbing painfully, but I had to finish the story and get the thing straightened out.

"Pete must have tailed him to Sue's apartment, maybe one of those goons down there in the canyon was with him. He probably didn't know where he was going and cared less. He saw his chance and took it. Pete seems the vendetta type. He would think first of revenge, and the money would come second. Her car evidently drove up before he had the money. Or maybe he didn't even try to get it."

Reardon nodded. "That's a place for us to start. I don't think you'll have to worry about the D.A." He grinned at me. "But when you took off to Dallas, you had me sweating!"

ALL THE WAY back to town, I nursed my shoulder and was glad to get to the hospital. The painkillers put me under and I dreamed that I was dying in a dark canyon under the crushing weight of a car.

When I fought my way back to life after a long sleep, it was morning and Sue Shannon was sitting there by the bed. I looked up at her thoughtfully.

"What?" she asked.

"I thought I was dying in a dream . . . and then I woke up and thought I'd gone to heaven."

She smiled.

"I was wondering if I'd have to wait until you found another corpse before I saw you again?" I asked.

"Not if you like a good meal and know of a quiet restaurant where we can get one."

My eyes absorbed her beauty again and I thought heaven could wait, living would do for now.

THE SUCKER SWITCH

WHEN JAKE BRUSA got out of the car, he spotted me waiting for him and his eyes went hard. Jake and I never cared for each other.

"Hi, Copper!" he said. "Loafing again, or are you here on business?"

"Would I come to see you for fun?" I asked. "It's a question or two; like where were you last night?"

"At the Roadside Club. In fact," he said, grinning at me, "I ran into your boss out there. Even talked with him for a while."

"Just asking," I told him. "But you'll need an alibi. Somebody knocked off the Moffit Storage and Transit Company for fifty grand in furs."

"Nice haul. Luck to 'em!" Jake grinned again and, sided by Al Huber and Frank Lincoff, went on into the Sporting Center.

The place was a combination bowling alley and billiard parlor. It was Jake Brusa's front for a lot of illegal activities. Jake had been operating, ever since his release from Joliet, but nobody was able to put a finger on him.

If James Briggs, my boss, had been with him the night before, then Jake might be in the clear, but in my own mind, I was positive this had been a Brusa job.

OLD MAN MOFFIT had been plenty sore when I'd showed up at his office earlier that morning. His little blue eyes glinted angrily in his fat red face.

"About time you got here!" he snapped at me. "What does Briggs think he's running, anyway? We pay your firm for security and this is the third time in five months we've taken a loss from thieves or holdup men."

"Take it easy," I said. "Let me have a look around first." I dug into my pocket for chewing gum and peeled three sticks. He had reason to complain. The robberies were covered by insurance, but his contracts to handle merchandise would never be renewed if he couldn't deliver the goods. Not that he was the only one suffering from burglary or stickups. The two rival firms in town had suffered a couple of losses each, and the police had failed to pin anything on anybody. All three of the companies had been clients of my boss's detective agency.

Moffit's face purpled. "I lose fifty thousand dollars' worth of furs and you tell me to take it easy!" he shouted. "I've got a good mind to call—"

"It wouldn't do you any good," I said. "Briggs only told me somebody knocked over the joint. Suppose you give me the details."

Moffit toned down, but his jaw jutted, and it was obvious that Briggs stood to lose a valuable client unless we recovered those furs or pinned this on somebody.

"My night watchman, a man investigated by your firm and pronounced reliable, is missing," Moffit told me. "With him went one of our armored trucks and the furs."

That watchman was Pete Burgeson and I'd investigated him myself. "And then what?" I asked. "Give me the whole setup."

"The furs were stored in the vault last night," he continued a little more mildly, "but when we opened it this morning, it was empty. The burglar alarm on the vault door failed to go off. The vault door and the door to the outer room were both locked this morning. So was the warehouse door.

"Our schedule called for the furs to be delivered to Pentecost and Martin the first thing this morning. The furs are gone and the truck is gone and Burgeson is gone, too!"

———

NATURALLY, AFTER I'D heard Moffit's story, I thought of Brusa and went down to see him. In his youth there had been no tougher mobster; he had a record as long as your arm in the Midwest and East. After his release from Joliet, he had come west to Lucaston and opened the Sporting Center.

Supposedly, he had been following a straight path since then, but I had my own ideas about that. Years ago, he had been a highly skilled loft burglar. Huber had been arrested several times on the same charge. Lincoff had been up for armed robbery and assault. The Sporting Center was the hangout for at least three other men with records.

Lucaston, while not a great metropolis, was a thriving and busy city near the coast and we had several select residential areas loaded with money. Such a place is sure to be a target for crooks, and I don't believe it was any accident that Jake Brusa had located there.

Well, I had seen Brusa and heard his alibi, and when I called my boss, Briggs told me that Brusa was right. He had talked with Briggs at the Roadside Club, and not only he but Huber and Lincoff had been there all evening. Their alibi was rockbound. But if they hadn't done it, who had? . . .

The warehouse itself offered little. It was a concrete structure, built like a blockhouse and almost as impregnable. A glance at it would defeat an amateur burglar, and the place was fairly loaded with alarms that we had installed ourselves and checked regularly. The fact that they hadn't gone off seemed to imply an inside job, but I knew that a skillful burglar can always manage to locate such alarms and put them out of action. Two doors and the vault had been opened, however, and there was no evidence of violence and no unidentified fingerprints.

During the war, an annex of sheet metal had been added to the warehouse. In this annex was the loading platform and the garage for the ten trucks employed by Moffit's firm. Two of these trucks were armored. This annex also housed the small office used by the night watchman. In one corner of the annex a window had been found broken, a window that opened on the alley.

Glass lay on the floor below the window, and a few fragments lay on a workbench that was partly under the window. The dust on the sill was disturbed, indicating that someone had entered by that means, and the glass on the floor implied the window had been broken from the outside. On the head of a nail on the edge of the window, I found a few threads of material resembling sharkskin. I put them in an envelope in my pocket.

Under the bench were a couple of folded tarps and some sacks. I flashed my light over them. At one end, those at the bottom of the pile were somewhat damp, yet there was no way for rain to have reached them despite the heavy fall the previous night. The outer door through which the truck would have to be driven was undamaged. It was then I started to get mad. Nobody goes through three doors, one with a combination lock, unless they are opened for him.

———

MOFFIT LOOKED UP, glaring, when I returned from my examination. "Well?" he demanded.

"Ghosts," I told him solemnly. "Spirits who walk through walls, or maybe Mandrake the Magician waved those furs out of the vault with a wand."

Hudspeth, Moffit's chief clerk, looked up at me as I came out of Moffit's office. "He's pretty worked up," he said, "he had a lot of faith in Burgeson."

I walked over to the water cooler. "Didn't you?"

"You can't be sure. I never trusted him too much. He was always asking questions that didn't concern him."

"Like what?"

"Oh, where we got our furs, what different coats cost, and such things." Hudspeth seemed nervous, like he was worried that I might not suspect the watchman.

When I got in my car, I sat there a few minutes, then started it up and swung out on the main drag, heading for the center of town. Then I heard a police siren, and the car slowed and swung over to me. Briggs was with them. He stuck his head out.

"Found that armored car," he called. "Come along."

———

THERE WAS A farmer standing alongside the road when we got there, and he flagged us down. It was on the Mill

Road, outside of town. The car was sitting among some trees and the door had been pried off with a chisel and crowbar. It was empty.

They had picked a good place. Only lovers or hikers ever stopped there. About a hundred yards back from the road was the old mill that gave the road its name. It was one of the first flour mills built west of the Sierras.

While Briggs and the cops were looking the car over, I walked around. There had been another car here and several men. The grass had been pressed down and had that gray look grass has when it's been walked through after a heavy dew. The trail looked interesting, and I followed it. It headed for the old mill. Skirting the mill, I walked out on the stone dock along the millpond. Even before I looked, I had a hunch what I'd find and I knew it wouldn't be nice. He was there, all right, floating facedown in the water, and even before I called the cops, I knew who it was.

When Pete Burgeson was hauled out of the water, we saw his head was smashed in. There was wire around him and you could see that somebody had bungled the job of anchoring him to whatever weight had been used.

"Burgeson was no crook," I said unnecessarily. "I knew the guy was straight."

For a private dick, I am very touchy about bodies. I don't like to hold hands with dead men, or women, for that matter. I walked away from this one and went back to the car. The cops would be busy so it gave me a chance to look around.

Backtracking from the car to the road, I found the place where it had left the pavement. There was a deep imprint of the tire, and I saw a place where the tread had picked up mud. Putting my hand down, I felt what looked like dry earth. It was dirt, just dry dirt. That brought me standing, for that car had been run in here after the rain ended!

Squatting down again, looking at that tread, I could see how it had picked up the thin surfacing of mud and left dry earth behind. If it had rained after the car turned off the road, that track would not be dry! Things began to click into place . . . at least a few things.

Without waiting for Briggs, I got into my car and drove

away. As I rounded the curve, I glanced back and saw Briggs staring after me. He knew I had something.

My first stop was Pete Burgeson's rooming house. Then I went on, mulling things over as I drove. It was just a hunch I had after all, a hunch based on three things: a broken window, dampness on a tarp, and a dry track on the edge of a wet road. At least, I knew how the job had been done. All I needed was to fill in a couple of blank spaces and tie it all together with a ribbon of evidence.

A stop at a phone booth got me Moffit. "What's the name of the driver of the armored truck that was stolen?"

"Mat Bryan. One of my best men. Why do you ask?"

"Just want to talk to him. Put him on the phone, will you?"

"I can't," Moffit explained. "He's getting married . . . he's got the day off but promised to make some morning deliveries for me. When his truck was missing we told him not to bother coming in."

It took me a half hour in that phone booth to get what I wanted, but by that time I was feeling sharper than a razor. Two things I had to do at once, but I dialed the chief. He was back in the office, and sounded skeptical.

"Why not take a chance?" I said finally. "If I'm right, we've got these crooks where we want them. I don't know what this bird looks like, how tall or short, but he's wearing a gray sharkskin suit, and it's been rained on. Try the parks, the cheap poolrooms, and the bars."

When I hung up, I hit the street and piled into my car. As I got into it, I got a glimpse of Huber coming down the sidewalk. He stopped to stare at me, and it was a long look that gave me cold chills.

WHEN I REACHED the warehouse, I headed right for the night watchman's office. Hudspeth was standing on the loading platform when I came in.

"Anyone been in Burgeson's office?" I asked him.

"No." He looked puzzled. "He always locked it when he came out, even for a few minutes, and it's still locked. I have the key here. Mr. Moffit wanted me to see if there was anything there that would help you."

"Let's look," I suggested, and then as he was bending over the lock, I gave it to him. "They found Burgeson's body. He was murdered."

The key jerked sharply, rattling on the lock. Finally, Hudspeth got it into the keyhole and opened the door. When he straightened up his face was gray.

Burgeson's leather-topped chair was where it always had been. The windows in the office allowed him to see all over the annex. His lunch box was open on the desk, and there was nothing in it but crumbs.

My eyes went over every inch of the desk, and at last I found what I had been looking for. On the side across from where Burgeson always sat, were a few cake crumbs. I looked at them, then squatted down and studied the floor. In front of the chair at that end of the desk was a spot of dampness. I got up. Hudspeth must have seen me grinning.

"You—you found something?"

"Uh huh." I looked right at him. "You can tell Moffit I'll be breaking this case in a few hours. Funny thing about crooks," I told him. "All of them suffer from overconfidence. This bunch had been pretty smart, but we've got them now. For burglary, and"—I looked right into his eyes—"murder!"

Then I went out of there on a run because when I'd said the last word, I had a hunch that scared me. I hit the door and got into my car, wheeled it around, and headed for the church. If I was right, and I knew I was, the phone from Moffit and Company would be busy right now, or some phone nearby.

There were a lot of cars at the church when I got there, and a bunch of people standing around as they always do for a funeral or a wedding.

"Where's Mat Bryan?" I demanded.

"We're waiting for him!" the nearest man told me. "He's late for his wedding!"

"Better break it to the bride that he probably won't make it today," I advised. "I'll go look for him." Without explanation, I swung my car into traffic and took off.

WHEN I PULLED up in front of his rooming house, I could see an old lady answering the telephone in the hallway.

As I walked up to her I heard her saying, "He should be there now! Some men drove up ten or fifteen minutes ago and took him away in a car!"

Taking the phone from her, I hung it up. "What did those men look like?" I demanded. "Tell me quick!"

She was neither bothered nor confused. "Who are you?" she demanded.

"The police," I lied. "Those men will kill Mat if I don't prevent them."

"They were in a blue car," she told me. "There were three of them—a big man in a plaid suit, and—"

"You call the police now," I interrupted. "Tell them what happened and that I was here. My name is Neil Shannon."

Racing back to my car, I knew it was all a gamble from here on. Bryan was an important witness, and unless I got to him he would go the way Pete Burgeson had gone. Mat Bryan was the one guy who could tip the police on what had actually taken place, and once they knew, they would have the killers in a matter of minutes.

Yet there was an even more important witness, and finding him was a bigger gamble than saving Mat Bryan.

All this trouble had developed because Jake Brusa had come out of Joliet determined to play it smart. This time he was going to be on the winning side, but now the sweetest deal he had ever had in his life was blowing up in his face, and when he was caught there he wouldn't have a chance if I could push this through.

If I'd expected to find him with Bryan, I was disappointed. He was just going in with Huber and Lincoff when I came in sight of the Sporting Center. I took a gander at my watch, then made a couple of calls to Briggs and the Roadside. They weren't necessary, for Jake Brusa had built his alibi the wrong way and for the wrong time.

Then I walked up to the Sporting Center and pushed the door open. Inside there was a cigar stand and a long lunch counter. You could bowl, play billiards or pool, and it was said that crap games ran there occasionally. You could also make bets on baseball, races, fights, anything you wanted.

Jake Brusa had a sweet setup there without going any further, but a crook never seems to know when he's got enough.

Huber was sitting at the counter with a cup of coffee. He turned when I started past him and grabbed at my wrist. I knocked the hand down so quick he spilled his coffee and jumped off the stool swearing.

"Where are you going?" he demanded.

"To talk to Jake," I told him. "So what?"

"He doesn't want to see anybody!"

"He'll see me, and like it."

"Tough guy, huh?" he said with a nasty smirk.

"That's right. You tell him I've come to get Mat Bryan!"

When I said that name, Huber's face went yellow-white, and he looked sick. I grinned at him.

"Don't like it, do you?" I threw it at him. "That was kidnapping, Huber. You'll get a chance to inhale some gas for this one!"

"Shut up!" he snarled. "Come on!"

I motioned him ahead of me, and after an instant's hesitation, he went. We went past a couple of bowling lanes, through a door, and up a stairway. The sound of the busy alley was only a vague whisper here. Soundproofed. That meant nobody would hear a shot, either. Nor a pushing around if it came to that. When he got to the door, he rapped and then stepped aside. "Think I'm a dope?" I said. "You first!"

His face went sour, but my right hand was in my coat pocket, and he didn't know I always carried my rod in a shoulder holster. He went in first.

Jake was behind a big desk, and Lincoff was seated in a chair at the opposite end. Brusa's face was like iron when he saw me.

"What do you want?" he growled.

"He said he wanted to see Mat Bryan!" Huber warned.

"He ain't here. I don't know him."

I leaned forward with both hands on the back of a chair. "Which one, Jake? Don't make me call you a liar," I told him. "Get him out here quick. I haven't much time."

Brusa's eyes were pools of hate. "No, you haven't!" he agreed. "What made you think Bryan was here?"

I laughed at him. I was in this up to my ears, and if I didn't come out of it, I might as well have fun.

"It was simple," I said. "You thought you had a good deal here. So what was it that gave you the idea you're smarter than everybody else? This time you thought you were going to be in the clear, and all you did was mess it up.

"You had a finger man point these jobs for you. You had a perfect alibi last night, and all the good it did you was to help you pull a fast switch. A sucker switch. You switched your chances at a cell for a chance at the gas chamber.

"When you drove that armored car off the road, Jake, you left a track, a track that was dry. That proved it was made this morning, after the rain had stopped. The rain stopped about seven A.M., and your alibi isn't worth a hoot. You took that truck out after the place opened up this morning!"

Brusa was sitting in his chair. He didn't like this. He didn't like it a bit. A crook can stand almost anything but being shown up as a fool.

"Smart lad!" he sneered. "Very smart! Until you walked in here!"

That one I shrugged off. Right now I wasn't too sure I had any more brains than he did, but I'd gambled that Bryan was here and alive. If I couldn't get him out, I could at least keep them thinking and keep them busy until the police followed up.

"You thought," I told him slowly, stalling for time, "you'd have the cops going around in circles over those locked doors. They'd all think the watchman had done it. But whoever sank that body did a messy job. It was already floating this morning."

Brusa's eyes swung around to Huber.

"He's lyin', boss!" Huber exclaimed in a panic. "He's lyin'!"

"He said the body was *floatin'*," Brusa replied brutally. "Why would he say that unless they'd found it?"

"You didn't go through those doors at all, Brusa," I broke in. "You didn't have to. The furs were all ready for you in the armored car, waiting to be driven away. Only two men knew how they got there, and one of them was honest, so you decided you had to kill him. Mat Bryan!"

Right then, I was praying for Briggs or the cops to get to me before the lid blew off. It was going to come off very soon and I was afraid I was expecting too much.

I kept on talking. "Bryan wanted to get off early because of the wedding, so your finger man hinted that he might leave the furs in the truck and have them all set to go in the morning, that would save time. All you had to do was wait until the plant opened in the morning, then go in and drive the truck away. Burgeson butted in, so you killed him.

"That was a mistake. According to the watchman's time schedule, he should have been inside the plant by then. Only something happened to throw him off, and he was there in the loading dock and tried to stop you.

"Murder changes everything, doesn't it, Jake? You weren't planning on killing, but you got it, anyway. If Burgeson and the furs disappeared, well, he would get credit for stealing them, only Huber here did a bum job of sinking the body.

"You picked the right man for the finger job, too. A smart man, and in a position where he could get all the inside information, not only from his own firm, but from others. But now I've got a feeling you've killed one man too many!"

"Then one more won't matter!" Brusa said harshly. "I'm going to kill Mat Bryan, but first I'm going to kill you!" His hand went to the drawer in front of him.

"Look out, boss!" Huber screamed. "He's got a rod!" He dove at me, clawing at that coat pocket. But my right hand slid into my jacket and it hit the butt of my .38, which came out of the armpit holster, spitting fire.

My first shot missed Brusa as Huber knocked me off balance. My second clipped Lincoff, and he cried out and grabbed at his side. Then I swung the barrel down Huber's ear and floored him.

Grabbing at the doorknob, I jerked it open and even as a slug ripped into the doorjamb over my head, I lunged out of the door with a gun exploding again behind me.

The stairs offered themselves, but I wanted Mat Bryan.

There was another door down the hall, and I hit it hard and went through just as Brusa filled the doorway of the room behind me. I tripped on the rug and sprawled at full length on the floor, my gun sliding from my hand and under the desk across the room.

There was no time to get it because Jake Brusa was lunging through the door. I shoved myself up and hit him with a flying tackle that smashed him against the wall, but he took it and chopped down at my ear with his gun. I slammed him in the ribs, then clipped his wrist with the edge of my hand and made him drop the gun.

I smashed him with a left as he came into me, but he kept coming and belted me with a right that brought smoke into my brain and made my knees sag. I staggered back, trying to cover up, and the guy was all over me, throwing them with both hands.

I nailed him with a right and left as he came on in, then stood him on his toes with an uppercut. He staggered and went to the wall. I followed him in and knocked him sprawling into a chair. It went to pieces under him, and he came up with a leg, taking a cut at my head that would have splattered my brains all over the wall had it connected. I went under it throwing a right into his solar plexus that jolted his mouth open. Then I lifted one from my knees that had the works and a prayer on it.

That wallop caught him on the jaw and lifted him right off his Number Elevens. The wall shivered as if an earthquake had struck and Brusa was out, but I was already leaving. I made a dive for my gun, shoved it into my belt, and went out the door and down the carpeted hall. My breath was coming in great gasps as I grabbed the knob and jerked the door open.

Lincoff had beat me to it, only I came in faster than he expected and hit him with my shoulder before he got his gun up. He hit the floor in a heap, and I grabbed up a paring knife lying beside some apples on the table and slashed the ropes at Bryan's wrists.

I got in that one slash, then dropped the knife and grabbed

at the gun in my waistband. Lincoff had got to his feet and had his gun on me by that time. I knew once that big cluck started to shoot, he'd never stop until the gun was empty, so I squeezed mine and felt it buck in my hand.

His gun muzzle pointed down as he raised on his tiptoes, and then it bellowed and the shot ripped into the floor. Lincoff dropped on his face and lay still. Thrusting the gun back in my pants, I wheeled to help Mat. He was almost free now, and it was only a minute's work to complete the job.

Down the hall there was a yell, then quiet, and then the pounding of feet. Briggs loomed in the door, a plainclothesman and a couple of harness cops with him.

"You!" Briggs's face broke into a relieved grin. "I might have known it. I was afraid they'd killed you!"

There wasn't much talking done until we got them down to Moffit's office. When we marched them in, he got up, scowling. Hudspeth was there, and I've never seen a man more frightened.

Jake Brusa and Huber, handcuffed, looked anything but the smart crooks they believed themselves to be. Brusa stood there glowering, and Huber was scared silly. But they were only the small fry in this crime. We wanted the man behind the scenes.

"All right," Briggs said, "it's your show." Most of the story he'd heard from me on the way over from the Sporting Center, and Bryan had admitted to the furs left in the truck.

"There's only one thing left," I said, watching one of our men come in beside a tall young fellow in a decrepit sharkskin suit, "and that's nailing the inside man, and we've got him. Dead to rights!"

Moffit sat up straight. "See here! If one of my men had been—" His eyes shifted to Hudspeth. "You, Warren?"

"No, Moffit," I said, leaning over the desk, "not the man you hired to be your scapegoat! You!"

His face went white as he sprang to his feet. "Why, of all the preposterous nonsense! Young man, I'll have—"

"Shut up, and sit down!" I barked at him. "It was you, Moffit. You were the man who informed these crooks when a valuable haul could be made! You were the man who cased the jobs for them! You knew the inside of every warehouse in town, and could come and go as you liked.

"We've got the evidence that will send you to prison if not to the gas chamber where you rightly should go! I'll confess I suspected Hudspeth. I know he had done time, but—"

"What?" Briggs interrupted. "Why, you investigated this man. You passed him for this job."

"Sure, and if I was wrong, we'd have to make the best of it. Hudspeth was in trouble as a kid, but after looking over his record, I decided he'd learned his lesson. I checked him carefully and found he had been bending over backwards to go straight.

"Nevertheless, knowing what I did and understanding it was my responsibility if anything went wrong, I kept a check on his spending and bank account. That day in the office when I first came in, he acted strangely because he knew something was going on and he was scared, afraid he'd be implicated.

"Another reason I originally let him stay was that I found that Moffit had hired him while knowing all about that prison stretch. I figured that if he would take a chance, we could, too. Now it seems Moffit was going to use him if anything went haywire."

"That's a lie!" Moffit bellowed. "I'll not be a party to this sort of talk anymore!"

Briggs looked at me. "I hope you've got the evidence." I looked at the man in the gray sharkskin suit and he stepped forward. "It was him, all right," he said, motioning toward Moffit. "He opened the doors this morning and he was standing by when the crooks knocked Pete out and took him away. He talked with this man," he added, pointing at Brusa.

"That's a lie!" Moffit protested weakly. "How would you know?"

"Tell us about it," I suggested to the man in gray.

He shifted his feet. "Pete Burgeson and me were in the same outfit overseas. But I got wounded and I've been in and out of the hospital for the last two years. He told me to come around and he'd give me money for a bed and chow. When I got here, the rain was pouring down and I couldn't make him hear. I tried to push up that back window and it busted, so I opened it and crawled in. Pete was some upset but said he'd take the blame. There weren't any burglar alarms on the annex.

"I was out of the hospital just a few days, and I got the shakes, so I laid down on those tarps under the bench after sharing Pete's lunch with him. Pete came along and put his coat over me.

"When I woke up, I saw them slug Pete. Moffit was standing right alongside. Every morning, I have to rub my legs before I can walk much and knew if I tried to get up they'd kill me, so I laid still until they left, then got away from there. One of the detectives found me this morning in the park."

"All right, boys," Briggs said, turning to the plainclothesman and the cops. "They're yours. All of them."

Jerking my head at Hudspeth, I said to one of the cops, "We represent the insurance company as well as this firm, so Hudspeth might as well stay in charge. The lawyers will probably want a reliable person here."

"Sure," Briggs said. "Sure thing."

We walked outside and the air smelled good. "Chief," I suggested, nodding at the man in the gray suit, "why not put this guy to work with us? He used to be an insurance investigator."

The man stopped and stared at me. Briggs did likewise. "How, how the devil did you know that?" he demanded. "You told me about the gray threads, the dampness on the tarp, the crumbs on the table, all the evidence that somebody was with Pete! But this—next thing you'll be telling me what his name is!"

"Sure," I agreed cheerfully. "It's Patrick Donahey!"

"Well, how in—" Donahey stared.

"Purely elementary, my dear Watson." I brushed my fingernails on my lapel. "You ate with your left hand, and insurance investigators always—"

"Don't give me that!" Briggs broke in.

"Okay, then," I said. "It did help a little that I found his billfold." I drew it out and handed it to Donahey. "It fell back of that tarp. But nevertheless, I—"

"Oh, shut up," Briggs said.

A FRIEND OF A HERO

THE GRAVEL ROAD forked unexpectedly and Neil Shannon slowed his convertible. On each side orange groves blocked his view, although to the right a steep hillside of dun-colored rock rose above the treetops. On that same side was a double gate in a graying split-rail fence.

He was about fifty miles northwest of Los Angeles, lost in a maze of orchards and small farms that was split by abrupt ridges and arroyos.

Neil Shannon got out of the car and walked to the gate. He was about to push it open when a stocky, hard-faced man stepped from the shrubbery. "Hold it, bud . . . what do you want?"

"I'm looking for the Shaw place. I thought someone might tell me where it was."

"The Shaw place? What do you want to go there for?"

Shannon was irritated. "All I asked was the directions. If you tell me I'll be on my way."

The man jerked his head to indicate direction. "Right down the fork, but if you're looking for Johnny, he ain't home."

"No? So where could I find him?"

The man paused. "Down at Laurel Lawn, in town. He's been dead for three days."

Shannon shook out a cigarette. "You don't seem upset over losing a neighbor, Mr. Bowen."

"Where'd you get that name?" The man stared suspiciously at Shannon.

"It's on your mailbox, in case you've forgotten. Are you Steve Bowen?"

"I'm Jock Perult. The Bowen boys ain't around. As for Shaw, his place is just down the road there."

"Thanks." Shannon opened the door of his car. "Tell me, Jock, do you always carry a pistol when you're loafing around home?"

"It's for snakes, if it's any of your business." He tugged his shirttail down over the butt of a small pistol.

Shannon grinned at him and put the car in gear. Scarcely three hundred yards further along the gravel road on the same side was the Shaw place. Marjorie Shaw saw him drive through the gate and came out to meet him.

The man who followed her from the door had a grizzle of gray beard over a hard chin and a short-stemmed pipe in his teeth. He looked at Shannon with obvious displeasure.

There were formalities to be taken care of. She read the contract standing by the car and looked at his private investigator's license. Finally she raised the subject of money.

"Let's not worry about that right now," he told her. "Johnny Shaw was a friend of mine; I'll do what I can for a couple of days and we'll see where we are. I'm warning you, though, on paper his death looks like an accident. I'm not sure there is much I can do."

"Come in, and I'll fix you a drink."

As he turned to follow he caught a tiny flash of sunlight from the brush-covered hillside across the way. Then he glimpsed the figure of a man, almost concealed. A man interested enough in what was going on to watch through binoculars.

Shannon glanced at the older man. "You're Keller? How about it? Did Johnny have any enemies?"

"Ain't none of my affair and I don't aim to make it so," Keller replied brusquely. "I'm quitting this job. Going to Fresno. Always did figure to go to Fresno."

———

MARJORIE SHAW WAS Johnny's sister, and though Shannon had never met her, he and John Shaw had been friends since the days before he had joined the police force. They had first met on a windy hillside in Korea. Now John was dead, his car crushed in a nearby ravine, and his sister thought that he had been intentionally killed.

The inside of the house was dim and cool. Shannon sat on the plaid sofa and listened to the girl moving about the kitchen. The door to the Frigidaire opened and closed; there was the sound of a spoon in a glass pitcher.

"After you called"—he spoke to her through the doorway—"I checked the report on the wreck. There was no indication of anything wrong. The insurance investigator agreed with the report. Clark, who investigated for the sheriff's office, said it was clearly an accident. Driving too fast or a drink too many."

She came in carrying a pitcher of iced tea and two glasses. "I didn't ask you out here, Mr. Shannon, to tell me what I've already heard. However, Johnny did not drink. Furthermore, he was extremely cautious. He had never had an accident of any kind, and he had been driving over that road two or three times a day for four years. I want it looked into. For my peace of mind, if nothing else. That's why I called you. Johnny always said you were the smartest detective on the Los Angeles police force."

"We'll see. . . . I'm not with the police force any longer."

———

AFTER THE ICED tea Marjorie Shaw drove Shannon out to the site of the wreck. They cut across the property on a dirt track and headed to where the county road came over the mountain from town. Emerging from Shaw's orange groves, they cut along the base of the hill. Although the car threw up a large cloud of dust, the track was well graded, and in the places where water drained, culverts had been installed. Obviously, Johnny Shaw had worked hard on his place and had accomplished a lot.

Marjorie pointed off to one side. "Johnny was going to dam that canyon and make a private lake," she explained. "Then, he intended to plant trees around it."

The canyon was rock-walled but not too deep. Dumped in the bottom were several junked cars.

"Did he intend to take those out?"

"Johnny was furious about them. He insisted the Bowens

take them out, and they said that if he cared so much he could take them out himself."

She paused. "This could be important, Mr. Shannon. . . . He tried to take it up with the county but the sheriffs and commissioners are all friends of the Bowens. I was with him when he went to the courthouse. They all got in a big fight and Johnny told that county commissioner that he would go to the DA if that was what it took and they got real quiet. After that we left. I was angry for Johnny and I didn't think about it much, but that's why I called you . . . it wasn't two weeks later that Johnny died."

"He mentioned the DA?" Shannon asked.

"Yes, why would he do that? Over junked cars, it doesn't make sense!"

"Unless he knew about something else and was making a threat."

"That's what I thought, but what could it be?"

"Well, if it has something to do with his death it's something that either someone in county government or the Bowen brothers don't want known."

The Bowen brothers . . . Shannon thought . . . and their buddy Perult who carried a gun inside his shirt.

———

THEY TURNED OUT onto the county road and within minutes were at the curve where Johnny had run off the cliff. She stopped the car and he got out. The afternoon shadows were long, but down below he could see the twisted mass of metal that had been Johnny's car.

"I'd like to go down and look around. I'll only be a few minutes."

At the edge of the road, starting down, he paused briefly. There was broken glass on the shoulder. Bits of headlight glass. He picked up several fragments, and the ridges and diffusers in them were not identical. Pocketing several, he climbed and slid down the cliff.

Examining the wreck, he could see why Johnny had been killed. The car had hit several times on the way down. The destruction was so complete that the sheriffs had had to use a torch to cut the body out. Surprisingly enough, one headlight was intact. Two pieces of the glass he had picked up conformed with the headlight pattern. The others did not.

The police and ambulance crew had left a lot of tracks, but there was another set that stood off to the side, and they turned off down the canyon. In two places other tracks were superimposed upon them.

Curious, he followed the tracks down the canyon where they met with the tracks of someone who had waited there.

He was back beside Johnny's car when there was a sharp tug at his hat and an ugly *whap* as something struck the frame and whined angrily away. Shannon dropped and rolled to the protection of some rocks. In the distant hills there was the vague echo of a gunshot.

It could have been a spent bullet . . . from someone hunting or shooting targets in the hills. Yet he knew it was nothing of the sort. That bullet had been fired by a man who meant to kill or, at least, warn. If he tried to get back up to the road, he might be shot.

He glanced up. Marjorie Shaw stood at the cliff's edge, looking down. "Get into the car," he called, just loud enough for her to hear, "and drive to the filling station on the highway. Wait there for me, in plain sight, with people around."

———

SHE LOOKED PALE and frightened when he got there a half hour later. His suit was stained with red clay and he showed her his hat.

"I called the sheriff," she said.

They heard the siren, and Deputy Sheriff Clark drew up. It was he whom Shannon had talked to about the accident.

He chuckled. "You city cops!" he scoffed. "That shot was probably fired by a late hunter, maybe a mile off. Now don't come down here trying to stir up trouble when there's no cause for it. Why would anyone try to kill someone investigating an accident?"

"What do you know about the Bowen outfit?"

Clark was bored. "Now look. Don't you go bothering people up here. The Bowens have got them a nice little place.

They pay their taxes and mind their own business. Furthermore, the Bowens are rugged boys and want to be left alone."

"Didn't Johnny Shaw complain about them once?"

Clark was annoyed. "Suppose he did? Shaw was some kind of a hero in the Korean War and he came out here thinking he was really going to do big things. He may have been quite a man in the war, but he sure didn't stack up against Steven Bowen."

"What's that? They had a fight?"

"I guess so, seein' that Johnny Shaw got himself whipped pretty bad. I think Steve got the idea that Shaw was throwing his weight around over those junk cars, comin' on high and mighty because he had a medal or two. They went at it out back of the hardware store in Santa Paula. I offered to take Shaw's complaint afterwards but I guess he was too proud."

Marjorie turned abruptly and got into her car, eyes blazing. Shannon put a hand on the door, then glanced back at Clark. "Tell me something, Clark. Just where do you stand?"

Clark was beside their car in an instant. "I'll tell you where I stand. I stand with the citizens of this community. I don't want any would-be hero barging in here stirring up trouble. And that goes double for private cops. The Bowens have lived here a long time and had no trouble until Shaw came in here. Now, I've heard all about these scrap cars and who wants who to tow them out of there. But I looked into it and there is nothing to prove that they ever belonged to Steve Bowen or anyone else on his place. If you ask me, that and this *investigation* of the car accident are just examples of city folks getting wild ideas and watching too much of those television shows."

THREE DAYS OF hard work came to nothing. Shaw had no enemies, his trouble with the Bowens was not considered serious, at least not killing serious, and as the Bowens had defeated Shaw all down the line, why should they wish to kill him? Of course there was that mention of the DA, but no one seemed to know what it meant.

The fragment of headlight glass he checked against the

Guide Lamp Bulletin, then sent it to the police lab for verification. The lens, he discovered, was most commonly used on newer Chrysler sedans but was a replacement for other models as well. He filed the information for future reference.

His next step was to talk with other farmers in the area. He drove about, asked many questions, got interesting answers.

The Bowens had two large barns on their place, which was only forty acres. They had two cows and one horse, and carried little hay. Their crops, if stored unsold, would have taken no more than a corner of the barn . . . so why two large barns?

Market prices for the products they raised did not account for the obvious prosperity of the brothers. All three drove fast cars, as did Jock Perult. At nearby bars they were known as good spenders. Some of the closest neighbors complained of the noise of compressors from the Bowen place and of their revving up unmuffled engines late at night, but these questions were soon answered—the Bowens built cars that they raced themselves at the track in Saugus and around the state at other dirt-track and figure-eight events.

At the county courthouse he researched the Bowen property, how long they had owned it and how much they had paid. While he was looking through the registrar's records a young man peered into the file room several times and had a whispered conversation with the clerk. The man had the look of someone who worked in the building, and Neil Shannon took a quick tour through the hallways on his way out. He spotted the young man sitting at a desk typing in the office of a particular county commissioner . . . a county commissioner who happened to be a neighbor of the Bowens.

Late at night—he was taking no chances with stray bullets this time—Shannon took a bucket of plaster back over to the crash site. While he was waiting for his casts to dry, he walked along the moonlit wash and into the canyon that Johnny had wanted to dam. The old rusted cars lay stark in the moonlight, and he used a pencil flash to examine them. One was a Studebaker and the other, not so old as he'd imagined, was a Chevrolet. Neither had engines; he searched hard for the Vehicle Identification Numbers on the body and could not find one on either car . . . they had been carefully removed. He pulled parts, the few that were left, off the Chevy and examined them carefully. They should have had a secondary date code on them, but every plate had been removed, the rivets meticulously drilled out.

———

HE MET MARJORIE Shaw for a drink in Santa Paula. "Little enough," he replied to her question. "Steve Bowen is a good dancer and a good spender, left school in the seventh grade, wasn't a good student, likes to drink but can handle his liquor. Likes to gamble and he drives in amateur races a little. Not sports cars . . . the rough stuff."

"So you think I'm mistaken?"

He hesitated. "No . . . I don't. Not anymore. I think your brother discovered something very wrong with the Bowens or their place. I think he was killed to keep him from causing trouble. Now that I know about the racing it fits too well; who better to force someone off a mountain road than a man who drives in demolition derbies!"

"Johnny once told me that the less I knew the better. That knowing about what went on out here could be dangerous."

"He was right. Keller knows it, too. I think that's why he is going to Fresno."

"Oh! That reminds me. He said he wanted to talk to you."

"I'll go see him." Shannon paused. "You know, Bowen was away from here for about six years. I wonder where he was?"

They left the bar and Shannon walked her to her car. They were standing on a side street when Steve Bowen walked up. Turning at the sound of steps, Shannon ran into a fist that caught the point of his chin. He was turned half around, and a second punch knocked him down.

"That'll teach you to mess around in other people's business!" Bowen said. He swung a kick at Shannon's face, but Shannon rolled over swiftly and got up. He ran into a swinging right and a left that caught him as he fell. He got up again and went tottering back into the car under a flail of fists. When he realized where he was again, he was seated in the car and Marjorie was dabbing at his face with a damp hand-kerchief.

"You didn't have a chance!" she protested. "He hit you when you weren't looking."

"Drive me to my car," he said.

Turning around a corner they stopped at a light, and along-side were Steve Bowen and his brothers. They were in a powerful Chrysler 300. The heavy car was stripped down for racing, and from the way the engine sounded they had hot-rodded it for even more horsepower. They looked at Shannon's face and laughed.

"Stop the car." Shannon opened the door and got out, despite her protests.

Ignoring the three, he walked to their car and studied the headlights. One had been replaced by glass from another make of car. When he straightened up, the grins were gone from their faces, and Joe Bowen was frightened.

"I see you've replaced a headlight," Shannon commented. "Was there any other damage?"

"Look, you . . . !" Tom Bowen opened the door.

"I'll handle this!" Steve Bowen interrupted. "You're look-ing for trouble, Shannon. If the beating you got didn't teach you anything, I'll give you worse."

Shannon smiled. "Don't let that sneak punch give you a big head. Is the paint on this fender fresh?"

There was a whine of sirens, and a car from the sheriff's department and also one of the city police cars pulled up.

"That's all, Shannon." Deputy Sheriff Clark stepped out. "It looks to me like you've had yours. Now get in your car and get out of town. You're beginning to look like a trouble-maker and we don't want your kind around."

"All right, Clark. First, though, I want to ask if Tom has a permit for that gun he's carrying. Further, I want you to check the number on it, and check the fingerprints of all four of them. Don't try putting me off either, I'll be talking to the DA and the FBI about why certain vehicle identification tags are missing and who's been bought off and who hasn't. Bowen, by the time this is over you're going to look back in wonder at how stupid you were when you refused to tow those cars like John Shaw asked!"

Clark was startled. He started to speak, and the Bowens stared angrily at Shannon as he got back into Marjorie's car.

They drove off. "I've talked a lot, but what can I prove?" he said. "Nothing yet. . . . The Bowens could explain that broken headlight, even if the make checks out perfectly. What we need is some real law enforcement and a search warrant for those barns."

"What's going on? What are you talking about?" Marjorie asked.

"Hot cars . . . and I don't mean the kind you race."

———

KELLER WAS NOT around when they rolled into the yard, but there was a telegram lying open on the table, addressed to Shannon. He picked it up, glanced at it, and shoved it into his pocket.

"That's it! Now we're getting someplace!"

Shannon seemed not to hear Marjorie's question about the contents. The message had been opened. Keller had read it. Keller was gone.

"Hide the car where we can get to it from the road, then hide yourself. No lights. No movement. The Bowens will be here as quick as they can get away from Clark. I don't have a thing on them yet, but they don't know it. Push a crook far enough and sometimes he'll move too fast and make mistakes."

There was little time remaining if he was to get to the barns before the Bowens arrived. They pulled the car behind the house, and Shannon made sure that Marjorie locked herself inside and turned out the lights. Then, careful to make no noise, he descended into the canyon and followed the path from near the junked cars through the wash and then an orchard to the barns back of the Bowen farmhouse.

By the time he reached the wall of the nearest barn, he knew he had only minutes in which to work. There was no sound. There were two large doors to the barn, closed as always, but there was a smaller door near them that opened under his hand.

Within, all was blackness mingled with the twin odors of oil and gasoline. It was not the smell of a farmer's barn, but of a garage. There was a faint gasping sound near his feet, then a low moan.

Kneeling, he put out a hand and touched a stubbled face. "Keller?" he whispered.

The old man strained against the agony. "I stepped into a bear trap. Get it off me."

Not daring to strike a light, Shannon struggled fiercely with the jaws of the powerful trap. He got it open, and a brief inspection by sensitive fingers told him Keller's leg was both broken and lacerated.

"I'll have to carry you," he whispered.

"You take a look first," Keller insisted. "With that trap off I can drag myself a ways."

Once the old man was out and the door closed, Shannon trusted his pencil flashlight.

Four cars, in the process of being stripped and scrambled. Swiftly he checked the motor numbers and jotted them down. He snapped off the light suddenly. Somebody was out in front of the barn, opposite from where he had entered.

"Nobody's around," Perult was saying. "The front door is locked and the bear trap is inside the back."

"Nevertheless, I'm having a look." That would be Tom Bowen.

The lock rattled in the door and Shannon moved swiftly, stepped in an unseen patch of oil, and his feet shot from under him. He sprawled full length, knocking over some tools.

The front door crashed open. The lights came on. Tom Bowen sprang inside with his gun ready. But Shannon was already on his feet.

"Drop it!" he yelled.

Both fired at the same instant, and Bowen's gun clattered to the floor and he clutched a burned shoulder. Perult had ducked out. Shannon stepped in and punched Tom Bowen on the chin; the man went down. With nothing to shoot at Shannon put two rounds into the side of one of the cars just to make them keep their heads down and ran out back.

He was down in the canyon before he found Keller, and he picked the old man up bodily and hurried as fast as he could with the extra weight.

He was almost at the house when Keller warned him. "Put me down and get your hands free. There's somebody at the house!"

Marjorie cried out and Shannon lowered Keller quickly to the ground, and gun in hand went around the corner of the house.

Shannon saw Steve Bowen strike Marjorie with the flat of his hand. "Tell me," Bowen said coldly, "or I'll ruin that face of yours."

Perult came sprinting in the front gate. "Hurry, boss! Tom's been shot."

Shannon stepped into sight and Perult grabbed for the front of his shirt, and Shannon lowered the gun and shot him in the thigh. Jock screamed, more in surprise than pain, and fell to the ground.

"Fast with the gun, aren't you?" Steve Bowen said. "I suppose you'll shoot me now."

"We're going back to your place," Shannon said, and then he whispered to Marjorie. "Get on the phone and call the district attorney. After you've called him, call the sheriff. But the DA first!"

"What are you going to do?" Marjorie protested.

"Me?" Shannon grinned. "This guy copped a Sunday on my chin when I wasn't looking, and he beat up Johnny, so as soon as you get through to the DA I'm going to take him back to that barn, lock the door, and see if he can take it himself."

———

TWENTY MINUTES LATER, Neil Shannon untied Steve Bowen and shoved him toward the door with his gun. They reached the barn without incident. Inside, Shannon locked the door and tossed the gun out of the window.

Bowen moved in fast, feinted, and threw a high, hard right.

Shannon went under it and hooked both hands to the body. The bigger man grunted and backed off, then rushed, swinging with both hands. A huge fist caught Shannon, rocking his head on his shoulders, but Shannon brushed a left aside and hooked his own left low to the belly.

Getting inside, he butted Bowen under the chin, hit him with a short chop to the head, and then pushing Bowen off, hit him twice so fast, Bowen's head bobbed. Angry, the big man moved in fast and Shannon sidestepped and let Bowen trip over his leg and plunge to the floor.

Bowen caught himself on his hands and dove in a long flying tackle, but Shannon moved swiftly, jerking his knee into Bowen's face. Nose and lips smashed, the big man fell, then got up, blood streaming down his face.

Bowen tried to set himself, but Shannon hit him with a left and knocked Bowen down again with a right.

Stepping in on Bowen, Shannon got too close and Bowen grabbed his ankle. He went down and Bowen leaped up and tried to jump on his stomach. Shannon rolled clear, got up fast, and when Bowen tried another kick, Shannon grabbed his ankle and jerked it high. Bowen fell hard and lay still.

There was a hammering at the door. Shannon backed off. "You're the tough guy, Bowen," he said, "but not that tough." Bowen didn't move.

The door opened and Clark came in followed by several deputies and a quiet man in a gray suit.

To the assistant district attorney he handed a telegram. "From the FBI. I checked on Bowen and found he had done six years in the federal pen for transporting a stolen car. I wired them on a hunch. I think you'll find that they were paying off certain people in county government to be left alone."

"Hey, now wait a minute!" Clark protested.

"Shut up," Shannon snapped. "They'll be looking at you, your boss, and a couple of commissioners, so you'd better start checking your hole card!

"Johnny Shaw got suspicious when he tried to get the county to make the Bowens move those derelict cars. He found out enough and Bowen ran him off the road. The headlight glass was a Chrysler lens and Bowen drives a 300. Perult and Steve

Bowen walked over to the wreck afterwards to be sure Johnny was dead. The tracks are still there, but I made casts of them to be sure."

Steve Bowen moaned and sat up.

"Come on, Steve," Shannon said. "I think we're all going to have to go to Ventura and answer a lot of questions."

Bowen winced as he stood up. "You broke my ribs," he growled.

"Count yourself lucky. If these boys hadn't come I'd still be at it. You beat up Johnny Shaw . . . he carried me out of a firefight in Korea when I was wounded. There were shells going off everywhere and he'd never even seen me before. They gave him a medal for it. Now, he wasn't a big guy like you, he didn't know how to box, and he'd become a medical corpsman because he knew he couldn't bring himself to kill. But when the chips were down he did what was necessary."

Shannon took a deep breath. "Plead guilty," he said. "Because if they don't have enough evidence to put you away, I'll find it. No matter how long it takes."

They were led to the waiting cars, and with the ambulances in the lead and Marjorie following, they headed for Ventura.

THE VANISHED BLONDE

ONLY ONE LIGHT showed in the ramshackle old house, a dim light from a front window. Neil Shannon hunched his shoulders inside the trench coat and looked up and down the street. There was only darkness and the slanting rain. He stepped out of the doorway of the empty building and crossed the street.

There was a short walk up to the unpainted house, and he went along the walkway and up the steps. Through the pocket of the trench coat, he could easily reach his .38 Colt automatic, and it felt good.

He touched the doorbell with his left forefinger and waited. Twice more he pressed it before he heard footsteps along the hall, and then the door opened a crack and Shannon put his shoulder against it. The slatternly woman stepped back and he went in. Down the hall, a man in undershirt and suspenders stared at him. He was a big man, bigger than Neil Shannon, and he looked mean.

"I've some questions I want to ask," Shannon said to the man. "I'm a detective."

The woman caught her breath, and the man walked slowly forward. "Private or Headquarters?" the man asked.

"Private."

"Then we're not answering. Beat it."

"Look, friend," Shannon said quietly, "you can talk to me or the DA. Personally, I'm not expecting to create a lot of publicity unless you force my hand. Now you tell me what I want to know, or you're in trouble."

"What d'you mean, trouble?" The man stopped in front of Shannon. He was big, all right, and he was both dirty and unshaven. "You don't look tough to me."

Shannon could see the man was not heeled, so he let go of the gun and took his hand from his pocket.

"Get out!" The big man's hand shot out.

Shannon brushed it aside and clipped him. It was a jarring punch and caught the big fellow with his mouth open. His teeth clicked like a steel trap and he staggered. Then Shannon hit him in the wind and the big fellow went down, his hoarse gasps making great, empty sounds in the dank hallway.

"Where do we talk?" Shannon asked the woman.

She gestured toward a door, then opened it and walked ahead of him into a lighted room beyond. Shannon grabbed the big man by his collar and dragged him into the room.

"I want to ask about a woman," he said, his eyes sharp. "A very good-looking blonde."

The woman's face did not change. "Nobody like that around here," she said sullenly. "Nobody around here very much at all."

"This wasn't yesterday," Shannon replied. "It was a couple of years ago. Maybe more."

He saw her fingers tighten on the chair's back and she looked up. He thought there was fear in her eyes. "Don't recall any such girl," she insisted.

"I think you're wrong." He sat down. "I'm going to wait until you do." He was on uncertain ground, for he had no idea when the girl had arrived, nor how, nor when she had left. He was feeling his way in the dark.

The man pulled himself to a sitting position and stared at Shannon, his eyes ugly.

"I'll kill you for that!" he said, his voice shaking with passion.

"Forget it," Shannon said. "You tried already." His eyes lifted to the woman. "Look, you can be rid of me right away. Tell me the whole story from beginning to end, every detail of it. I'll leave then, and if you tell me the truth, I won't be back."

"Don't recall no such girl." The woman pushed a strand of mouse-colored hair from her face. Her cheeks were sallow and her skin was oily. The dress she wore was not ragged from poverty, merely dirty, and she herself was unclean.

Disgusted, Shannon stared around the room. How could a girl, such as he knew Darcy Lane to be, have come to such a place? What could have happened to her?

———

HE HAD LOOKED at her picture until the amused expression of her eyes seemed only for him, and although he told himself no man could fall in love with a picture, and that of a girl who was probably dead, he knew he was doing a fair job of it.

Right now he knew more about her than any woman he had ever known. He knew what she liked to eat and drink, the clothes she wore and the perfume she preferred. He had read, with wry humor, her diary and its comments on men, women, and life. He had studied the books she read, and was amazed at their range and quantity.

He had sat in the same booth where she had formerly come to eat breakfast and drink coffee, and in the same bar where she had drunk Burgundy and eaten Roquefort cheese and crackers. Yet despite all the reality she had once been, she had vanished like a puff of smoke.

Alive, beautiful, talented, intelligent, filled with laughter and friendship, liked by both men and women, Darcy Lane had dropped from sight at the age of twenty-four as mysteriously as though she had never been, leaving behind her an apartment with the rent paid up, a closet full of beautiful clothes, and even groceries and liquor.

"Find her," Attorney Watt Braith had said. "You've three months to do it, and she has a half million dollars coming. You will get twenty-five dollars a day and expenses, with a five-hundred-dollar bonus if you succeed."

Whatever happened to Darcy Lane had happened suddenly and without preliminaries. Nothing in all her effects gave any hint as to what such a girl would be doing in a place like this. Yet it was his only lead, flimsy, strange, yet a lead nonetheless.

The police had failed to find her. Then their attention had

been distracted by more immediate crimes; the disappearance of one girl who, it was hinted, had probably run off with a lover, was forgotten. Now, he had a tip, just a casual mention by a man he met in Tilford's Coffee Shop, to the effect that he had once seen the beautiful blonde, who used to eat there, living in a ramshackle dump in the worst part of town. The description fit Darcy Lane.

Six months after she disappeared, prospector Jim Buckle was killed in a rockslide that overturned his jeep and partially buried him, and Darcy Lane sprang into the news once more when it turned out that Buckle had two million dollars' worth of mineral holdings and that he had left it to four people, of whom Miss Lane was one.

———

"TALK," NEIL SHANNON said now to the disreputable-looking pair before him, "and you might get something out of it. Keep your mouths shut and you're in trouble. You see," he smiled, "I've a witness. He places the girl in your place, and you both were seen with her. You"—he pointed a finger at the man—"forced her back into a room when she wanted to come out."

The man glared balefully at him. "She was sick," he said, "she wasn't right in the head."

Neil Shannon tightened, but his face did not change. Now he had something. At all costs, he must not betray how little it was, how the connection was based on one man's memory, a memory almost three years old. "Tell me about it."

He reached in his pocket and drew out a ten-dollar bill, smoothing it on his knee. The woman stared at it with eager, acquisitive eyes.

"He found her," she said. "She was on the beach, half naked, and her head cut. He brought her here."

"Shut up, you old fool!" The man was furious. "You want to get us into trouble?"

"Talk, and maybe you can get out of it. You're already in trouble," Shannon assured them. "If the girl was injured, why didn't you take her to a hospital? Or report it to the police?"

"He wanted her," the slattern said malevolently. "That's why he did it. She didn't know who she was nor nothin'. He brung her here. He figured she'd do like he said. Well, she wouldn't! She fought him off, an' made so much fuss he had to quit."

"What about you?" the man sneered. "You and your plans to make money with her?"

Sickened, Shannon stared at them. What hands for an injured girl to fall into! "What happened?" he demanded. "Where is she now?"

"Don't know," the man said. "Don't know nothin' about that."

Neil got up. "Well, this is a police matter, then."

"What about the ten?" the woman protested. "I talked."

"Not enough," Shannon said. "If you've more to say, get started."

"She'd been bumped or hit on the head," the woman said. "First off, I thought he done it, but I don't think he did from what she said after. She was mighty bad off, with splittin' headaches like, an' a few times she was off her head, talkin' about a boat, then about paintin', an' finally some name, sounded like Brett."

"Where did you find her?" Shannon asked the man.

He looked up. "On the beach past Malibu," he said. "I was drivin' along when I thought I saw somebody swimmin', so I slowed down. Then she splashed in an' fell on the sand. No swimmin' suit, nor any dress, either, nor shoes." He wiped his mouth with the back of his hand. "She was some looker, but that gash on her head was bad. I loaded her up an' brung her on home."

"What happened to her?" Shannon watched them keenly. Had they murdered the girl?

"She run off!" The man was vindictive. "She run off, stole a dress an' a coat, then took out of here one night."

"You ever seen her again?"

"No." Shannon felt sure the man was lying, and he saw the woman's lips tighten a little. "Never seen nor heard of her after."

WHEN HE WAS back in the street, he walked a block, then crossed the street and came back a little ways, easing up until he could slip close to the house, the dripping rain covering his approach. Listening, he could hear through a partly opened window, but at first nothing but the vilest language and bickering.

Finally, they calmed down. "Must be money in it," the man said. "Mage, we should've got more out of that feller. Private detective. They ain't had for nothin'."

"How could we ever git any of it?" the woman protested.

"How do I know? But if there's money, we should try."

"I told you that lingerie of hers was expensive!" Mage proclaimed triumphantly. "Anyway, she ain't writ this month. She ain't sent us our due."

"This time," the man said thoughtfully, "I think I'll go see her. I think I will."

"You better watch out," Mage declared querulously. "That detective will have an eye on us now. We could git into trouble."

There was no more said, and he saw them move into a bedroom where the man started to undress. Neil Shannon eased away from the window and walked down the street. He was in a quandary now. Obviously, the two had been getting mail from the girl, and from the sound of it, money. But for what?

They had found her with a cut on her head. That part would fit in all right, but what would she be doing in the sea? And who had hit her? If she had been struck, she might have amnesia, and that would explain her not returning to her apartment. That she was an excellent swimmer, he knew. She had several clippings for distance swimming, and others telling of diving contests she had won.

She must have come from a boat. Yet whose boat, and what had she been doing on it? One thing he resolved. These two must never learn that she was Darcy Lane, and heiress to a half million—if they did not already know it.

Before daylight, he was parked up the street, and he saw the man come from the house and start in his direction. From where he sat, he saw the man draw nearer and, without noticing him, drop a letter in a mailbox. As soon as the man was out of sight, Shannon slid from his car and, hurrying across the street, he shoved a dozen blank sheets of paper from his notepad after it.

They would, he knew, provide an effectual marker for the letter he wanted to see. It was almost two hours later that the mail truck came by, and he got out of his car and crossed the street again. He flashed his badge.

"All I want to see is the top envelope under those blank pages I dropped in."

"Well"—the man shrugged his shoulders—"I guess I can let you see the envelope, all right, but only the outside."

From their position, there were three letters that it could have been. He eliminated two of them at once. Both were typewritten. The third letter was written in pencil, judging by the envelope, and it was addressed to Miss Julie McLean, General Delivery, Kingman, Arizona. The return address was the house down the street, and the name was Sam Wachler.

"Thanks," Shannon said and, noting the address, he climbed into his car and started back for his office.

<hr>

When he opened the door, a tall, slender man with sharp features and a white face rose. "Mr. Shannon? I am Hugh Potifer, one of the Buckle heirs."

Shannon was not impressed. "What can I do for you?" he asked, leading the way into his private office.

"Why, nothing, probably. I was wondering how you were getting along with your search for Darcy Lane?"

"Oh, that?" Shannon shrugged. "Nothing so far, why?"

"There isn't much time left, Mr. Shannon, and she has been gone a long time. Do you really think it worthwhile to look?"

Shannon sat down at his desk and took out some papers. His mind was working swiftly, trying to grasp what was in the wind.

"I get paid for looking," he replied coolly, "it's my business."

"Suppose"—Potifer's dry voice was cautious—"you were given a new job? Something that would keep you here in town? Say, at one hundred dollars a day?"

Neil Shannon looked up slowly. His eyes were darker and he felt his gorge rising. "Just what are you implying? That I occupy myself here, and stop looking for Darcy Lane?"

"At one hundred dollars a day—that would be seven ... no. ... six hundred dollars." Potifer drew out his wallet. "How about it?"

Shannon started to tell him to get lost, then hesitated. A sudden thought came to him. Why should Potifer call on him at this time? What was the sudden worry? It was easy to understand that he might not want Darcy to show up now and lay claim to her share, which otherwise would be divided among the remaining three heirs. But why come right now? There was little time left and no indication that the girl would ever be found. So what did Hugh Potifer know?

Shannon shrugged. "Six hundred is a nice sum of money," he admitted, stalling. "On the other hand, you'd stand to make well over a hundred thousand more if she doesn't appear. That's a nicer sum, believe me!"

Potifer pursed his thin lips. "I'll make it a thousand, Mr. Shannon. An even thousand."

"Why," Shannon asked suddenly, "did you specify that I stay in town? Do you have reason to believe she is alive, but out of town?"

From Potifer's expression, Shannon knew he had hit it. Certainly, Potifer knew something, but what? And how had he found out? Suppose he had been the one who—but no. None of these three admitted to knowing each other or Darcy before becoming heirs to the Buckle estate. Further, Darcy had vanished six months before Buckle died, and none of them had known about the will. Or had they?

"You forget," Shannon said quietly, "there's a five-hundred-dollar bonus if I find her—and one would suspect that she might be quite grateful herself. Why, she might give a man four or five thousand dollars for finding her in time!"

"Well?" Potifer got to his feet. "You're trying to boost the ante. No, Mr. Shannon. You have my offer."

Neil Shannon tipped back in his chair. "So you know something about Darcy Lane's whereabouts? If I were you, I'd do some tall talking, right now and fast!"

"You can't frighten me, Shannon," Potifer said coldly. "Good day!"

When the door had closed behind Potifer, Shannon rose. Thrusting all the papers into a briefcase, he raced around to his apartment and hurriedly packed a bag with the barest necessities for a two-day trip. Then he went down to his car.

He was afraid to take the time, but he drove by Braith's office to check in. He met the attorney coming toward the street. Braith was a tall, handsome man with a quick smile.

"Any luck, Shannon?" he asked. "Only a week left, you know."

"That's what I was coming to see you about," he said. "I got a lead."

"What?" Watt Braith was excited. "You don't mean it!"

"Yes, I'm going to investigate now. I'm driving over to Kingman."

"Arizona?" Braith stared at him. "What would a model be doing over there?"

"Well, she was a secretary before she was a model, you know. Anyway, I've a good lead in that direction. I think," he added, "that Potifer knows something, too. He dropped around today and tried to bribe me to lay off."

"I'm not surprised. He stands to make more money if she's not found; however, I doubt if he had anything to do with her disappearance. What information do you have?"

"Not enough to be definite. But, from what I know, I'm fairly certain that we have our girl."

"Kingman, eh? Any idea what name she's using?"

Shannon hesitated, then he said, "If I did, I'd be a lot better off. But there will be lots of ways of finding out, and she's a girl who is apt to be remembered."

Watt Braith studied him sharply. "You know anything you're not telling, Shannon? I hired you, and I want whatever information you have."

Shannon just looked at him.

Braith didn't like it. "Have it your own way. It's probably a wild-goose chase, anyway. If she had been able to, she would have communicated with us long since."

"She may not have known anything about this Buckle will. Even if she has returned to her right senses and normal attitude, she may have decided to stay on."

Braith shook his head. "I doubt it. This trip to Kingman seems a wild-goose chase. Probably the girl drowned or something, and her body simply wasn't recovered."

"Drowned?" Shannon laughed. "That's the last thing I'd believe."

"Why, what do you mean?" Braith stared at him.

"She was a champion swimmer. It was an old gag of hers to tell new boyfriends that she couldn't swim, and seven or eight of them gave her lessons, and Darcy Lane started winning medals for swimming when she was twelve!"

Watt Braith shrugged. "Well, a lot of other things could have happened. I hope none of them did. Let me know how you come out."

———

AFTER THE ATTORNEY had left, Neil Shannon stood there in the street, scowling. Braith acted funny; that part about the swimming had seemed to affect him strangely.

He was imagining things. Only three people stood to gain from an accident to Darcy Lane, and they were Amy Bernard, Stukie Tomlin, and Hugh Potifer. There was no use considering Braith, for that highly successful young lawyer stood to profit in no way at all. And, anyway, Darcy Lane had been missing for six months before the death of Jim Buckle brought the matter to a head.

Neil Shannon stood there scowling, some sixth sense irritating him with a feeling of something left undone. It was high time that he started for Kingman, yet walking down the street he debated the whole question again, and then he got on the telephone.

When he hung up, he sat in the booth, turning the matter over in his mind, and then he dialed another number and still another. He placed a call to the Mojave County sheriff's office, in Kingman. Another to a real estate agent, and a third to a lawyer that he sometimes worked for. Details began to click together in his mind, and as he worked, he paused from time to time to mop the sweat from his face and curse telephone booths for being so hot.

His last call convinced him, and when he left the booth, he was almost running. He made one stop, and that a quick one at his own apartment. There he picked up the diary of Darcy Lane and hurriedly leafed through it. At a page near the end, he stopped, skimming rapidly over the opening lines of the entry. Then he came to what he was seeking.

. . . At the Del Mar today, met a tall and very handsome young man whose name was Brule. One of those accidental meetings, but we had a drink together and talked of yachting, boating, and swimming. He noticed my paints and commented on them, expressing an interest. Yet, when I mentioned Turner, he was vague, and he was equally uncertain about Renoir and Winslow Homer. Why do people who know nothing about a subject seem to want to discuss it as an expert with someone who is well educated?

Shannon closed the diary with a snap and locked it away, and then ran for his car. He took Route 66 toward Kingman and drove steadily, holding his speed within reason until he was in the desert and then opening the convertible up.

He glanced at his watch. It was not so late as he had believed. He had got the address from the letter Sam Wachler had mailed at some time around eight in the morning. Potifer had been in his office when he arrived there, which was nearly an hour later. Potifer had been with him awhile, and then he had gone to his own apartment. Having been up much of the night, and at his post so early in the morning, the day had seemed much advanced to him when actually it was quite early. And that meant that Braith had been leaving his office early, too. Or for a late lunch.

The check of the diary had taken a little time, but now he

was rolling. He drove faster, turning the problem around in his mind. It was lucky that he knew something of Kingman, and knew a few people there. It would make his search much easier.

As the pavement unwound beneath the wheels, he studied the problem again and was sure that he had arrived at the correct conclusion. Yet, knowing what he did, he realized that every second counted, for Darcy Lane . . . if alive as he believed, was again in danger.

———

HE WAS ALONE on the road now, and the setting sun was turning the mountains into ridges of pink and gold, shading to deeper red and then to purple. A plane moaned overhead, and suddenly realizing that one of those involved might travel by air, he felt sick to the stomach and speeded up, pushing the convertible even faster.

Hugh Potifer was a mystery. How much did the man know? He seemed to know that Darcy was alive, and even to have some hint as to her whereabouts, yet how could he have found her? It could, of course, have been an accident. Potifer was an assayer and, though based in Las Vegas, was in touch with many miners and prospectors in the Kingman area.

Old Jim Buckle had been a lonely man, without relatives, and interested solely in the finding of gold. Potifer had accommodated him a number of times. Amy Bernard had done some typing for him and had forwarded things to him at various places in Arizona and Nevada. Stukie Tomlin had been a mechanic who kept his jeep in repair, and Darcy Lane had merely been a girl who talked to him over coffee, then took him out to show him the Los Angeles nightlife and had secretly hoped that he might meet a woman and settle down.

Shannon recalled that part of the diary very well. How Darcy had found herself seated beside the old man. He had seemed very lonely, and they had talked. He had shamefacedly confessed it had always been his wish to go to the Mocambo or Ciro's—places he had read about in the papers. Touched, Darcy had agreed to go with him, so the kindly old man and the girl who had just become a model had made the rounds. From the diary and from Watt Braith, Shannon had a very clear picture of Buckle. He had been a little man, shy and white-haired, happy in the desert, but lost away from it. Darcy's thoughtfulness had touched him, and none of the four had known of the will—except maybe Potifer. He might have.

Kingman's lights were coming on when he swung the car into a U-turn and parked against the curb in front of the Beale Hotel. For a moment he sat there thinking. It was well into the evening. The chances were that Darcy would be at home, wherever that might be. He got out of his car and went in, trying the phone book first.

No luck. He called the operator, asking for Alice, whom he had known years before. She was no longer with the phone company, moved east with her husband, and he could get no information about Julie McLean. And then he remembered someone else. Johnny had been a deputy sheriff here in Mojave County. His father had been one of the last stage drivers in the West. Time and again he had regaled Shannon with stories of his father's days on the Prescott and Ash Fork run. He was the kind of man who knew what was going on around town, even in retirement.

———

HUALAPI JOHNNY ANSON sat on his porch watching the last blue fade from the western sky. He greeted Shannon with a wave and offered him a White Rock soda from a dented cooler sitting on a chair beside him.

"Haven't seen you in a while," he said.

"Haven't been here in a while." Shannon went on to tell Anson what he was up to. In ten minutes he was back in his car and headed back up the road and Hualapi Johnny was dialing the sheriff's office in Kingman.

Johnny had reminded him of a box canyon they had once visited many years ago. There was a gravel road that led to it and a bottleneck entrance. It was a cozy corner where people went for picnics when he had last seen it. There was a house there now, and it was rented to a young lady.

Strangely, his mouth felt dry and there were butterflies in

his stomach. He knew it was not all due to the fact that he was in a race with a murderer. It was because, finally, he was about to find Darcy Lane.

He slowed down and dimmed his lights, having no idea what he was heading into. And then, almost at the entrance to the small canyon, he glimpsed a car parked off the road in the darkness. It had a California license, and it was empty. He was late—perhaps too late!

He drove the car into the canyon, saw the lights of the house, then swung from the car and ran up the steps. The door stood open and on the floor lay a dark, still figure.

Lunging through, he dropped to his knees, then grunted his surprise. It was a man who lay there, and he lay in a pool of blood.

Shannon turned him over, and the man's eyes flickered. It was Stukie Tomlin.

"Shannon!" The wounded man's voice was a hoarse whisper. "He's—he's after her. Up—up on the cliffs. I tried to—help. Hurry!"

"Listen," Shannon said sharply, bringing the wounded man back to consciousness. "Help is on the way. Where is she? Did she go up on the cliffs tonight?"

"No"—the head shook feebly—"this—afternoon. To paint. I warned her. I came myself, tried to stop him. He shot me, went up cliffs—sundown."

Sundown! Hours ago! Feebly, Tomlin gasped out directions and, vaguely, Shannon recalled the path up the cliffs. To go up there at night? With someone waiting with a gun? Shannon felt coldness go all over him, and his stomach was sick and empty.

He left the house, moving fast, stumbled on the end of the path more through luck than design, and then started up.

———

WHEN HE WAS halfway up, the path narrowed into an eyebrow that hung over the box canyon, with a sheer drop of seventy feet or so even here, and increasing as the path mounted. Probably, he reflected, there was some vantage point from the cliff top where she could paint. Yet by this time, whatever the killer had come to do was probably done, and the man gone, long since.

Cool wind touched his face, and then he heard a voice speaking. He stopped, holding his breath, listening intently. He could make out no words, only that somewhere ahead, someone was talking.

On careful feet, he moved to the top of the cliff, holding himself low to present no silhouette. Before him were many ledges of rock, broken off to present a rugged shoulder some fifteen feet high, all of ten feet back from the promontory. He crouched, for the voices were clearer now.

"You'd better come out, Julie. Just come out and talk to me. It will be all right."

That voice!

Choking anger mounted within Neil Shannon, and he shifted his feet, listening.

"Go away." Her voice was low and strained. "I'm not coming out, and when morning comes, people will see us."

The man laughed. "No, they won't, Julie. It's hours until morning, and you can't hang there that long. Besides, if you don't come out, I'm going up higher where I can throw rocks down. People will just think you got too near the edge, and fell."

There was no reply at all. Trying to reconstruct the situation, Shannon decided that Darcy had seen the man before he got to her. She must have got around the cliff on some tiny ledge where he could not follow or reach her.

There had to be an end now. He rose to his feet and took two quick steps, then stopped.

"All right!" His voice rang sharply. "This is the end of the line! Come away from there, your hands up!"

The dark figure whirled, and Shannon saw the stab of flame and heard the gun bellow. But the man fired too fast, missing his shot. Involuntarily, Shannon stepped back. A rock rolled under his foot and he lost balance. Instantly, the gun roared again, and then the man charged toward him. Shannon lunged up, swinging his own gun, but the man leaped at him feet first.

Rolling dangerously near the cliff edge, Shannon scrambled as the man dove for him. Shannon slashed out with the pistol barrel, but caught a staggering blow and lost his grip on his gun. He swung a left and it sank into the man's stomach. He heard the breath go out of him, and then Shannon lunged forward, knocking the other man back into an upthrust ledge of rock.

They struggled there, fighting desperately, for the other man was powerful, and had the added urgency of fear to drive him. All he had gambled for was lost if he could not win now, and he was fighting not only for money, but for life.

A blow staggered Shannon, but he felt his right crash home, took a wicked left without backing, and threw two hard hooks to the head. He could taste blood now, and with a grunt of eagerness, he shifted his feet and went in closer, his shoulders weaving. His punches were landing now, and the fellow didn't like them, not even a little. This was a rougher game than the other man was used to, but Shannon, who had always loved a rough-and-tumble fight, went into him, smashing punches—until the man collapsed.

It was pitch dark even atop the mountain, and Shannon was taking no chances that the man was playing possum. When he felt the man go slack under his punches, he thrust out his left hand making a crotch of his thumb and fingers and jammed it under the fellow's chin, jerking him erect. Then he hooked his right into his midsection again and again. This time when he let go, he wasn't worried.

Swiftly, in a move natural to every policeman, he rolled the fellow on his face and handcuffed his hands behind his back. Then, at last, his breath coming in painful gasps, sweat streaming from him, he straightened.

"It's all right, ma'am," he said quietly. "You can come back out."

Her voice was strained. "I—I can't. I'm afraid to let go. I—"

Quickly, he went to the cliff edge, then worked his way around. Only the balls of her feet were on a narrow ledge, and her fingers clutched precariously at another. Obviously, she had clung so long that her fingers were stiffened. He moved closer, put his left arm around her waist, and drew her to him.

Carefully, then, he eased himself back until they stood on the flat rocks, and suddenly she seemed to let go and he felt her body loosen against him, all the tension going out of her. He held her until she stopped crying.

"Better sit down right here," he said quietly then. "We won't try the path for a little while, not until you feel better. I've got to take him down, too."

"But who—who are you?" she protested. "I don't know you, do I?"

"No, Miss Lane." He heard her gasp at the name. "You don't. But I know all about you. I'm a private detective."

He told her, slowly and carefully, about Jim Buckle and his will, about the search for her, about Hugh Potifer, Stukie Tomlin, and Amy Bernard. From a long way off a siren approached, red lights flashed against the rocks. He'd worry about the sheriffs in good time. . . .

"Now," he said, "you tell me, and then we'll get this straight, once and for all."

"I can't!" There was panic in her voice. "I—I don't know . . ."

"Take it easy," he said sympathetically, "and let's go back to the day you met that chap Brule. It was him, wasn't it?"

He saw her nod. The moon was coming up now, and the valley off to the right and the canyon below them would soon be bathed in the pale gold beauty of a desert night. The great shoulders of rock became blacker, and the face of the man, who lay on the rocks, whiter.

"After I met him, only a few days after, I was painting. I was on an old oil dock—where there was one of those offshore wells, you know? He came along in a motorboat and wanted me to come for a ride, offered to drop me back at Santa Monica. I had come up on the bus, so I agreed.

"We started back, but he kept going farther and farther out. I—I was a little worried, but he said there were some sandbars closer. Then he stopped the boat and said something about a lunch. He told me it was under a seat. I stooped to get it, and something struck me. That was the last I remembered. The last, except—well, I felt the water around me. I remember then that when he struck me I fell over the side and went down."

"Nothing more—until when?"

"It was"—she hesitated—"days later. I was on a bus, and—"

"Wait a minute," he said quietly. "Before that. You remember Sam Wachler?"

Her gasp was sheer agony, and he took her hand. She tried to draw it away, but he held it firmly.

"Let's straighten this all out at once, shall we?" he insisted. "There's a bunch of people down below who are going to want to know what's been going on. So, no secrets anymore. And let me promise you. You have nothing to be worried about, frightened of, or ashamed of."

"You—you're sure?" she pleaded.

"Uh-huh," he said carefully, "I've followed your every footstep for the last year; I would know. But I've an idea that Wachler told you something, didn't he?"

She nodded. "Both of them. It was—that second day. I was beginning to remember, but was all—all sort of hazy about it. I saw the calendar, and it didn't make sense to me until later. They told me that I'd killed a man, that they were my friends, and they had brought me away to safety, and that if I did as they told me to, they would keep my secret."

"You didn't believe them?"

"Not really, but they showed me blood on my clothes. Afterwards, I thought it was from my cut head, but I couldn't be sure. So I ran away. I stole a dress, and they had taken my watch off, but I stole it back. I pawned that and bought a ticket out of the state.

"I didn't know where to go, but this place was in Arizona, and Jim Buckle had owned it, so I came here. They traced me somehow, and I had to—I sent them money. It was all very hazy. They sent me some clippings about a man found dead, and I didn't know what the truth was, and couldn't imagine why that Brett Brule had struck me like that, so I was really scared they were right."

An ambulance arrived, adding to the flashing lights in the canyon. Questioning voices drifted up to them.

He stood up. "Let's go down below. Better to go to them before they come to us." Catching the bound man by the coat collar, he dragged him after them. At the bottom, he said, "There's another thing. What about Stukie Tomlin?"

"Oh." She turned sharply around. "I'd forgotten him. He came here a few days ago and said I was in danger. He told me that I was to inherit a lot of money, but that somebody was asking a lot of odd questions and that I should be careful. I didn't know what to believe. But, you see, I'd met Stukie before—when I was with Mr. Buckle."

TOMLIN WAS AWAKE when they came in; a medic was working on him, and he grinned weakly when he saw Darcy. Shannon dropped his burden on the floor, then looked down into the face of Watt Braith.

"I thought so," Shannon said. He turned to Darcy. "This is Brule, isn't it?"

She nodded. "Yes . . ."

"Hey, mister!" A deputy sheriff stepped forward. "You going to explain all this?"

"Give him a minute and I expect he will, Hank." Hualapi Johnny spoke up from the doorway.

Shannon turned back to Darcy Lane, but he spoke for the others, too. "His real name is Braith. He was Buckle's lawyer. If anything happened to one of the heirs, that estate would be in his hands for five years. With five years and two million dollars to work with, a man can do plenty. So he decided to kill you, Miss Lane. He probably figured on sinking your body, but his blow knocked you over the side. You'd told him you couldn't swim, so he figured he was pretty safe."

"But Buckle was alive!" she protested.

"Sure. He was alive for six months. You hadn't showed up, so Braith went ahead and killed Buckle."

"You'll have a time proving that," Braith growled.

"I can already prove it," Shannon said quietly. "Within twenty minutes after I left you yesterday, I knew it."

"That's like I figured," Tomlin interrupted. "I'd lent the old man some tools, stuff I needed. I drove over here to get them back, and saw where he died. I prowled around and found that slide might have been caused by somebody with a crowbar. I told the sheriff about it and we both looked around, but there was nobody around then who seemed to have a motive, so we dropped it."

"And then the will came out in the open?"

"Yeah," Hank said, "and the boss still couldn't figure it. We all liked that old man. He was mighty nice. Potifer knew about the will. Buckle had told him, but he didn't fit the other facts."

They picked Stukie Tomlin up and were carrying him out. He caught Darcy's sleeve. "I saw him in town. I didn't know what was up but I never trusted him so I thought I'd warn you."

Darcy touched his shoulder. "Thank you."

Shannon sat down and lit a cigarette. "I made some calls and checked into the guy. I found he had made a lot of money with real estate he had handled, and his success began with the death of Buckle. Then, I got in touch with the Mojave County sheriff, and he told me somebody else had been suspicious, also, and that he had checked all strangers in and out of the county at that time. One of them answered the description of Braith, here. He said if I could produce the man, he had the men to identify him. We know one of them is Tomlin."

"We'll meet with the sheriff in the morning," said Hank. "But it doesn't sound like we'll have to spend much time explaining what happened. You-all need to be here for that meeting, though." He shoved the cuffed Braith ahead of him out the door.

Darcy Lane sat, her legs still trembling from her ordeal on the cliffs.

"You must have done a lot of work on this to locate me," she said.

"Uh-huh." He grinned at her. "I even read your diary."

She blushed. "Well," she protested defensively, "there was nothing in it to be ashamed of."

"I agree. In fact," he added seriously, "there was a lot to be proud of. So much that I often found myself wanting to meet you . . . even if I couldn't find you."

She smiled at him and laughed, and after a moment, he did, too.

BACKFIELD BATTERING RAM

L EANING ON THE back of the players' bench, "Socks" Barnaby stared cynically at the squad of husky young men going through their paces on the playing field.

"You've got plenty of beef, Coach," he drawled, "but have you got any brains out there?"

Horace Temple, head coach at Eastern, directed a poisonous glare at the lean, broad-shouldered Barnaby, editor of the campus newspaper.

"What d'you care, Socks?" he said. "Aren't you one of these guys who thinks football is overemphasized?"

"Me? I only think you've placed too much emphasis on sheer bulk. You need some smarts, that's all."

"Yeah?" The coach laughed. "Why don't you come out then? You were good enough at track and field last year."

"I haven't got the time."

"Crabapples!" Temple scoffed. "You've got time for more activities and fewer classes than any man on the campus. Editor of that scurvy sheet, president of the Drama Club, Poetry society . . . Writing that thesis on something or other is the only thing that keeps you from graduating!"

Coach Temple glanced back at the football field, and instantly he sprang to his feet.

"Kulowski!" he called. "What's the matter with you? Can't you even *hold* a football?" He glared at the lumbering bulk of "Muggs" Kulowski. "Of all the dumb clucks! Kulowski, get off the field. When you aren't fumbling, you're falling over one of my best men and crippling him. Go on, beat it!"

Muggs Kulowski looked up, his eyes pleading, but there was no mercy in Temple now. Slowly, his head hanging, Muggs turned toward the field house.

"That guy!" Coach Temple stared after him. "The biggest

man I've got. Strong as an ox, an' twice as dumb. We're going to get killed this year!"

———

THOUGHTFULLY, BARNABY STARED after Kulowski. The man was big. He weighed at least forty pounds over two hundred, and was inches taller than Socks himself. But despite his size there was a certain unconscious rhythm in his movements. Still, in three weeks he hadn't learned to do anything right. For all his great size, Kulowski went into a line as if he was afraid he'd break something, and his fingers were all thumbs.

"You cut us a break, Barnaby. All you do is use that sheet of yours to needle everybody who tries to do anything. A lot you've done for Eastern."

Socks grinned. "Wait until after the Hanover game," he said. "I'm just trying to save you from yourself, Coach. If you get by Hanover, we'll say something nice. I'd like to be optimistic but I've got to call it as I see it."

———

BARNABY WALKED OFF the field, heading for the quad. Kulowski was shambling along ahead of him, and something in the disconsolate appearance of the huge Pole touched a sympathetic chord in him. More, he was curious. It seemed impossible that any man with all his fingers could be as clumsy as this one. Stretching his long legs, Socks Barnaby quickened his pace to catch up with Kulowski.

"Hey, Kulowski, rough going today?" he asked, walking up beside the big fellow.

"Yeah." Muggs looked at him, surprised. "Didn't know you knew me."

"Sure," Socks replied. "Don't let this get you down. Tomorrow you'll do better."

"No," Muggs said bitterly. "He told me yesterday that if I messed up one more time I was through."

"Can't you get the hang of it?"

"No." The guy's brow furrowed. "I don't know what's wrong."

"Well, football isn't everything."

"For me it is," Kulowski said bitterly. "If I lose my scholarship, I'm finished. And I want a degree."

"That's something," Barnaby agreed. "Most football players don't care much about finishing. They just want to play ball. But if you lose the scholarship you can always get a job."

"I've got a job, but the money has to go home." He glanced at Socks. "I've got a mother, two sisters, and a kid brother."

———

BARNABY LEFT KULOWSKI at the field house and started across the campus to the *Lantern* office in the Press Building. He was turning up the walk when he saw Professor Hazelton, and he stopped. The two were old friends, and Barnaby had corrected papers for him a few times, and written reviews for a book page the professor edited.

"Prof, don't you have Muggs Kulowski in a couple of classes?"

"Yes, of course. Why do you ask?" Hazelton was a slim, erect man of thirty-five and had been a crack basketballer.

"An idea I've got. Tell me about him."

"Well." Hazelton thought for a moment. "He always gets passing grades. He's not brilliant, mostly a successful plodder."

"How about recitations?" Barnaby asked.

"Very inferior. If it wasn't for his paperwork he wouldn't get by. He's almost incoherent, although I must say he's shown some improvement lately."

After a few minutes, Socks Barnaby walked on into the office. He sat down at the typewriter and banged away on a story for the *Lantern*. It was several hours later, as he was finishing a letter to a girl in Cedar Rapids, when he remembered that Kulowski was working at the freight docks. On an inspiration, he got up and went out.

He liked Coach Temple. He and the coach had an old-time feud, but underneath there was a good deal of respect. Knowing a good many of the faculty and alumni, Barnaby had heard the gossip about the coach being on his last legs at

Eastern. He had to turn out a team this year or lose his contract.

The fault wasn't wholly Temple's. Other schools had more money to spend, and were spending it. Yet, here at Eastern, they expected Temple to turn out teams as good as the bigger, better financed schools.

Temple had a strategy. Digging around in the coal mines and lumber camps he had found a lot of huskies who liked the game, and many of them had played in high school and the Army. He recruited all he could but the teams he fielded were often uneven. This time it was his backfield where the weakness lay. They lacked a hard-hitting offensive combination. Kuttner was a good steady man, strong on the defense, and a fair passer and kicker. Ryan and DeVries were both fast, and fair backs, but neither of them was good enough to buck the big fast men that Hanover and State would have.

———

THE FREIGHT DOCK was dimly lit and smelled of fresh lumber, tar, and onions. Socks walked out on the dock and looked around. Then he saw Kulowski.

The big fellow hadn't noticed him. In overalls and without a shirt, with shoulders and arms that looked like a heavyweight wrestler's, he trundled his truck up to a huge barrel, tipped the barrel and slid the truck underneath, dipped the truck deftly, and started off toward the dim end of the dock.

Socks walked after him, watching. There was no uncertainty in Muggs Kulowski now. Alone here in the half-light of the freight dock, doing something he had done for months, he was deft, sure, and capable.

"Hi, Muggs," Socks said. "Looks like you're working hard." Kulowski turned, showing his surprise.

"Gosh, how did you happen to come down here?" he asked.

"Came to see you," Socks said casually. "I think we should get together on this football business."

Kulowski flushed: "Aw, I'm just no good. Can't get it through my head. Anyway, Coach is dead set against me."

"D'you play any other games?" Socks asked.

"Not exactly." Kulowski stopped, wiping the sweat from his face. "I used to play a little golf. Never played with anybody, just by myself."

"Why not?"

"I guess I wasn't good enough. I could do all right alone, but whenever anybody got around, I just couldn't hit the ball. I couldn't do anything."

Socks sat around the dock, strolled after Kulowski as he worked, and talked with the big fellow. Mostly, he watched him. The big guy was doing a job he knew. He was not conscious of being observed, and as he worked swiftly and surely, there wasn't a clumsy or awkward thing about him.

"I had trouble with games ever since I was a kid," Muggs Kulowski admitted finally. "My old man used to say I was too big and too awkward, and he made fun of me. I guess I was clumsy, growing fast and all."

"Muggs." Socks stood up suddenly. "We need you out there on that field this year. We need you badly. You know where Springer's barn is?"

"You mean that old red barn out there by the creek?"

"That's it. You meet me out there tomorrow. Bring your football suit, and don't tell anybody where you're going. We're going to work out a little."

They settled the time, and then Socks walked back to his room. He knew what it meant to grow fast and be awkward. His own father had been understanding, and had helped him get by that awkward period. But he knew how shy he had been, himself, how it embarrassed him so terribly when anyone had laughed.

———

SOCKS, IN A faded green sweater and slacks, walked out on the field the next afternoon. He paced off a hundred yards, and then walked back to the cottonwoods that divided the field from the edge of the campus. In a few minutes he saw Muggs, big as a house, coming up, grinning.

"Hi, Coach!" Muggs said. "What do I do first?"

"First we try you for speed," Socks said. "No use fooling with you if you're slow." He pointed. "See that stake down there? That's an even hundred yards. You go down there, and when I give you the word, shag it up here as fast as you can."

Muggs shambled down the field, turned and crouched in a starting position. At the barked command, he lunged forward.

Socks clicked the stopwatch as Muggs thundered past him, and looked thoughtful. Thirteen seconds, and there was a lot Kulowski didn't know about starting.

Barnaby dug out the football from his bag of gear.

He walked over to his pupil.

"You've got big hands," he said, "and long fingers, which is all to the good. But when you take hold of the ball, grip the thing, don't just let it lay in your hand. Take it between the thumb and fingers, with the fingers along the laces, just back of the middle. Press it well down into your hand with your left. When you pass, throw it overhand, right off the ear. You know all this, but we're going to work on it until it's automatic . . . until you can do it whether you're self-conscious or not."

———

IT WAS ALMOST dark when they left the field. For two hours Kulowski had practiced passing and receiving passes, and he had fallen on the ball until he seemed to have flattened every bit of grass on the field. They walked back toward the field house together, weary but cheerful.

"You'll do," Socks said quietly. "Don't let anything Coach said bother you. You're big and you're fast. We'll have you faster. All you need is confidence, and to get over being afraid of other people looking on."

Muggs looked at him curiously.

"How come you aren't playing football?" he asked. "You seem to know plenty about it."

"Too many other things, I guess." Socks shrugged. "A man can't do everything."

———

THE HANOVER GAME was three weeks away. Sitting beside Muggs in the stands, Socks saw Eastern outplayed by Pentland, a smaller and inferior team.

BACKFIELD BATTERING RAM / 339

It had been pretty bad. Socks glanced at Temple's face as the big coach lumbered off the field, and he didn't have the heart to rib him. Kuttner, battered from sixty minutes of play, looked pale and drawn.

One thing was sure, Socks decided. Hanover or State would ruin them. Hanover had an aerial game that was good, and as strong a line as Eastern's. Unless something happened to develop a behind-the-line combination for Eastern, an awful drubbing was in the cards.

———

DAY AFTER DAY, Barnaby met Kulowski in the field by the red barn, and worked the big guy and himself to exhaustion. Kulowski grinned when he got on the scales. His big brown face was drawn hard. He had lost almost twenty pounds in three weeks of work.

"Well, the Hanover game is tomorrow," Socks said, watching Kulowski curiously.

"What d'you think? Want to try it if the coach says yes?"

Kulowski's tongue touched his lips. "Yeah, I'll try," he said. "I can't do any more than mess it up."

"You won't mess it up. You're plenty fast now. You've cut two seconds off that hundred. And you know how to use your hands and your feet. If you get out there, just forget about that crowd. Just remember what we've been doing here, and do the same things."

Kulowski hesitated, staring at Barnaby, one of the most popular men in school. In those three weeks of bitter work, he had come to know him, to like him, and to respect him. He had seen that lean body lash out in a tackle that jarred every bone in his huge body. He had seen passes rifle down the field like bullets, right into his waiting arms.

Time and again Kulowski had missed those passes. They had slipped away, or dropped from his clumsy fingers, yet Socks had never been angry. He had kidded about it in friendly fashion, and encouraged him, flattered him.

Now, Kulowski wasn't missing the passes. He was taking kicks and coming down the field fast. Socks had shown him how to get to full speed at once, how to get the drive into his powerful legs. He had shown him how to tackle. He had taught him to use his feet and his hands.

For the first time, Kulowski felt that somebody believed in him, that somebody really thought he could do something without making a mess of it. Taunted and tormented so long for his size and awkwardness, Muggs had never known what it meant to be encouraged.

On his end, Socks knew that he had actually done little. Kulowski was a natural. All he had ever lacked was confidence. He liked doing things. He was big, and he was rough. Once confidence came to him, he threw himself into the practice with a will, his movements, day by day, became more sharp, more sure.

———

SOCKS STOPPED COACH Temple outside the field house. "Hi, Coach," he said, grinning. "Why so glum?"

Temple scowled. "You trying to irritate me? How would you feel going into that Hanover game without anything good in the backfield but Kuttner? They'll beat our ears off!"

"Can I quote you on that?"

"No!"

Socks dodged playfully backward as Temple rounded on him. "Are you willing to take a chance, Coach?"

"What d'you mean?"

"Put Kulowski in there, at half."

"Kulowski?" Temple exploded. "Are you crazy? Why, that big ox—"

"I said it was a chance," Socks interrupted. "But I've been working with him, and that boy is good."

"*You've* been working with him? What do you know about football?" Temple sneered, yet in the back of his eyes there was a hopeful, calculating expression.

"I read a book once." Socks grinned. "Anyway, what have you got to lose?"

Temple shrugged. "You got something there," he said wryly. "What?"

———

THE STADIUM WAS jammed when the team trotted out on the field. Sitting on the bench beside Muggs Kulowski, Socks Barnaby talked to him quietly.

"This crowd is so big, it's impersonal. You just go out there and play a careful, steady game. You'll have your chance, and if you make good, you're back in."

Barnaby knew the huge crowd of fans hadn't come to see Eastern. There was little hope after the Pentland game that Eastern could win, and playing in the Hanover backfield was Pete Tarbell, two hundred pounds of dynamite and twice an All-American. Besides that, in the Hanover line were two tackles said to be likely prospects for the All-American this year, and there was Speed Burtson, at right half, a former high school flash, and one of the most talked-of players in the college game.

Hanover was a star-studded team. Looking at them thoughtfully, Socks found himself wondering if they weren't a little too star-studded. And he found his eyes going again and again to Tarbell in his red jersey. He had known Pete Tarbell and didn't like him.

Kuttner kicked off to Hanover and Burtson took the ball on his own twenty yard line and ran it back to the forty yard line before he was downed by DeVries. Then Hanover began to roll.

They came through Hunk Warren, big Eastern tackle, for two first downs. Then Tarbell came over guard for six. Tarbell tried Hunk again, but Kuttner came down fast and Tarbell was stopped dead. They passed on the third down.

The pass was good, plenty good. Speed Burtson, living up to his name, went down the field, evaded Kuttner, and took the pass over his shoulder. He went over into the end zone standing up for the first score. Tarbell kicked, and Hanover had a lead of seven to nothing.

The rest of the first quarter was murder. Eastern could hold their opponents in the line, but the Hanover aerial attack was beyond them. Twice Burtson got away for long gains, and Tarbell came around the left end and crashed into DeVries, taking him over into the end zone with him. Hanover missed the kick, but when the play was over, DeVries was on the ground. He got up and limped off the field.

Coach Temple paled and he swore under his breath. He looked at Kulowski, then at Socks. "All right, Muggs," he said grimly. "You go in at full."

Ryan was at quarterback for Eastern, Kulowski at full, Kuttner at left halfback, and Hansen at right half.

Socks glanced up at the stands. President Crandall was there, and the short, fat-jowled man beside him would be Erich P. Wells, head of the Alumni Association. Socks glanced at Temple and saw the big coach was kicking his toe into the turf, his face drawn. Temple had expected defeat, but this was going to be slaughter.

The tension was getting to him. Socks wanted Kulowski to do well but he didn't have a good feeling about this game. He slid off the bench and took a walk around the stands; he had another thought but it was crazy . . . the coach would laugh at him. . . .

When he got back, Temple glowered at Socks.

"Kulowski's fumbled once already," the coach growled. "Kuttner made a recovery."

Socks's heart sank. Eastern was lining up again. He could see the uncertainty in the big Pole. The ball was snapped and Kuttner started around the end. Kulowski came in, hurled himself halfheartedly at Tarbell's feet as the big back lunged through. Tarbell merely sidestepped neatly, then launched himself in a tackle that brought Kuttner down with a thud they could hear on the sidelines.

"I'm going to take that big lug out of there!" Temple barked. "He's yellow!"

"Let me go in," he suggested. "I can make him work."

Temple turned, staring.

"You, Socks? Where'd you ever play football?"

"I played against Tarbell," Socks said. "I was with the Gorman Air Base team."

Temple looked at him cynically. "Gorman Air Base, eh? You ain't lyin'? All right, Socks, but you aren't writing poetry out there. Suit up!"

When Socks trotted out on the field he suddenly felt as

Kulowski must. It had been four years and when he looked at Hanover's big line, he felt his heart go down into his stomach. Those huge guards! And that center, as enormous as a concrete pillbox!

Then, behind the line, Socks saw big Pete Tarbell staring at him. Then the stare changed to a wolfish smile.

"Well, well!" he said, "if it isn't the bomber boy. What do you think this is, badminton?"

Socks ignored him. He trotted up and grabbed Kulowski. "Listen," he said, "I'm here now, and I'm going to be playing with you. But you've got to focus . . . let's play this one just like out behind the barn. You can do it."

Kulowski flushed, "I'll try," he said.

"Crabapples!" Socks grinned. "Turn loose on these guys an' you can wreck that team. Let's go out there and bust 'em up!"

He trotted over to Ryan and whispered for a moment. Ryan nodded, looking doubtful.

"Okay," he said, "if Coach says so."

KULOWSKI TOOK THE ball. For a wonder, his big fingers clamped on it and he started moving. Behind him he heard Socks's voice and saw the lean redhead move in ahead of him. Hunk had a hole and Kulowski went through, his big knees lifting high.

Pete Tarbell saw him coming and angled over, but suddenly Socks knifed across and Tarbell hit the ground with a thud. He got up slowly, and looked at Barnaby.

"Hi," Socks said, grinning, "how's the badminton?"

Tarbell glowered and his face set. Kulowski had been downed on the thirty yard line. He had made six yards.

KULOWSKI GOT UP grinning. It was the first successful thing he had ever accomplished in front of a crowd. He looked at Barnaby, and as Socks passed Ryan, Socks said, "Give it to Muggs again."

Ryan barked the signals. Muggs Kulowski took the ball

running and hit the line hard. He went through for four yards. Kulowski was getting warmed up. Ryan worked Kuttner on a reverse and he got away for ten yards before he was downed.

Socks had thrown a wicked block into Burtson and as he got up he saw Tarbell rising shakily from the ground and glowering at Kulowski. The big Pole was grinning from ear to ear.

The Eastern team was working now. Kulowski's face was sweat-streaked and muddy, but he was still grinning. He was hitting that line with power and whenever he hit, something happened. He wasn't missing any passes, and all the fear of the crowd, the fear of being laughed at was gone. He was in there, driving, and his two hundred and twenty pounds was making itself felt.

Eastern worked smoothly and marched down the field. They got to the thirty, and there Hanover smashed them back three times. Hanover was concentrating on Kulowski now, sensing his power and drive.

"You think we ought to pass it?" Ryan whispered to Socks.

"Yeah." Socks glanced around. "Give it to me in the corner."

Socks Barnaby slid around an end and went down the field fast and took the ball on the three. There Tarbell hit him like a tank, and Socks went down and rolled over. Tarbell got up.

Ryan called for Kulowski. The big Pole tucked the ball under his arm and put his head down and drove. The Hanover line bulged, and then it gave way all of a sudden. Kulowski powered through, and they had the score.

Kuttner dropped back and kicked the point. The score was 13 and 7 at the half.

To OPEN THE second half it was Hanover's choice, and they elected to receive. Kuttner again toed the ball. Ammons, Hanover's big right tackle, took it coming fast, but Kulowski was moving and he drove the bigger Ammons back on his shoulder.

Hanover lined up, Tarbell came plunging through, and Kulowski hit him.

Tarbell got slowly to his feet, and he looked wonderingly at the big guy. Tarbell, twice All-American, had lost a yard on the play!

Tarbell came in again like a battering ram and there was murder in his drive. Hunk was ready this time and he hit Tarbell at the knees, then Kulowski hit him high, and Tarbell went down, hard.

Tarbell had lost two yards, and he was mad clear through. Socks ran back to position, laughing at the puzzled, angry face of the Hanover star.

Then Hanover got tough. Eastern drove at the line three times and made only three yards.

Burtson kicked. He lived up to reputation, booting a low whirler that hit and rolled over and over. The wind helped it, but Socks finally downed the ball on the Eastern sixteen.

They made three first downs, then Hanover got hot and swamped them. Taking Kuttner's kick, Hanover began to hammer. They sent Tarbell through the line, and ganged Hunk Warren to make the hole. They made it. Tarbell came through, his head down, driving like a locomotive, but Muggs Kulowski was coming in. He had an urge to ruin Tarbell and they both knew it. They hit hard and bounced apart, both of them shaken to the heels.

———

EASTERN TOOK POSSESSION of the ball on downs and powered it straight down the field as the quarter neared its end. They got to the seven, and Kulowski had been doing most of the work. Socks took the ball off tackle with Kulowski and Ryan clearing the way, and went over the line standing up.

Kuttner missed the point and the score was tied.

———

THE LAST QUARTER opened and the big Hanover team came out for blood. They were against a team that seemed to be playing way over its head, and it had Hanover desperate for fear the mounting confidence of Eastern would smear them.

Then it happened. It was Eastern's ball on their own forty yard line. Eastern lined up and Kulowski went off tackle for four. Then Kuttner started around the end, but Sinclair, a Hanover end, cut in for him, and with a quick shift, Kuttner went through the messup at guard, charging the center of the field.

A huge Hanover tackler missed him, got a hand on his leg, and Kuttner spun around, staggering three steps and then went down under a rib-cracking tackle from Speed Burtson.

They lined up and Ryan sent Kulowski through the line for four. The big fellow got up, and he grinned at Socks.

"We're doin' it!" he said. "This is fun!"

"We got a chance," Kuttner said. "We got a good chance. It's with you, Socks, or Kulowski."

"It's Kulowski," Socks said. "Listen, Muggs. Remember those long passes out there by the creek? You get away this time and get off down the field, but fast. Go around the left end and when you get down there, angle across the field. Wherever you are, you'll get that pass."

Socks glanced at Ryan.

"Okay," he said. "Let's go!" He spun on his heel and said to Muggs, "All right, let's see the deer in those big feet of yours!"

The center snapped the ball back to Socks, and he dropped back for the pass. Kuttner started around the end, and Burtson, thinking the pass was for Kuttner, started after him. Ryan had gone through the middle, and suddenly, Socks, still falling back, saw Kulowski away off down the field. He was really running. It would be forty yards, at least.

As a big tackle lunged toward him, Socks shot the pass in a rifling spiral that traveled like a bullet, just out of reach of leaping hands. Then Kulowski went up, the ball momentarily slipped through his hands, and a terrific groan went up from the stands, but then he recovered and was running!

Tarbell had been playing far back, and he started slow as Kulowski came toward him. Then the big All-American's pace changed suddenly, his toes dug in and he hurled himself in a dynamite-charged tackle at Muggs.

Kulowski made a lightninglike cross step, and at the same moment, his open hand shot out in a wicked stiff-arm, backed by all the power of those freight-handling muscles. That hand flattened against Tarbell's face and the clutching hands grasped only air.

Two men got Kulowski on the two yard line, bringing him down with a bone-crushing jolt.

They lined up again, and Ryan looked at Muggs and Kulowski grinned. They snapped the ball, and he went through the middle with everything he could give. They tried to hold him, but for the first time in his life, Muggs Kulowski was playing with everything he had in him. He put his head down and drove.

With four men clinging to him, he shoved through. The ball was over.

The rest was anticlimax. Socks Barnaby dropped back and booted the ball through the goal posts, and the whistle blew.

It was 20 to 13!

"Well," Barnaby said to Temple as the big coach stood waiting for them, "what did I tell you?"

"You tell me?" The Coach grinned. "Why, I knew that you were all brains an' he was all beef. What d'you suppose I needled you for? Don't you suppose I knew that thesis of yours was on the sense of inferiority?"

"Crabapples!" Socks scoffed. "Why, you couldn't—!"

"Listen, pantywaist," Temple growled. "D'you suppose I'd ever have let you an' Muggs on that field if I didn't know you could do it? Don't you suppose I knew you an' him were down behind that barn every night? What d'you suppose I kicked him off the field for? I knew you were so confounded contrary you'd get busy an' work with him just to show me up!"

"Well," Socks grinned, "it wasn't you who got showed up. It was Hanover."

"Yeah," Temple agreed, "so go put that in the *Lantern*. And you, Kulowski. You get out for practice, you hear?"

"Okay," Kulowski said. Then he grinned. "But first I got to write an article for the *Lantern*."

Coach Temple's eyes narrowed and his face grew brick red.

"You? Writing for the *Lantern*? What about?"

"Coaching methods at Eastern," Kulowski said, and laughed.

He was still laughing as he walked toward the field house with his arm across Barnaby's shoulders.

MORAN OF THE TIGERS

FLASH MORAN TOOK the ball on the Rangers' thirty yard line, running with his head up, eyes alert. He was a money player, and a ground gainer who took the openings where he found them.

The play was called for off tackle. Murphy had the hole open for him, and Flash put his head down and went through, running like a madman. He hit a two-hundred-pound tackle in the midriff and set him back ten feet and plowed on for nine yards before he was downed.

Higgins called for a pass and Flash dropped back and took the ball. Swindler went around end fast and was cutting over when Flash rifled the ball to him with a pass that fairly smoked. He took it without slowing and started for the end zone. Weaving, a big Ranger lineman missed him, and he went on to be downed on the two yard line by a Ranger named Fenton, a wiry lad new in pro football.

"All right, Flash," Higgins said as they trotted back. "I'm sending you right through the middle for this one."

Flash nodded. The ball was snapped, and as Higgins wheeled and shoved it into his middle, he turned sharply and went through the line with a crash of leather that could be heard in the top rows. He went through and he was downed safely in the end zone. He got up as the whistle shrilled, and grinned at Higgins. "Well, there's another one for Pop. If we can keep this up, the Old Man will be in the money again."

"Right." Tom Higgins was limping a little, but grinning. "It's lucky for him he's got a loyal bunch. Not a man offered to back out when he laid his cards on the table."

"No," Flash agreed, "but I'm worried. Lon Cramp has been after some of the boys. He's got money, and he's willing to pay anything to get in there with a championship team.

He's already got Johnny Hill from the Rangers, doubled his salary, and he got Kowalski from the Brewers. He hasn't started on us, but I'm expecting it."

"It'll be you he's after," Tom Higgins said, glancing at the big halfback. "You were the biggest ground gainer in the league last year, and a triple-threat man."

"Maybe. But there's others, too. Hagan, for instance. And he needs the money with all those operations for his wife. He's the best tackle in pro football."

POP DOLAN WAS standing in the dressing room grinning when they came in. "Thanks, boys," he said, "I can't tell you what this means to me. I don't mean the winning, so much as the loyalty."

Flash Moran sat down and began to unlace his shoes. Pop Dolan had started in pro football on a shoestring and a lot of goodwill. He had made it pay. His first two years had been successful beyond anybody's expectations, but Pop hadn't banked all the money; he had split a good third of the take with the team, over and above their salaries. "You earned it," he said simply. "When I make money, we all make it."

Well, Flash thought, he's losing now, and if we take the winnings we've got to take the punishment. Yet how many of the players felt that way? Tom Higgins, yes. Dolan had discovered Tom in the mines of Colorado. He had coached him through college, and the two were close as father and son. Hagan?

He didn't know. Butch Hagan was the mainstay of the big line. An intercollegiate heavyweight wrestling champ, he had drive and power to spare. Ken Martin? The handsome Tiger tailback, famous college star and glamour boy of pro football, was another doubtful one. He was practically engaged to "Micky" Dolan, Pop's flame-haired daughter, so that would probably keep him in line.

Flash dressed and walked outside, then turned and strolled away toward the line of cabs that stood waiting.

A slender, sallow-faced man was standing by a black car as he approached, and he looked up at Flash, smiling. "Hi,

Moran!" He thrust out a cold limp hand. "Want a ride up-town?"

Flash looked at him, then shrugged. It wasn't unusual. Lots of sports fans liked to talk to athletes, and the ride would save him the cab fare, as his car was in the shop. He got in.

"You live at the Metropole, don't you?" the stranger asked. "How about dropping by the Parkway for a steak? I want to talk a little. My name is Rossaro. Jinx Rossaro."

"A steak? Well, why not?" They rode on in silence until the car swung into the drive of the Parkway. It was a twenty-story apartment hotel, and quite a place. The kind of place Flash Moran couldn't afford. He was wondering, now . . . Jinx Rossaro . . . The name sounded familiar but he couldn't place it. He shrugged. Well, what the devil? He wasn't any high-school girl who had to be careful about pickups.

The dining room was spotless and the hush that prevailed was broken only by the tinkle of glass and silver. Somewhere, beyond the range of his eyes, an orchestra played a waltz by Strauss. They did things well here, he reflected. This Rossaro—

Another man was approaching their table. A short, square man who looked all soft and silky, until you saw his eyes. Then he looked hard. He walked up and held out his hand. "How are you, Jinx? And this is the great Flash Moran?"

There was no sarcasm in the man. His hard little eyes spanned Moran's shoulders and took in his lean, hard two hundred pounds. "I'm happy to meet you. My name is Cramp, Lon Cramp."

Flash had risen to acknowledge the introduction. His eyes narrowed a little as they often did when he saw an opposing tackler start toward him.

They sat down and he looked across at Cramp. "If the occasion is purely social, Mr. Cramp, I'm going to enjoy it. If you got me here to offer me a job, I'm not interested."

Cramp smiled. "How much money do you make, Mr. Moran?"

"You probably know as well as I do. I'm getting fifteen thousand for the season."

"If you get paid. To pay you Dolan must make money. He's broke now, and he won't win any more games. I think, Moran, you'd better listen to what I have to say."

"I wouldn't think of leaving Pop," Flash said quietly. "I'm not a college boy. I came off a cow ranch to the Marines. After the Marines, where I played some football in training, Pop found me and gave me all the real coaching I had, so I owe a lot to him."

"Of course," Cramp smiled, then he leaned forward, "but you owe something to yourself, too. You haven't long, no man has, in professional football. You have to get what you can when you can get it. Pop's through. We know that, and you must realize it yourself. You can't help him."

"I'm not a rat. If the ship sinks I'll go down with it."

"Very noble. But impractical. And," Cramp leaned forward again, "it isn't as if you would have to leave Dolan."

Flash straightened. "Just what do you mean?"

"My friend, we are businessmen. I want the professional championship. You would be infinitely more valuable on Dolan's team than on mine—if you were on my payroll, too."

"You mean—?" Flash's face was tight, his eyes hard.

"That you play badly? Certainly not! You play your best game, until, shall we say, the critical moment. Then, perhaps a fumble, a bad kick—you understand?" Cramp smiled smoothly.

Flash pushed back his chair, then he leaned forward. "I understand very well. You're not a sportsman, you're a crook! I not only won't do your dirty work, but I'll see nobody else does!"

Cramp's eyes were deadly. "Those were hard words, Moran. Reconsider when your temper cools, and my offer stands. For two days only. Then—watch yourself!"

Moran wheeled and walked out. He was mad, and mad clear through, yet underneath his anger there was a cool, hardheaded reasoning that told him this was something Dolan couldn't buck. Dolan was honest. Cramp had the money to spend . . . if Flash wouldn't cooperate, there were others.

There was Hagan, who needed money. Hagan who could fail to open a hole, who could let a tackler by him, who could run too slowly and block out one of his own players. Would Butch do it? Flash shook his head. He wouldn't—usually. Now his wife was ill and he was broke as they all were. . . .

Higgins? He would stand by. Most of the others would, too. Flash walked back to his room, and lay down on the bed. He did not even open his eyes when Higgins came in, undressed, and turned in.

———

DOLAN MET HIM in the coffee shop for breakfast. He looked bad, dark circles under his eyes, and he showed lack of sleep. Tom Higgins was with him, so was Ken Martin. Ken, looking tall and bronzed and strong, beside him, Micky.

Flash felt a sharp pang. He was in love with Micky Dolan. He had never deceived himself about that. Yet it was always the handsome Martin who was with her, always the sharp-looking former All-American.

"Well, it's happened!" Pop said suddenly. "Cramp raided me yesterday. He got Wilson and Krakoff."

Moran felt himself go sick. Krakoff was their big center. He had been with the team for three years. None of them were working under contract this year, not in the strictest sense. Pop leaned over backwards in being fair. Any agreement could be terminated if the player wished. Krakoff at twenty-two was a power in the line. Wilson had been a substitute back, but a good one. They had been shorthanded before this happened.

Martin looked at Flash thoughtfully. "Didn't I see you going off the field with Rossaro?"

Moran looked up and said quietly, "Rossaro met me with an offer to drive me home. When we got up to dinner, Cramp was there. He made me an offer."

Micky was looking at him, her eyes very steady. "I told him nothing doing."

Ken Martin was still staring at him. So was Micky, but neither of them said a word.

———

IT WASN'T UNTIL they met the Shippers on Friday that the extent of the damage was visible. The Shippers were big and rough. Dolan's Tigers had beaten them a month before in a hard-fought game, but hadn't beaten them decisively. Now it was different.

Jalkan, the big Shipper fullback, carried the ball through the middle on the first play. He went right through where Krakoff had stopped him cold a month before. He went for five yards, then Higgins nailed him.

They lined up, and Jalkan came right through again for four yards. Then on a fake, Duffy got away for fourteen, and the Shippers really began to march. They rolled down the field and nothing the Tigers could do would stop them. Duffy got away again and made twenty yards around end before Moran angled downfield and hit him hard on the eight yard line.

But it was only a momentary setback, for Jalkan came through the middle again, nearly wrecking Burgess, a husky Tiger guard, in the process. He was downed by Martin on the two yard line, but went over on the next play.

Then they repeated. Duffy got in the clear and took a pass from Jalkan and made twenty yards before he was doomed by Martin. The Tigers lined up and began to battle, but they weren't clicking. Even Flash, fighting with everything he had, could see that. Krakoff had left a big hole at center, a hole that Worth, the substitute, could never begin to fill. Burgess, the right guard, was badly hurt. They were working him, deliberately, it seemed to Moran. The center of the line was awfully soft.

At the half, the score was twenty to nothing, and the team trooped into the dressing room, tired and battered. Burgess had taken a fearful beating. Dolan looked at him, and shook his head. "No use you going out there again, Bud," he said. "We'll let Noble go in."

Ken Martin looked up, and then his eyes shifted to Flash. They all knew what that meant. Noble was big and strong, but he was slower than Burgess. That hole at center was going to be awfully weak.

"We'll be taking the kick," Dolan said simply, "let's get that ball and get on down the field."

————

MORAN TOOK THE kick and started down the field. Every yard counted now, and he was making time. He was crossing their own forty yard line when Jalkan cut in toward him. He cross-stepped quickly, in an effort to get away, and smacked into a heavy shoulder. Thrown off balance, he was knocked squarely into Jalkan's path and the big Shipper hit him like a piledriver with a thud they could hear high in the stands.

Rolling over and over, Flash was suddenly stopped when the pile-up came. He got slowly to his feet, badly shaken. Martin stared at him. "What did you run into me for? You could have gotten away from Jalkan!"

"What?" Puzzled, he stared at Martin. Then he noticed Butch Hagan looking at him queerly. Frowning, he trotted back into position. Higgins called for twenty-two, and that meant Flash was to go around the end for a pass, and he went fast. He got down the field, saw Ken drop back with the ball, and then it came whistling over!

He glanced over his shoulder and saw with wild panic that he was never going to make it. It was leading him too much. Hurling every ounce of speed he had, he threw himself at the ball, missed, it hit the ground and was recovered by the Shipper tailback.

Schaumberg, the rangy Tiger end, glanced at him. "What's the matter?" he asked sharply. "Cramp got to you, too?"

His answer froze on his lips. Hot words would do no good at this time. He started to reply, but Schaumberg was trotting away. His head down, Flash rounded into position. He noticed Higgins glance at him, and Ken Martin was smiling cynically.

————

THE TIGERS KEPT trying. They made two first downs through the Shipper wall with Ken Martin's twelve-yard reverse sparking the drive. Then a Shipper end spilled through and squelched a spinner, and the Tigers had to kick.

Higgins toed the ball into the corner, and it didn't bounce out.

Duffy fell back as if for a kick, but the Shippers' Jalkan took the ball and powered it through for five yards. They continued to feed him the pigskin for three downs, and he ran the ball back out of danger.

Then Duffy got loose. The flashy Irishman got into the secondary, and he was running like Red Grange. When Flash drove for him he met a stiffarm that dropped him in his tracks. Duffy was away and going fast. He was a wizard on his feet, anyway, and today he was running as if possessed.

Ken Martin cut down the field heading for him, but Duffy had a hidden burst of speed, and he pulled the trigger on it and cut back across the field. Martin swerved, lost distance, gained, and then made a dive that left his arms empty and Duffy went across the goal line standing up.

———

IT WAS SHEER murder. Duffy was playing way over his head, and Jalkan seemed to have more drive than normal. Against the weakened Tiger line even less worthy opponents would have had a field day; as it was, Jalkan pulverized them, and Duffy kept the backfield in a dither.

Then, with four minutes to go, Flash got away and Martin dropped back for a pass. The ball came over like a bullet, and Flash glimpsed it, then let his legs out. He was in an open field and there wasn't a man between him and the goal posts. The ball was leading him; he ran like a madman, stretched and got his fingertips on it, almost had it, then it eeled from his fingers and dropped, hitting the ground. Pounding feet warned him, and with a frantic dive he made a recovery.

When the pile untangled he got up slowly. Schaumberg stared at him, but said nothing. Makin, a Shipper end, stood looking at him and then said, "We don't need any help. We can win it without you."

Flash froze. Then he wheeled and started for Makin. Somebody yelled, and Makin said, "All right, come an' get it!" He threw a right. Flash slipped it, and smashed him in the ribs with his own. A left caught him over the eye, but it bounced off the padding of his helmet, and then he was jerked back and the referee was yelling at him. "Cut it out or get off the field!"

Without a word he pulled himself free and walked back. Tom Higgins took the ball and went through tackle for three, then Martin for two, and then Higgins took it over for their only score of the game.

Slowly, Flash started for the dressing room. Higgins was limping. As if it hadn't been enough to lose Wilson and Krakoff, now Burgess and Higgins were both hurt. He started toward Schaumberg, but the big German deliberately walked away from him, and Moran stopped.

Pop Dolan was standing by the door with Micky. His face was pale. Ken Martin was talking to him, then Martin shrugged and walked into the dressing room. Flash stopped.

Micky looked at him, her eyes scornful. "Well," she said, "you probably earned *your* money!"

Moran felt himself turn sick inside. He turned to her. "What makes you say that?" he demanded. "I do my best!"

"Do you?" she inquired. "But for whom? Dad, or Lon Cramp?"

Moran stared at them, pale and helpless. Even Pop suspected him. "What are you thinking of me?" he burst out. "Men have missed taking passes before!"

"After talking with Cramp?" Micky demanded. "And you, Moran, you who were supposed to be so grateful! You, who never missed a pass!"

For a moment, he stared at them, and then he turned and walked inside. There was dead silence when he came in, and he walked across to his locker and began to strip. He didn't even bother to shower, just dressed, and no one spoke, no one said a word.

———

MICKY AND POP had gone when he got outside. He walked slowly across the street and got into his car. Rossaro was leaning against it, waiting for him. "See how it goes when you don't play ball?" The smaller man arched an eyebrow and sauntered off and Flash watched him go.

Just what, he asked himself suddenly, had Rossaro meant by that? Those passes. . . . But that would mean that Ken Martin was taking a payoff from Cramp. And Ken was going to marry Micky Dolan. It didn't make sense. Even from a selfish standpoint, it would be much better to marry Micky if Pop owned a successful club.

On the inspiration of a moment, he swung his coupe into a side street and turned it to face the highway. Who had Rossaro been waiting for?

He had only to wait a minute. Rossaro came by in the big black car, and there were two men in the backseat with him. Who they were he couldn't make out. He waited what seemed a full minute, then swung out and began to follow them. Up the drive and down the street toward the Parkway. Suddenly they turned sharp left and went down a street that led toward the country. He fell back a little further, puzzled, but alert.

The black car swung off the highway and took to the woods. He waited an instant, then followed. Ahead of him, the car was stopped. Hastily, he swung his own car into a side road and got out.

He was almost up to the black car when he heard a slight noise. He moved forward, through the brush, and then he saw Rossaro. The Italian was turning, then recognition caused a sneer to curl his lips. "Well, Moran! I guess you asked for it. Take him boys!"

Flash tried to turn, then something slugged him, and he staggered. In staggering, he turned. The man he was facing was Makin. Something slammed over his head with terrific force and he fell, tumbling away into an awful, cushiony blackness that smelled strangely of damp earth and pine needles.

————

WHEN HE OPENED his eyes it was dark. His head was one great throbbing burst of pain. He got his hands under him and pushed up, then lifted to his knees. He could see the dim marks of a dirt road, and then, overhead, the stars. He got shakily to his feet.

It came back, slowly. He had followed Rossaro to see who was with him. They must have guessed who he was, or known, and had turned off and led him into this trap. Makin had been one of them, and they had hit him. When he was facing them, Rossaro must have stepped up and hit him on the head.

He got back to his car. It was there and unharmed. He got in, started the motor, and drove back to his room. When he got to the door, he opened it, staggered in and fell across the bed.

———

IT WAS DAYLIGHT when Flash was awakened by the sound of movement. He turned his head and groaned. He heard somebody walking over, and looked up to see Butch Hagan. "What happened to you?" Butch demanded.

Stumblingly, he told him. Hagan stared at him, then got up and dampened a towel. When he came back he went to work on the cut on Moran's head. A long time later, when Flash had bathed and shaved, the two men looked at each other.

"Well," Butch said, "I'll admit, they had me doubting. You always got everything Martin threw and missing two passes, the same way, it didn't look reasonable. Martin swore he put them just as he always had."

"You said 'they' almost convinced you. Who did you mean?"

"Martin and Schaumberg. Both of them said you'd sold out. They said the offer Cramp made you was to fumble or do something to mess up."

Suddenly, Flash looked up. "Butch, I got an idea that can save the Tigers. Are you with me?"

"Yeah," Hagan said. "I need the dough. I'll admit, I told 'em I'd think it over. But I've got a kid, and—You know how it is, you've got to set an example."

"Yeah." Flash leaned forward. "Butch, did you know Deacon Peabody was working at Denton Mills now?"

"Peabody? Used to be All-American? Why, he was a pal of mine!"

"I know. Now here's what I want you to do. We've got a week until the game with Cramp's Bears. Let's get busy."

———

FLASH CAME DOWN the stadium steps to the box where Pop Dolan sat with Micky. Pop saw him, and his face got red. Micky saw him, too. She started to speak, then tightened her lips and deliberately turned her back on him.

Flash sat down. "Pop," he said, "it's nearly game time. In a few minutes you'll have a crippled team going out on that field for a beating. You've only got sixteen men down there, and I know for a fact that two of them have sold out."

Pop stared at him, and Micky turned suddenly, her eyes angry, but before she could speak, Flash leaned forward and grabbed Pop Dolan's arm. "Listen, Pop! I know what they told you. But it was all lies! Give me the word and I'll have a winning team on that field when the game starts. They're all here, ready to go!"

"What do you mean?" Pop demanded. "What kind of a team?"

"Pop," Flash said, "you're a square guy. You got friends. Well, I've got them, too. So has Butch Hagan."

Flash stood up and waved, and down on the field near the door to the dressing room, Butch Hagan turned and went through the door. Suddenly, there was a roar, and out on the field came the Bears. They were big, and they were the favorites in today's game, and Flash knew that, even at the odds he had to give, Cramp had bet heavily. The true facts of the Dolan team weren't out, and the fans still believed in them.

There was another roar as the Tigers ran out onto the field. Flash was watching Cramp, and suddenly he saw the gambler stiffen and come erect. There weren't sixteen men out there—there were thirty-five!

Micky sat up suddenly. "Pop, look! That man with the twenty-two on his jersey! Why, it's Red Saunders!"

"Saunders? But he's not playing football anymore!" Pop

said. "He hasn't played since he quit the Tigers two years ago to practice law!"

"And there's Larry Simmons, twice All-American end! And Lew Young, ex-Navy center, and—!"

"We've got you a team!" Flash said. "We've got a team that will win if you give me the word. So what do you say?"

"Why, son," Pop smiled suddenly, "I couldn't make myself believe that you would go back on me!"

"Then we've got a game to play!" Flash said, and slipped away before they could say any more.

He knew it was a good team. Right now there were more stars on that field than there had been in years. Of course, they hadn't all played together, but some of them had. Simmons had played on an Army post team, and Lew Young had played with the Navy, and Saunders had just come back from a hunting trip and was in rare condition. It was a chance, and a good chance.

The Bears had everything in the books. Lon Cramp was out for a title, and he hadn't spared money. He had a big fullback, a ten-second man named Brogan. And the Bears' captain was a lad named Chadwick who ran like a ghost. Their other backs, both triple-threat men in college ball, were Baykov and Chavel.

The line was bigger than that of the Tigers, and they had power to spare. There was a big tackle named Polanyi, and an end with long legs and arms who could run like a streak and was named Monte Crabb. They had others, too. They had Leland, Barnes, Wilson and, at center, Krakoff.

Red Saunders kicked off for the Tigers and they started down the field. Flash Moran was playing tailback, and he was hanging far back, looking over the team.

Monte Crabb took the ball on the Bear twenty-five yard line and running behind perfect interference got down the field for twenty yards before Larry Simmons cut in, evaded a halfback and dropped Crabb with a bone-jolting tackle.

They lined up and Brogan powered through the center for five yards. Then he took the ball again, and hitting the line, went through for three more before they stopped him.

They drove on until they had rolled the Tigers back to their own ten yard line, but the Tigers were playing good ball. They were getting used to each other, and they were looking over the opposition.

Brogan started through the line, but Butch Hagan shoved Polanyi on his face in the dirt and hit Brogan with everything he had. Brogan clung to the ball, however, and they lined up with a yard lost.

The Tigers held them again, held them without the ball moving an inch, and then on the next play the Tigers' Lew Young and a guard named Corbett hit Krakoff and drove him back on his heels. Krakoff got up mad and took a swing at Young, and Lew, who had been some shakes as an amateur heavyweight, dropped him in his tracks.

They broke that one up, but Krakoff was mad clear through. He snapped the ball, then drove at Young, and Lew jumped back and Krakoff sprawled forward off balance and Corbett went through that hole and nailed Brogan before he could get out of his tracks. Saunders cut around and as the ball slipped from Brogan's hands, he nailed it and went to the ground.

The Tigers had the ball. Higgins called the signals and Saunders took it around the end for five yards, then they snapped it to Flash and he went off tackle for six. They lined up, and Moran took the ball again, and Red Saunders, running like a deer, got off ahead of him. They went down the sidelines, and he was crossing the Bear forty yard line when he was downed by Chavel.

He was feeling good now, and the team was beginning to click. They liked Pop Dolan, and they didn't like Cramp, and they were out for blood. They weren't saving themselves for another game because most of them weren't expecting to play another.

Flash went around end on the next play and Ken Martin passed. The minute he saw the pass he knew he couldn't make it. He ran like a wild man, but his fingers just grazed the ball. It went down and Chadwick recovered.

Flash turned and started back up the field and saw Schaumberg and Ken Martin standing together. He started toward them, and they stood there waiting for him.

"You deliberately passed that ball out of range!" Flash accused Martin.

"Moran, you're a fool!" Martin said. "If Lon Cramp gets this club you stand to make more money than you ever did!" Suddenly Flash was sure he knew who the other men had been that day in the woods. It had been Makin and Rossaro . . . and, in the car, where he could barely be seen, Ken Martin!

"Yeah?" Moran's eyes narrowed. "You seem to know a lot about it!"

"I do," he said harshly. "I'm going to be the manager!"

Unseen by Schaumberg or Martin, Red Saunders had come down behind them and stood listening. Suddenly, he stepped up. "Who's captain of this team?"

"I am," Martin declared flatly. "What about it?"

Red turned abruptly and walked to the edge of the field where he began to talk to Pop. "You get off the field," Flash told Martin. "Captain or not, you're finished!"

"Yeah?" Martin sneered. "You've had this coming for a long time!"

The punch started, but it was a left hook, and too wide. It came up against the padded side of his helmet and Flash let go with an inside right cross that dropped Martin to his haunches. Ken came up fast, and Flash caught him full in the face with one hand then the other! He felt the nose bone crunch under his fist. Then Schaumberg started a punch that was suddenly picked out of the air by Lew Young, who returned it, and Schaumberg went down.

Pop came out on the field then, and his eyes were blazing. The umpire came up, shouting angrily. There were a few words, and Ken Martin and Schaumberg were rushed off the field.

———

THE TEAMS LINED up. Brogan tried to come through the center, but Krakoff had taken a beating by then, and when Young hit him he went back on his heels and Higgins went through after Corbett and they dropped Brogan in his tracks.

Flash saw Chadwick catch up a handful of dust and rub it

on his palms. It was a habit the swift-footed runner had before he took the ball. Even as the ball was snapped, Flash saw Butch Hagan dump his man out of the way. Then he drove through the hole like a streak and hit the red-jerseyed Chadwick before he could even tuck the ball away!

He knocked Chadwick a dozen feet, the ball flying from his hands. Lew Young was in there fast and lit on the ball just as the pileup came.

They lined up and it was the Tigers' ball on the Bear thirty yard line. Flash got away and Saunders shot a pass to him. He took the ball running and saw Brogan cut in toward him. He angled across toward Brogan, deliberately closing up the distance, yet even as the big fullback hurled himself forward in a wicked tackle, Flash cross-stepped and shoved out a stiffarm that flattened Brogan's nose across his face, and then he was away.

Chadwick was coming, and drove into his pounding knees, clutched wildly, but his fingers slipped and he slid into the dirt on his face as Flash went over for a touchdown!

Simmons kicked the point and they trotted back to midfield. Krakoff took the ball on the kickoff but Higgins started fast and came down on Krakoff like a streak. He hit him high and Butch Hagan hit him low, and when they got up, Krakoff was still lying there. He got up, after a minute, and limped into position.

There was smeared blood on Brogan's face from his broken nose and the big fullback was mad. Chadwick was talking the game, trying to pull his team together.

They lost the ball on the forty yard line and Higgins recovered for the Tigers. They were rolling now and they knew it. Flash shot a bulletlike pass to Saunders and the redheaded young lawyer made fifteen yards before he was slammed to the ground by Chadwick.

Chadwick was the only man on the team who seemed to have kept his head. Wilson came in for Brogan and when they lined up, Butch Hagan went through that line like a baby tank and threw an angle block into Wilson that nearly broke both his legs! Wilson got up limping, and Butch looked at him. "How d'you like it, quitter?"

Wilson's FACE FLUSHED, and he walked back into line. On the next play Hagan hit him again with another angle block, and Wilson's face was pale.

Flash rifled a long pass to Simmons and the former All-American end carried it ten yards before they dropped him. On the next play Higgins went through tackle for the score.

The Bears had gone to pieces now. Wilson was frankly scared. On every play his one urge seemed to be to get away from Butch Hagan. Krakoff and Brogan were out of the game, and the Tigers, playing straight, hard, but wickedly rough football, rolled down the field for their third straight score.

They lined up for the kickoff, and Flash took it on his own thirty-five yard line, angled toward the sidelines and running like a madman hit the twenty yard line before he was downed. They lined up and Saunders went through center for six. On a single wing back Higgins made six more, and then Simmons took a pass from Flash and was finally downed on the five yard line. Then Flash crashed over for the final score, driving through with five men clinging to him.

And the whistle blew as they got up from the ground.

Flash WALKED SLOWLY toward the dressing room, his face mud streaked and ugly. Pop was standing there, waiting for him.

"You saved my bacon, son," he said quietly. "I can't thank you enough!"

"Forget it," Moran said quietly, "it wasn't me. It was those friends of yours. And give Butch Hagan credit. He lined up six or eight of them himself, to say nothing of what he did on the field."

He turned to go, and Micky was standing there, her face pale and her eyes large. She lifted her chin and stepped toward him.

"Flash, I'm sorry. Pop never believed, but for a while, I did. He—Ken—made it sound so much like you'd done something crooked."

"It was him," Flash said quietly. "I'm sorry for your sake."

"I'm not," Micky looked up at him, her eyes wide and soft, "I'm not at all, Flash."

"But I thought—?"

"You thought I was in love with him? That I was going to marry him? That was all his idea, Flash. He never said anything to me about it, and I wouldn't have. I went with him because the man I really wanted never asked me."

"He must be an awful fool," Flash said grimly. "Why, I'd—!"

"You'd what, Flash? You better say it now, because I've been waiting!"

"You mean—?" Flash gulped. Then he moved in, but fast.

Lew Young stuck his head out of the door, then hastily withdrew it. "That Moran," he said, grinning, "may be slow getting an idea, but when he does—*man, oh man!*"

About Louis L'Amour

"I think of myself in the oral tradition—as a troubadour, a village taleteller, the man in the shadows of the camp-fire. That's the way I'd like to be remembered—as a storyteller. A good storyteller."

I T IS DOUBTFUL that any author could be as at home in the world recreated in his novels as Louis Dearborn L'Amour. Not only could he physically fill the boots of the rugged characters he wrote about, but he literally "walked the land my characters walk." His personal experiences as well as his lifelong devotion to historical research combined to give Mr. L'Amour the unique knowledge and understanding of people, events, and the challenge of the American frontier that became the hallmarks of his popularity.

Of French-Irish descent, Mr. L'Amour could trace his own family in North America back to the early 1600s and follow their steady progression westward, "always on the frontier." As a boy growing up in Jamestown, North Dakota, he absorbed all he could about his family's frontier heritage, including the story of his great-grandfather who was scalped by Sioux warriors.

Spurred by an eager curiosity and desire to broaden his horizons, Mr. L'Amour left home at the age of fifteen and enjoyed a wide variety of jobs, including seaman, lumberjack, elephant handler, skinner of dead cattle, miner, and an officer in the transportation corps during World War II. During his "yondering" days he also circled the world on a freighter, sailed a dhow on the Red

Sea, was shipwrecked in the West Indies, and stranded in the Mojave Desert. He won fifty-one of fifty-nine fights as a professional boxer and worked as a journalist and lecturer. He was a voracious reader and collector of rare books. His personal library contained 17,000 volumes.

Mr. L'Amour "wanted to write almost from the time I could talk." After developing a widespread following for his many frontier and adventure stories written for fiction magazines, Mr. L'Amour published his first full-length novel, *Hondo,* in the United States in 1953. Every one of his more than 120 books is in print; there are more than 300 million copies of his books in print worldwide, making him one of the bestselling authors in modern literary history. His books have been translated into twenty languages, and more than forty-five of his novels and stories have been made into feature films and television movies.

His hardcover bestsellers include *The Lonesome Gods, The Walking Drum* (his twelfth-century historical novel), *Jubal Sackett, Last of the Breed,* and *The Haunted Mesa.* His memoir, *Education of a Wandering Man,* was a leading bestseller in 1989. Audio dramatizations and adaptations of many L'Amour stories are available from Random House Audio publishing.

The recipient of many great honors and awards, in 1983 Mr. L'Amour became the first novelist ever to be awarded the Congressional Gold Medal by the United States Congress in honor of his life's work. In 1984 he was also awarded the Medal of Freedom by President Reagan.

Louis L'Amour died on June 10, 1988. His wife, Kathy, and their two children, Beau and Angelique, carry the L'Amour publishing tradition forward with new books written by the author during his lifetime to be published by Bantam.

FORGET THE LAW OF THE JUNGLE...

The Worst
Drought In
Memory . . .

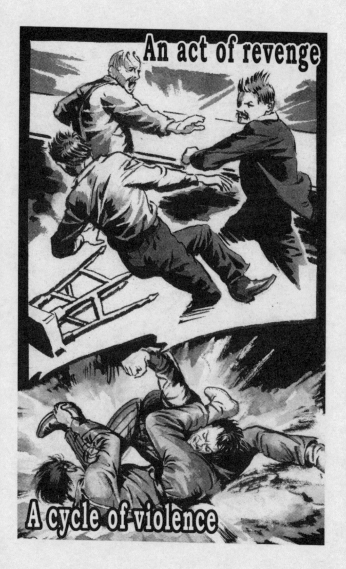

In Louis L'Amour's classic tale of loyalty and betrayal . . .

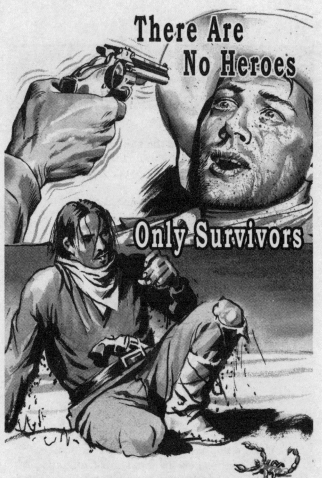

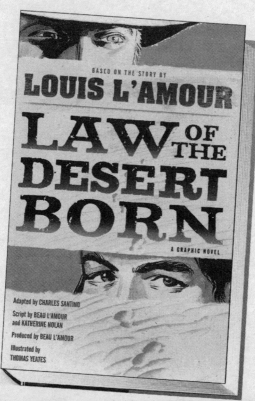